MOONLIGHT, MADNESS, AND MAGIC

MOONLIGHT, MADNESS, AND MAGIC

by

SUZANNE FORSTER

CHARLOTTE HUGHES

OLIVIA RUPPRECHT

LOVESWEPT®
DOUBLEDAY
NEW YORK
LONDON
TORONTO
SYDNEY
AUCKLAND

L OVESWEPT ®
PUBLISHED BY DOUBLEDAY
a division of Bantam Doubleday Dell Publishing Group, Inc.
1540 Broadway, New York, New York 10036

DOUBLEDAY, LOVESWEPT, and the portrayal of the wave device
are trademarks of Doubleday, a division of
Bantam Doubleday Dell Publishing Group, Inc.

Grateful acknowledgment is made to the following for permission to
reprint the epigraph from previously published material:

Reprinted by permission from the Putnam Publishing Group for
Mastering Witchcraft by Paul Huson. Copyright © 1970 by Paul Huson.

Book design by Dorothy Kline

Library of Congress Cataloging-in-Publication Data

Forster, Suzanne.
Moonlight, madness, and magic / Suzanne Forster, Charlotte Hughes,
Olivia Rupprecht. — 1st ed.
p.   cm.
"Loveswept."—Colophon.
1. Love stories, American.   2. Supernatural—Fiction.   I. Hughes,
Charlotte.   II. Rupprecht, Olivia.   III. Title.
PS3556.O7443M6   1993
813'.54—dc20   92-40756
CIP

ISBN 0-385-46832-6

Printed in the United States of America
May 1993

1   3   5   7   9   10   8   6   4   2

First Edition

Table of Contents

Night is jealous of her secrets and guards them
in many ways;
but those who succeed in wooing her
may reap many rewards.

—PAUL HUSON

OXFORD VILLAGE, MASSACHUSETTS—1690

Rachael Deliverance Dobbs had been beautiful once. The flaming red hair that often strayed from her morning cap and curled in wispy tendrils about her face had turned more than one shopkeeper's head. Today, however, that red hair was tangled and filthy and fell against her back and shoulders like a tattered woolen shawl.

Prison had not served her well.

"The woman hath *witchcraft* in her," an onlooker spat out as Rachael was led to the front of the meeting house, where a constable, the governor's magistrate, and several of the town selectmen waited to decide her fate. Her ankles were shackled in irons, making her progress slow and painful.

"She's the devil's own!" another called out as the burly, gap-toothed jailer shoved Rachael toward a bench facing the authorities.

Rachael staggered, struggling to catch her balance as the magistrate peered over his spectacles at her. He stood out like a beacon against the somberly dressed crowd with his embroidered white gloves and ruffled cuffs. The laws forbade the ordinary citizens of Oxford to wear such finery.

Clearing his throat, the magistrate began to speak, giving

each word a deep and thunderous import. "Rachael Deliverance Dobbs, thou hast been accused by this court of not fearing the Almighty God as do thy good and prudent neighbors, of preternatural acts against the citizenry of Oxford, and of the heinous crime of witchcraft, for which, by the law of the colony of Massachusetts, thou deservest to die. Hast thou anything to say in thy defense?"

Rachael Dobbs could barely summon the strength to deny the charges. Her accusers had kept her jailed for months, often depriving her of sleep, food, and clean water to drink. In order to secure a confession, they'd whipped her with rawhide and tortured her with hideous instruments. Though she'd been grievously injured and several of her ribs broken, she'd given them nothing.

"Nay," she said faintly, "I know not of which ye speak, m'lord. For as God is my witness, I have been wrongly accused."

A rage quickened the air, and several of the spectators rose from their seats. "Blasphemy!" someone cried. "The witch would use *His* name in vain?"

"Order!" The magistrate brought his gavel down. "Let the accused answer the charges. Goody Dobbs, it is said thou makest the devil's brew of strange plants that grow in the forest."

"I know not this devil's brew you speak of," Rachael protested. "I use the herbs for healing, just as my mother before me."

"And thou extracts a fungus from rye grass to stop birthing pains?" he queried.

"I do not believe a woman should suffer so, m'lord."

"Even though the Good Book commands it?"

"The Good Book also commands us to use the sense God gave us," she reminded him tremulously.

"I'll not tolerate this sacrilege!" The village preacher slammed his fist down on the table, inciting the onlookers into a frenzy of shouting and name-calling.

The crowd's fear and hatred washed over Rachael, battering at her defenses like a gale wind. She hitched her chin up and stiffened her spine, though the pain of her injuries stabbed her. Did not these people see that she was a decent, honorable woman who'd struggled to keep her children after their father's death? She'd given her time to the aged and the infirm, and not once had she ever loitered in the marketplace with the town gossips.

As the magistrate called for order, Rachael turned to the crowd, searching for the darkly handsome face of her betrothed, Jonathan Nightingale. She'd not been allowed visitors in jail, but surely Jonathan would be here today to speak on her behalf. With his wealth and good name, he would quickly put an end to this hysteria. That hope had kept her alive, bringing her comfort even when she'd learned her children had been placed in the care of Jonathan's housekeeper, a young woman Rachael distrusted for her deceptive ways. But that mattered little now. When Jonathan cleared her name of these crimes, she would be united with her babes once again. How she longed to see them!

When she finally spotted Jonathan at the back of the crowd, she was overcome with relief. A smile wreathed her gaunt features and warmed her starved body, burning away her fears and the bone-deep chill of the jail.

"Speak thou for me, Jonathan Nightingale?" she cried, forgetting everything but her joy at seeing him. "Thou knowest me better than anyone. Thou knowest the secrets of my heart. Tell these people I am not what they accuse me. Tell them, so that my children may be returned to me." Her voice trembled with emotion, but as Jonathan glanced up and met her eyes, she knew a moment of doubt. She didn't see the welcoming warmth she expected. Was something amiss?

At the magistrate's instruction, the bailiff called Jonathan to come forward. "State thy name for the court," the bailiff said, once he'd sworn him in.

"Jonathan Peyton Nightingale."

"Thou knowest the accused, Goody Dobbs?" the magistrate asked.

Jonathan acknowledged Rachael with a slow nod of his head. It was indeed sad to note the changes that had taken place in his betrothed these last months. Rachael was piteously thin, and her emerald eyes, once so vital and alive, were as cold and bitter as a winter morning. Neither were there any signs of the fiery passion that had induced him to bed with her before her elderly husband had been in the grave a year. Was God punishing them both for their haste? For surely Jonathan was being punished too. His family had suffered grievously from the scandal, and his once prosperous business was flagging.

"Mistress Dobbs and I were engaged to be married before she was incarcerated," Jonathan told the magistrate. "I've assumed the care of her children these last few months. She has no family of her own."

"Hast thou anything to say in her defense?"

"She was a decent mother, to be sure. Her children be well mannered."

"And have ye reason to believe the charges against her?"

When Jonathan hesitated, the magistrate pressed him. "Prithee, do not withhold information from the court, Mr.

Nightingale," he cautioned, "lest thee find thyself in the same dire predicament as the accused. Conspiring to protect a witch is a lawful test of guilt."

Startled, Jonathan could only stare at the stern-faced tribunal before him. It had never occurred to him that his association with Rachael could put him in a hangman's noose as well. He had been searching his soul since she'd been jailed, wondering how much he was morally bound to reveal at this trial. Now he saw little choice but to unburden himself.

"After she was taken, I found this among her things," he said, pulling an object from his coat pocket and unwrapping it. He avoided looking at Rachael, anticipating the stricken expression he would surely see in her eyes. "It's an image made of horsehair. A woman's image. There be a pin stuck through it."

The crowd gasped as Jonathan held up the effigy. A woman screamed, and even the magistrate drew back in horror.

Rachael sat in stunned disbelief. An icy fist closed around her heart. How could Jonathan have done such a thing? Did he not realize he'd signed her death warrant? Dear merciful God, if they found her guilty, she would never see her children again!

" 'Twas mere folly that I fashioned the image, m'lord," she told the magistrate. "I suspected my betrothed of dallying with his housekeeper. I fear my temper bested me."

"And was it folly when thou gavest Goodwife Brown's child the evil eye and caused her to languish with the fever?" the magistrate probed.

" 'Twas coincidence, m'lord," she said, imploring him to believe her. "The child was ill when I arrived at Goody Brown's house. I merely tried to help her." Rachael could see the magistrate's skepticism, and she whirled to Jonathan in desperation. "How canst thou doubt me, Jonathan?" she asked.

He hung his head. He was torn with regret, even shame.

He loved Rachael, but God help him, he had no wish to die beside her. One had only to utter the word *witch* these days to end up on the gallows. Not that Rachael hadn't given all of them cause to suspect her. When he'd found the effigy, he'd told himself she must have been maddened by jealousy. But truly he didn't understand her anymore. She'd stopped going to Sunday services and more than once had induced him to lie abed with her on a Sabbath morn. "Methinks thou hast bewitched me as well, Rachael," he replied.

Another gasp from the crowd.

"Hanging is too good for her!" a woman shouted.

"Burn her!" another cried from the front row. "Before she bewitches us all."

Rachael bent her head in despair, all hope draining from her. Her own betrothed had forsaken her, and his condemnation meant certain death. There was no one who could save her now. No woman so grievously accused of consort with the devil had ever been spared. She would hang, regardless. The furor around her went unheeded as she faced that terrible knowledge. Weighed down by the horror of it, she felt as if her heart were being crushed. And yet, in the depths of her desolation, a spark of rage kindled.

"Coward," she whispered, glancing up at Jonathan. "Why did thou not defend me? Why hast thou wished this damnation upon me?" Tears blurred her eyes as the bewilderment she felt ignited into fiery pain. Witnessing the guilt and the deep shame in his eyes, she sprang to her feet. Suddenly she understood what had happened. "It's the harlot who keeps thy house, isn't it? Thou desires her! Has she replaced me in thy heart?"

Jonathan rose to deny it, but she wouldn't let him speak. "So be it," she said, seized by a black hysteria. She was beyond caring now, beyond the crowd's censure or their grace. No one could take anything more from her than had already been taken. Jonathan's engagement gift to her, a golden locket, hung at her neck. She ripped it free and flung it at him.

"Thou shall have thy desire, Jonathan Nightingale," she cried. "And pay for it dearly. Since thou hast consigned me to the gallows and stolen my children from me, I shall put a blood curse on thee and thine."

The magistrate pounded his gavel against the table, ordering the spectators to silence. "Mistress Dobbs!" he warned, his voice harsh. "I fear thou hast just sealed thy fate."

But Rachael would not be deterred. Her heart was aflame with the fury of a woman betrayed. "Hear me good, Jonathan," she said, oblivious of the magistrate, of everyone but the man she'd once loved with all her being. "Thou has damned my soul to hell, but I'll not burn there alone. I curse the Nightingale seed to a fate worse than the flames of Hades. Your progeny shall be as the living dead, denied the rest of the grave."

Her voice dropped to a terrifying hush as she began to intone the curse. "The third son of every third son shall walk the earth as a creature of the night, trapped in shadows, no two creatures alike. Stripped of humanity, he will howl in concert with demons, never to die, always to wander in agony, until a woman entraps his heart and soul as thee did mine—"

"My God, she is truly the devil's mistress!" the preacher gasped. A cry rose from the crowd, and several of them surged forward, trying to stop her. Guards rushed to block them.

"Listen to me, Jonathan!" Rachael cried over the din. "I've not finished with thee yet. If that woman should find a way to set the creature free, it will be at great and terrible cost. A sacrifice no mortal woman would ever be willing to make—"

She hesitated, her chin beginning to tremble as hot tears

pooled in her eyes. Glistening, they slid down her cheeks, burning her tender flesh before they dropped to the wooden floor. But as they hit the planks, something astonishing happened. Even Rachael in her grief was amazed. The teardrops hardened before everyone's eyes into precious gems. Flashing in the sunlight was a dazzling blue-white diamond, a blood-red ruby, and a brilliant green emerald.

The crowd was stunned to silence.

Rachael glanced up, aware of Jonathan's fear, of everyone's astonishment. Their gaping stares brought her a fleeting sense of triumph. Her curse had been heard. For a moment, at least, her composure and dignity were restored to her. "To all who would sit in judgment of me," she said, "let it also be known this day. The curse will go on, Jonathan Nightingale, until every tear I have shed is returned to me, and I am whole again."

"Rachael Dobbs, confess thy sins before this court and thy Creator!" the magistrate bellowed.

But it was too late for confessions. The doors to the courtroom burst open, and a pack of men streamed in with blazing pine torches. "Goody Brown's child is dead of the fits," they shouted. "The witch must burn!"

The guards couldn't hold back the vigilantes, and Rachael closed her eyes as the pack of men engulfed her. She said a silent good-bye to her children as she was gripped by bruising hands and lifted off the ground. She could feel herself being torn nearly apart as they dragged her from the meeting room, but she did not cry out. She felt no physical pain. She had just made a pact with the forces of darkness, and she could no longer feel anything except the white-hot inferno of the funeral pyre that would soon release her to her everlasting vigil.

She welcomed it, just as she welcomed the sweet justice

that would one day be hers. She would not die in vain. Her curse had been heard.

Long after the courtroom had emptied, Jonathan Nightingale stood alone in the terrible stillness, staring at the locket Rachael had flung at him. Opening the clasp, he gazed at the miniature portrait of her. Three tear-shaped holes were burned into the flesh of her cheek. Startled, he searched the floor where her tears had transformed to precious stones, but he found nothing. The gems were gone, vanished without a trace. Had they been lost in the crush of bodies, he wondered, or had he only imagined he'd seen them? With a sudden and gripping sense of dread, he closed the locket, aware of its strange, pulsating warmth in his hand.

Rachael, my beloved . . . what hast thou done?

MOONLIGHT

Suzanne Forster

1

OXFORD FOREST—1785

An eerie howl rose from the shadows, awakening the red oak forest from its nocturnal slumber. Neither human nor animal, the sound shivered on the wind, carrying with it the soul-loneliness of the ages. Above the forest, adrift in a fathomless sky, the full moon glowed huge and transparent.

A great black wolf with golden eyes and a riotous mane stopped to heed the call, then moved on noiselessly through the night, compelled by a more powerful lure, the scent of living prey. The animal was as supple as it was muscular, a beast of such magnificent proportions that it outweighed the largest of its kind by fifty pounds. And yet not even a dying leaf crackled under its enormous paws.

The wolf hesitated again, sniffing the wind and pinpointing with swift and deadly accuracy the direction of the tantalizing scent. His nostrils dilated. Every sense came alert, every nerve fiber went taut. The odor of his prey excited ancient instincts, and his mouth watered copiously. He would feast tonight.

The fertile aroma of moist earth rose to greet him as he loped along, and its rich, loamy textures cushioned his paw pads. Wind ruffled his glossy black coat, and his ears pricked as sounds came to him on the breezes, the deep croaking of toads, the startled slithering of deer mice, and the hot urgent coupling of night creatures making furtive love.

A faint but riveting heartbeat drew his attention back to the hunt. He narrowed his focus consciously, selectively, homing in on that one irresistible pulse. He had not yet caught sight of his quarry, but he'd identified the scent with its first ghosting on the wind. His prey was human, a woman. She was young, but not a child. Her body was fertile, her health good, and her essence called to him, the sweetest, most fragrant lure he'd ever known.

The muscles of his jaw rippled in anticipation, and a hunger more ancient than Nature itself surged painfully. The pursuit of human prey brought him the most pleasure and the deepest agony imaginable. The pleasure itself was agony, filled with a terrible knowledge of life and death, of hell eternal. Even the scent of humans forced him to face what he'd become. At first he'd fought the clawing urgency to stalk the creatures that worshiped daylight. He'd known that to prey on humans was to destroy the last vestiges of hope he clung to and to lose what little remained of his innocence for all time. But ultimately he'd been driven by overmastering forces to accept his destiny. The gods of darkness had made him what he was. They had given him no quarter. And he gave none in turn to those who became his victims.

He saw her then, kneeling near the river's edge, her back to him as she gathered herbs in the moonlight. She was less than a hundred feet away, but he might have thought her a vision if his preternatural senses hadn't picked up the soft hush of her breathing, the steady rate of her pulse. Her hooded cape flowed around her, making her look pale and inviolable in the moonlight. But she was protected less by the light summer cape than by the fragile cloak of her own virtue, he realized. Goodness and honesty emanated from her like tangible things. And perhaps it was that aura of virtue that told him she was a maiden still, untouched by the carnal desires of men, a virgin to sex, to life and death.

A growl locked in his massive jaws. His animal soul quivered. He would be the one to initiate her. Perhaps that was why he'd been led here, to bring her the rapture of living and dying in one glorious crescendo of passion and bloodlust. For a few moments at least, he could give her everything she'd ever longed for . . . and then he would take what he longed for.

He left the cover of the forest cautiously, his nostrils flaring with the lush scent of her. It would be better to keep her unknowing for as long as possible. When she saw him, she would be frightened. Her eyes would fill with terror, and the sharp burst of fear that flooded from her pores would drive him wild. Human fear acted as a potent aphrodisiac, all the more irresistible because he knew what followed in its pungent wake. Surrender. Ecstasy. The yielding of flesh, of life, of the shuddering soul with its arms outstretched to him.

He came upon her cautiously, hanging back to watch her pluck the herbs and fill her basket. Her quick white hands were all he could see of her. The hooded cape hid everything else from his eyes. Curious, he doubled back and angled around, compromising his quest for a glimpse of her face. He wanted to view her serenity, to witness the virtue he'd sensed. He wanted to know who she truly was before he altered her life forever. But her chestnut hair hung forward, falling over her face and hiding even her profile from him.

The wind shifted suddenly, bringing him another odor, bitter and brackish. It pierced his nostrils and seared his windpipe as he drew it in. It was a scent all wolves loathed and feared. She was gathering monkshood, the deep-blue poison-

ous flowers also known as wolfsbane. The snarl rattling in his
throat became a whine as he backed off.

She dropped the basket of herbs and whirled to her feet,
staggering backward as she saw him. A gasp caught in her
throat, but she didn't run. She was caught in the glare of his
yellow eyes, as mesmerized as she was terrified. He knew from
experience that he could hold her spellbound with the power
of his glowing stare alone, while fear flowed from her like rich
red wine.

Quelling the hot frenzy inside him, he bored through her
fear and resistance to the naked wonder of her soul. This was
the most beguiling moment of the hunt, the seconds when a
wolf offered its prey not the chance to escape, but the chance to
accept its fate with dignity. He told her with his eyes that he
was about to take her on a sacred journey, to introduce her to
the exquisite caress of life and death.

Her breathing fell to an imperceptible hush as she joined
him in the silent dance of death that linked them. Her eyes
swam with darkness, and he knew that she was deeply in thrall.
She was slowly being sapped of the strength to flee, gradually
losing even the will to save herself. When her volition was
gone, she would do more than let herself be taken. Like all the
others before her, she would offer herself to him wantonly,
surrendering everything to his demon lust.

Blood rushed into the chambers of his heart, pounding
furiously. He wanted this good and virtuous woman, wanted to
taste her sweet flesh, to lick her human fluids and know the
profound release of conquest. But even more than release, he
wanted to be set free of his hellish sins, if only for an instant to
be cleansed by the purifying touch of her flesh. He wanted that
savagely. It was an agony that swelled thickly in his loins.

The wolfsbane held him at bay. The acrid stench of the

herbs choked him, but he began to advance on her anyway, a deadly growl shaking in his chest. Perhaps he could drive her farther away from the basket. If she broke and ran, her fate was sealed.

She stumbled backward, into a shaft of moonlight that illuminated her features. Suddenly she was drowning in white iridescence, more lovely than he could ever have imagined. The sight of her quickened every fiber of his being. But in some place other than his mind, a ripple of recognition shivered through him. The hackles raised along his powerful neck, and his lips curled back, revealing gleaming white fangs.

This woman was known to him.

Another scent ripped the dawning recognition away. He could smell human sweat—male sweat—rife with fear. He could detect the gunpowder in the musket even before it ignited. Someone else was there. Behind him. A hunter! He whirled, snarling viciously, and leapt.

The man who'd come up behind him took aim, the deadly muzzle of his musket glowing in the light. The gun went off as the wolf hurtled through the air, exploding seconds before he hit the man's chest and knocked him to the ground. Pain seared the wolf's body, tearing through flesh and sinew, but the adrenaline rampaging in his veins propelled him over the man's sprawled form. Moist earth ripping up under his claws, he sprinted for cover. As he disappeared into the darkness of the trees, a streak of white-hot fire singed his muzzle. Another shot rang out. And then another. The forest was alive with hunters!

"Are you hurt, Katherine Downing?"

Obed Springer's voice broke through Kit Downing's dazed confusion. "No, I don't think so," she said, suddenly aware that the wolf was gone and she was surrounded by a circle of men from the village, all of them carrying muskets and dressed in their buckskin hunting shirts.

"You're sure? The wolf didn't attack you?"

"No, he didn't attack, but his eyes, Obed, his eyes!" Kit pressed a fist to the hollow throb in her chest. "They were terrible evil."

"Have no fear, girl. We'll shoot the beast and have his head mounted above the door of the Meetin' Hall by day's break."

Kit shivered at the thought. As frightening as the wolf had been, she could hardly rejoice at the prospect of seeing its magnificent black head nailed above the Meeting Hall door. Wolves were as deeply feared and loathed as Indians and fire in the back country of northeastern Massachusetts. A dead wolf brought a high bounty because of the threat it posed to local livestock, but for the life of her, Kit didn't understand the jubilation involved in disfiguring a beautiful wild creature after its death.

Asa Hubbard, the village gunsmith, pushed through the pack of men, his voice gruff. "What are you doing out this time of night, Katherine?" he demanded to know. "You've got no call to be taking a stroll in the forest when there's a wolf about. That scurvy beast could have sunk his teeth into you, or one of us might have shot you."

"The Widow Fletcher over the hill needed me," Kit hastened to explain, improving on the truth a bit as she crouched down to retrieve her basket of herbs and draw it under the cover of her cloak. It was true she'd paid a visit to the Widow Fletcher's place, but she'd also stopped on the way back for some special herbs whose powers were reputed to be stronger if collected by moonlight.

"Her middle boy, Gideon, was stricken with stomach flux-ions and a gripping fever," she added, hoping the angels weren't listening in on her sinful exaggerations. "So I administered a decoction of the pink beet and dosed him with feverfew tea. It was the oldest boy come to fetch me. He said Gideon was ailing bad and might be gone to his Maker by morn." That last part was true at least.

Asa seemed grudgingly willing to accept her explanation. The whole village was aware that Kit had been gradually assuming more and more of her elderly aunt's midwifery duties. Parthenia Pott's rheumatism had left her unable to travel long distances, and she couldn't possibly have made the trip to the Fletchers', so Asa could hardly argue with Kit's reasoning.

"Get one of the boys here to fetch you home," Asa told Kit, nodding a brusque dismissal as he turned back to the waiting men. Kit knew by "one of the boys" he meant Obed, the thin, bespectacled town clerk. She liked Obed well enough, even if he was taking on the airs of a suitor lately, but for some reason, she didn't want his company or his protection tonight.

The baying of hounds signaled the arrival of another group of hunters on horseback. A dozen of them thundered to a stop at the riverbank, their horses snorting, their hunting dogs wild-eyed and quivering with excitement. In all the confusion, Kit took the opportunity to slip away and start for home.

"Kit, wait!" Obed called after her. "I'll walk you."

"No, Obed, go ahead with the others," she said, hurrying on. "It's only a short distance. I'll be all right."

She gathered up the skirt of her linsey-woolsey dress and set off at a quick pace to discourage him from following her. If she had concerns that night, they weren't about her own safety. It was the wolf on her mind. She truly hated to think of a wounded animal being run to the ground by a pack of snarling hounds. It pained her to imagine any wild creature being hunted down for doing what came naturally to it. And yet she knew wolves were a grave threat to a back-country village like Oxford, where a goat and some chickens might mean the difference between eating and starving once winter hit.

As for her own safety, she had the wolfsbane with her, securely tucked under her cape. She was small of stature, barely an inch over five feet in her worsted stockings, but for the better part of her twenty-two years, she'd heard herself described as having enough grit for several individuals. "Sand in her soap, that's my Kit," her mother used to say. Kit was fairly certain that she herself could frighten off a wild beast sooner than a gentle soul like Obed could.

She also wanted to be alone with her thoughts for a few moments before she reached the small clapboard house she shared with her mother's maiden sister. When Kit's mother and father and her two younger brothers had moved their ironworks business to Boston to aid the patriots' cause in the Revolution, Kit had stayed on to help Aunt Parth, who was already ailing with rheumatism. Parthenia was a good soul, and a devoutly religious woman who'd dedicated her life to helping others, but Kit knew the minute she entered the house that night, her aunt would be after her for every detail of the Fletcher boy's condition.

Little Gideon had simply eaten too many green-apple tarts was all. But if Kit was to admit how she'd exaggerated the seriousness of the boy's complaint for the gunsmith's benefit, or that she'd been picking herbs by moonlight, her aunt would probably insist on holding evening devotions immediately so that Kit could petition the heavens for forgiveness. And if her aunt was to learn about the wolf, she'd have them both on their knees praying for the safe deliverance of their immortal souls.

A distant cry brought Kit to a halt. It rose out of the bowels of the forest, an animal's howl so fraught with anguish, it made the skin rise on her arms. Had the wolf been shot? No, surely not. She hadn't heard the report of guns.

An icy breeze swirled up under her cape, spurring her into motion again. She began to walk hurriedly, glancing over her shoulder, her heart racing as she picked her way through the undergrowth and fallen logs. She'd wandered off the path, and something was wrong, terribly wrong, she could sense it. An owl hooted mournfully, and the wind shivered through the trees, but there was something more. The darkness stirred with an unknown threat. She felt as if some evil presence were closing in on her.

She slipped her hand inside her cape and took a stalk of wolfsbane from the basket. She could feel the wolf's presence, as if it were out there in the night somewhere, watching her, waiting for her. The creature's glowing eyes haunted her mind, drawing up the same rapt terror, the same horrified shiver of excitement she'd felt when she'd been caught in its gaze. The animal had a beguiling intelligence, but there was something diabolical beneath it, something paralyzing. And yet she'd been strangely compelled. Surely she was being fanciful, but she'd felt as if the wolf had been trying to communicate with her, trying to soothe her, in much the same way that a cat often licked its victims before destroying them. For the wolf had meant to kill her, she was certain of that.

Another howl split the silence. Startled, she dropped the basket of herbs and began to run blindly, stumbling over her dress and trying to lift her skirts. Leafy limbs slapped at her body, and spidery tendrils clung to her face. As she blundered through the darkness, she realized there was nothing in her clenched fist. She'd lost the wolfsbane! A branch snagged her petticoat, ripping a jagged strip from the homespun linen as she jerked herself free.

When at last she saw the flickering glow of candlelit windows, she flew toward her aunt's small clapboard house as if banshees were shrieking at her heels. The sight of a haven heightened the terror of being enveloped by some unspeakable evil. She reached the house in a shuddering rush and heaved open the heavy wooden door.

Her Aunt Parth dropped the ball of yarn she'd been rolling.

"Katherine Mercy Downing!" she cried, struggling to rise to her feet as the yarn rolled across the floor. "Whatever is wrong with you?"

Kit bolted the door behind her and tried to stop the terrible shaking that had invaded her whole being. She didn't want to frighten her aunt needlessly, and she was already beginning to feel a little foolish. Despite her pounding heart she had an uncomfortable feeling she'd been running from nothing but the terrors of her own imagination. Everything was more frightening after dark. Deep in the forest even a hoot owl sounded ominous, but that was nothing to be mortally terrified of, certainly nothing evil.

"I'm all right," she said, trying to reassure her aunt with a wan smile. "I caught my skirt on a branch and took a spill."

Parthenia scrutinized her niece with piercing gray eyes as she made her way over to where Kit stood. "Well, you certainly did, child. Look what you've done to your slip. Why didn't you stay the night with the Fletchers as we agreed?" She groaned with the effort of crouching to pick up her yarn. "You're a strange one, Kit, traipsing around in the dead of night. If the Almighty weren't watching over you, surely the Indians would have had you by now . . . or the wolves."

Kit shuddered. "Next time I will stay over," she said with complete sincerity. It was common practice that midwives would stay the night when they were called out at a late hour or had to travel a great distance, but the moon was full tonight, and she'd wanted to gather the herbs. Too bad she'd dropped her basket in the woods.

"Go on over to the fire and get warm," Parthenia suggested, unable to suppress the fond tone that crept through her exasperation. "I'll get you a bit of currant tea and some corn cake. You must be famished. I don't suppose the Widow Fletcher fed you anything, did she, what with that screeching brood of hers underfoot?"

Aunt Parth didn't hold with those who were imprudent in any way, which included having more children than they could reasonably care for. She'd been a spinster all her years and preferred it that way, so it was a source of great perplexity to her why a man and his wife might want to seek out the comforts of the bed for anything other than sleeping to restore their soul. Moderation in all things, and abstinence when moderation didn't suffice, that was her credo.

Kit hung her cape on a peg by the door and went to stand at one side of the huge stone fireplace that dominated the back wall of the small room. While her aunt raked the glowing coals to boil a kettle of water, Kit took the bellows that were propped against the edge of the hearth and fanned the smoldering embers at her end.

She loved the crackle of a good warm fire and the smell of burning pine pitch. Lifting her skirts to ward off the chill of their dampness, she watched her aunt bustle around, getting the food ready. A moment later she and Parthenia were facing each other on two settles, the narrow, high-backed benches that sat before the fire, and Kit had begun recounting the details of Gideon Fletcher's mysterious illness. Once she'd reassured her

aunt that the boy would survive to eat more apple tarts, they
began to talk about the calls Kit would need to make the following day.

"You must remember the dock root for Shubal Potter's
itch," Parthenia reminded her. "And the burdock leaves for
Martha Wright's sore shoulder."

Kit made a mental note of both. "I'll need more feverfew
tea for Mrs. Hamlin," she added, "and plenty of soap pills, of
course. Did I tell you old Mr. Learned wanted me to bleed a
cat to make a poultice for his shingles?"

Parthenia snorted. "Who's been filling his head with such
nonsense? That daft neighbor of his, Phoebe Tupper? If I were
him, I wouldn't listen too hard to a woman who drops chickens
down the chimney so their beating wings will clear the soot."

Kit laughed, savoring the currant tea. Her aunt had sweet-
ened it with a nugget of maple sugar, which added a soothing
richness to the piquant flavor. "Phoebe told Mr. Learned the
cat had to be pure black without a single white hair—like that
big old tom that sleeps among the flour sacks at the general
store."

"You've got no time to be bothered with such things,"
Parthenia decried. "There's more than enough to keep you
busy these days, child. I sometimes wonder how you do it
all."

Kit often wondered that herself, and she was already feeling
a little weary about the day that awaited. She toyed with the
corn cake. It was studded with blueberries, her favorite kind,
but she delayed the pleasure of partaking. Truth be told, she
always seemed to be putting off pleasurable things in favor of
more pressing demands. "The Lord loveth not idleness," she
murmured, quoting her aunt.

"Amen to that," Parth concurred.

"I'll need some ingredients for a poultice," Kit said at last. There was one other visit she would be making tomorrow, but she'd avoided mentioning it until now. "How are we fixed for onions?"

Parthenia glanced up from her tea. "An onion poultice? Whatever for?"

"I'm going up to the Cloud Castle tomorrow morn."

"The Nightingales' place? Kit, not again!"

For as long as Kit could remember, the Nightingales' mansion had been called the Cloud Castle by the children in the village, perhaps because of its mysterious grandeur. It sat on a majestic hillside overlooking the Indian River, and its gabled roof and dormer windows always seemed to be shrouded in mists. Rumors still abounded that the house was haunted and the family cursed, rumors with which Kit was all too familiar because of her own ancestry.

It was her great-great-grandmother, Rachael Deliverance Dobbs, who was said to have put a curse on the Nightingale bloodline because of the betrayal of her betrothed, Jonathan Nightingale. Rachael had been tried and executed in the witchcraft hysteria of the 1690s, and although the tragic incident was nearly one hundred years old, it had opened a chasm between the Dobbses and the Nightingales that hadn't been bridged to this day.

"I have to go, Aunt Parth," Kit insisted. "The boy is languishing of fever, and there's no one else to care for him. You know what it says in the Scriptures about helping the sick and infirm."

"But not at the risk of our lives! Even the Almighty wouldn't expect that of you, Kit. You're a Dobbs on your mother's side. If you're caught at the Nightingale place, I don't know what they might do to you."

"Who's to catch me? There's no one left now but the boy and the caretaker."

The older woman set her tea down, suddenly saddened. Her shoulders rose and fell with a sigh. "It's a terrible shame what's happened to that family," she admitted. "What with the youngest brother so ill and the oldest dead. Tragedy about the parents, too, ambushed by redcoats the way they were. Folks are always talking about the suffering that family's had to endure."

"That's why I have to go, Aunt Parth."

Parthenia looked up sharply. "What do you mean, child?"

"Surely we bear some responsibility to the Nightingales, at least for whatever our part might have been in their suffering."

The older woman's eyes flared almost frighteningly. "Don't ever say that, Kit! I pray every morning and night for the souls of that unfortunate family. And I pray just as fervently for the souls of our own forebears. Have you forgotten what happened to your great-great-grandmother Rachael Dobbs? They burned that poor wretched creature at the stake!"

With effort Kit swallowed the bit of corn cake she'd been chewing and carefully settled her spoon in the earthenware bowl. "What they did to our kin was cruel and inhuman, Aunt Parth, I'd be the first to agree with you on that. But has it ever occurred to you that there might have been a measure of truth in Jonathan Nightingale's accusation?"

"No such thing, Kit! All of your mother's people were decent, diligent, and honorable, Rachael foremost among them. She was widowed at a young age with two babes to raise. You should be singing the woman's praises."

"I have nothing but sympathy for Rachael's hardships," Kit assured her aunt. "But how do you explain what's happened to the Nightingales, the bad fortune they've suffered over the years?"

"It's not for me to explain the crosses others must bear," Parth said, her voice growing almost fierce as she struggled to get up from the settle. "Or for you either, Kit. The Lord chasteneth those he loves, and we shouldn't be questioning such things. We shouldn't even be talking of them."

She pulled her shawl around her tightly and bent to pick up Kit's bowl. "My heavens, just look at the chill you've given me," she said, picking up the other dishes and carrying them off.

Parthenia's reaction told Kit how badly she'd upset her aunt, and though she regretted having done so, the history of their family's feud with the Nightingales weighed heavily on her mind now that she was caring for Ephraim, the fourteen-year-old boy who was perhaps the only member of the family left.

Her aunt returned moments later, a stern but not unkindly expression on her face. "There will be no more talk about witchcraft and curses. I forbid it, child, do you hear? You take after me, Katherine Mercy. You're strong-minded, but you're a sensible girl, and if you feel you must go see the boy, then I won't be the one to tell you otherwise. But have a care while you're there. That old man—their caretaker—especially bears watching. There's something unsavory about him."

With that said Parthenia took her torn and tattered Bible off the mantel and returned to the settle. "Now, let us proceed with our evening devotions and be off to bed."

Kit nodded, happy to oblige her aunt. As Parthenia began to read aloud from her favorite passages, Kit's thoughts drifted to her own concerns and to the concerns of the people she would be seeing tomorrow. She said a quiet prayer, remembering each of the infirm by name, and asking for their improved health and well-being, and then she put in an especially heartfelt plea for Ephraim Nightingale.

As she finished her prayers, she caught a faint sound from somewhere outside the cabin, a plaintive howl echoing in the distance. She clasped her hands tighter as a shiver raised the delicate hairs on her nape. A spontaneous and surprisingly passionate request ended her prayer: *Please don't let them kill the wolf.*

2

The horizon glowed golden with the promise of the rising sun as Kit made her way along the rocky path that bordered the Indian River. It was a considerable distance to the Nightingale estate, and a trip through the woods would have shortened her journey by half, but she'd chosen the river path for safety's sake.

A part of her regretted having to take such measures. She had some wolfsbane tucked in her basket, and it was common knowledge that wolves hunted by moonlight. That alone should have kept her safe enough, but Aunt Parth's cautions were ringing in her head. Still, she felt strongly drawn to the forest this morning. The light slanting through the giant oaks gave it the look of a huge, serene cathedral, and she found herself peering into the emerald-green depths, wondering if the wolf had been spared.

Distracted, she was barely aware of the mists rolling off the river and rising toward the cliffs in the near distance. She was also oblivious of the hoary figure those mists shrouded. The cloaked apparition stared down at her from its vantage point in a jagged pulpit of rocks, its dark eyes lit with unearthly intensity. When Kit finally did glance up at the cliffs, it was a full moment before the shock of it hit her.

"Michael?" she breathed.

The figure evanesced into the vaporous clouds, gone like a

mystical vision. Kit's heart pounded wildly as she struggled to make sense of what she'd seen. For a moment she'd thought it was Michael Nightingale, the family's eldest son. But it *couldn't* have been, for he'd died three years ago. And yet Kit couldn't escape the chilling feeling that she had seen him—or his ghost. Even more frightening, she'd had an eerily similar vision once as a child—years *before* Michael's death.

She and two adventurous friends had decided to sneak into the grounds of the Cloud Castle one spring morning and learn for themselves if the house was haunted as everyone claimed. As they'd approached the bridge that crossed the river, they'd seen a dark figure standing on the cliffs in front of the house. Shrouded in mist, he'd looked mysterious and otherworldly. The mere sight of him had brought all three of them to a halt, and Kit had been even more transfixed when she'd realized the vision was Michael Nightingale. The other girls had found him forbidding, but Kit had been fascinated. She'd imagined him as a spirit of the river haunting the cliffs. Perhaps even then she'd sensed some premonition of doom surrounding him.

A shiver crawled over her skin, compelling her to shake off all thoughts of visions and ghosts and be on her way. She had so much to do today, so many calls to make! She was grateful she'd dressed warmly as she began to climb the winding trail that led to the Cloud Castle. Though it was late spring, the early-morning air held a biting chill that wouldn't burn off for several hours. Frost laced the delicate blackberry vines like icing, and the bramble roses were coming into bud.

As the mansion itself came into view, she was taken aback as always by its stark grandeur. With its latticed windows and darkly peaked gables, the Cloud Castle had a funereal gloom about it. But the wooden structure had always given Kit the feeling of some inner life, some trapped emotion, as if the house itself were longing to be set free. Lonely and somehow stormy-looking, it was hauntingly peopled with secrets, or so its diamond-faceted windows suggested. Only when the mists burned off, and sunshine bathed the cliffs, did the house seem at peace.

Otis Pettingill, the caretaker, was coming out of the stables as Kit approached the house. The leather jerkin he wore was stained with sweat, and the gnarled muscles of his arms bulged with the burden of the heavy saddle he was carrying. His hair was long and unkempt, and his dark beard was sprigged with reddish casts. Though everyone described him as old, Kit suspected he was younger than his looks might indicate. There was a litheness in his movements and a strange energy in his eyes that was frightening if you tarried too long under his observation. Kit had actually heard folks in the village whispering about the oddly shaped white crescent on his forehead, calling it "the Devil's mark."

Otis hesitated when he saw Kit. He looked her over sullenly and nodded once, though it was less a greeting than reluctant permission for her to enter the house. She nodded in return and started toward the door. The boy's bedroom was in the north wing at the back of the house, overlooking terraced gardens that must have been splendid once, but were now overgrown with weeds, nettles, and thistles.

She went straight to Ephraim's room as she always did, though she'd often wanted to explore the rest of the house. The maze of dark paneled hallways encouraged fanciful thinking, and she'd imagined secret passageways and hidden compartments. It disturbed her that a place so grand had been neglected so badly. Aunt Parth would have chastised the owners for not appreciating what their Maker had given them, especially when He'd been so bountiful.

Kit had actually done some cleaning on her last visit, just a bit of washing up in the boy's bedroom and some polishing in the front hall, which included the graceful newels and balustrades of the splendid mahogany stairway. It had given the place a little cheer.

Now she let herself quietly into the boy's room. Ephraim was dozing in the canopied bed, his eyes closed, his breathing steady. At first glance he seemed improved from her last visit a few days ago, when he'd been chilled and headachy with a fever. But on closer inspection, Kit saw what she'd been dreading. The blood-red patches creeping up his neck confirmed her worst fears. He was coming down with the canker rash, an affliction that had taken the lives of a half dozen of her patients in the last few months, most of them children.

She would have to forgo the blistering onion poultice because of his rash, but she hurried to set out the cold water tincture and the other herbal remedies she'd prepared, calming herself with the activity. It wouldn't do to let him see that she was alarmed. What he needed now was her reassurance and her strength.

He opened his eyes as she sat down beside him on the bed.

"How are you today, Firefly?" she asked, using the nickname she'd coined for him when she found him on the shores of the river one evening, trying to trap the glowing insects. She put her hand to his forehead. His fever had dropped with the cool of the morning, but it would undoubtedly rise as the day went on.

Pain turned his smile into a grimace. "My throat hurts."

"I know it does," she said sympathetically. "Here, let me look."

He made a valiant attempt to accommodate her, opening his mouth as wide as he could. His throat was raw and painfully ulcerated, and Kit set about immediately to bring him some relief. She had him gargle her tincture, rolling the liquid around in his throat to bathe it thoroughly. And when she'd eased his pain enough that he could swallow, she took the chicken broth she'd been warming by the fireplace and spooned some of it down him, all the while making a great story of the excitement she'd had with the wolf the night before and warning him to tread carefully when he himself was well enough to go out again. She was hoping to spark his sense of adventure. Though the boy was plucky, he was also frail, and she'd sensed a profound loneliness in him since the loss of his family.

Kit hadn't admitted it until now, even to herself, but she was deeply afraid that Ephraim was to be the next in a series of tragedies that had all but wiped out the Nightingales. His parents' deaths at the hands of British sympathizers had forced his brother Michael to move to Salem to oversee the family's shipbuilding venture there. Michael had donated several of their vessels to the patriots' cause, and because of the lack of trained naval officers, he'd been commissioned to captain one of the ships himself. When his merchantman was lost at sea, the word came back that none of the crew was found, including Michael.

Kit's heart had gone out to the family, and though she'd told herself she didn't believe in curses, the enormity of their misfortunes had given her cause to wonder. She had wanted to find a way to lend her support, but the opportunity hadn't come until late last year when the preacher's wife paid a call on Aunt Parth with the news that young Ephraim had suffered a riding accident. Since there was no doctor in Oxford and Aunt Parth wasn't well enough to go, Kit had felt an obligation to offer her help, even if it wasn't welcome.

Otis had grudgingly allowed her to treat Ephraim, and she'd soon formed an attachment to the frail boy with his guileless blue-gray eyes and sweeping black eyelashes. She'd continued to visit and bring him nourishing food, though she was keenly aware of Otis's hostility. But the boy had responded to her attentions over the months, his weight increasing and his color improving. He'd begun to thrive until this new and frightening epidemic of the canker rash had struck him down.

Kit glanced out the window occasionally as she continued to feed Ephraim both nourishment and news from the village. She was watching for the sun to break through the clouds, but what she glimpsed instead as she scooped up the last spoonful of broth was a shadowy form in the gardens. A chill shivered across her shoulders.

"Excuse me, Ephraim!" She jumped up for a cloth, realizing she'd spilled the soup on his bedding. "I thought I saw someone out the window. I'm sorry."

"Must have been Otis," Ephraim said. "He's the only one here—unless that crazy Moses Partridge has come by again, trying to sell us his lame horse."

"No, it wasn't Moses," she assured him, daubing at the spilled soup. She set down the bowl, but by the time she got to the window, the gardens were deserted. Whoever she'd seen was gone. Or maybe she'd been imagining things again. Perhaps it was nothing more than a shadow, the sun passing behind a cloud. And yet the icy chill had left her trembling, and her palms were damp. It had given her quite a fright, probably because no one ever came out this way anymore. With the exception of Moses, who drank to excess, the villagers seemed as uneasy about visiting the Nightingale estate as she was.

Before gathering up her things to leave, she swathed Ephraim's neck with warmed tow, an absorbent cloth made of flax, and left him some hyssop tea to sip. She'd already put some warm cornmeal mush on the table near his bed in case he felt strong enough to eat. He was faring a little better than when she'd arrived, but now that he had the canker rash, or what some of the villagers were calling scarlet fever, she would need to check on him every day.

She let herself out of his room and started down the hallway, preoccupied with how she was going to make Otis understand the urgency of Ephraim's condition. She couldn't imagine why the Nightingales' attorneys hadn't appointed a guardian for Ephraim, rather than leaving a youngster in the care of such an uncivil man. She had never considered Otis a proper influence on the boy. He rarely spoke and was greatly disposed to surliness. But since there was no one else, the caretaker would have to be told how to tincture the boy's throat periodically and be sure that he took some nourishment.

Hesitating at the top of the stairway, Kit fastened her cape around her. As she secured the hook in its loop, an odd stirring of awareness stilled her fingers. She glanced up, not sure what she'd heard, or if she'd heard anything. It felt as if something imperceptible had moved, a ripple in the air currents or some subtle shift in the natural order of things. Her senses seemed to want to play tricks on her today. Or were they trying to tell her something, to warn her?

She waited for the sensation to fade, but instead it heightened, prickling her skin. Despite the warmth of her cape, an icy chill crept through her once more, and something compelled her to turn and look back down the hallway that led to Ephraim's room. As she did, the shadows lengthened and swelled with the movements of something alive. Kit's heart careened wildly, and she stumbled backward, teetering on the edge of the landing.

"Who's there?" she cried softly.

A figure emerged from the darkness. The man's face was

hidden in gloom, unrecognizable to Kit, but her mind registered other frightening details. He was tall and strongly built, his body shrouded in a cloak that made him seem massive across the shoulders. Pooled in shadows, he looked like all the looming monsters of her childhood imagination. Her first impulse was to run, but her legs felt leaden and clumsy.

"Who is it?" she asked.

He said nothing, but his spectral presence filled the hallway like a malevolent force. Kit might have thought she was having another vision, except that he seemed to radiate an aura of terrifying evil. Her mind was racing, trying to imagine how she would ever escape him, when suddenly his black cloak flared like wings and he started toward her.

Kit lurched back, hitting the post at the top of the stairway, barely aware of the pain that streaked through her hip.

"Stop," she whispered, sensing that nothing could stop him, certainly not words. To her horrified eyes, he looked like a winged emissary from hell, swooping down to snatch her up in his talons. And yet even with the fear of death churning in her stomach, she didn't try to bolt. Something about the threatening figure riveted her. She strained to see the details of his face as he approached, but it wasn't until he'd passed from the hallway's darkness and the light struck his features that she realized who he was.

"Michael?" His name was a strangled gasp, torn from her in disbelief.

Kit sagged against the railing, afraid she was going to faint. She searched the man's face as he came to stand before her. Was it really Michael? Alive? How could that be? She was too astounded to be frightened at that moment, although his harsh countenance would certainly have terrified her under any other circumstances.

"They told us you were lost at sea," she managed.

"My ship was lost," he corrected coldly.

"But where have you been? Why didn't you return? Or get word to your family?"

"What are you doing here?" he demanded, ignoring her questions.

She began to shake her head weakly, refusing to go on until he answered her. "What happened to you, Michael? My God, we thought you were *dead* these last three years."

"Did it ever occur to you that I haven't returned because I couldn't? I was taken captive by the British frigate that attacked my ship, and by the time I escaped, they were in the West Indies, and I was desperately ill with malaria."

"But why haven't you written or sent word?"

"What would you have had me do? Write home that I was terminally ill, dying of malaria?"

"Yes! At least we'd have known you were *alive*." Kit checked herself, aware that she was reacting as if he'd forsaken her personally. She and Michael had never even been friends— their families wouldn't have allowed such a thing—but they'd had an unforgettable experience once, or at least that was how Kit thought of it. She'd foolishly gone wading in the river one spring when the floods were rushing, and she'd been dragged in by the currents and knocked unconscious against the rocks. It was Michael who'd found her and pulled her out. He'd held her tightly, quieting her shuddering sobs. When she'd tried to thank him, he'd touched his lips to her forehead . . . so gently, it had made her light-headed. She would never forget the sweet confusion of that moment, the utter tenderness of his gesture. The incident had aroused feverishly romantic daydreams that had plagued her ever since.

But there was no tenderness in him now. His eyes bore into

hers, their dark depths shot through with strange amber lights. She'd never remembered them being so concentrated with menace or so frighteningly reminiscent of fire.

"What are you doing here?" he pressed.

"Your brother is sick. I came to treat him." Kit knew she ought to warn him of the dangers of Ephraim's illness, but she was too struck by Michael's physical changes to go on. He looked to have aged at least ten years in the three he'd been gone. His striking features were etched with fatigue and ravaged by turmoil. He even seemed physically larger, as if some malevolent energy had burst forth in him, causing his body to burgeon in order to contain it.

And yet there were hints of the handsome, reclusive young man she remembered. His mouth still conveyed the innate sensitivity of a dreamer, and though his wild, wavy black hair had been forced into the ponytail at his nape as if to curb its rebellious streak, errant tendrils had pulled free. A graceful shock of ebony drooped toward his eyes.

"I asked you what was wrong with my brother!"

"I'm sorry—" Kit hadn't even realized he'd been talking to her. She was still suffering the shock of seeing him alive. "Ephraim's got the canker rash," she explained. "It's already killed more than a half dozen in the village—"

"Scarlet fever? Good God!"

He stepped forward in a way that frightened Kit, darkness glowing in his features. At first she couldn't tell if it was from anger or concern, but the violence breathing in his voice left her no doubt that some inner rage was fueling him.

"Get off my property," he warned her savagely. "I own this land now, and you're not welcome here. You've *never* been welcome."

Kit was stunned to silence. When his parents were alive, they had refused to acknowledge the existence of her or her family. But Michael, though he'd been remote, had never been hostile.

"You don't understand," she told him, hoping that if he saw the urgency, he'd relent. "The rash is deadly, and I'm the only one in these parts who knows how to administer the remedies. I've been treating the sick for nearly two years now. My Aunt Parth has been teaching me."

"No, it's you who doesn't understand, Katherine Downing. You're the last person I want caring for my brother. You've got the blood of witches running in your veins. If Ephraim's sick, it's probably because of you."

The accusation stung Kit deeply. "Michael, surely you can't believe that. It's nothing but superstition, the fanciful whisperings of gossips and overimaginative children."

"I can and I do believe it," he said emphatically. "I've lived with the destruction brought about by your kind. I've seen it destroy my family, and I want you out of my house. I won't have a Dobbs on my land."

"But you must let me come back," she implored. "There's no one else. The nearest physician is hundreds of miles away. I'm the only one who can help Ephraim."

"Don't make me use force."

Something in the soft menace of his voice froze Kit's blood to ice. It seemed to hold the hush whisperings of the dead. She clutched the stairway railing behind her and stumbled down two steps before she turned and descended the rest of the way.

Otis was out by the woodshed splitting logs for kindling as she rushed out of the house. Kit pulled the hood of her cape up, too distraught to deal with him. She would have to think about how to handle the predicament of Ephraim's illness later. For now, all she wanted was to be as far away from this frightening place as possible.

Her hood blew back as a gust of wind caught it, whipping tendrils of chestnut-gold hair from the thick braid she'd coiled at her nape. She glanced up at the sky, praying it wasn't a storm blowing up. She had so many people to see today, so much to do. Gathering the cloak around her, she hurried along the path, anxious to be down the hillside and on her way to her next call that day.

The path ahead of her passed through a stand of oaks, and the dark tunnel of trees filled her with foreboding as she entered it. Kit's pulse began to race as she searched the shadows, not at all sure what she was looking for. A rustle of leaves made her heart rocket. "Ahh!" she cried, wheeling around as a hand touched her shoulder.

"You lose this?"

Otis Pettingill was holding out the basket she'd dropped the night before. The herbs had all spilled out, including the wolfsbane, but the strip of linen she'd torn from her petticoat was lying limp as a dead thing on the woven birch bark.

"Maybe you best not come back," he said gruffly.

"But I have to," she told him, taking the basket. "Who's to care for Ephraim? He's dangerously ill."

"I'll deal with the boy. We don't need you."

"Deal with him?" she said incredulously. "Are you prepared to make poultices and tinctures and sit up nights, swabbing his throat and seeing that he takes nourishment? For if you don't, he'll surely expire, Otis. He has the canker rash."

She could hear the shake of fear and anger in her voice. But Otis didn't respond. He just glared at her with his piercing dark eyes, warning her off with such cold, mute fury that she turned and bolted down the path. She couldn't imagine that he was capable of caring for the child, and she knew that worry would tear at her heart if she didn't return. But as she struggled to keep her footing on the steep incline, another question flashed into her mind. *How had Otis found her basket?*

3

The wine-red glow of twilight was pouring through the library windows as Michael entered the oak-paneled room that evening. Night was falling swiftly, and he could already feel a restlessness mounting inside him. Golden waves of light rose and fell as he approached the fireplace, took a lantern from the mantel, and lit its candle in the flames. He was reasonably sure of being undisturbed with Otis upstairs tending to Ephraim, but he would still need to act quickly. The moon was already on the rise.

On the wall opposite the fireplace, a cherrywood pilaster with a roaring lion's head at the top divided the bookcases. Michael walked to the regal column, hooked his fingers into a groove in the elegantly carved wood, and pulled until the pilaster gave way. It swung back from the wall, revealing a dark compartment. Michael quickly stepped into the passageway and shut the column behind him.

The lantern he carried barely held back the tidal wave of darkness that engulfed him. Its flame flickered wildly as he descended a steep stairway and made his way down a narrow, twisting corridor. The air, though rank and musty, held the icy chill of a subterranean tomb.

A heavy, iron-bolted oak door came into view at the end of the passageway. Rusted hinges groaned and creaked as Michael heaved the huge structure open and stared into a gaping pitch-black void. He held up the lantern, illumining a tiny room that looked as if it had been torn apart by vandals. Books were strewn about the floor, many of them lying open, some crumbling nearly to dust, they were so old.

Wall sconces bordered the doorway, and as Michael lit the candles, the room flared with a shadowy light that revealed shelves of ledgers, account books, and journals, some of them the personal diaries of his forebears. His mother had once told him there was a journal hidden away in the family archives, an account of the witchcraft trial, which had been carefully preserved by Michael's great-great-grandfather, Jonathan Nightingale. The patriarch had believed fervently that the curse would manifest itself in some tragic way, and he'd recorded the details of the incident in an attempt to forewarn his progeny.

Michael needed desperately to find that account. He himself was the vandal who'd torn the room apart. He'd been searching through the books on a daily basis since he returned home a week ago. He'd found nothing so far, but he was about to renew his assault. Wincing, he reached up to pull an armload of heavy volumes off the shelves. He'd forgotten about the flesh wound on his upper arm. He'd done a hasty job of dressing it, and the injury was beginning to fester. He knew he ought to have taken more care with it, but that would have to wait.

As he scanned the volumes, he felt something stir in the very depths of his soul, an elemental shudder that spoke of ancient evils, a primeval shriek that had no origins, no end. A chill flashed over him, prickling his flesh with a thousand white-hot needles. It was beginning again, that terrible awakening within him to things no man should ever have to experience.

Enraged, he began dragging books off the shelves, searching

through them and throwing them aside. Where the bloody hell was it? His own father had never spoken of the curse, and it was forbidden to mention the name of Dobbs within the man's hearing, but surely he would have preserved the journal among his vital papers.

It was through Otis that Michael had learned the details of the witchcraft trial. The story had become part of Oxford's folklore, and on many a chill winter's night, Michael had been well entertained and thoroughly frightened by the caretaker's tales. And yet despite Michael's fears, he'd never truly countenanced the idea of demons and curses.

Sadly, he'd been made a believer when the first primeval shriek had ripped through his body over a year ago. He'd been in the West Indies, still desperately ill with malaria. At first he'd thought it was some deadly complication of that disease. But the convulsions had gained force until they'd literally torn him apart, rending him limb from limb and recreating him as a living, breathing monster, a predator of his own kind. At first the transformation had occurred only when the full moon called, giving him a way to predict the madness. Now it came upon him without warning, rarely subsiding until his animal lusts were satisfied. And it always started in the same painful way—vertebrae shattering into fragments and arcing into a bony chain, dense black hair erupting in glowing strips down his back.

He could feel the pressure along his spine now, the tiny puncture wounds where hair was growing, the fragile bones tightening as if to burst. His muscles had already begun to throb with tension. Before long the pain would be so excruciating that he would be writhing in agony, praying for some kind of salvation, even the release of death. His body would be torn and twisted beyond recognition. But once the pain had passed, no one would be safe from him. He would ravage and devour with the careless lust of devils, a hideous son of the moon.

He tore the books from the shelves, ripping through them, determined to find the one that would tell him what was happening to him, the words that would release him. Moments later he'd emptied the shelves, but the ancient journal still eluded him. With a roar of despair, he scooped up a handful of ledgers and threw them at the wall.

His heart was thundering, his body contorting with the internal explosion that snapped bones and twisted muscles into wiry sinew. He could feel the skin of his back and belly toughening into hide, the sharp bristles of hair piercing through it like tiny spikes. His jaw locked involuntarily, teeth gritting as pain ripped his shuddering frame. The agony had begun, and he was helpless against it!

The archives were in shambles, but the rage he felt could not be contained. He began to rip the books to shreds, stopping only as he realized what he was doing to his family's written history. Spent and shuddering, he dropped to his knees, choked by a tortured sound. *Sweet Jesus, what have I done to deserve this torment? How do I end it?* When he opened his eyes, the candlefire was wavering, flickering over him and pooling on the surface in front of him. In the throes of utter despair, he saw the loose plank in the wooden floor. A flung journal had dislodged it.

He sprang into action, pulling up the boards as he realized it was a false floor. A strongbox, coated with a thick layer of dust, was hidden there, and with one savage heave, he brought the box up by its iron handles. The curse had given him superhuman strength, but he'd had little reason to be glad of it until now. The latch broke with one blow of his clenched fist, and the rusted lid flew open.

There was a single bound volume inside. He removed it carefully, aware of a strange sensation of heat in his fingertips, as if the leather were reacting to his touch. He was surprised as he opened the book at how well preserved its pages were. The ink was dark, the parchmentlike paper strong. Unlike the other journals, this one could have been written yesterday. The strongbox alone couldn't have accounted for its pristine state, Michael realized, but he didn't want to think about the other more disturbing reasons the book might not have aged.

The opening page read, "Personal Diary of Jonathan Peyton Nightingale, The Year of Our Lorde, Sixteen Hundred and Ninety." Each day was neatly accounted for with a few terse sentences describing the weather and other events considered worthy of note. His ancestor's style was factual. No emotion was evident until Michael turned to that fated day when Jonathan's betrothed was accused of consorting with demons. The trial was set down in excruciating detail, seemingly a word-for-word account. And then scrawled in barely legible letters was Rachael Dobbs's curse, as if Jonathan himself had been in the clutches of demons while writing it.

Michael read the words avidly, fearfully, murmuring the first few lines aloud. "The third son of every third son shall walk the earth as a creature of the night . . . Stripped of humanity, he will howl in concert with demons, never to die, always to wander in agony . . ."

As he read on, his reaction was rage and despair. His mother had lost two children before him, both males. He was the third son of a third son, and because of that accident of birth, he was the one doomed "to wander in agony." Pain seared his rib cage, stabbing like hot wires as if to prove the immutable truth of his ancestor's account. Sweat filmed his body as he read Rachael's last words. " 'The curse will go on,

Jonathan Nightingale, until every tear I have shed is returned to me, and I am whole again.' "

He slammed the journal shut. What sort of Faustian bargain was that? How in the name of God could he or anyone else hope to find the bitter tears of a woman long dead? In her spurned rage, Rachael Dobbs had wished on him—on all the Nightingale men—a fate worse than burning in everlasting hell.

Dust flew as he dropped the journal into the strongbox, exposing a small fabric-covered jewelry case that was hidden in a corner of the chest. Michael picked it up swiftly, opening it to discover a locket as beautifully preserved as the journal. As he touched the precious metal, he was aware of a sensation of heat so intense, he feared at first that it might sear his flesh. But the delicate clasp gave easily, and the miniature portrait inside was of a woman of striking and unusual beauty. Her hair was fiery red, and the deep, rich green of her eyes was flecked with a color so silvery, it seemed to be made of moonlight. But it wasn't her loveliness that took him by storm. It was her countenance. If this was Rachael Deliverance Dobbs, her resemblance to Katherine Downing was staggering.

The wild beat of his heart echoed deafeningly in his temples. Perhaps the similarity shouldn't have surprised him. She was Katherine's kin, just as Jonathan was his. And yet none of the other Dobbs women bore such an uncanny likeness, certainly not Katherine's aunt. He'd accused Katherine of having witch's blood, but his fury with her that morning had more to do with his fears for Ephraim than with any deep belief that she actually practiced the dark arts.

He wondered now if he'd been more right than he knew.

Studying Rachael's portrait, he compared it with the image of Katherine in his head. Rachael's hair was the color of hellfire, whereas Katherine's was the antique gold of ripening wheat fields and September leaves. But her differences from Rachael were more than physical. She was a midwife and a healer. Even as a child she'd had a seemingly ungovernable need to help others, sometimes in peril of her life. He could remember her climbing roofs to rescue a child's toy and shooing feral dogs away from a broken-winged bird.

No, he couldn't believe Katherine Mercy Downing was demonic. If anything, it was her strength and her purity that attracted him. He closed the locket, recalling the riveting moment that attraction had first surfaced. He'd been hunting game one sweltering summer afternoon when he came upon her at the river. He kept to the trees, realizing she wasn't aware of his presence. He hadn't meant to spy, but there was something odd and secretive about her movements, and within seconds he realized what it was. She was undoing the laces and hooks of her dress.

He could hardly believe his eyes when she finally shimmied out of the calico garment and dropped it onto a rock beside her. If any one of the villagers had seen her standing there in her coarse linen petticoat, she would have been marched before the church elders and severely reprimanded, perhaps even pilloried or given a dunking in the stool. Oxford was a God-fearing, law-loving Congregationalist community.

As she waded into the water, he realized she was on a mission to retrieve her sunbonnet. A gust of wind must have taken the hat off her head and sailed it out to a tree branch in the river. The sun was shining from behind her, glowing through her petticoat and outlining her body with a soft aura. The effect was so remarkable, it had made him take a deep breath. He could see the gentle curve of her breasts and the flare of her hips, and he'd felt a stirring of something deep within him. He'd never thought of her in that way before, or noticed she was developing a woman's body.

The river was rough that day, swollen by spring floods, and the turbulent water spumed and sprayed. Within seconds her slip was soaked, wet linen shivering against her flesh, clinging in ways that made him almost light-headed with excitement. Her small breasts bounced tantalizingly, and her thighs rippled with lithe, quivering muscle. He could see the intimate details of her body as if she were naked, and the sight riveted him as nothing else ever had in his nineteen years.

Suddenly she splashed deeper, trying to prevent the branch from being tugged into the rapids. It was a reckless move, and the white water knocked her off her feet almost immediately. Michael bolted into action as he saw her being dragged toward an outcropping of jagged rocks. She would be ripped to shreds if she hit them!

He crashed into the water and caught hold of her hand, pulling her into his arms. She'd nearly knocked herself unconscious, but as he carried her to shore, a sodden bundle of trembling wetness, nothing had ever felt quite so good to him before. And when he set her on her feet, she clung to him in a way that made him want to do more than soothe and comfort her with gentle words. He'd kissed her temple that afternoon, but there were so many other places he wanted to press his lips. . . .

A rusty door hinge creaked mournfully, jolting Michael out of his reverie. Pain shot through his legs and spine as he sprang up and moved into the shadows. It was Otis standing in the doorway. The caretaker knew nothing of Michael's affliction, and Michael was reasonably sure the older man wouldn't be able to discern his physical changes in the low light. They were largely internal so far, though he could feel the bones of his face working, aching with the need to splinter and shift.

"What is it?" Michael asked.

"Ephraim—" The caretaker's voice cracked. "The boy's terrible sick, sir. He's coughing up blood and babbling with the fits. He bucks so hard, I can't hold him still."

"Ephraim," Michael echoed. He shuddered with the gut-deep pressure of his own writhing flesh. The change was accelerating. The muscles in his hands were thickening, his nails toughening into claws. He had to do something to help his brother, but what could he do in this state? Half man, half animal?

Summoning whatever might still be holy inside him, he willed the transfiguration to stop. He willed himself to stay a man, but it was too late. His nerves and sinew answered him with searing agony. The violence couldn't be checked.

"It's like that Downing woman said," Otis warned. "I fear the boy is dying."

Michael clenched his jaw savagely, knowing what had to be done. "Ephraim won't die," he told the caretaker. "I won't let him."

Kit awoke to a thunderous explosion and the deafening clatter of horse's hooves. For a moment she thought it must be the Revolution all over again, and the British were riding down upon them. Then she realized it was someone pounding furiously on the front door.

She threw off the heavy quilt and pulled her shawl around her without a thought for her own safety or her undressed state. She and her aunt shared the house's only bedroom, and Parthenia was stirring as Kit left the room. But Kit knew that whatever was wrong, she would have to deal with it alone. She couldn't count on her aunt in a crisis. Poor Parthenia could hardly get around the house anymore.

"Who's there?" she shouted as she approached the door.

Unable to make herself heard over the racket, she unfastened the iron bolt and heaved open the door. A scream bubbled in her throat as she stared at the wild-eyed, gesticulating man on the stoop. "Otis?" she said. "Whatever is it?"

"It's the boy—he's dying!" The caretaker grasped her by the wrist. "You must come with me."

"The boy? Ephraim?"

"Yes—come!"

"Wait!" she cried, but the man had her halfway out the door and was pulling her with him toward his cart before she was able to twist free of his grip. "Calm yourself, Otis," she said, trying to soothe him with her voice. "Of course I'll come, but let me get my clothes and the remedies I'll need."

A short time later, she was huddled with her baskets in the back of the caretaker's cart, enduring a ride that was one of the most jarring, frightening experiences of her life. She couldn't doubt that Ephraim must be mortally ill by the way Otis was driving his horsecart. The crack of his whip over the animal's back was a lash to her nerves. Several times the cart's wheels caught in ruts and they were nearly overturned.

Otis lifted her out of the cart the moment they arrived and hurried with her to Ephraim's room. He hadn't exaggerated the boy's condition. She found Ephraim ravaged by fever and nearly strangling from the fits and spasms that were shaking him.

"Fill up a tub with ice-cold water," she told the caretaker. "Hurry! And keep bringing fresh buckets from the well. We're going to bathe him to bring the fever down."

While Otis went for the water, Kit strained hyssop into the tepid liquid from the wash basin and began to bathe Ephraim's face with it. She had to prepare the boy for the icy bath to come, or he might not live through the shock of it. She spoke to him in gentle tones as she smoothed the rag over his violently red skin, crooning softly, praying silently. Every gasping breath he took tugged at her heart. Seeing him so ill brought home to her how young he was, how terribly frail, and how much she cared about him.

Don't take him yet, Lord, she thought. *He's seen enough pain for a lifetime, but not enough joy. Let him have his fair share of happiness in this world before he goes on to another. It can't be a sin to ask for that much, can it, Lord? Don't let the child die before he knows love. . . .*

Her eyes burned with tears as she realized what she was doing. She was praying for herself too. At twenty-two she was already considered a spinster, and perhaps she'd come to believe that she would never have the things she wanted in life—the love of a good man, a brood of babies to cuddle, and a home of her own. Aware of the emptiness clutching at her, she forced the thoughts from her mind. Somehow it did feel like a sin asking for that kind of love for herself.

Ephraim's spasms had eased a little by the time Otis had the tub of water ready, but the boy's fever was still raging high. He began to thrash violently as Otis lowered him into the water, and Kit feared she'd made a terrible mistake. If the boy didn't stop fighting, he would soon exhaust himself, jeopardizing whatever will to survive he had left.

Within moments Ephraim had slumped into shuddering unconsciousness, and Kit was sure she'd lost him. She drew him to her breast, struggling to hold him up and murmuring to him fervently as she bathed him with cool water. She could see a heartbeat flickering in his throat, and she prayed the faint pulse would not give out.

As soon as the heat of his fever had eased a little, Otis carried him to his bed, and Kit began to treat him with her special remedies. She tinctured his throat with cold water root and swabbed his blistered skin with a compound of hyssop, slippery elm, and dragon's blood. Following that, she applied vinegar to his lips, temples, and palms, and onions to the soles of his feet.

She'd treated Martha Cool's swooning fits with a vinegar bath, and it had brought her great relief. But Ephraim didn't respond to her ministrations. He lay limp under the bed covers, barely breathing. Kit tried everything she knew to revive him, and finally, in desperation, she resorted to one of the cures her aunt had warned her never to use.

She sent Otis from the room as she took a small blue cloth bag from her basket. She'd learned about the herbal charm from a midwife who'd visited Oxford one summer to sit with a dying relation. The woman had warned her to use great caution invoking healing spells, and she'd frightened Kit so badly, Kit had never had the courage to try one. Now she had no choice. There was a life at stake.

A strong, ethereal smell permeated the air as she passed the bag over the candle flame, charging the herbs with fire. Once that was done, she breathed on the bag, charging the herbs with air. "This is the spell that I intone," she murmured. "Flesh to flesh and bone to bone, sinew to sinew and vein to vein, and each one shall be whole again."

Finally she opened Ephraim's nightshirt and passed the charm over his body, murmuring the ancient chant. The candles guttered and the curtains rustled as if a foul wind had blown open the shutters. Kit knew she was tempting Providence, but she'd reached that point where reason gave way to blind hope, where no risk was too great. She cared deeply about all her patients, but Ephraim held claim to the tenderest part of her heart. Perhaps she saw her own frailties in the boy, or maybe it was the resemblance he bore to his brother, Michael. All she knew was that she would gladly have suffered anything, even the wrath of Lucifer himself, to bring Ephraim back.

"Take my strength to heal you," she murmured. "Take my heart to seal it. In the depths of my strength, you will find rest and renewal. In the balm of my heart, you will find comfort and consolation—"

The winds grew hotter and sharper, stinging her skin and whipping her dress against her legs. Dear God, what had she done? It seemed she'd kindled the hellfires of the nether world with her chant. If she continued, she would surely unleash its demons. The winds moaned with a terrible sound, a cry to wake the dead. And yet through it all, the boy lay as still as stone.

Kit continued chanting until her throat was too dry and raw to go on. As the words died on her lips, she turned away from Ephraim's corpselike body in despair. Her head bowed, she sank into the chair by the boy's bedside, knowing there was nothing left but to wait and pray.

Her vigil went on into the small hours of the morning until she finally dozed off fitfully in the chair. As she drifted between waking and sleeping, trapped in some kind of limbo, the candles flickered out one by one, and the room around her fell ominously dark and still. She knew she must be dreaming, and yet it felt as if she were wide awake, caught in a strange and threatening place. She couldn't seem to rouse herself even as the darkness turned into a jungle of shadows. The ghostly nightscape rustled with luminous wisps of smoke and haunted whisperings.

She watched in mute horror as a huge hooded figure in a billowing black cloak walked to Ephraim's bedside and hovered like an evil spirit over the boy's barely breathing body. She heard a wolf's mournful howl and saw its bright yellow eyes glowing in the gloom. . . .

"Miss Downing!"

Kit woke up with a start, bewildered at the sight of Otis standing before her. The bedroom was bright with candlefire, and the shadowy figures had vanished. Had she been dreaming? "What is it?" she asked, seeing the anguish on the caretaker's face.

"The boy—he's coming round!"

Kit sprang from the chair. Ephraim was stirring, his eyes fluttering open. She touched her fingers to his face and neck. His skin was cold and clammy, but his pulse was strong, and the brilliant red of his rash had faded a bit. She felt a trembling surge of relief.

Energized, she hurried to heat some water for tea and to warm some broth. The boy would need nourishment. He'd come through the worst of it, but the ordeal was far from over. Still, if they could keep his fever down, he might survive, after all.

"Is he going to be all right, miss?" Otis asked as Kit returned to Ephraim's bedside with the food.

"I hope so." She spooned some feverfew tea through Ephraim's cracked lips, grateful to see that he could swallow it.

"Thank God for that," Otis said, his voice breaking emotionally. "I'll go tell the master."

The master? Michael? Kit felt a quick flash of indignation as she realized Ephraim's brother hadn't bothered to appear. Where had Michael been through all of this, she wondered? What could have kept a grown man away from his own dying brother's bedside? It was unforgivable!

"No, wait!" she called to Otis. "I'd like to tell the *master* myself." Michael would no doubt be furious to find her here, but she almost welcomed the encounter. She could hardly wait to inform him what she thought of his selfish behavior. Their last meeting was still vivid in her mind—his anger and disdain when she'd tried to tell him how ill Ephraim was.

"I wouldn't if I were you, miss. The master hasn't been well. He's probably in bed."

"In *bed?*" Kit could hardly believe her ears. Michael had been sleeping peacefully while his brother was struggling for his life? "In that case I insist on speaking to him, Otis. Tell me where he is, or I'll search this house until I find him."

"His bedroom's in the tower room, but I wouldn't, miss. Please, for your own safety—"

The caretaker's anxiety was evident, but Kit was unmoved. She walked to the wash basin and splashed some water on her face. Dawn was breaking outside the window, and she wanted to be the one to awaken Michael Nightingale from his lonely repose.

4

Kit curled her hand around the guttering flame of the candle she carried, trying to protect it from the drafts that moaned and whistled in the tower's spiral stairway. The light it provided was weak, but without it, she would have been plunged into dizzying darkness, stranded in the steep and narrow well. She told herself that her shortness of breath was due to the exertion of climbing, but she knew the real reason was something closer to raw fear.

She had never believed the tales the villagers told about the Cloud Castle, certainly not their accounts of people disappearing in the mists and returning as river spirits. But some of the stories, especially those about the ghouls that haunted the tower room and the fanged bats that hung in the darkness, had left a stark impression on her young mind. Even now she found herself peering into the gloom ahead and checking over her shoulder. It must have been the events of the last few days that had made her imagination so excitable.

But she had another reason to be wary, a flesh-and-blood reason—Michael. His blatant indifference to his brother's welfare had spurred her anger, but now that she was about to confront him, the wisdom of such a move seemed questionable. She was not only invading his home, but his private quarters. She couldn't imagine why he was staying in the tower room, but the fact that it was in an isolated part of the house made her all the more uneasy. Still, Michael must be told about Ephraim —and made to understand how perilous his brother's condition was.

When she reached the arched doorway, she rapped on it soundly, not allowing herself to hesitate. The door creaked open slightly, and she realized it wasn't latched or barred. She waited to see if Michael would open it himself or perhaps call to her to enter. When he did neither, she eased the door open wider and held her candle up. The flame threw an eerie, flickering light, but she refused to let her imagination make devils out of shadows. From what she could see of the circular room, it had oculus windows at each point of the compass. The only furniture was a four-poster bed that showed no signs of having been slept in, a wing chair, a mahogany wardrobe, and a highboy dresser.

Other than some carelessly discarded clothing, there was no sign of Michael, either. But as she stepped over the threshold, her focus was drawn immediately to the far end of the room, where a man stood before a bay window that looked as if it had been flung open to the night's biting chill. Dawn was breaking over the hills, and its first pale light flooded his body, washing out the details, yet holding him in a strange, silvery nimbus.

Kit hesitated, her eyes slowly registering the sight, her brain refusing to take in the information. Was fatigue assailing her senses, visiting her with fantastical visions? The man's dark hair was stormblown and wild. Even more astonishing, his body was totally naked. It was Michael, she realized, and yet he barely resembled the man she'd seen yesterday.

She tried to step back, to leave the room unseen, but her shoe caught and she stumbled, dropping the candle. As the pewter candlestick clunked against the hardwood floor, Mi-

chael whirled, glaring at her malevolently. His body was muscled and magnificent, glowing with dark power. Kit had witnessed male nakedness before. She treated the sick and had as
many male patients as female, but she'd never seen anything
like this.

With his hair exploding around him, as black and turbulent
as a thunderhead, he could have been one of the man-beasts of
ancient mythology. His features held a strange feral energy. His
body was lean and rippling with dark chest hair that accented
the flow of broad shoulders to narrow hips. Another flowering
of dark hair at the juncture of his thighs drew her attention. To
her total shock, the thatch of blue-black crowned a male member that was semierect.

A frisson of sensations ran the entire length of her body. In
its wake a painful clutch of excitement caught low in her belly.
Her awareness of him as a male was so instantaneous, so pierced
with erotic confusion and shocked heat, she could scarcely
breathe.

"I'm sorry," she said, backing away. "I didn't mean to—I
didn't realize—"

The glare of his eyes said he didn't know what she meant,
perhaps didn't even know her, and yet he stared at her with an
intense, preternatural interest. Her heart pounded wildly. Was
he ill? Had he gone mad?

His eyes frightened her. They held no recognition, but they
were beautiful, wild, and hungry. They spoke of every elemental impulse known to man, of violence and dark passions, of
conquest and ecstasy. But it was their beauty that held her . . .
his wild beauty. She'd never seen the like of it.

He made a sound that snagged in his throat, escaping on his
breath like a low, predatory snarl. Kit felt a stab of cold terror.
What was happening? She'd witnessed the miracle of life and

the ravages of death in her twenty-odd years. She had delivered wailing babies and closed the eyelids of the deceased, but she had no experience with whatever was taking place in this room.

Her throat went dry as flax, and the hair on her scalp drew tight, painfully tight. Quivering with the nerves of a stalked animal, she watched him, ready to bolt if he moved. To her relief he remained by the window, haloed by the rising light. He seemed more interested in studying her than attacking her, at least for the moment. His dark gaze slid over her face and hesitated on the frantic tick that dominated her slender throat. A growl worked softly in his jaw, its timbre thickening, deepening, as he took in the laced bodice of her dress, the soft dip and flare of material from waist to hips.

A horrible fascination took hold of Kit as she noticed that one of his hands was hovering near the darkness that crowned his thighs. His fingers rode upward, flesh upon flesh as he absently acknowledged his own aroused body, grazing the black thatch of hair and gliding along the rampant length.

He seemed to have done it unconsciously, with no more thought than a child would give to touching itself pleasurably or an animal to licking its own fur. But it was the very animal naturalness of the act that told Kit what was in his mind. She knew it with utter certainty. He was going to ravish her, perhaps even take her by force if she fought him. It was imbued in the unholy glow of his eyes, in the tension that ridged his muscles. There was no decision involved, no moral choice. This was an inalienable right, bequeathed to him by whatever force had taken possession of his soul. He meant to plunder and pillage with the wanton disregard of the mythical gods for their mortal captives and with as little concern for her fears and desires.

Her mind shouted at her to run, but fear and shock had drained her of strength. She was pinned where she stood, weighed down by a terrible premonition of what was about to happen. She'd had her chance to bolt earlier. Now it was too late. The pull of his eyes froze her in their paralyzing glow.

He stepped out of the light and into the shadows. It took her a moment to realize that he was coming toward her, and by the time she did, he'd almost closed the gap between them. She veered away instinctively, and her foot hit the pewter candlestick. Her first instinct was to pick it up, to fling it at him. She could use it as a weapon!

She lunged for it, recklessly aware that he was almost upon her. It was her only chance. But as her fingers grasped the heavy candlestick, his foot came down on her wrist and pinned her to the floor. "No, please!" she cried. "Let me go!" She twisted and jerked back, fighting to free herself, but his strength was stunning.

Gathering her wits, she crouched silently, trying to decide what to do. He was naked and aroused, which might work to her advantage if she could get free. She could rear up, strike a blow where he was vulnerable.

"You're hurting me," she told him.

"Then don't fight me. . . ."

The sound of his voice startled her. It was rough and guttural, but it was a man's voice—Michael's voice—not a demon's or a monster's.

He reached down and buried his hand in the chestnut wealth of her hair, gathering its silky mass into his grip. Kit ducked her head, refusing to give in to the impulse to look up at him. At the same time he released the pressure on her wrist and urged her toward him. Her heart began to pitch wildly, but her mind grew very still as he drew her head up, not roughly, but firmly, compelling her to face him. What was he going to do?

She glanced up the length of his body, struck by several frightening things at once, the gleaming ferocity of his long hair and his dark eyes, the virile evidence of his arousal. It stunned her that she was so close to him, that she could have brushed her cheek up against that angry, swollen part of him.

He touched her cheek, a shudder going through him as if he could hardly comprehend her softness. His eyes flared with the glittery pain of desire, and his hand dropped back, gliding along his own hardness for a brief electrifying second before he brought his fingers to her lips. She sensed instantly what he wanted her to do, but it was unthinkable. Her stomach clenched and turned over. Nerves sparked in a shower of raw, churning excitement.

She turned her head away, defying him as he urged her back. "No!" she cried. "I won't! I *can't.*"

His fingers contracted in her hair, and his hands became fists. She stiffened against him, but he drew her closer, forcing her lips toward his hot flesh.

Rearing back, she glared up at him. "I won't!" she rasped, but a painful catch of excitement filled her throat. He was so dark, so beautiful. Her imagination went wild, nearly paralyzing her as she realized that some part of her, some terrible curiosity, wanted to know what it would be like to do this sinful thing he wanted. No, she couldn't! But she lowered her gaze slowly, and a strange, gleaming pleasure flooded her in places that she touched only when she bathed. In the next flurry of seconds, she felt as if she'd stepped outside her own body, as if she were watching herself bend toward him, watching herself as she touched her lips to a hardness that felt like silk and throbbed like molten iron.

He let out an anguished sound and gripped her face with both hands, his thumbs sinking into the flesh of her cheeks. His fingers curled into her hair, drawing it tight against her scalp.

"You're hurting me!" she cried.

"Hurting you?" His voice was harshness itself, studded with aching, tortured contempt. "You don't know what pain is."

He brought her to her feet, his hot breath pouring over her. Before she'd caught her balance, he'd already begun pressing her backward, forcing her to move awkwardly with his steps until she came up against the wall that loomed behind her. A gasp welled in her throat as light flickered from the window. That was when she saw the torment swimming in his eyes, the quivering glimpses of an agony so deep, she couldn't begin to fathom it.

"You're in pain," she whispered, searching his face. The suffering was so profound, so inherently mortal, she was seized with the need to comfort him.

"No!" He towered above her, beautiful, wrathful. "Save your pity for those in need of it."

"I feel no pity, only compassion."

He gripped her by the arms as if to lift her off the floor, as if her very compassion were the cause of his pain and rage. Anger shook through him for a long, terrifying moment, and then he released her. "Do as I say," he warned her harshly. "Submit to me, or I'll give you some of this pain I carry. I'll make you scream in the night the way I do."

Though his voice was anguished, his fingers caressed her throat irresistibly. He tilted her chin high and gazed at her as if he meant to kiss her, to give her a taste not only of his power, but of the staggering pleasure he could bring her. Kit's first impulse was to resist him, but something more potent swept her. He was graced with the dark beauty of the devil himself.

He radiated sinfulness, and though it did repel her, it also attracted her in a way she was afraid to contemplate. She felt as if some dark heartbeat were compelling her, some seductive force she didn't understand and couldn't fight.

"And if I do what you say?" she asked breathlessly. "If I submit?"

"I'll show you the wonders of life and death, an ecstasy beyond all your imaginings."

He stroked along her lips with his fingers, drawing up sensations that made her shudder with a new knowledge of the responsiveness of her own flesh. Expectation soared within her like the bells in the meeting-hall tower. Their peeling cries signified either tragedy or joy, and though she feared he would bring her both, her mind was rushing with a much more elemental question. She didn't understand why he was hesitating. Why he hadn't taken what he wanted, a kiss at least. He must know she was waiting to be transformed in some way by the touch of his lips. Surely he could see that her cheeks were feverish, her eyes bright with desire? Surely he'd heard the whimper of anguish in her throat?

"Submit to me," he said again, softly.

She looked up at him through lowered lashes, bewildered. She didn't understand what he wanted, but she knew it was something far more ruinous than a kiss. This man wasn't Michael. He was darkness itself, an incarnation of hell's own prince.

He bent toward her and hesitated, hovering near her lips, prolonging the anticipation until she trembled with it. *Kiss me,* her mind cried softly. *Kiss me, Michael. I can feel your mouth on mine.* Her breath hissed out, and she slumped against the wall, grateful for its solid support. What was this wildness trembling through her? She wanted to believe it was black magic compelling her, and yet her responses were so profound, she knew the desire must be coming from within. He'd given her a taste of ecstasy, and she was irresistibly drawn by it, yearning to experience more, no matter how much she feared the other side, the evil. But what was he asking in exchange for the rapture he promised? She had to know what price she would pay.

She had her answer the moment his mouth touched hers. His darkness enveloped her, saturating her senses, while his lips stroked over hers like an angel's sigh. It was enthralling. She'd never known a kiss could hold such bright rapture. The sweet ache of longing filled her whole body.

Submit to me . . . drink from the cup of ecstasy.

She could hear him as if his thoughts were speaking to her, promising her everything she'd ever wanted. She felt as if she were drowning in bliss, sinking like a stone into the fathomless depths of the Indian River, just as she had that day when he'd found her and saved her life. Only this time it was he weighing her down. He was the river, the deep and irresistible suction. He was dragging her into oblivion, spiraling her down toward some dark, deadly ecstasy only he could give her.

She felt his tongue slide into her mouth, heard the serpent's hiss of his breath, and suddenly she knew what price she would pay for rapture. She would pay with her very soul. This man, this demon, would be satisfied with nothing less.

The will to resist him had nearly ebbed from her. She was weakened to the point of faintness. And yet if she didn't act now, she would never find the strength. "Michael—" Her voice was thick, throaty with desire. "Michael, please! You're named for the angels. Don't do this, don't destroy me."

He drew back slowly, hovering near her lips, reluctant to break the kiss. "You're mine," he said softly. "Even the angels can't deliver you from this sweet hell."

"No!" Denial sparked her waning strength. "I won't submit. I can't."

She wrenched away from him and saw the blood coating her hand. A drop of crimson splattered to the floor, horrifying her. *What had he done to her?* She screamed, but the cry locked in her throat. And at the same time that she went silent, the room exploded with brightness. A shaft of sunlight knifed through the window. Michael flinched back from its bright rays as if their heat and purity could burn him to cinders. He blinked to clear his vision, staring at Kit in confusion and looking around him as if he were coming out of a trance.

As he backed away from her, Kit saw the oozing wound on his upper arm. It looked as if he'd been grazed by a bullet or a knife blade. "Michael, what happened? You're hurt!"

He touched the wound, gazing at the blood for a moment as if he didn't understand the reason for it any better than she did. The flow had already begun to stem, and within seconds he seemed to have forgotten the injury, apparently more concerned with where he was and with covering his nakedness. A pair of silk breeches had been thrown over the back of the wing chair. By the time he had them on, he seemed to be coming out of his disoriented state.

He looked at Kit as if he hadn't realized she was there. "What happened?" he asked. "What are you doing here?"

Kit was beginning to realize that he didn't know what had just occurred between them. It was as if he'd awakened from some dark dream he couldn't remember. She'd seen this kind of behavior in the delirious and the elderly, but in the physically sound it was considered a sign of insanity. One of the men in the village who'd fought with Washington at Valley Forge still suffered nightmares and fearful delusions. Michael had fought in the Revolution, too, but she prayed it wasn't that,

that he wasn't going mad. Yet somehow even madness didn't disturb her as much as the possibility that this might be the curse manifesting itself again.

"I've been at the house all night," she told him, deciding to say nothing more. "Your brother nearly died from the canker rash. He's desperately ill, Michael. You must go see him."

Michael pulled a coverlet from the bed and blotted the blood from his arm. "No one knows I've returned except you and Otis," he said tonelessly. "Ephraim thinks I'm dead. And maybe it's just as well that he does."

"What earthly purpose does it serve for Ephraim to think you dead? If he knew you were alive—here!—it might give him a reason to fight. He's so lonely, Michael. He's lost everything. His parents, you—"

A creak on the stairway silenced Kit's attempt to reason with him. Michael tautened expectantly, staring at the open door. They both waited as a figure materialized from the depths of the stairwell. It was Otis, his face flushed as he hurried into the room.

"You're needed downstairs," he said, speaking to Michael. "There's a gang from the village on horseback. They're saying a killer wolf's on the prowl. It took two of Asa Hubbard's sheep last night, and they followed its tracks onto our land." He gestured for Michael to hurry. "Come quickly!"

Michael pulled on a pair of black riding boots, then went to the highboy and dug a shirt out of one of the drawers. "You'll have to take care of it, Otis," he told the caretaker. "I don't want it known that I've returned. And when you're done with the villagers, you can drive Miss Downing home."

Kit spoke up immediately. "I'm not going home," she declared flatly, addressing herself to Otis. "Please inform my aunt for me that I'm staying here until Ephraim's out of danger. And if she's up to it, perhaps you could take her around in your cart so that she can see to my other patients."

"Otis, take Miss Downing home," Michael said abruptly. He rose from the bed, an impressive figure in his skintight breeches. "She's not needed here any longer."

"If I go, that boy will die!" Her face flushed red with fury, she stood her ground. "But perhaps you don't care about that. Perhaps saving your own brother's life is too much bother!"

Michael glared at her and swept on his shirt, shaking his head as he stalked from the room. Kit took it as a sign of concession. Relief swept through her, leaving her weak but triumphant. She glanced up at Otis, her voice trembling. "I'm staying and that's that. There'll not be another word said about it."

5

"You must be hungry, miss."

Kit turned from the mortar and pestle she'd been using to crush herbs and saw Otis standing in the doorway of Ephraim's bedroom.

"I've got some dinner ready for you down in the dining room," he said. "I can sit here with the boy if you like." Kit was surprised and pleased at Otis's thoughtfulness. She was famished, and she also wanted a chance to speak with Michael again. It was probably useless, but she had decided to try once more to convince him to see his brother. She'd spent all day with Ephraim, and though the boy didn't seem to be approaching another crisis, he wasn't rallying as she'd hoped.

"Thank you, Otis." She favored the caretaker with a warm smile as she indicated the chair by the boy's bed. "The tincture is there on the table. I'd be grateful if you'd take the time to swab his throat while I'm gone."

Kit stopped to glance in a hallway mirror on her way to the dining room. She looked wan and tired from lack of sleep, but the depths of her blue eyes concealed a hidden quiver of anticipation. Sighing, she smoothed the collar of her blouse, wishing her clothing weren't so plain, her hair so severely coiled at the nape of her neck.

"Foolish thing," she muttered. Who was she primping for?

Michael? If she had any sense at all, she'd be frightened to death of the man. She'd barely escaped his onslaught alive. Her blood ran hot at the memory of what had happened between them, and she turned away from her reflection in disgust, refusing to acknowledge her flushed cheeks and bright eyes.

Her heartbeat quickened as she descended the stairway and hesitated at the bottom, wondering if she dare risk his company again. Well, perhaps it wasn't her life at stake, she admitted. Her imagination was running rampant these days. But her virtue had been in some considerable jeopardy. There was no denying that.

She found him standing alongside the dining-room fireplace, a silver wine goblet in his hand as he gazed into the roaring inferno. Surprise stirred pleasurably within her. He looked rakishly elegant in black silk breeches and a snowy white shirt with a fringe of lace at the wrists. Etched in profile against the golden flames, his features were especially striking. He'd drawn his hair back into a ponytail, but as always, dark tendrils strayed with a sweet recklessness that made her want to smooth them back, to tend to him with a woman's caring hand. Why did he draw such tender feelings from her? What could she be thinking about, wanting to touch him so? He was a dangerous, frightening . . . beautiful man.

She hurried to smooth her own flyaway hair into the coil at her nape, but he turned with quick, offhand grace and caught her in the act. "Miss Downing." His smile was dark, faintly arch. "I'm pleased you could join me."

"Kit," she corrected stiffly. Everything considered, his formality seemed a strange thing indeed. Was it possible that he still didn't recall their encounter that morning? She decided it was best if he didn't and turned her attention to the table. She was beginning to wonder if Michael Nightingale was not one man, but several, all distinctly different.

The food was already served, two generous plates of venison, roasted potatoes, turnips, and pine nuts, one at each end of the long table. Convinced now that he'd been expecting her, Kit took the chair he indicated. Unfailingly courteous, he waited for her to be seated before taking his place at the table's head. Like the very master of the house, she thought.

She reached for her wine, answering him with a cool smile as he raised his goblet in a silent toast. She could play this game of highbred manners if that's what he required. It would be an improvement on being accosted by a naked madman.

The food was delicious. Kit murmured her delight as she sampled the venison, savoring its richness. The roasted turnips were wild and sharp with flavor, and the red wine flowed down her throat easily, warming her blood. Despite a ravenous appetite, she ate slowly, glancing up from time to time to gauge Michael's mood. To her dismay, he seemed more interested in watching her than in eating.

"Apparently Otis was able to divert the villagers from their wolf hunt this morning," she said, deciding that conversation was preferable to his silent scrutiny.

"He tells me it wasn't too difficult. He agreed to notify them directly if he saw any sign of intruders on Nightingale land, and then he sent them on their way."

"And they went that easily?"

He shrugged and settled back in his chair. "Apparently they were anxious to be on with their search for the demon creature that took Asa Hubbard's sheep."

"Creature?" She set down her fork, suddenly curious. "I understood it was a wolf."

He laughed and reached for his wine. "Some of them seem to think there's something demonic at large." A dark magnetism was evident in his eyes as he tipped up the goblet, gazing at her briefly over its silver rim.

Kit concentrated on her own wine, drinking perhaps too much of the heady brew in an attempt to relax. "Why did they think that? What did they say?"

She tossed out the questions so quickly, he began to smile. She wished he hadn't. She could hardly endure it when he smiled. The heat of his being seemed to concentrate darkly in his eyes and his lips, making it impossible not to go nearly breathless until she'd adjusted herself to the intensity of it.

"Are you quite sure you want to hear it?" he asked. "I'm afraid it isn't pleasant dinner conversation."

"Yes, if you would." She settled her fork on the plate and nodded. "I've finished eating."

"Very well. Apparently the animal kills in an unusual way. It severs an artery in the sheeps' necks, then it opens their chest cavities and removes their hearts."

Kit shuddered inwardly. Her work involved things others would have found grotesque, including observing an autopsy on one occasion when a physician had visited Oxford. But what Michael had just described sounded decidedly gruesome. "A wolf couldn't manage that, could it? Don't they simply hunt for food?"

"That's exactly the point, Kit. A wolf couldn't have managed such a thing, not very neatly, anyway. Some of them believe the creature is a human who takes the form of a wolf. They said they found animal tracks that eventually became the footprints of a barefoot man."

"Oh . . . yes, I see."

"A werewolf," he murmured.

Kit felt her breath crowding her chest as she stared at him. The images filling her head were of a naked man with haunted eyes and wild hair, a man who looked for all the world as if he were in the grip of some demonic spell. "Your arm was bleeding this morning," she said, her voice falling off nervously. "You never told me what happened."

He rubbed the arm in question as if to show her that everything was fine. "It's nothing. I was doing some repair work in the tower room and got careless."

"Perhaps I should look at it," she offered.

He gazed at her across the table for a long moment, then smiled again and swept his hand toward her. "If you like."

What Kit would have liked was another swallow of wine, but she was already feeling a bit woozy. What could she have been thinking about, asking to look at his injury? He would have to remove his shirt, or at the very least roll up his sleeve. She would have to touch him. Knowing whether or not he was telling the truth didn't seem worth the risk of putting herself that close to him again.

She hesitated, studying the delicate flowered designs on the china plate in front of her. "I saw the wolf two nights ago in the forest," she said suddenly, wondering why she was making such an admission. And why she felt so fuzzy-headed. She couldn't seem to stop the words that were spilling out of her mouth. "The men from the village were hunting it down. I prayed they wouldn't kill it."

In the silence that followed, the fire crackled loudly in the hearth, and the scent of bayberry drifted from the tapers in the candelabra centerpiece. Kit traced the plate's blue flower petals with her eyes, detailing them again and again with exacting precision. She already regretted the impulsive comment, but what concerned her more was Michael's lack of reaction. Why hadn't he said anything? When at last she glanced up at him, her heart took a strange, painful leap. He was leaning back in the chair, gazing at her, his eyes reflecting the flames from the fire.

"Tell me about the wolf," he said.

She couldn't seem to catch up with her own jumbled thoughts as she recounted the incident, but somehow she knew that it was very important to tell him everything, to get the details right. "I couldn't look away from the wolf's eyes," she said after she'd told him all the rest. "They were hypnotic. I felt as if they could entrap me, devour me alive. I think the villagers may be right about it being more than a wolf. There was an intelligence there I've never seen before in any animal."

"The wolf was stalking you . . . but it didn't attack you?"

"No . . . no, he didn't."

"He? You're sure the wolf was a male?"

She nodded. "Yes, I'm sure."

"A male wolf with intelligent eyes." He picked up his goblet, but didn't drink from it. Instead he rubbed his thumb along its silver base as if he were lost in deep contemplation. When he looked up, his gaze was slow, probing. "Tell me, Kit . . . the truth now. I must have the truth. Did you want the wolf to entrap you? Perhaps even to . . . *devour* you? Did that thought ever occur to you? At any time? Even if only for a moment?"

A strange sweet pain sparkled in her throat, flaring through her like honeyed fire. Her jaw ached softly as the words finally came. "Yes . . . there was a moment."

"When?"

"It was just before the hunters arrived, I think. I lost touch with everything except the wolf's eyes and what they were telling me."

"And what was that?"

"That he was going to take me . . . on a mortal journey."

A log burst and the fire flared, enveloping the room in vermilion waves. Michael sat forward, his hair and face sheened by the rippling light. "And you wanted that?"

"Yes, I wanted it. I knew it would be beautiful, a kind of death, but more than that, a release of the spirit, a fulfillment of the soul."

"Do you understand what you're saying?"

She nodded, caught in the beauty of the flames that played in his eyes. Everything about him seemed to glow darkly, reflecting the firelight. The room itself appeared to be cast in a golden aura, the richness of it spreading like a glimmering mist that gilded her, too. She could feel her heart slowing, yet working harder. In that moment she felt as susceptible to the incandescent gleam in his eyes, as drawn to it, as she had been to the wolf's gaze.

He touched his injured arm, and she sensed immediately what he was going to ask.

"You offered to look at this," he said. "Would you?"

"I don't think—" She'd intended to refuse, but she found herself rising from the chair. As she straightened, she realized something was wrong. The room began to swirl, forcing her to catch hold of the table edge. She must have risen too quickly.

"You probably should look at it," he pressed. "Just to make sure it hasn't festered."

"Very well," she agreed. Steadying herself against the table, she concentrated on fighting off the dizzy spell. It seemed to take an enormous amount of strength and coordination to push back her chair, and the floor dipped under her feet as she began to walk toward him. Too much wine, she told herself. Or too little sleep. Perhaps that was what was making her feel so odd and say such strange things. What had they been talking about? Wolves? Death? Fulfillment?

"Are you all right?" he asked.

"I think so." She nodded, but the room began to spin madly. "No, perhaps not—" The Persian rug beneath her undulated like water, coming up at her in waves. Closing her eyes, she tried to block out the flood of impressions, and suddenly she was caught in the frantic suction of a whirlpool. It spun her around and pulled her down with a force that was paralyzing. She could feel her legs going out from under her, the floor dropping away, but there was nothing she could do to save herself, no way to hold back the crashing darkness. . . .

Michael sprang to his feet and caught her as she sagged to the floor. A dull stab of pain reminded him of his injury as he hooked an arm under her knees, lifted her into his arms, and carried her toward the stairway. The powder he'd dissolved in her wine had taken effect surprisingly slowly. He hadn't expected her to get through dinner, much less an account of her ordeal with the wolf. He'd been fairly certain she wouldn't remember their conversation, so he'd risked asking her some deeply intimate questions. But it might have been better if he hadn't. She'd aroused more than his curiosity with her answers. She'd aroused his blood.

A less adventurous soul would have been frightened off by the events of the last few days, but Kit was a woman of nerve and spirit, a child of curiosity. She'd tasted the ecstasy the wolf could bring her. She had imagined the soaring thrill of release, and now he feared she would never be satisfied until she'd experienced it for herself. That was why he'd had to drug her. He couldn't take the chance of arousing her curiosity any further, perhaps even have her become suspicious and decide to investigate his comings and goings.

He carried her to a room he'd had Otis prepare in the east wing and settled her on the canopy bed. She lay so still against the blue damask coverlet, it alarmed him, and he sat next to her for a moment, watching her breathe. Her chestnut hair shimmered with a natural light that made him think of clover honey. Her cheeks were flushed and warm, the color of pink bramble roses.

The longing that stirred inside him as he gazed down at her cut into him like a blade. His hand was less than steady as he unwrapped the coil of hair at her nape and spread the wild honey over the pillow. She made him want sweet, impossible things, all those things he could never have with a woman. He longed to unlace the bodice of her dress and free her breasts to his touch. He wanted to suckle at her budded nipple like a child, to plunder her flesh like a normal man. More, he wanted to steal every pink rose petal, every precious bit of life she possessed, even knowing that he would certainly destroy her when he took it.

He began to unlace the ties at her bodice, marveling at the milk tones of her skin as he laid open the material. Her linen shift was poignantly familiar to him. It could have been the one she wore when he pulled her out of the river. As he drew down the strap, baring one small, voluptuously rounded breast, his heart quickened painfully. Heat flooded the most excitable part of his body. He could feel it pooling there, hot and ready, filling him with tender lust.

She aroused his blood. Her soft flesh called to the man in him, promising savage fulfillment, aching release, even spiritual healing. He wanted desperately to make love to her, even now, while she slept. But he couldn't risk it. Her flesh called to the man, but her innocent soul called to the beast.

The longing rose fresh and sharp as he drew up the strap of her slip and touched his fingers to the faint pulse at her throat, acknowledging the life force that ebbed and flowed there. What was he to do with this tender-hearted woman? She'd come here for Ephraim, knowing her devotion to the boy might put her in danger. She'd prayed for the wolf to be spared even though she must have known the creature meant to kill her. Her compassion astonished him. It was boundless. But it wasn't compassion that would be her undoing, he realized. It was her other qualities—her nerve, her spirit, and especially her curiosity.

As he stroked the softness of her throat, he felt something dark awakening inside him. The beast was stirring from its shadowed sleep. *You're already half in love with the danger, Kit. How can I protect you from that, darling? How can I protect you from me, if I can't even protect you from yourself?*

He left her side and went to the window. The moon was rising and it would call him soon. It was time to go, time to lose himself in the heart of the forest. Desire still throbbed sweetly in his loins as he turned back to her. He wanted to lie with her, to feel the rage of human love, the grace, but he didn't know if he could without endangering her. The transformation was accelerated by arousal, whether emotional or sexual. Even now he could feel the energy tingling and tightening in his groin, rippling up his spine. He was hardening with the swift, uncontrollable instincts of an animal. If he didn't leave soon, it would be too late.

6

It was a howl to ice the blood and shrivel the heart.

Kit sprang up in the canopy bed, bewildered. She searched the shadows with her eyes, combing the bedroom for the source of the haunting shriek. The glowing coals in the fireplace provided the only light, casting the small, elegant chamber in eerie pools of crimson. Every flicker seemed an apparition. Every dark corner held a hobgoblin, waiting to pounce.

She gathered the coverlet around her, scarcely able to breathe for the grip of fear in her chest, but she could find nothing amiss. The solid oak door was closed, the heavy damask curtains undisturbed. Still, she didn't move from the meager protection of the coverlet until she'd assured herself that she was truly alone in the bedchamber. Had she been dreaming?

No, she couldn't have dreamed that harrowing sound.

It began to dawn on her as she glanced around at the crumpled bed, and especially at her own unlaced bodice, that she didn't know how she'd come to be in this room. Oddly, nothing about that evening came back to her beyond the fact that she'd had dinner with Michael Nightingale.

She touched a hand to her breast, trying to imagine what had happened. With a flush of chagrin, she realized that her hair was falling free and unrestrained around her shoulders. She must have drunk too much wine. But who had carried her here and taken the liberty of freeing her hair *and* her bosom? Michael?

Her concerns about propriety vanished as she remembered Ephraim's plight. Praying that Otis had stayed near the boy, she slipped from the bed, took a candle from the fireplace mantel, lit the wick in the flames, and let herself out of the room. The huge house seemed a dark and bewildering labyrinth until she found the main hallway, which took her directly to the north wing and Ephraim's room.

She was relieved to find the boy sleeping comfortably and the caretaker dozing beside him. Though it surprised her that the howl hadn't awakened them, she was grateful they were both undisturbed. But the haunting cry still concerned her, and she decided to have another look around before relieving Otis of his watch.

It took considerable courage to steal about the corridors of the Cloud Castle at night with nothing more than a candle to light her way. She went first to the dining room, where except for the fire burning low in the grate, she found nothing to indicate that her dinner with Michael had ever taken place. Even the tapers in the candelabra looked new and unused.

Perplexed, she continued her exploration of the main floor, wandering through the kitchen and the pantry. Something about the stillness of the library made her uneasy, and as she held her candle up to scan the rows of leather-bound volumes, she noticed that one of the carved pilasters had been disturbed. It appeared to have been pulled away from the wall on one side.

She approached the column cautiously, startled as she realized the opening concealed a passageway. With a little effort, she pulled the column back far enough to slip inside. She hesitated at the steep stairway and peered into the darkness below, keenly aware that if the thing that had howled was down there, she would be quite defenseless against it.

She drew in a breath and started down, taking care not to stumble. One false step, and she would plummet to the bottom. The stairway creaked with every step, heightening her apprehension. She certainly couldn't count on taking anyone by surprise. When she finally came upon the vaultlike door at the end of the passageway, she didn't know whether to be relieved or alarmed. It appeared sealed shut, but as she stepped up to it, the door creaked open.

She clung to the candle as a chilly gust of air swept past her. The flame guttered wildly, sending Kit's heart into her throat. From what she could see of the small room beyond the door, it was strewn with books and journals, as if someone had broken in and torn it apart in a rage.

A premonition swept Kit as she stood on the threshold of that door. She couldn't escape the feeling that to enter the room, to cross the portal, would somehow change her life, that it would transform her destiny in some unalterable way. Suddenly frightened, she wanted very much to turn and run, to forget she'd ever seen this place, but she forced herself to stand fast. There was something terribly wrong at the Nightingale mansion, and she seemed to be the one intended in some way to discover the truth, perhaps because she was a Dobbs. At any rate, she'd started this unholy quest, and now she had to follow through.

The small room came aglow as she entered it and set her candle down on one of the shelves. Refusing to let herself conjure up any more fears, she knelt and scanned the account books and business ledgers on the floor, trying to understand why someone would want to destroy them.

As she rose, she saw a strongbox that had been pushed beneath one of the lowest shelves, and then she noticed a hole in the wooden floor that looked as if it had been torn open by pillagers or thieves. She struggled with the strongbox until she'd pulled it free of the shelf. A leather-bound journal and a gleaming gold locket were the only contents.

The locket's clasp was unfastened, and as she opened it, she had the oddest sense that someone else had opened it recently. The exquisite portrait inside made her draw in a breath. Although she'd never seen a painting of Rachael Dobbs, she was immediately aware of the similarities she bore to the woman in the painting. This must be her ancestor.

She felt a prickly sensation of heat as she set the locket down and picked up the journal. The leather seemed to sting her fingertips, filling her with a sudden sense of dread. Somehow she knew that the journal held the source of her premonition, and she couldn't bring herself to open it. She didn't dare. Her quickening heart was telling her that something terrible and unforeseen would happen if she did.

The courage that had brought her to this room failed her utterly as she returned the journal to the strongbox. Tears of sadness welled in her eyes, bewildering her, and her heart suddenly felt as if it might break. As she set the book down, it fell open, seeming almost to glow as the pages began to turn. They flew, one after the other, until the book finally lay still, and the page before her eyes read: "The Year of Our Lorde, Sixteen Hundred and Ninety."

Unable to stop herself, Kit began to read, and as she did, she realized it was a firsthand account of her ancestor's witchcraft trial. She could see the hideous event in her mind as vividly as if she were there in the courtroom, watching it. She could hear the screamed accusations and her great-great-grandmother's tremulous curse. She could see the fires of hell that had consumed the shrieking woman's body.

Horrified, she realized the village folklore was true. A woman had been burned at the stake, a man's bloodline had been cursed, and probably all of the tragedies the Nightingale family had suffered since were because of it.

Rachael's words were there on the page, undeniable and indelible. The Nightingale men were doomed to walk the earth as creatures of the night. But what frightened Kit nearly as much was the reference to the women who must sacrifice themselves in order to set the men free. The locket lay open next to the journal, and as Kit gazed at Rachael Dobbs, she feared her uncanny likeness to her ancestor was not coincidental.

It was still dark as Kit made her way up the winding stairway to Michael's room in the tower. Her heart was beating frantically, but she had no choice. She had to find him. Only he could answer the questions tumbling through her head.

The door was hanging open as she reached the top of the stairs, and though the room was unoccupied, she saw his clothes strewn about and knew he'd been there. The first light of dawn crept through the open shutters of the bay window, and she hurried toward it, intending to post herself there and watch for any sign of him.

Her trembling urgency began to ease as she waited, watching the mists rise off the river. It was a lovely sight, calming somehow, and her thoughts were drawn back to that one unforgettable spring morning in her childhood when she'd seen a dark figure hidden in the haze. . . .

A breath of cool air against her neck startled her.

"Michael?" She turned to the room, expecting to see him standing there. But there was no one, nothing. It was as still as a tomb, and yet she felt his presence so strongly that she found herself walking to the doorway.

The fine hair along her nape prickled as she hesitated on the threshold and searched the darkness of the stairwell, repelled by its coiled emptiness. He was nearby, she could feel it. His presence was as palpable as the icy finger of air on her neck. The intuition grew so powerful that she wheeled around, her heart beating uncontrollably.

"How did you get in here?" she cried.

He was standing by the bay window as if he'd materialized out of the river mists. He didn't answer, but even in Kit's confusion, she'd already begun to realize there must be a passageway in the tower, one that led to this room. She was guardedly aware of the wildness of his dark hair and the bloodstains on his clothing. He looked as if he were caught in the grip of madness again. His breeches were ripped in several places, and his shirt was hanging open. "Are you hurt?" she asked.

"Someone was hurt." He turned away from her in apparent self-disgust, pulled off his shirt, and let it drop to the floor. "But it wasn't I."

"Who then? What happened?"

"It's not your concern, Kit. Leave it alone."

"I can't leave it alone!" Too distraught to hold back, she came out with the rest of it. "Michael, I found the hidden stairway, and I read the journal. I want to know what's happening to you."

He whirled and she screamed, backing away as he lunged and caught her by the arm.

"What's happening to me?" he breathed. "Why don't you tell me, Kit? *What the hell is happening to me?*"

His fingers cut into her flesh, forcing tears and even more dangerous questions out of her. She couldn't help herself. "Your mother lost two children before you, didn't she, Michael? Were they both boys?"

"Yes!"

He shouted the word as if he meant it to silence her. She saw the rage in his eyes, the need to deny, and she knew what must be behind it, what kind of torment he must be suffering. But she couldn't stop. No matter what he did to her, she couldn't stop. "Who were you the night you attacked me?" she asked. "What kind of monster had taken possession of your mind?"

"Is that what you want to hear, Kit—that I've become some kind of monster? That I prowl the night and prey on the weak? Well, it's true. Goddammit, it's true!"

"Oh, no," she cried softly.

He shook her as if inflamed by her emotions, infuriated by them. "My victims are legion," he warned her. "Maybe you should get out of here, before you become one of them. Or do you *want* to be one of them?"

Caught in his flaring eyes, she was aware of something she'd never noticed before. Golden starbursts radiated from the depths of his eyes, vibrant against the deep, rich black of his irises. They were spiky and beautiful, animal-like. *"You're the wolf, aren't you?"* She whispered the question. "That night in the forest when I was gathering herbs, it was you—"

He released her abruptly and walked away, as if he didn't want her to see him. "You're not safe here," was his terse reply. "You're not safe with me. Do you have any idea what kind of destruction I'm capable of? I destroy living things. I rip their beating hearts from their bodies!"

She had her answer then. It was everything she dreaded

hearing. She didn't doubt that he was telling the truth any more than she doubted the wolf had meant to kill her that night. It was all true, but none of it seemed to matter anymore. Though she was inwardly terrified, though fear pounded her like the black waters of the river, nothing mattered except the pain she'd seen in his eyes the first morning she'd found him here. Now she understood the anguish, the unfathomable rage. He'd been turned into a predatory fiend by her own ancestor, and his suffering cut into Kit as deeply and profoundly as if it were her own. No, she realized, nothing mattered but freeing him from whatever hell imprisoned him.

"Let me help you," she said. "The journal spoke of a woman. It said she—"

"Kit, don't be foolish. There's nothing you can do."

Her voice broke softly, but she went on. Suddenly she understood what she must do. "It said this woman must entrap his heart and soul."

"That assumes he has a heart and soul."

"It also said she must find a way to set him free, that she would make some kind of sacrifice."

His voice went cold. "A sacrifice? How dramatic. Perhaps you'll fling yourself off the cliffs?"

"Don't mock me, Michael. I'm the woman in the curse. I must be! I even look like Rachael Dobbs."

He searched her face. "There's truth in that."

"There is," she said breathlessly, stepping nearer him. "And I have things worthy of sacrificing."

Darkness moved over him like a shadow. "And what would those be?" he asked.

"The same as any other chaste, unmarried woman. I have my courage, my honor . . . my virtue."

He moved closer, all the while staring into her eyes and

mesmerizing her with his wolf's hungry gaze. "And which of those things would you sacrifice for me?"

"Any of them . . . all of them." The words whispered out of her, nearly cut off by the fierceness of her surging blood. And yet they were the God's truth. She would do anything to save him. Some sharp, sweet pain was compelling her to take any risk. "Please, Michael, don't disdain what I'm offering."

When he didn't respond, she began to unlace the strings that hung loosely from her bodice. Though her body trembled with anticipation, her fingers were amazingly steady in their task. Their sureness convinced her that this dangerous course she'd taken must be the right one.

His expression flared with disbelief as he saw her intention. "Kit, stop this madness. You can't save me. It's too late for that."

"Then I can comfort you. Let me do that at least. I know I'm not as beautiful as Rachael. My hair isn't red and flaming like hers, but my body is soft." When she had the strings free, she pulled the linsey-woolsey dress off her shoulders. It fell to her hips, and she let it hang there, knowing somehow that it would entice him. She was glad her hair was hanging free, that her voice was soft and warm with her trapped, shaking breath.

"I know you still want women in that way, Michael. I saw it in the wolf's eyes. And the other night, when I found you up here, you were naked and—" She flushed, then said the word. "Erect."

His darkening eyes frightened and excited her. They made her breasts swell and her belly throb. "You wanted me then, Michael. You were stiff with wanting me, savage with it."

"Good God, Kit," he said softly. "Where's your shame?"

"Shame is a fine thing in a sinner, Michael. But it won't profit either of us now. I must do what's crying out inside of me to be done." She pressed a hand to her stomach, startled by the riot of sensation there. "Oh, Michael, I wish you could feel it, this sweet wanting in my belly. It isn't dangerous, it's beautiful. It's telling me what to do."

"It's not you who's dangerous." Michael glared at her, but try as he would, he couldn't infuse his words with the harsh conviction they deserved. "It's I." She was tender and tempting in her coarse linen slip, and as he gazed at her, his own body responded involuntarily. He remembered well how soft she was. His muscles tautened and his body grew harder, making him ache with that memory. Could she save him with the sacrifice of herself?

Her dress fell to the floor, pooling around her bare feet. She was trembling visibly as she drew the strap of her slip off her shoulder, yet something that was mesmerizingly reminiscent of a smile awakened her lips. She had one breast nearly bared before he could stop her.

"Be warned," he said, staying her hand. "You'll push me past my limits. I can't be responsible."

"It's my body, Michael. If I want to bare it, I have the God-given right."

"You'd have a right to leap off the cliffs, too, but I couldn't let you do it." He reached out with every intention of drawing her strap back up, but instead his hand grazed the side of her breast, and he let it linger there, staring into her eyes. Desire rose wildly inside him as he felt her flesh quiver. She gave off a scent that made his jaws ache and his mouth water. It was the irresistible musk of a female sweetly aroused.

"Kit, have you ever done anything like this before? Have you even been with a man?"

Fear and excitement mingled explosively in her blue gaze,

and the combination was ravishing. She flushed, then shook her head, averting her eyes. "No," she admitted.

The wolf in him stirred. He could feel the creature's presence, silent and watchful, aroused at the thought of virgin prey. Longing rose sharply inside him. But was it the wolf, longing for another innocent soul? Or the man in need of her innocent love? The impulses were inseparable, he realized. Both animal and man were hardening, responding to her lush scent, to the call of her untouched flesh.

Kit quaked inwardly as his fingers began to stroke her. They moved caressingly against her skin, and the feelings they spurred were so exquisite, she wanted to cry with joy. Nerves shivered, dancing like moonbeams on the surface of the river. No, she'd never done this with a man. She'd never done anything, but she'd dreamed of it, and it was always Michael in her dreams, always Michael's hands making her feel this way.

"Can you feel what's happening to me?" she asked him. "My heart is wild, and my skin comes alive wherever you touch it. There's so much pleasure, I can hardly bare it."

His fingers stilled, and she let out a gasp of regret as his hand dropped away. "I didn't mean it," she said imploringly. "I'm sure I could stand a little more pleasure."

"Oh, Kit—" He threw his head back, sighing deeply, shaking dark hair off his face. "I don't know whether I can make love to you without endangering you. I never know when the bloodlust is going to take over. Passion could reduce me to something deadly. What if I hurt you? Or something worse?"

What if the wolf devoured her? Was that what he was trying to say? She began to shake so hard, she could scarcely speak. "If you become the wolf . . . then that will be my sacrifice."

"Are you insane, woman?"

"Not insane, Michael." She hesitated, but her heart was fairly bursting with the words. "In love, perhaps . . . yes, I think that's what it is, *love.*"

"In love with me? God help you, how could you be in love with a monster?"

The self-loathing in his voice made her ache for him. She suspected anything she said would be construed as pity, but she wanted him to know he wasn't monstrous in her eyes, quite the opposite. He was richly endowed with masculine grace, broad across the shoulders and muscled in the lean, sleek way of a forest creature. Dark hair cascaded to his shoulders like a hawk's mantle, and on his chest and stomach, it flared like unfurling wings. "You're not a monster, Michael. You're quite the most beautiful man I've ever seen."

"You're seeing what I was, not what I've become."

"I'm seeing everything, even the wildness, even the wolf."

If she couldn't make him believe her words, she would have to show him the truth of them. She walked to him, sensing instinctively what she must do. "You are beautiful, Michael. And very desirable, I swear it. You're built in a way to make any woman blush with wanting. Looking at you now, bared to the waist, makes me feel strange inside, high and tight when I breathe. But down deep, in the softest part of me, I'm trembling."

With some pleasure she saw him draw in a breath. A faint ripple fanned out from the muscles of his stomach, and his nipples turned to ruddy pebbles. Some ancient feminine instinct told her he was succumbing to her, that he liked what she was saying, despite his terrible need not to.

Emboldened, she let herself glance down at his lower body, taking in the blunt force of hipbone and thigh. If she was a little frightened by what she could see was happening inside his form-fitting breeches, she was careful not to show it. He must think her entirely sure of herself. Very deliberately, she drew up her hand and grazed his thigh with her fingertips, lingering as he had at her breast. "You were beautiful the other night, too, so wild, so hard when I kissed you . . . here."

"Sweet God, Kit!" He grabbed her wrist as if he couldn't decide whether to shove her away or press her hand to his throbbing body. With a soft groan of regret, he did the latter. Triumph mingled with Kit's fear as he imprisoned her hand in the groove between his thigh and groin. He felt like granite to her surprised senses. The hardness quivering against her knuckles sent a thrill of discovery through her. It was her first conquest. She prayed it would not be her last.

"Damn you for what you're offering, girl," he said roughly. "And damn me for taking it."

Before she could answer him, he'd buried his hand in her hair and pulled her to the heat of his mouth. The force of his embrace, the power that swept through his body and into hers, left her weak and dizzy with fearful pleasure. It seemed to come from the deepest part of his being, from some molten and timeless core. His mouth was kindling a fire within her, burning her flesh like a windswept blaze. The urgency of it sharpened until it was almost piercing, and yet it was exquisite too. Utterly beautiful, just as she'd imagined sensual love would be.

She moaned deep in her throat, wanting more of it, this sweet hurting he gave her. Instead, he pulled back, leaving her startled and breathless.

"Kit, you must promise me one thing and one thing only," he said, his eyes searching hers. "It's all I'll ever ask of you."

"What is it? Anything."

"You've got it in your mind to save me somehow, and unholy bastard that I am, I can't bring myself to stop you. But no matter what happens between us in this room, you must never follow me into the darkness."

She stared at him, bewildered. "The darkness?"

"The forest, Kit. If I should go there tonight, or any night, you're not to follow me, do you understand?"

"Yes . . ." She nodded, but in truth, she couldn't grasp the gravity of his warning. She couldn't think beyond this one moment. Her life seemed to have started and ended with the touch of his lips. She was already deeply in thrall, as lost to logic and reason as the night she'd stared into the wolf's eyes. Perhaps she'd surrendered to her fate that night, and this was simply the culmination. But she knew in her heart that whatever her sacrifice was to be, she would give herself over to it willingly . . . even if that meant being ravished by a great black wolf with golden eyes, *even if it meant being devoured.*

A low snarl reverberated in his throat, and the sound sent a shock of alarm through her. "Michael?"

"What is it?"

"That sound, I thought you were changing."

"The sound was passion," he told her, soothing her with a caress of his knuckles along her cheek. "I want what you're offering, Kit. Lord knows how much, but I don't know how to take it without hurting you. It can be uncomfortable for a woman the first time."

Kit knew all about the discomfort a woman went through. She'd seen the result of it. She'd delivered the babies. "If there's pain, I'll rejoice in it," she told him. "But there won't be much, I'm sure of it." She touched the strap of her shift. "Am I to take this off soon? I want to be naked when we do all those things that men and women do."

Michael could hardly believe that this was Katherine Mercy Downing he was about to make love to, the odd little sprig who'd grown up across the river. But she was also the budding young woman he'd spied on, and he'd never forgotten her ravishing sensuality. Regret gripped him as he realized that she would make some lucky man a very spirited mate. But it wouldn't be him. It could never be him . . . unless by God's grace this was indeed sacrifice enough.

Now she was gazing at him with blue eyes full of longing and innocent faith, as if there were nothing in the world she wouldn't do for him, nothing too abhorrent. And it was her very innocence that made her impossible to resist, he realized. But did he dare let himself believe that she could make a difference, that she could stay the hand of Fate with her virginal flesh?

"What's it to be?" she murmured.

The throaty catch in her voice made him quicken and jerk inside. If she was innocent, she was also a born temptress. "So you want to be naked," he said, fingering her strap. "Then let's take this off, so you'll have nothing to be disappointed about."

She caught her lower lip between her teeth nervously, as though waiting for him to draw the strap off her shoulder. Instead, he reached down and slowly raised the hem of her linen shift, revealing her strong, slender thighs and the golden mound of curls between her legs. Her belly tautened and her breasts shivered as he exposed them to his gaze. She was as lovely as he remembered, so lovely, she made him ache. He had rediscovered the sensual water nymph beneath the plain clothing.

"Raise your arms, Kit, above your head."

She flushed slightly, but did as he asked, gracefully elongating the milky fullness of her flesh before his eyes. The sight of her budding nipples elicited a sharp clutch of pleasure in his groin. By the time he had the petticoat over her head, his body had tightened painfully with desire. He was throbbing with it, hardening all over again. A growl of pleasure stirred within him, reverberating in the depths of his chest as he flung the slip away. Had he told her the truth? Was this passion, just passion?

Gazing at her nakedness aroused him even further, to the point of swift and agonizing tension. A nerve sparked near his eye, and his jaw clenched, aching like fire as he imagined how sweet her full-breasted body would taste. He wanted to take her into his mouth, to drink of her female essence. He wanted to open her thighs and sheathe himself in her innocent, forgiving flesh. He wanted all of that! But not just for now, *forever*. He clenched a fist as the longing ripped through him again, coming from somewhere deep and hungry. He wanted what could never be, and that knowledge enraged him.

A frightening impulse flashed in his brain, rousing prehuman instincts and impelling him to take her in a way that was savage and primitive. "Kit, it's not safe," he warned her, stepping back. "I can feel the violence coming over me."

"But, Michael—" She came to him impulsively, ignoring his efforts to ward her off. "We have to make love," she told him. "If you won't take what I'm offering, then what more can I do? It's all I have to give."

Pain gripped him as she began to caress him, her fingers gliding over muscle and bone, fluttering down his body until she reached the core of his desire. Hunger rose from that dark place like a living, breathing thing. It was as if the wolf were crouching in wait, muscles coiled to spring.

"Kit, no!" he groaned.

"I have to, Michael."

"Then God help us both," he said as he caught her by the arms. He took her mouth with a trembling ferocity he could barely contain. And though she didn't resist him, he shook her as if she had, gripping her as though she might try to escape him. A savage sound burned in his throat, flaring up from his groin. She reached to touch him, but he wouldn't let her. He wanted none of her tender touches and female wiles. He wanted soft flesh and hard, shuddering satisfaction. Penetrating her lips, he plundered her with his tongue, stroking deeply into the vault of her mouth, showing no mercy until he'd subdued and mastered that trembling part of her, until she flowed against him helplessly.

The wildness between his thighs urged him to take her quickly, ardently, by force or whatever means necessary. But for all his frantic hunger, a semblance of sanity remained. It was still human blood flowing through his veins. The tether that held him back was slender, but some part of him was still human! With a shudder of awareness, he realized he was gripping her so fiercely, he could feel the bones under her flesh. It had to be hurting her, but cutting through all the other signals that bombarded him was the strange, wild moaning in her throat. It told him she was frightened.

He broke the kiss, denying the reckless hunger—denying the beast his ravishment—at least for the moment. A violent shudder racked him as he gathered her up in his arms. He hated himself all the more for frightening her.

"Michael, we must make love," she pleaded. "We must."

He held her tighter, struck by the urgency in her voice, touched by it. After a time, when he'd calmed a little, he drew back to look at her. The longing in her eyes was so sharp, it hurt him. Perhaps there was a way he could maintain some control and protect her at the same time. Lord knew he wanted that.

"Come with me," he told her suddenly, impulsively, drawing her with him to the bed. He stripped off his breeches and tossed them aside, then positioned himself on the edge of the bed.

"Open your legs," he said, gentling his voice as he drew her to him. "Straddle me. Yes . . . that way. Relax now, just sit on my lap for the moment."

Kit felt terribly vulnerable as she settled herself on his naked thighs. It was difficult not to stare at the virile length that rose between them, and even more difficult not to think about what all that dark, pulsing flesh might do to her tender, inexperienced body. She shuddered, and the involuntary response rippled through her, shaking her breasts.

His eyes changed as he watched her move, and she realized how hopelessly wanton she must look with her thighs opened to his gaze and her breasts so readily available. Not moments ago she'd been trying to entice him. Now she was afraid of inflaming him again. His rough passion had excited her, but it had frightened her too. He'd warned her it would be impossible to make love with him without arousing the beast. Was he right?

"Come here, Kit, kiss me," he said. He stroked her face, urging her to bend toward him. And when she did, he captured the weight of her breast in his palm. His touch sent a hot, sweet thrill twisting through her. Deep inside, she coiled and quivered and tightened.

His lips were gentle but demanding as they closed over her taut nipple. He began to pull rhythmically on her flesh, and she let out a cry, tangling her fingers in his hair, needing his mouth on hers. At her urging, he reared up suddenly, reasserting his claim on her lips. She opened to him spontaneously, groaning softly as she accepted his tongue. She could barely control the impulse to squirm as he filled her mouth, making her anticipate the rampant pleasure that would surely come when he penetrated her in a more intimate way.

Michael sighed out his deep, shuddering pleasure. Drawing her closer, he cupped the back of her head and locked her mouth to his. He couldn't get enough of her lips, couldn't go deep enough with his tongue to satisfy himself. Every sound she made, each throaty whimper, brought him a punishing jolt of desire. She hadn't touched him, and yet it felt as if she were gently stroking the hardest part of him with a switch. The pain was as sweet as the pleasure, and finally he could bear no more of it.

"Come closer, Kit," he said, cupping her buttocks. "Move with me." He lifted her up and guided her onto him, settling her over the sensitive crest of his flesh. Steadying her with his hands, he stretched up and kissed her startled lips, murmuring reassuringly.

"Now you're in charge," he told her. "I'm yours for the taking, as much or as little of me as you want."

Kit felt as if she were precariously balanced on the tip of a quarterstaff. "Oh, Michael," she said, "I don't know if I can do this. You feel . . . enormous."

"I am enormous," he said, his voice roughening. "And it's you who made me that way. You can't stop now, Kit, or I'll go up in flames. My whole body will explode in flames."

Though he was smiling, Kit knew he must be serious. The desire in his features was etched with sweet torment, and she knew exactly how that felt. It mirrored the excitement that clutched at her vitals. And if the size of him alarmed her a little, it thrilled her too. Her muscles were already fluttering tightly, trying to draw him in.

She began to slide down on him, gasping with every new

sensation of fullness. And though he quivered and jerked inside her, seeming to grow bigger with every move she made, her body was finding a way to accommodate him. She'd never felt anything quite so exquisite. She'd never wanted anything so badly as she did this new and thrilling experience. Her muscles worked and ached against his hardness, and by the time she came up against her body's natural barrier, she couldn't stop, even at the sharp tweak of pain.

"Help me, Michael," she cried, kissing him fiercely.

"Easy," he cautioned, steadying her with his hands. "Don't force it. Let me help."

She gripped his shoulders as he thrust up gently, probing into her petaled softness in a way that felt as if he were caressing her from the inside. Once he'd soothed and teased her muscles into accepting him, he began to flex slowly inside her, persisting until he'd worked the obstruction away with a minimum of discomfort.

Kit let out a moan of pure delight as the pressure eased and she slipped down the entire length of him. "Good Lord," she breathed softly, "and all the saints in heaven too. It feels like a miracle." She was impaled by him, unable to move for the startlingly deep sensations. Her muscles wanted to contract around him, but they couldn't. She was too full of him, too sweetly stuffed with his flesh.

"I can't move," she said, crying softly. She felt a clutching need to be even closer to him, to be in his arms, and as she fell toward him, he pulled her into an embrace, tangling his hands in her hair.

"I'll move for you," he said, thrusting into her gently.

He did, again and again, bringing her such pleasure, she cried with the sheer joy of it. They stayed that way for a time, she paralyzed with pleasure, he bucking gently, both of them reveling in the half thrusts and sharp, sweet kisses. They were completely attuned to each other, delighting in the astonishing intimacy of each other's bodies and enjoying the gentle build to a climax that neither of them was prepared for when it actually came.

Kit began to feel something taking over her as he stroked inside her. Each buck of his muscular body created a wave of stimulation that pierced her like sunbeams through a gathering storm. She felt it begin in the reaches of her belly and fan through her, darkness and light shimmering like spokes of the same eternal wheel. Suddenly she began to cry and to clutch at him, every part of her body drawn into the beautiful maelstrom.

Michael soothed her, holding his own pleasure back, knowing it was her first time and what she needed was his control. But his body craved release, and it took all of his strength to contain the torrent in his loins. By the time she'd stopped shuddering, he was lodged deeply inside her, but he couldn't thrust freely or powerfully enough to satisfy himself. He wanted her on her back. He wanted to take her in the time-honored way of men and women, a sacred mating ritual.

"Hang on to me," he told her. "Tightly, Kit. Lock your arms and legs around me."

She clung to him, rolling with him onto the softness of the bed. Gazing into her misty, dreamstruck eyes, he rocked into her, slowly at first, then thrusting with increasing power. The energy that surged into his loins was as primal as anything he'd ever felt. Raw joy shook through him as he plunged and pumped, his dark flesh sinking into her golden triangle of curls.

Kit lay beneath him, dazed with pleasure and languidly glorying in the sight of his magnificent body above her. He loomed like a phantom, and though she was absently aware of

the darkness enveloping him, his deep strokes gave her indescribable satisfaction, a rippling completeness she'd never felt
before. He was beautiful, made of shadows. She was too bliss-
fully weak to think about stopping him even as his eyes caught
the light, glowing yellow like a wolf's in the dead of night.

"Michael . . . ?"

Her question was lost in his sudden tortured groan.

Aroused by a soft jangling of alarm, she watched him move
above her and began to register the subtle changes. The muscles
stood out against his neck, and his nostrils flared with every
thrust of his hard, naked body. A harsh, hissing sound burst out
from him, more snarl than groan, and suddenly his lips curled
back in a terrifying grimace.

"Michael! What is it? What's happening?"

She reached up, more out of concern than fear, but he
caught her wrists and pinned them over her head. Some kind
of rage shook through him as he pressed her to the bed and
began to plunge faster, driving into her deeply, almost violently. His breath rose harshly, and just as suddenly his body
began to toss and buck in the throes of release. With a harsh
cry, he gathered her into his arms, nearly crushing her in an
explosion of primordial agony.

He sounded as if he were in excruciating pain, but as he
dropped to the bed, still holding her, still deeply inside her, Kit
saw the darkness slip away from him. Trembling, she wondered
if she'd just witnessed a struggle between the man and the wolf
for domination. And the man had won! Triumph stirred within
her, bringing the quick heat of tears. Did that mean her sacrifice had satisfied the curse? Praying it had, she caressed his
turbulent features and pressed her lips to his brow.

"You're named for the angels, Michael," she whispered,
her voice catching. "I love you."

7

Kit awoke to a dreadful commotion on the stairway. "What is it?" she murmured as someone shouted her name. Dazed with sleep, she sat up and hugged the bed covers around her, vaguely aware that Michael was gone.

"The boy, miss!" Otis said as the tower door exploded open and the caretaker slammed into the room. "Maybe you ought to come see about him."

Ephraim! She'd been gone from his bedside all night and most of the day. "Is he all right, Otis?" *Oh, please, let him be all right.*

"He's wanting to eat Indian pudding, miss, and I don't know if he should."

Indian pudding? The boy had barely had the strength to swallow broth before. "I'll be right there, Otis," she said reassuringly, aware that the caretaker was at a loss. "You go on back."

She slipped out of bed once Otis was gone and hurriedly put on her clothing. The way the sun slanted through the windows told her it was late afternoon. She could hardly believe she'd slept that long, or worse, that she'd been found in Michael's bed by Otis. And yet she felt no guilt. Only hope. If the boy wanted to eat solid food, it must mean he was getting better. That was enough to rejoice over, but she was already daring to attach an even deeper meaning to it. Though it frightened her that she might be tempting Providence, she wanted to believe that things were turning around, that the years of tragedy for the Nightingale family were finally over.

As she was leaving the room, she caught a glimpse of her face in the windowpane and hardly recognized herself. There was a smile on her face! "Whether mercies great or small," she said softly, recalling one of her aunt's many recitations, "we thank thee for them all."

Buoyed by optimism, she rushed into Ephraim's bedroom moments later to find sunlight pouring through the windows and the boy sitting up in bed. His dark hair was mussed, and his angular features were drawn and pale, but he managed a wan smile. The sight of him so frail and brave brought a painful constriction to Kit's throat. His resemblance to his brother was remarkable, almost stunning to the senses. He could have been Michael at that age. Tears stung Kit's eyes. This was the first time since the illness struck that she'd allowed herself to hope Ephraim would live to be as strong and handsome as his older brother.

"Indian pudding is it, Ephraim?" she said, feigning sternness. "So you think you're up to that?" What she truly wanted was to take the boy in her arms, hug him breathless, and tell him how very much she loved him. But she imagined that might fluster him a bit. And perhaps it would fluster her too. She hadn't realized how deeply she'd come to care for Michael's younger brother.

"I could eat a dragon," Ephraim assured her shakily. "Even if Otis cooked it."

"Shhh." Kit hushed him fondly as she walked to his bedside. She held her hand to his forehead, then touched her fingers to his mouth. His forehead was dry and cool, his lips moist and soft, just as she'd hoped. "I think we'll settle on pudding for now," she said, allowing herself to rejoice silently. Her heart felt as if it might burst with relief. The fever had left him!

She busied herself with bathing Ephraim, getting him into a fresh nightshirt, and changing his bedclothes. Just as she was finishing with the boy, Otis appeared with a tray of food, including a huge bowl of the steaming cornmeal-and-molasses mixture commonly called Indian pudding. She wanted to ask the caretaker if he'd seen Michael, but she refrained, remembering that Michael had kept his return a secret from his brother.

The sun was setting by the time Kit had Ephraim fed, dosed with herbals, and settled for the evening. Increasingly concerned about Michael, she beckoned for Otis to join her in the hallway. "Have you seen the master?" she asked as soon as they were out of earshot.

"No, miss, I thought you might know where he was." He flushed slightly. "Being as you were . . . in his room."

Kit flushed too. Apparently now that the urgency of Ephraim's situation had passed, she wasn't to be spared the burden of guilt. She had no idea whether Otis knew of Michael's frightening secret, so she couldn't hope to justify her behavior in the caretaker's eyes. And her more immediate concern was with finding Michael. She prayed he was all right, especially now that the last light of day was fading and the moon would soon be on the rise. She couldn't imagine where he'd gone. Or that he wouldn't know she'd be worried, especially after what had happened between them.

"Otis, can I ask you to stay with the boy again? I think Michael should know about Ephraim's condition."

"I'll sit with the boy, but you ought not to be going out, miss," the caretaker warned. "With it getting dark and all. It's not safe."

Kit searched the old man's face, wondering how much he knew. She was sorely tempted to take him into her confidence. Right now she needed an ally, but she couldn't risk it. If he didn't know, he would either be terrified or think she'd taken leave of her senses. And she would have lost valuable time trying to explain the unexplainable.

"I'm sure Michael can't have gone far," she said. "I'll just check the grounds."

Moments later she had on her cape and was letting herself out the front door. She hadn't bothered with a candle because though the moon was still low, it was nearly full and very bright. Drifting across a wine-dark sky, it illuminated the mists that rose from the river like ascending spirits. The beauty of the eerie vision did nothing to calm Kit, but she was grateful for the light.

She called out Michael's name, half expecting to find him shrouded in the mists by the cliff. But there was no sign of him anywhere as she walked the grounds, and the longer she searched, the more she feared the worst. Perhaps she'd been naive to think that making love with him could break the curse. How could it have been a sacrifice to lie with Michael when she'd wanted it so badly?

The hope that had surged sweetly in her that day was dwindling rapidly as she stood at the edge of the forest that surrounded the grounds. She searched its tomblike darkness, fearing what she might see. She had no concern for her own safety, only the need to find out what had happened to Michael. Perhaps he was hurt somewhere and couldn't get back to the house. That thought frightened her, but not nearly as much as the possibility that he was still in the devil's grip of her ancestor's curse.

The crack of a gunshot whirled her around. It had come from the direction of the woodshed, but before she could react, a nerve-shattering shriek ripped through her startled heart.

"Michael?" Kit picked up her skirts and broke into a run. As she neared the shed, she heard frantic moans coming from the ravine that ran behind it.

"Help me!" a man gasped as she reached the side of the shallow gorge. She could see someone thrashing in the dry riverbed below and started toward him, stumbling over rocks and brambles. His whiskey-soaked breath and ragged, dirty clothing told her it was Moses Partridge even before she was close enough to see his features.

"What happened, Moses?" Kit asked, kneeling over him. "Are you hurt?" He was bleeding from a gash to his arm and badly scratched up by the brambles, but he didn't appear to be seriously injured.

"I shot it," he sobbed drunkenly, slurring the words as she helped him sit up. He grabbed the rusty musket that lay next to him, clutching it to his chest. "Black devil! It would have killed me if I hadn't shot it!"

Kit's hands went still on the hem of her petticoat. She'd been about to tear off some material to clean his wounds. "You shot *what?*" she asked.

"I couldn't see the damn thing clear." He choked back another sob. "But it had the fangs of a wolf and the strength of a grizzly bear. Mebbe I killed it! It howled like a banshee from hell and then it ran off."

"Which way did it go? Into the forest?"

He nodded, still clutching the gun. "Mebbe it'll bleed to death."

"Can you walk, Moses?" she cried, rising to help him up. "Please, hurry! You have to show me where it went."

Kit was exhausted by the time she had Moses up the hill. "Stay here until I come back," she told him firmly after she'd found him a place to rest against the woodshed. "Now, which way did it go, Moses? Show me, quickly!"

He nodded toward the east, past the mansion.

Kit stared at the expanse of forest, wondering how she would ever summon the courage to penetrate its inky depths. But before the thought could frighten her off, she was already hurrying toward the trees. The image of Michael lying wounded and bleeding to death spurred her on. For she knew it was Michael who'd attacked Moses. Her stitching heartbeat told her that much.

"Grant me the courage of lions, the craft of foxes," she murmured as she entered the dark ocean of trees and whispering shadows. She quickly realized that the forest was different this night than it had ever been before. The moon's rays couldn't penetrate the dense foliage above her, giving her the still, suffocating feeling of being enveloped. The air was vaporous with a seeping, low-lying mist, and though the leaves shivered on their stems, she could feel no breeze. Even the crickets were silent.

She hadn't gone far when a strange thick cry stopped her midstride. It quickly soared to an ear-splitting wail, and the unearthly sound seemed to come from the very entrails of the forest. Kit felt as if the ground were shaking under her feet. She looked around frantically, expecting to see the golden eyes of the wolf and bracing herself for the impact of its hurtling black body.

But there were no terrifying yellow orbs, no bloodcurdling

snarls or flashing fangs. Instead as she searched the gloom, she saw a pale light glowing through the trees. Still some distance away, it was as lucent as a shaft of moonlight, with particles that flashed and sparkled like diamond dust. Thinking it might be a camp fire or even a lantern, she began to move toward it. Toward safety, she prayed.

An ethereal scent crept around her, circling her, clinging like smoke as she neared. It pierced her nostrils, and the diamond dust grew so painfully bright, she had to shade her eyes. She could see that it was coming from a clearing in the trees, and she could also see a dark figure spinning slowly in the light's brilliant center.

The brightness became a shimmering barrier as she reached the clearing. She hesitated as the figure began to turn toward her. Though he stood on two feet like a man, his naked body was contorted, and his skin was bristling with strips of black hair. And his face, when she finally got a glimpse of it, was grotesquely deformed, the muscles and bones writhing and twisting beneath his skin. A scream strangled in Kit's throat, never reaching her lips. He glowed with darkness, and his eyes were incandescent, the most ungodly yellowish green she'd ever seen.

"Michael?" she breathed.

"Kit! Don't look at me. Turn away!"

His voice seemed to come from some source other than his body. It was hoarse and guttural, infused with the low rumble of thunder. It resonated like the word of God—or the devil. He was changing before her eyes, becoming a monster.

"Don't look at me!" he roared.

She wanted to turn away desperately, but his eyes blinded and transfixed her. She knew that to let herself stare at him was to risk a hideous fate. She would be seduced into surrendering to his savagery, to his bloodlust. But she was frozen in horror. Dear God, was this to be her sacrifice? Was she to die for him?

"Kit—get away from here. Run!"

He was trying to save her, telling her to flee. Why didn't she? *Why couldn't she?* It was her life at stake, and yet whatever held her there was even more powerful than the raw, paralyzing fear. The creature transforming before her eyes was Michael! It was Michael in the throes of some shattering nightmare. Though his teeth were curving into deadly fangs and his nails sharpening to claws, all she could see was the man, his flesh-and-blood agony. When the pain ripped through him, it ripped through her too. And he was in pain. She could hear it in his voice. She could see it beneath the blinding glare of the wolf's eyes. He was suffering, being torn limb from limb. Bones were breaking, muscles tearing from their moorings.

"What can I do?" she cried. "How can I help you?" She started toward him, unable to stop herself. The pull was stronger than her sense of self-preservation.

"No, Kit, stay away!"

"Michael, *please*—" Tears glittered and stung. She longed to touch him, just to touch him, no matter how grotesque he was. She was sure she could heal him if he would only let her near.

He met her gaze for a moment, and his dark pupils reflected her longing. They swam with marrow-deep sadness and profound regret. And then the shaft of moonlight brightened, bathing him, and he grimaced as if the agony were unbearable. His features contorted and he clutched his stomach, doubling. The sound that came out of him was more animal than human, a hiss of pain, a guttural snarl of rage. His facial features began to distort even further, and the muscles of his arms and legs bulged.

It was horrible to watch. Kit had never felt such anguish, but still she couldn't turn away. "What can I do?" she asked. "Michael, please tell me!"

"There's nothing—it's too late."

"It can't be!"

"Go!" he bellowed. "While you still can."

She held fast, terrified, torn. "No, the curse said a woman would save you."

He looked up at her, his muscles twisted and misshapen, tendons writhing under his skin like wires. His dark beauty had become demonic, his voice a serpent's rasp. "You can't save me," he told her. "Nothing can. There's only one thing left."

"What is it? I'll do anything!"

He knelt and drew something from the clothing that lay at his feet. It was a coin-silver dagger, its blade rapier-sharp. He gazed at the flashing metal for a moment, then tossed it at her feet. "Use this," he said. "And do it quickly."

Kit glanced down at the deadly weapon in disbelief. "Use it for what?" Her voice was whispering, soft.

"Use it on me."

She began to shake her head. He couldn't mean it. He didn't mean it. "You're asking me to—"

"Yes!" He grimaced, fighting to stand erect. "Pick up the dagger, Kit!" he ordered harshly. "Do it! It's too late for anything else now."

"Michael, I *can't.*" What he was asking was impossible. He must know that. He wanted her to use the knife on him—to take his life! But she couldn't kill anything. She abhorred killing. She stepped back, feeling as if she'd moved out of her own body, just as she had that night in the tower room. For an instant, she felt as if she were somewhere else, somewhere safe, watching all this happen.

"Use it, Kit." His eyes were burning a sulfurous yellow as he looked up at her. "You have to."

"No, I can't!"

He struggled to his feet, and a tortured sound shook through him, racking him as though he were being struck, brutally beaten. His body convulsed into the same soul-deep shriek she'd heard before, a wail of such heartrending despair, it was unendurable.

It tore through her own body, searing her with pain. "Michael," she pleaded. "Don't—"

"Kill me!" His voice caught and shattered. "Because if you don't, *I'll kill you.*"

She fell to her knees, sobbing. "Michael, no—"

His voice was butchered, broken. "Kit, you know I will. The wolf wants your blood, your soul. There's nothing you could do to escape him. He'll kill you! He'll rip out your jugular and take your heart."

"Then am I to die? Is that my sacrifice?"

"No, I'm the one who must die. Pick up the dagger!" Caught by another convulsion, he roared the command at her, then turned his fury on the heavens, railing at the cold and silent moon for letting such a deadly aberration of nature occur.

Kit's hands shook violently as she reached for the knife. It felt icy against her fingers as she touched it, heavy as she picked it up. The dead weight of it repulsed her. She could hardly hold on to it as she rose to her feet.

"I can't," she said, looking up at him. "Michael, I could *never* do what you're asking."

"Please, Kit. I'll destroy you if you don't. And I couldn't live with that."

She shook her head, knowing it was his life or hers and willing to let it be hers. "Destroy me, then. You don't have to take my life. I give it to you."

"Kit, no!" he raged at her. "Don't you understand? I can't live like this any longer, killing like a rabid animal, slaughtering whatever crosses my path, even if it's someone I love. If I could end it, I would. God knows I've tried."

He turned his arms out, exposing the scars—ugly red welts on his wrists that she hadn't noticed in the gloom of the tower. Her heart twisted as she stared at the self-inflicted wounds. *He'd tried to kill himself.* She couldn't deny it any longer, not in the face of this brutal evidence. She couldn't pretend that miracles or magic would save him, or that she was the one with the healing touch. Why hadn't she seen how desperate he was?

Another spasm shook him, and he began to writhe out of control, muscles contorting inside his skin, bones popping. The wail that ripped out of him was so sharp, so agonized, Kit couldn't bear it any longer.

"I'll do it, Michael," she promised, a sob choking her. "I'll do it, if that's the only way." She clutched the knife as if to stab him, but all she could do was shake her head. Tears flooded her eyes, and shuddering sobs racked her body. How was she to kill someone she loved?

Suddenly his lips curled back in a frenzied snarl, exposing the gleaming fangs. Foam spilled from the corner of his mouth, and his eyes glittered acid-yellow as he whirled on her, glaring at her.

Her knuckles whitened on the knife handle. Horror froze in her throat, strangling off a scream as he strode toward her. "Michael, don't!" she cried, pleading with him. She raised the blade instinctively as he lunged at her, desperate to ward him off. She didn't even realize she'd stabbed him until it was done.

He stopped and shuddered as the knife blade impaled him, agony rippling through him. Tears welled in his eyes. "Deeper, Kit. Finish it! Release me from the pain."

"No!"

Kit tried to withdraw the knife, but he gripped her hands together around the handle. "I love you," he whispered as he thrust himself against the blade, forcing it deeper.

Kit's wail was as anguished as his had been, a sound so lonely and terrible, so full of despair, it made the earth tremble.

Michael sagged to the ground, blood spilling from the wound. It flowed in a crimson stream from his ravaged body, a sight so beautiful and terrible that Kit was paralyzed by it. She was pinioned by horror, deafened by the screaming inside her mind. It was the sharp, tiny shriek of a lost child, a plea for help from the uncaring universe. *Please don't let him die this way! Not at my hand! I loved him. I only wanted to help him.*

But by the time she'd dropped to her knees beside him, his last shudders had stilled. The life had ebbed out of him.

Blinded by tears, her throat aching so fiercely she could barely speak, she rasped out a few broken words of intercession. "Please, God," she said, touching his misshapen face. "Let him be at peace now. Let him be whole again."

Her tears fell, bathing him. Above her, the leaves shivered on their stems, filling the clearing with silvery music. As she watched, a wisp of white smoke curled from the beast's mouth and rose in the darkness, drifting toward the river. As if in response to her prayer, he began to change before her eyes, to transform. But it wasn't Michael's face taking shape. His distorted features elongated into the wolf's sleek muzzle, and his skin became glossy black fur. The transformation took only an instant, and when it was done, the wolf lay lifeless at her feet. She stared down at the beautiful animal and felt her heart shatter. He was so peaceful in death, she knew he was truly gone. Michael was gone. The wolf was dead.

She slumped to the ground beside him, unable even to cry, her grief was so great. "Forgive me," she whispered brokenly. She stroked the animal's muzzle, his graceful jaw. And finally she drew the wolf's proud head into her lap and sat that way through the night, inconsolable.

The thunder of horses' hooves roused Kit from her mourning. Hounds were baying and men shouting as a group of riders crashed through the forest, their pine torches blazing against the darkness. There must have been twenty or more, and the first of them came within a hundred feet of where she sat with the wolf's body. No one noticed her in the predawn gloom. By the direction they were taking, they appeared to be heading for the Nightingale mansion.

"To hell with a trial!" one of them shouted. "Let's string him up."

Asa Hubbard, who was leading the pack, called back to the others. "If Otis Pettingill is the werewolf, he can't be killed by hanging. He's in league with the devil."

"He cuts the heart out of his kills. He's a son of Satan himself!"

Kit couldn't see who'd screamed the last statement, but the moment she spied Moses Partridge riding among the men, she understood what had happened. Moses must have gone back to Oxford and told the villagers about being attacked by a "monster" on Nightingale property, somehow implicating Otis. Perhaps Moses actually believed the caretaker was the werewolf everyone was looking for, but more likely it was an act of revenge. Otis had run Moses off the property several times. Whatever the reason, she had to get back to the Cloud Castle and stop the onslaught before someone was hurt.

She felt battered and bruised, as if grief had nearly torn her apart. Staring down at the wolf, she wondered if she could move, and how she could possibly leave the animal to the forest's scavengers. Promising herself she would come back to bury its body, she rose stiffly.

The bloodstained dagger would be her proof that she'd killed the werewolf, but she would never reveal the animal's real identity, not even to Otis. She owed Michael that much at least. She would protect his secret. Ephraim believed his older brother was a hero of the Revolution, a ship's captain lost at sea. She would make sure he continued to believe that.

The sky was beginning to lighten by the time she reached the mansion. Her throat was raw from having run so far, making every breath she took a searing punishment. Her greatest fear was that she would be too late to prevent them from doing harm to Otis. After what had just happened to Michael, she couldn't bear the thought that someone else might be hurt—or killed—because she couldn't prevent it.

As the estate came into view, she could see that the violence had already erupted. The pack of men were congregated around a huge black oak, and Otis was tied to the trunk of the tree. Accusations were flying, and one of the men was menacing the caretaker with his riding crop.

"Hanging's too good for him," the man shouted as he brandished the whip. "He bears the mark of the devil!" He stabbed the crop at the oddly shaped scar on Otis's forehead.

Fear and outrage rippled through the restless group. A second man stepped forward and raised his musket, aiming it at the caretaker. "The evil bastard needs a bullet through the heart!"

Asa Hubbard shouldered the man and his musket aside as he strode to the center of the group. "There'll be no killing until we've proved his guilt. Moses Partridge, where are you? Come forward, man!" he ordered. "Is this the wretch who attacked you?"

Kit burst through the crush of bodies just seconds after Moses appeared. "It isn't Otis you're after," she told Asa breathlessly. "It's a wolf, a huge black wolf."

Moses looked appalled at having his thunder stolen from him. "She wasn't attacked, I was!" he blurted. "Besides, Otis can transform into a wolf. I seen him do it!"

Kit turned on Moses, glaring at him until he blanched. "You didn't see anything, Moses Partridge," she snapped. "You were blind drunk. It was I who found you, remember?" She held up the bloody dagger for everyone to see. "It's a wolf you want and it's already dead. I killed it with this!"

The uproar died to a hush. Kit could sense the group's skepticism, but she rushed on, her voice shaking with conviction. "The creature I killed transformed before my eyes," she told them. "He changed from human form to animal and died that way."

"Who was he?" Obed Springer asked.

"He's not from these parts," she assured them all. "Come with me if you don't believe it. I left the body in the forest."

Moments later they were riding into the woods, Kit on the back of Obed's horse. She felt an odd mix of pain and relief as they came upon the wolf's body in the clearing, still lying where she left it. Otis's life depended on the men believing her.

"That'll make a fine trophy for the meeting-hall door," Asa

said, circling the dead animal on his horse. "I don't know how you brought it down, Kit. It's the biggest wolf I've ever seen."

Kit slipped off the back of Obed's horse and faced the men. "No one's touching this animal. It was me who killed it, and I'm claiming it."

"What's *she* going to do with the beast?" someone shouted.

Asa's laughter relieved the mounting tension. "What does it matter?" he said. "She's right. The kill was hers. Now let's escort our fearless huntress and her black devil-wolf back to the Nightingale place."

Kit's heart was heavy as they began the journey back to the Cloud Castle. It pained her greatly to see the wolf's limp body tied to the back of Asa's horse. She told herself the first thing she would do when they reached the estate was free poor Otis, and together they would bury the animal.

As they reached the river and started across the bridge, Kit found herself gazing up at the cliffs with their graceful veil of white mists. The magical beauty of the morning struck at her heart, and through a film of tears, she saw a shaft of sunlight pierce the river, scattering diamonds across its surface. As she blinked away the moisture, she imagined that she saw something, a figure shrouded in the haze of the cliffs. Breezes rose off the river, and the veil of mists began to part, but it wasn't until her vision had cleared that she let herself believe what she was seeing.

His hair was as black as a deep forest night, and his amber eyes seemed to blaze from some mysterious inner source. He was standing at the edge of the cliffs, looking over the river, just as he was when she'd seen him as a child. Michael! It was Michael, and he was as real and riveting to her senses as he had been that day. She wanted to cry out his name, but she didn't dare alert anyone else.

She hoped Obed wouldn't detect her trembling as she searched the cliffs, trying to discern every facet of Michael's face. Did he see her? Surely he could hear the way her heart was thundering. Everyone must hear it. *Look at me, Michael!*

But the breezes stilled and the veil of mists dropped, shrouding him again. No! she cried silently, realizing it was only an illusion. She could do nothing but watch helplessly as the image faded. Though she tried to hold him with her mind, to keep some semblance of him intact, by the time they reached the end of the bridge, there was nothing left but the pale morning haze and the diamonds dancing on the river.

Her disappointment was crushing. To ease it, she sought a pain even greater than the heartbreak of losing him a second time. She flayed herself with the brutal truth. Michael was gone, dead for all time, and she had destroyed him. The image she'd seen was a vision brought to life by her longing, a ghost. She had wished him into existence.

The dagger flashed into her mind, and she was grateful she didn't have it in hand. She imagined the blade piercing her rib cage and puncturing her heart as it must have Michael's, and she knew it would be the sweetest, cruelest pain she could ever feel. She wanted that peace, but it wasn't to be hers. He was gone, to something better, she prayed. And she was alive, left with memories as jagged as daggers. Her only comfort was in knowing that she could never lose him again. She had lost him forever.

8

Kit awakened with a start and glanced around the small bed-chamber. The light filtering through the open shutters had the pale glow of dawn about it, but it wasn't sunlight that had teased her awake. She had the strongest sense that something had been altered in the room. Had the morning breeze lifted a curtain? Or a lace doily slipped off the lowboy and fallen to the floor? She scanned the room, relieved when it seemed that everything was in place, but the feeling persisted.

Moments later, as she patted her face dry after washing up, she was still musing the change. Perhaps something had altered in her. The ordeals of the last twenty-four hours had been emotionally devastating. Last night she and Otis had dug a deep grave in a shady oak grove near the edge of the forest and laid the wolf's body to rest there. Otis hadn't asked her to explain her bitter sadness. He'd seemed to understand in some way.

But the sadness lingered even now in her expression as she gazed into the wall mirror. There was a gravity in her blue eyes that told her she had been altered from within, that some new and solemn understanding had been instilled in her. She would never have believed she could take a human life, but she had finally come to understand the tragedy for what it was, an act of mercy. Michael had begged to be released from his agony, but she hadn't had the strength of heart to help him until she'd seen the depths of his despair. Compassion was love in its purest and most unselfish form, she knew that now. But her heart also knew the terrible cost of taking a life, any life, even if fate demanded it. If Michael had found peace, she could be happy for that. But she wondered if she would ever again know its solace.

She dressed quickly, grateful to have the fresh clothing Otis had brought back from Aunt Parth's. She was going home today, but of course she had to see Ephraim first, one last visit to reassure herself that the boy was all right before she left him in Otis's care.

As she gathered up her things and turned to smooth the bed covers, she noticed something lying on the pillow next to hers. It glittered brightly as an errant beam of sunlight struck it. As she gazed at it, Kit felt that odd sense of movement again, of breezes blowing and curtains shifting.

Nestled against the bleached-white linen pillowcase like something priceless, the antique locket invited her to pick it up. Preparing herself for the pale countenance of Rachael Dobbs, she freed the clasp. But as she lay the locket open, it wasn't Rachael's face that made her breath snag in her throat. It was a tiny perfect gem. Grooved into the highest tear-shaped burn on Rachael's cheek was a sparkling blue-white diamond. It flashed as brilliantly as sunlight shattering on the river.

The curse will go on, Jonathan Nightingale, until every tear I have shed is returned to me, and I am whole again.

Rachael's own words sounded in Kit's mind as she stared at the jewel in astonishment. What manner of wizardry had brought this about? Even if Otis had found the locket in the archives and placed it on her pillow, perhaps thinking it should be returned to the Dobbs family, he couldn't have replaced the diamond. That would have taken a jeweler, a master craftsman.

Was the diamond meant to be the first tear restored?

She clutched the locket in her hand as that question seared through her thoughts. A sudden urgency compelled her, and before she quite understood what had seized hold of her, she found herself rushing out the bedroom door and down the great stairway. She ran through the halls like a woman possessed.

The door to the tower stairway was closed against her, but she flung herself at it, slamming it open with all her might. She plunged into the gloom without a candle, climbing the circular stairway by some magical combination of faith and memory. Her lungs were bursting by the time she reached the landing at the top, and she had to stop and gather herself together before she could open the door.

The image of him standing in the light of the window had formed during her flight, and now it was so vibrantly alive in her mind that she cried out his name even before she'd entered the room. As the door swung open and she stepped across the threshold, she hesitated, paralyzed by the possibility that her vision had come true—and terrified it was only that, a vision.

The windows were thrown open, but instead of sunlight, mists from the river rolled into the room like a thick, silky fog. At its shimmering heart a figure moved, and though Kit couldn't see clearly, she knew with the certainty of Solomon who it was. But was he real this time? Or another trick of the river spirits?

"Michael?" Her voice broke. "Is it you?"

The silk began to swirl and rise like a veil, drifting up his body. Kit could hardly endure the pain of waiting to see if her premonition would be confirmed. When the veil was gone, she began to shake. For all of her fear, the sight of his beautiful face and glowing dark hair nearly split her heart wide open with joy. "Michael!" she cried. "Please say something. *I'm so afraid that I'm dreaming you.*"

His silence gripped her like death itself. She couldn't bring herself to approach him. What if he vanished again?

"Michael . . . ?"

"I may be named for the angels," he said at last, his voice echoing softly, "but I'm real enough. Come and see."

She dragged in a great sob of relief. "I was afraid I'd wished you back to life."

"Something wished me back to life. It must have been you." He held out his hand. "Come, Kit. See for yourself if it's flesh and blood."

His voice had a gentle tug in it, like a warm wind pulling at thistledown. She let herself be drawn by it, though she was still reluctant to let herself believe in it. But his hand was warm and strong as she took it, pulsing with life. Surely he was made of human flesh and bone and blood, just as she was.

"Convinced?" he asked, squeezing her hand.

"Nearly . . . but do you think we might kiss? I expect that would settle my mind once and for all."

His smile set her heart afire. There was such dark beauty and sensuality in it, she didn't need to be kissed to believe he was real. He was thrumming with life and love and desire, all of it directed at her.

"Whatever it takes," he said, laughing softly as he drew her into his arms. He stroked her face, smoothing back the golden tangle of her hair as he gazed at her. Passion sparked in his eyes and tingled hotly on his lips as he bent and took her trembling mouth. Kit felt the power of him shiver through her and allowed herself to go weak and loose in his arms, to rejoice in the wonder of realized dreams. He was alive. He was hers, forevermore. Oh, please let that be true!

She broke away, gasping softly at the sweet ache that filled her throat. She wanted to kiss him forever. She never wanted to let go, but there was so much she needed to know. Their very future was at stake. "So it's done, then?" she asked him, touching his face, thrilling at the warmth of him. "This thing that has plagued both our families for a hundred years? The curse is broken?"

"Not broken, Kit. I'm afraid it may continue to haunt the Nightingale lineage in some way, but you've released me from it. We can be thankful for that, at least. It was your sacrifice that brought back the first tear."

"My sacrifice?" Suddenly Kit understood. "Then it wasn't giving up my own life as I first believed. It was taking yours—the life of the man I loved. That was the sacrifice no mortal woman would ever make."

At his nod she realized she was still clutching the locket in her hand. "I found this on my pillow," she said, uncurling her fingers to show him. "Did you put it there?"

"Yes, I hoped it would prepare you for my return. I didn't want to frighten you again, after everything you'd been through." He closed her hand over the necklace and brought her fingers to his lips, kissing her knuckles. "The locket is yours, Kit. You were meant to have it. I hope you'll think of it as a symbol of my love. And as my promise that I will never betray you as my ancestor betrayed yours."

Kit let out a shaky sigh. She felt as if a lifetime's longing might burst the seams of her heart. The naked tenderness that moved in his eyes gave his features an entirely different aspect. It didn't soften the strong, solemn lines, it lent them depth and texture and character. Surely this man the fates had chosen for her was a good match, she thought. He had love in him, great compassion. For he knew the true value of those qualities now, as she did.

"I think you should turn, Kit," he said, taking the locket from her hand. "And let me put this on you."

She did as he asked, shivering a little as he drew the silky chain around her neck and fastened it at her nape. When he had it secured, he grasped her shoulders gently, nuzzling her hair and her neck.

Kit arched at the touch of his lips, closing her eyes and luxuriating in the bliss of it. His hands stroked her arms, and his lips drifted up the curve of her neck. It was so startlingly sensual, she was nearly dizzy with pleasure when she heard something that made her eyes fly open. There was a growl rumbling in the depths of his throat. "Michael?"

She turned, searching his face. "That sound! I thought you were changing."

He laughed softly. "It means passion too, remember? Tell me the truth, Kit. Didn't you like the wolf a little?"

"Yes, I did."

"And didn't you want to be devoured, just a little?"

She nodded.

"Good, because there's still some wolf in me."

"Just a little?"

His dark eyes flickered with amber fire as he tipped up her chin and kissed her lightly. "Just enough," he assured her.

MADNESS

Olivia Rupprecht

AUTHOR'S NOTE

Being a contemporary romance author, I acquired great respect for the historical novel in the writing of "Madness." The research involved was time consuming, but several professionals contributed to making my job much easier. I thank them and do gratefully acknowledge their individual contributions:

Brian Tautges, who allowed me access to his extensive knowledge of American history. Nanci Rinehart, RN, MSN, for her invaluable insights into hysterical blindness. Dr. Kerri Scarbrough, who generously shared her medical expertise, including the historical context of visual testing and medical technology. Barbra Jamieson of the Todd Wehr Library, Medical College of Wisconsin, for referencing information on optokinetic nystagmus.

Nystagmus, I learned, was treated in Rome as early as the fifth century B.C. There are, however, various forms of this symptom, the optokinetic variety being one of them. Since the Index Medicus didn't start until 1895, I was unable to determine an American physician's awareness of this particular form in 1872, the year in which "Madness" is set. Needing this symptom in the telling of the story, I took the liberty of using it.

Writing fiction is what I best love to do, and it's a good thing that I understand it better than the science of medicine. Medicalese is lost on me. The aforementioned professionals simplified their explanations as much as possible, but there is a chance I erred in some way. If I did, be it in terminology or historical correctness, any and all mistakes are the sole responsibility of this author.

1

EUGENE, OREGON—1872

Annabelle Rawlings fingered the locket between her breasts, and felt the coolness of the smooth metal she remembered as being a gleaming gold. The clean, woodsy scent of towering pines tantalized her nostrils. A soft summer wind moved through the branches overhead, and prickly needles rustled like a freshly starched petticoat.

As she rocked on the porch of the log cabin, she wished once more that she could see the sleek, green beauty of a slender blade of grass, or lightning, like crow's feet, stitched across an indigo sky.

She sighed. To see nature was no more possible than to read the books she cherished with the intensity of a lover, their pages worn ragged from her fingers' brush.

Refusing the bite of bitterness, she exulted in the sun's waning rays. They warmed her face, danced against her lids, and warded off the creeping shadows of dusk—and the blinding fear that night brought.

A faint snapping noise caused her to stop rocking. Someone or something large enough to break a twig on the grass-covered ground was approaching.

"Pa?" she called anxiously, feeling for the stick he'd whittled for her with equal measures of love and skill.

"It's me, Annabelle. Gettin' late in the day. Don't you want to go in?"

"In a minute, Pa. The sun's not down yet." She felt his hand pat her shoulder, the callused tips of his fingers creating soft friction against the cheap cloth of her calico dress.

"I'll stir up the fire and put the candles to light. Scoop some of that stew you've been brewing all day. Sure smells tasty, Annabelle. You do good, girl—so good, your Pa's taking you to town tomorrow. Got you a dandy surprise."

"A dandy! You mean that mail-order groom I asked for last Christmas finally arrived?" With a saucy toss of her head, she added drolly, "If he's uncomely, no need to send him back. Even sight unseen, I'll gladly take his ring."

"Don't you start that old-maid nonsense with me. Some man's going to count his lucky stars the day he gets you for a wife. You're a fine-looking woman, the spitting image of your ma, and not the flighty sort."

"Like Lorna? Lord knows she went through more beaux than hair ribbons before tying the knot." Annabelle wished her little sister had settled on a suitor whose home was closer than a half day's ride away. At times she even wished that one of Lorna's castoffs had taken notice of the elder sister, who now hid her envy with a too-bright laugh.

"You're fretting, girl, and I reckon you've got cause. But just remember, all good things come to those who wait."

Annabelle bit back the obvious retort, that as long as she'd likely have to wait for a man who would take her, she should indeed have grand prospects ahead.

She heard Pa's boots scrape against the wood planking, then the rusty groan of hinges as he passed through the cabin door.

Her smile vanished, and she fingered the locket until the sun kissed her farewell. Grabbing her walking stick, she got up. The tap-tap of the cane, the swish of her skirt, and the soft tread of her leather shoes on the wooden porch blended with the shrill call of a bird.

Only a bird, Annabelle told herself, not an anguished shriek piercing the darkness—a darkness that had come seventeen years ago and never left.

Annabelle quickened her pace. Pa would have the fire raised high and candles lit all around. But it would do no good, because the creatures that stalked her would find where she hid in dreams.

They always found her. Always . . .

At night.

"Say, 'ahh.' "

"Ahhh . . ."

Ahh-hah! Just as he'd suspected. Heath Nightingale adjusted the gaslight reflector strapped around his head and quickly finished his inspection of the young woman's tonsils.

"See anything wrong, Dr. Nightingale?" asked the mother who'd brought the patient in—along with a basket of cookies.

"Nothing out of the ordinary." Not unless he counted the fact that this was the tenth pretty skirt this week to claim to have a tickle in her throat but not to have a sign of infection. After turning down yet another dinner invitation, he saw the pair out and prepared for his next appointment.

Jacob Rawlings, a giant of a man Heath had literally bumped into at the dry-goods store, was bringing in his daughter. It seemed that old Doc Adams, whose practice he'd taken on, had made the diagnosis she was blind, and that was that.

Jake Rawlings hadn't been convinced, had said he'd even taken her from Eugene to San Francisco, where another doctor had done all sorts of tests, then, instead of confirming Adams's opinion, suggested they travel east for further evaluation. The problem was, the farm couldn't tend itself and money was too tight for railroad fare, not to mention his "little girl had been poked and probed so much she'd have to be hog-tied before she'd let anyone else look at her."

Heath had sympathized with the man and was more than happy to accept his payment in chopped wood for the fireplace. Such a deep satisfaction he'd felt when Jake nearly unhinged his arm in a parting handshake of gratitude. That's when Heath knew that his decision to venture west had been wise, not "madness, sheer madness" as his colleagues had insisted.

As he poured water from a pitcher into a washing bowl and soaped up, he had to admit that his office and the adjoining room he used for living quarters weren't anything to write home about. However, a frontier town's lack of amenities was a minor trade-off for freedom from Boston high society and family power struggles.

Stealing a quick glance in the mirror, Heath noticed something flash near his reflection. He turned, but saw nothing. At the same time there arose a whiff of a scent that seemed familiar, but before he could place it, it was gone as well.

He felt a vague unease but decided he'd merely been imagining things. Returning his attention to the mirror, Heath recognized the expression he wore whenever he couldn't make a ready diagnosis. His perplexed frown made him laugh, revealing slightly crooked front teeth. Otherwise, the mirror wasn't unkind. He wasn't the most handsome man in the world, but he'd never sent a woman running in the opposite direction.

A brisk knock on the open door to the examination room alerted him that he'd been caught in his self-study. His slight embarrassment was forgotten as his gaze veered from Jake Rawlings, with his hat in hand, to . . . the woman beside him. Heath had expected a timid teenager, not a striking creature with flaxen-colored hair spilling in all directions. As he walked toward them, he watched as she fanned herself with an agitated sweep of her hand and took several shallow breaths.

She was, he decided, manifesting a nervous reaction.

His own reaction to her flushed cheeks and the rapid rise and fall of her breasts was altogether too male.

"Please, do come in." Heath hoped his warm greeting passed for that of a physician setting a patient at ease.

"Why, thankee," Jake responded. Gripping his daughter's arm, he took a step forward but stopped when she dug in her heels. With an expression that silently begged Heath to back him up, Jake said pointedly, "Come meet *Mr.* Nightingale."

"Don't you mean *Doctor?*" The fineness of her voice contrasted with the harsh sound of her walking stick striking the floor twice. "You tricked me, didn't you, Pa? Don't deny it, I can smell antiseptic from here. A 'dandy surprise,' indeed."

Jake Rawlings's "little girl" was wearing an expression of fury that said she was old enough to know her own mind. Heath guessed her to be in her midtwenties.

"You must be . . . Annabelle, isn't it?" In the wake of her silence and Jake's apologetic head shaking, Heath called upon his best bedside manner. "I understand that you don't care to visit doctors any more than I care to sit in a dentist's chair. So why don't we forget my profession for a while and, if your father doesn't mind, put aside formalities. Call me—"

His attention was suddenly riveted by her gold locket. He was inexplicably mesmerized, caught by a vision of that locket nestled between bare breasts and dangling from a slender, graceful throat. Locket, breasts, and throat seemed to merge and become one, and the image was bewitching, erotic and—

Heath blinked. He must need to see a doctor. His eyes were playing tricks on him today, as if his firm grip on reality were loosening and he was being led in some very strange directions.

"Call me Heath," he invited her in a tone that he recognized as unsuitably intimate. Clearing his throat, he commanded his befuddled brain to do the same and asked politely, "Would either of you care for tea?"

"None for me, thank you." Annabelle gripped the locket.

Realizing his gaze had become an outright stare, Heath forced his attention to Jake, who said, "I'd be much obliged for a cup."

"You don't like tea, Pa. Unless it's spiked with a shot of whiskey."

"I have whiskey," Heath said. "I also have a box of chocolates. Would you care to sample a few, Annabelle?"

"Trying to sweeten me up so you can check me out?"

"Annabelle!" Pa gripped her wrist when she again tapped her cane. "That's enough, young lady. I taught you better."

When she tried to retreat, Heath caught her shoulders. Immediately he was enveloped by the sweet, dank scent he'd detected earlier. There was a pounding in his chest as if something inside was frantic to get out. His heart raced. So did his blood. It seemed to pool in his thickening loins and left him lightheaded, giddy, as if he'd taken opium.

She jerked away, and that quickly he was released from the drugging sensations. Her gasping breaths made him wonder if she'd felt them too. Or was she simply affronted by his touch? That was the logical assumption, considering her aversion to doctors. Equally as logical was his conclusion that she inspired his hormones to rise to new heights of chemical reaction.

"Please stay," he entreated her. "You were right, I was trying to bribe you with chocolates. Since that didn't work, I'm asking for an hour of your time. Alone. If you still want to leave, fine. I won't agree to see you again unless you make the next appointment yourself."

Quite unexpectedly, he was rewarded with a sly smile.

"Pa, didn't you need a few things from the feed store?"

With a muttered "Sorry, Doc," Jake departed.

After shutting the door, Heath spent a minute indulging himself by watching Annabelle tap the length of his examining table. She shuddered visibly before moving on to trace her fingertips along the shelf where his pharmaceuticals were alphabetically lined.

"If you turn left and walk ten paces, you'll find a closet. The chocolates are on the top shelf."

"Aren't you going to offer to fetch them for me?"

"Why should I? You're perfectly capable of managing by yourself."

"Thank you," she said quietly, and he knew full well she didn't mean for the chocolate. It told him a lot about her. Annabelle Rawlings had dignity; she'd also had it hurt.

Heath, taking note of the graceful back-and-forth sweep of her cane and the even more graceful sway of her hips, decided that she did a lot for a simple dress. Certainly more than the pampered heiress he'd refused to marry had done for the lacy confections she'd habitually worn.

Candy in hand, Annabelle found the couch and sat. With a flick of her wrist, she flipped aside the bunched folds of her skirt. Heath's eyes widened. She had revealed not only a shapely calf, but a *bare* calf. No stockings? *Good Lord.*

After a deep breath to steady himself, he breached the silence. "So tell me, Annabelle, what might I do to sway your aversion to doctors? I much prefer for you to like me."

"So tell me, Heath Nightingale, do you always stand while ornery patients eat up your profits? This is very fine chocolate, and though I appreciate your willingness to share, I'm afraid it's wasted as a means of persuasion." She smiled a lush, teasing, sensual smile that was disconcerting because it was unstudied, then sank her teeth into a bonbon. Licking vanilla cream from a tapered finger, she informed him, "You should have saved these for your wife."

"I'm not married."

She shrugged indifferently. "In that case, to gain the favor of any woman you fancy."

"If I can gain your favor, I should be able to gain the Queen of England's . . . with nary a chocolate," he replied, sitting beside her.

She laughed. A throaty laugh that was pure and deep and a refreshing relief from coy twitters and false giggles hidden behind gloved hands that had never done an honest day's work.

Truth to tell, *she* was the first woman to catch his fancy in some time. He had the distinct impression that Annabelle Rawlings didn't consider herself a potential candidate for any man's attention, which only managed to further capture his.

A bit too well. Again he realized he was staring at the locket and the breasts it rested between. Lucky for him she couldn't see; she'd have good reason to slap his face!

"Want one?" She extended the box to him, the movement causing locket and breasts to come temptingly close. He reached out a hand—but not for the candy.

What the hell was the matter with him? Heath stared dumbly at his hand, which hovered over the locket. With difficulty, such difficulty he felt as if he were fighting the logical order of nature, he withdrew.

"I—" Struggling to make sense out of nonsense, he said, "None for me. I'd rather that you tell me about yourself."

"You mean about my blindness." She sighed wearily, as if resigned to an inquisition.

"No. I was wondering about you. If you're always so . . ."

"Impertinent? Persnickety? Fortunately for Pa, no."

"Delightful, was actually the word I was searching for."

Annabelle snorted at that. "I've tired of this parlor game. You may examine me. All I ask is that, please, unlike the last doctor, don't give my father false hope."

He should be taking advantage of her permission before she changed her mind. He should be peering into her eyes without the fanciful notion in his head that her irises were the blue hue of wildflowers in bloom. And surely he should soon be waking from this dream that had him forsaking professional behavior for personal interest.

"I give no hope unless it's warranted. I give no compliments unless they are, as well. Has anyone ever told you that you are a very lovely woman to look at?"

"Pa." She bit off the single syllable as if vexed by false flattery and then bit her bottom lip as if desperate to believe it was true. "You've proved far kinder than necessary, and for that I'll allow you to do your job. You'd best make it quick. Time's short."

2

He wasn't a man who believed in things unseen. Neither was it his nature to act rashly. Later, when she was gone and the world again righted itself, he would contemplate his impulsive actions and mystifying reactions.

But right now, sure of his intent, though he was no longer sure of much else, he couldn't stop himself from asking, "What are you doing this Saturday?"

"Chores. Shelling peas, feeding hogs, and doing the wash."

"If I lent a hand, would you agree to join me for a buggy ride? With your father's permission, of course."

"Stop it!" she cried in sudden distress. She clutched at the locket. It seemed to give her the fortitude she needed to still her trembling chin and snap, "I hate to be patronized."

"So do I," he countered. "May I come call?"

"Why?" Annabelle demanded.

"Because . . ." What could he say? That he'd never felt such a forceful pull to a woman? Or that the locket she wore had the effect of a hypnotist's pendulum, making the urge to touch her breasts seem a command? "Because by riding quickly past fence posts, I can test you for pattern stimulation."

"Of course," she said slowly. "Why else?"

Heath was relieved to hear the disappointment in her voice, and he hurried to reassure her.

"But that's not the only reason. I find you intriguing. I also think you're . . ." *Beautiful* didn't exactly describe her. Her features were indeed pleasing, but she was more arresting than pretty, more lush than delicate. And her hair, that glorious swirl that was the color of sunshine, begged to be strewn over a pillow by a man's hand. Her complexion bore a glowing, healthy tint, which declared that she disdained bonnets, preferred the outdoors, and didn't give a tinker's damn about what society expected from a woman.

He wondered if the blindness, by setting her apart, had granted her a certain freedom. Whatever the reason, she gave new dimension to his definition of a desirable woman. And it was that uniqueness he found undeniably beautiful.

"Beautiful," he whispered to himself.

She drew back as if he'd slapped her. Heath quickly decided that if he could inform dying patients to make their peace with God and man, he could surely advise Annabelle Rawlings that she'd vastly underestimated herself.

"Yes," he said firmly, "you *are* beautiful."

"No I'm not!" She gripped the pendant tighter. His gaze alternated between the alluring jewelry and her stricken expression.

"I beg to differ," he countered. "Were you to look into a mirror, I'm sure you'd have to agree."

She thrust the box of chocolates away and felt for her walking stick. Heath quickly intercepted her hands.

"What kind of doctor are you?" she gasped, taking quick, uneven breaths. "How dare you bait me with compliments, then taunt me with the reason I'm here?"

"The reason you're here is because your father thought I might be of help. As for your accusations, why is it easier for you to believe that I'd trifle with your feelings, rather than genuinely desire your company?"

Annabelle had never had a man ask her if he could come call. After all, in these parts a woman was needed for more than the ability to bear children who could help work the land. Annabelle couldn't even see to mend, and had a local merchant taken a shine to her, she couldn't figure change. Then there were the rumors she was "tetched," so scared of the dark that she wouldn't venture to a town social, where she couldn't dance even if a man took pity and asked.

The doctor was new in town and apparently wasn't aware she had a reputation. He'd find out sooner or later, so she'd save him the embarrassment of making his excuses and dashing her hopes.

"You strike me as an honorable man." Yes, she did believe he was. And given that, she preferred to think he'd been sincere with the compliment she'd rudely rebuked him for. "I thank you for your kind words too. But I don't think you really want to call on a woman who's considered to be . . . different."

"Different," he murmured. "Yes, so I've noticed."

She could feel his gaze on her like a touch. It moved from her hair to her bare legs, then returned to where she'd felt it most acutely before—on her bosom and throat. She'd nearly exposed them earlier when she'd been standing in the office doorway. The need to undo her dress buttons had been strong, because the terrible dread sensation she'd had upon climbing the stairs had thickened to a suffocating darkness. It seemed to emanate from the room she'd feared to enter even before she realized the man Pa was taking her to was a doctor.

As for that stranger than strange experience of his hands on her . . . Annabelle shivered. She'd smelled the funereal scent of flowers honoring the dead. She'd felt a draining, as if his fingertips were letting blood while her insides contracted with pleasure and a gentle sucking tugged at her breasts and in her most private reaches. Never in her life had she been so unnerved, or so exquisitely excited.

Maybe she *was* tetched. His hands were holding hers now, and she felt no fear. Large and warm and steady, they were doctor's hands, smelling of soap, not death-room flowers. His person smelled clean as well, touched with the hint of a subtle cologne.

Honesty demanded she set him straight, and Annabelle knew a deep regret. Because once she told him, he wouldn't come knocking at her door.

"You don't seem to understand what I mean by *different,* um, Heath. You see, some folks say I'm . . ." Forcing the word, she whispered, "Crazy."

"Are you?"

His curious tone and wry chuckle had her wondering if he must be a little mad himself.

"I'm no crazier than you are. But you have to forget this nonsense about calling for me and see to the reason I'm here."

In disbelief she felt him lift her hands to his face and say quietly, "Tell me what you see."

Could Pa have been right? He'd always said that some man would have the good sense to realize *she* was special.

"Describe me," Heath urged when she hesitated. "You can see me in a way no one else does. It's a rare opportunity for me, and I *would* be crazy if I let this one pass me by."

His words echoed her thoughts, and she felt a peculiar

bonding with this stranger, who didn't seem a stranger at all.
There was a hauntingly familiar texture to his skin, and the
stubble on the hollows of his cheeks lightly abraded her palms.

"You won't have trouble growing a heavy beard," she said
with certainty.

"It's my curse." He chuckled. "Twice a day I shave, and
even then, it's a losing battle. I wonder, do you think a beard
might suit me?"

He wanted her opinion on his appearance! For the first
time in her life a man was asking her to take notice and leaving
no question that he'd definitely noticed *her!*

It was a heady realization. She'd never had reason to tame
her hair into a bun, protect her skin from the sun she cherished,
or stain her lips with berry juice. But he seemed to like her just
fine the way she was. That was a blessing, since she couldn't
change her ways at this late date.

Tracing the planes of his cheeks with fingertips that had
started trembling, she judged the shape of his face to be angular, a framework of prominent bones and taut muscle. A few
age lines were grooved between his brows and fanned from his
eyes.

"What I think is, whether you shaved or not, you'd still be
very nice looking. And you're not as old as you sound. Mid-
thirties, are you?"

"Observing the miracle of life and the worst of death can
prematurely age a man. I'll be thirty next month. As for my
looks, I'm not homely. But even if I were, I've always been of
the opinion that real beauty resides within. Unfortunately, like
anyone else, I have my moments of ugliness."

She brushed away from his brow a thick shock of hair that
promptly fell over her searching fingers.

"What color is your hair?" she suddenly asked.

"Do you remember colors? Your father said you could see when you were a small child."

"Colors . . . Yellow as a daffodil, or a streak down a coward's back. Blue as the sky or a melancholy mood. White as a sheet or a lie meant in kindness. Orange as a setting sun or sweet as juice from the fruit."

"And what is green?"

"It's a shade moving over my head before the leaves fall. But now I see it as the way I feel. . . ." *Right now. Unsure of myself and younger than my years.* "Green is the way I feel when I slop the hogs, miss the trough, and feel them rooting at the hem of my skirt."

His gentle laughter assured her that even if she sometimes made a mess of her dress, she wasn't making a fool of herself in this conversation.

"And black? Do you remember black?"

"I've lived in it most of my life."

"But not always."

"No, not always. Only after—"

"Yes?" Heath gently prompted.

"I can't remember," she said quickly. That wasn't exactly the truth. She could remember some things. Mama. Parts of that night when she gave her the locket, just before the darkness came and never left. And the dreams, they were bits and pieces of memory that ended with a hideous twist. The creatures always found her hiding spot, and just as she cried out to Mama, she awoke.

Perhaps she'd tell Heath one day, should they ever become true friends. For now, the moment was too precious to taint with reality and bad dreams.

"Like most people, I've forgotten a lot of things about my childhood. But yes, I do remember colors."

"Then paint me in your mind. Unlike yours, my hair isn't remarkable. It's, well, just black. Except for a little gray at the temples. As for my eyes, they're fairly ordinary. Brown, with amber flecks. Hazel."

"There's nothing ordinary about your eyes. They're wide set and deep." His hands were lightly touching hers, and if she didn't know better, she'd swear he was stroking them, creating a formidable excitement that made her fingers quiver. "Your lashes are very thick."

"So's my skull, according to my family."

"It would seem, Heath, that we come from similar stock." His gentle grip tightened, and before her prickly pride could intrude, she confessed, "Please forgive me for taking my anger out on you earlier. My sharp tongue gets away from me."

"Does it?" There was a subtle intimacy in his tone that caused her to inhale sharply, and then softly gasp when he guided her hands to either side of his mouth. His lips were smooth, firm and well shaped. She'd never been kissed on the mouth, but she suddenly knew she wanted Heath to be the first.

She also knew he'd likely had a lot of practice at it. Why, he was actually gliding her fingertip over his front teeth, allowing her to see they were slightly crooked! Such familiarity was most improper.

"I believe you to be a worldly man." As usual she said what she thought before thinking. Heat spread down her neck until it reached her breasts, which felt unusually sensitive and tight. "What must you think of me?" she blurted. "Ladies don't say such things."

She cringed at her own words. This was terrible—she'd

stuck one foot in her mouth only to open it up and put the other one in for good measure.

"What I think, Miss Rawlings, is that you're highly perceptive, delightfully honest, and every inch a lady."

"And you, Dr. Nightingale, are very kind." She knew she should take her hand away from his lips, but they felt too good to stop touching just yet.

"Not always. My only saving grace is that I usually regret my unkindnesses. Almost as much as I regret that those I've hurt most are the people closest to me."

"I hear sorrow in your voice."

"And in yours I hear the wish to ease it."

"You hear rightly. Tell me what's on your mind."

"It's a long story," he murmured in a tone that sounded awfully crafty. "Ride with me Saturday? Take pity on a lonely doctor whose soul is in dire need of confession."

Annabelle felt a wondrous thrill. She was having trouble catching her breath. "That depends . . ." Oh, but this was fun! Amazing! That *she* was engaged in a game of flirtation, the kind she'd so envied as she eavesdropped on her sister playing hard to get with her beaux. How many nights had she wept into her pillow, wishing for a beau of her own? Her tears had run dry years ago, but now she was suddenly fighting tears of joy.

"Miss Rawlings, it seems that you have an aptitude for unkindness yourself, leaving me in this terrible suspense. Tell me what depends upon your acceptance, and I'll agree to any condition you set forth."

A mischievous grin curved her lips. "Will you help me shell peas?"

"Only if you do the wash while I'm slopping the hogs."

Together they laughed, an easy laughter of connection and

fast friendship. But as their mutual humor lulled, she again felt that pang of discomfort in her woman parts, and her cheeks warmed.

Was that a kiss she felt against her fingertips, that light pressure that was no wetter than a dewdrop and too fleeting for her to believe he'd actually touched her with his tongue? A small silence came between them as her hands fell to her sides.

"How long before Pa's due back?"

"Too soon, but there's time to eat a chocolate or two."

"Time enough for you to check my eyes?"

"If that's what you want."

"It is. I trust you." He was so unlike the other doctors who'd stretched her lids and debated her odd affliction until she felt like a freak that belonged in a carnival tent. Though she trusted Heath, apprehension rose as she heard him moving about. She smelled the fumes of a gas lamp. He was so close, she could feel the low heat of the instrument.

"You're very tense," he observed.

"I can't help it."

"I'd like you to relax." He gently kneaded the taut muscles in her shoulders, and she caught a hint of roses that mingled with the clean scent of soap on his hands.

She felt other things that she didn't understand: sensations akin to those she'd experienced the first time he touched her. The fleeting sense of darkness and deadly danger, a draining from her and into him, a sucking at the tips of her breasts and deep inside, where she clenched and grasped . . . nothing.

"Do you feel strange?" she whispered.

"Strange, yes. But strangely wonderful."

His rich, cultured voice mocked the eeriness she couldn't reconcile with this special man. A man who was making her belly grow taut as a bowstring while a hollow achiness settled between her thighs, causing her to squirm.

"I promise not to hurt you, Annabelle. A few deep breaths and you'll be fine. Breathe with me. In . . . and out. Again. Ah, that's good."

Why was he suddenly too still? Why was he making that puzzled sound and opening wider first one of her eyes and then the other, then repeating the procedure until his last "hmmmm" pronounced him done?

"What is it?" she asked anxiously. "What do you see?"

His thumbs traced the arch of her brows, then rested lightly against each temple.

"What I see is no less than a phenomenon of nature." He paused, and she measured the terrible wait for his next words with the swishing beat of her pulse. "My diagnosis is, Annabelle, of all the eyes I've looked into, yours are the first I could get lost in."

3

AMAZING ANOMALY STOP PATIENT TRUE BLIND STOP PUPIL REACTION TO LIGHT NORMAL STOP ANTERIOR CHAMBERS CLEAR STOP RETINAL BLOOD VESSELS HEALTHY STOP OPTIC NERVE NO DETECTABLE INJURY STOP TESTING FOR OPTO-KINETIC NYSTAGMUS TWO DAYS

"That all?" asked Mr. Mahony. Hand poised above the transmitter, the local telegraph operator peered curiously over his spectacles at Heath.

He'd almost forgotten the most important reason he was sending a wire to his instructor turned colleague, Dr. Purdue.

"Not quite." Quickly scribbling down the item he needed, Heath added his request that it be sent with all due haste and the promise to advise of any new findings.

"That all?"

Heath considered tacking on the fact that since he'd met Annabelle Rawlings the day before, he was suffering from some very peculiar symptoms himself: thinking about her when he should be concentrating on other patients. Dreaming about the locket and the breasts it nestled between. Counting the days till he saw her again. Humming. Wearing a big, sappy smile.

Realizing he was doing it again, Heath said, "That will be

all," paid the man, and made for the exit. He was turning Annabelle's symptoms, or rather her lack of them, over in his head for the untold time, when the brilliant noon sun hit him full in the face.

Heath felt as if he'd been slammed into a wall. Everything went black and he swayed. Slumping against the doorway, he heard Mr. Mahony's distant voice calling, "Doc! Doc Nightingale, you okay?" Though Heath could feel him shaking his arm, something wasn't right. His skin was acutely sensitive at the same time it felt anesthetized.

He opened his mouth to speak but shut it when a sharp pain in his upper gums coincided with a wave of nausea.

Both receded as quickly as they came.

He blinked. His eyes stung, but even that passed as soon as he raised a hand to block the sun.

"You okay now, Doc?"

"Fine. I'm . . . fine." Heath let go of the door frame and straightened. Still averting his eyes from the sun, he glanced at Mr. Mahony, who didn't look as if he believed the doctor's claim. Heath managed a laugh and a lie. "I was a little dizzy, but it serves me right for not eating since yesterday's lunch. Bachelor that I am, I'm sometimes guilty of working late and being too lazy to see to my meals."

"Why ain't you eatin' plenty? The way I hear it, every dadburn mother in town with a marriageable daughter's been asking you to join their tables."

"I appreciate their invitations, but I've had the good fortune to meet a lady whose company I've asked to keep."

"That a fact! And who might be this envy of Eugene?"

Heath was so relieved to be feeling perfectly fine once again and to have gotten Mr. Mahony's mind off the embarrassing episode, that he told him outright.

"Annabelle Rawlings?" Mahony exclaimed. *"The blind girl? Well if that don't beat all, I don't know what does."*

The man's hoot of laughter and slap to the knee had Heath grinding his teeth. *The blind girl.* Was that how the residents referred to her among themselves? The need to protect her was fierce.

"You obviously find my interest in Miss Rawlings a matter of great amusement." His voice was as tight as the fist he clenched. "Perhaps you wouldn't mind sharing the joke?"

"Why, sure. It's just that nobody else would have her. And here you go taking to the likes of a strange old maid when you could have your pick of the lot." Wiping tears of mirth from his eyes, Mahony sobered when his gaze connected with Heath's.

"Miss Rawlings might lack the gift of sight, but I'm *sure* you'll agree that she's more intelligent and attractive than the pick of the lot in Eugene and Boston combined. You are right, of course," he said coldly. "I *have* taken to the likes of Annabelle Rawlings. And I highly advise you to remember that in the future."

Before he could punctuate his warning with a punch, Heath strode down the boardwalk to the general store where he bought a hair ribbon and a lacy handkerchief. Nothing too extravagant, but acceptable tokens of his esteem. In two weeks he hoped to have a gift for Annabelle that was more priceless than gold.

How would she describe gold? he mused.

Golden as a sunrise, or an anniversary marked by fifty years together of watching it set.

Heath paused at the door, suddenly wary of going outside.

"Did you forget something, Dr. Nightingale?"

"Yes, Bud, I did," he told the shopkeeper. "Would you please order another box of those fancy chocolates for me?"

"Glad to. Mind if I ask if they're for anyone special?"

"They are." Heath anticipated again coming to Annabelle's defense but instead was rewarded with Bud's wink.

"Miss Annabelle's a fine woman, and if I wasn't married with grown children of my own, I'd be racing you to her door. You'll probably hear some rumors about her, but don't you believe 'em. Folks just tend to get uneasy when others have different ways than they do." Bud grinned. "Sure you don't want to order two boxes of those chocolates? An extra one for her pa. His approval's sure to be harder to earn than hers."

"If she was my daughter, I'd be much the same. As for that order . . ." Heath remembered the sweet treat of watching Annabelle lick vanilla cream from her finger. The only thing better would have been to do it himself, but such an intimate privilege was at least several boxes away. "Make it three and—" Much as he wanted to put off the inevitable, Heath knew he couldn't stay until sunset. "And I'll be saying good day."

Bracing himself, he shielded his eyes until he'd climbed the stairs that led to his office. Resting his head against the door, he breathed a "whew" of relief. Tension ebbed from him as the dim room soothed his rattled composure. He felt a sense of well-being in the wake of disquiet. The atmosphere surrounding him was much like that of another place and time he held most private and dear.

A dark, still room in Boston. Alone, except for the old man whose hand he held. Sitting beside the sickbed, after months of agonizing over his inability to stop the inevitable, he'd watched Grandpapa depart with a long, whispering sigh.

And then, peace. No more pain. No more piteous pleas

that his beloved grandson be spared the curse of fate or frantic cries of "The journal! The journal! Take warning, *believe.*" The delirium had been a horrid thing, the worst memory Heath possessed. And though he missed his grandfather fiercely, the utter stillness and tranquillity of that final breath was etched in his heart as a moment of wonder, of a bond they shared that death could never steal.

Heath shook his head at the unusual turn of his thoughts. Death was a fact of life in his profession, but even now he felt altered by its visit to his home. Two years had gone by, and the memory was still poignantly keen. Perhaps that's why he'd been imagining the smell of roses and death. Both had surrounded him as Grandpapa lay in state at Cloud Castle.

A cloying sensation, the same he'd felt in the drawing room at the old family mansion after Grandpapa had been buried in the family plot nearby, prompted him to go wash his hands. As he dried them, he chanced to look up in the mirror. Something that was too fleeting to grasp had been superimposed over his image. He was left with a disturbing impression of malevolent sweetness and calculated seduction. Terrible, wonderful.

Like poisoned candy offered to a trusted friend.

Like the last breath of a loved one gently embraced by the angel of death.

Heath blinked. Looking closer, he noted a vacuous quality to eyes that were his, but somehow not his, then wondered if they needed to be examined. He swiped the towel over his reflection. Judging from the smudge of dust the towel picked up, he needed to get himself a wife who was a more particular housekeeper than he.

His stomach growled, and he suddenly wondered if Annabelle was a tolerable cook. If she was, that was more than he could say for himself. And if she wasn't? The hell if he cared.

Laughing, thrilling even to the illogical thought processes she summoned from him, Heath passed through the open door joining office to apartment. He went straightaway to the pantry, but the light was too meager to take inventory. Going to the window, he gripped the drawn drapes, then hesitated as the memory of his near swoon and anxious rush home came back to him. The unmanliness of his behavior stung his pride.

Heath jerked open the heavy brocade.

The blinding assault was immediate, and he quickly shut his eyes. But his skin didn't hurt. Neither did his teeth. No nausea, just the rumble of his stomach.

Carefully, he opened one eye and then the other. Squinting against the glare of the tin roof across the street, he laughed at his own foolishness and opened the window wide.

Annabelle raised her skirt as Heath helped her into his buggy.

"The clouds are hanging low," Jake said for the third time in as many minutes. "Much as the crops could use a good rain, I wouldn't want the two of you caught in a storm. Sure you wouldn't rather keep company with me and take this ride another day?"

"Oh, Pa, don't be such a worrywart." Annabelle laughed gaily, scarcely able to contain her excitement.

"No need to worry, sir, I'll turn the buggy around if the wind whips up. And even if it doesn't, I'll have your daughter home before dark."

Annabelle's smile faltered as Heath sat down beside her. Of course he'd have her home before dark, she hastily assured herself. A gentleman would see to it, and a gentleman he was. She felt Pa's hand squeeze her own in reassurance and reluctant parting. Heath's arm brushed against hers as he shook out the reins and shouted "Giddap!"

The buggy lurched and so did her heart. Its beating matched the clip-clopping of the horses' hooves upon the dirt road, and it turned over and over just like the wheels beneath them. She had an irrational urge to demand they go back where she was safe, because she didn't feel safe at all now that she and Heath were without other company.

That had to be it. She'd never been alone with a suitor, and inexperience was making her imagine danger where there was none. Silently chastising herself for such silly apprehension, Annabelle said politely, "Thank you for helping me shell peas." She nervously clutched the lace hankie Heath had given her and rushed on. "And I know Pa appreciated your lending a hand with—"

"I'd appreciate you lending me yours." Heath lifted her hand for a quick kiss, then squeezed it before letting go. "Did you think of me this week?"

"You're all I was able to think about." She winced at her passionate declaration. Hadn't Lorna reminded her just yesterday that a woman ought to let a man chase her till she caught him? "What I mean is, you did cross my mind once or twice."

"I liked your first answer better. After all, I've been counting the days until I could see you again. And as for helping your father, my motives weren't completely admirable. The sooner he ran out of those chores he said the two of you do each Saturday, the sooner you and I could be alone." His chuckle relaxed her and she laughed aloud.

"Well, sir, that is a great relief, and I do thank you."

"For what? Confessing to my less-than-honorable nature?"

"For allowing me to honor mine. I lied. You *were* the only thing on my mind, and we'd still be doing chores if I hadn't gotten up before the cock crowed to knead dough and wash my hair while the sun rose." She touched the bun at her nape that she'd fiddled with forever, it seemed, feeling for hairpins sticking out, and pushing stray tendrils in. The wind caught at the flyaway strands framing her left temple. With a start she realized that Heath was sifting through the loose curl.

"Did you fix your hair this way for me?"

"I—yes, I did."

"I wish you hadn't. Pretty as it is, I much prefer to see it a little wild."

"But wouldn't you rather keep company with a woman who at least appears respectable? That's why I spent an hour getting this mess to mind."

"Appearances," he said firmly, "are often lies. Don't ever change to meet the expectations of those who could learn from you. That in mind, I brought a ribbon that won't look nearly as right on a prim and proper bun as it would if your hair was loose and windblown. I was hoping you'd wear it for me today."

She was breathless.

"You actually bought a ribbon for me?"

"I did. Would you like to see it?"

"Yes! Yes, of course, but I—" *Can't see.* Oh, how she longed to be free of this curse, to turn to him now and assure herself that there wasn't pity in the gaze she felt on her.

"You're wrong, Annabelle, you *can* see. It's just that you see differently." His voice was gentle, but she heard no trace of pity in it. "We'll stop soon, but first I want you to look right and slightly down, keeping your eyes open. Pretend you're staring at the fence we're passing."

"Why?"

"Because I'm testing for optokinetic nystagmus. A fancy term for an involuntary reflex. And once that's done, I'd like to put this ribbon to good use." His second reason was ample inducement for her to agree readily to the first.

Annabelle was still beaming when the carriage veered to the side and his "Whoa" halted the horses. With his palms on her shoulders, he turned her until she faced him. He framed her jaw with strong fingers, and his breath was so close, she wondered if he might kiss her. The smell of roses wafted between them.

Had he brought her flowers? Hope filled her even as she had a sense of all-consuming darkness. Perhaps his body was merely blocking the sun, his body that was so near he surely meant to kiss her! She was simultaneously terrified and thrilled —until he drew back and made that curious sound of interest. A kiss, she feared, was not to be.

"Amazing," he whispered. Heath couldn't believe it; her eyes were twitching from pattern stimulation. It was a normal reaction and one that couldn't be controlled.

"What's amazing?"

What could he tell her? That his initial findings had just been supported and her visual system was perfectly intact? That somehow her brain was refusing all messages from her optic nerves? Farfetched as it was, there was no other logical explanation for her blindness.

Annabelle, he concluded, was no more blind than he.

The problem was, if her brain refused to listen to her body's signals, it certainly wouldn't listen to his logic. At least not until he could find out what had triggered her loss of sight. A memory, perhaps? He had no way of telling, but if he could isolate the cause, he could search for a cure. Any answers would have to come from Annabelle, and those wouldn't be forthcoming if he didn't have her trust.

At the moment, he didn't completely trust himself. Even as his mind went through the array of information that could point to an explanation for her condition, he fought the compulsion to plant his mouth against the pulse point at her throat.

"What's amazing?" she asked again, her voice a whisper.

"What's amazing? You are." Heath deemed it prudent to withhold his diagnosis. Equally as prudent was for him to busy his hands and keep his mouth to himself. "Do you mind if I take down your hair?"

"I'd like you to, very much, only Pa's sure to ask how my bun got loose. He teased me about wearing one for the first time in as many years as I've got fingers."

"He won't ask any such thing." Loosening pins from her hair, he assured her, "I'll fix it back once we turn the carriage around. If I can thread catgut to a needle, I should be able to manage a few hairpins and . . . *Lord.*"

Quickly pocketing the pins, he wound his fingers through the most extraordinary hair he'd ever touched. The texture was thick and silky. It shined bright as a dazzling sun.

Annabelle gripped the seat and said shakily, "Good gracious, whatever are you doing? A man's never made my hair feel like it was breathing."

"I'd be horribly jealous if another man had. Especially when touching you makes me feel . . . I can't even describe it." Heath reveled in the sensual pleasure reserved for a husband in the arms of his wife or a mistress. With Annabelle he knew the proprietary, protective emotions of the former and the rutting lust of the latter.

There was more: a sense of familiarity that he couldn't explain.

"Do you feel what I do?" he whispered.

"I'm not sure. Is your heart beating too fast?"

He pressed his fingertips to the pulse at her throat. "It's beating as fast as yours."

"Then does your stomach feel like a thousand frogs are loose? Are your palms wet, and do you have a peculiar sensation low in your belly?"

"I do."

"You're a doctor, Heath. Is something wrong with us?"

"Nothing that a kiss wouldn't make worse. And better."

"You want to kiss me?" she said, both hesitant and eager.

"More than I've ever wanted to kiss a woman before."

"Then by all means, go right ahead. If a kiss is what you prescribe, we must surely be in need of the tonic."

He bent to kiss her, but stopped short. Her eyes were squinched tight, and her lips were puckered up.

"Annabelle, have you never been kissed by a man?"

"No one's ever so much as tried," she confessed.

Heath felt his loins responding to a devious thought. If she didn't know how to kiss, she probably wasn't aware it could encompass varying degrees of intimacy.

"Lucky for me to claim rights as the first. Would you, perchance, be agreeable to an impromptu lesson?" Heath decided if she kissed as vigorously as she nodded, Annabelle would prove a most astute student. "In that case, I want you to wrap your arms around my neck . . . umm, very good. Next, it's important that you part your lips. Wet them a bit . . . that's perfect."

"What's next?"

"The rest is easy as matching what I do to you." He fit his mouth to hers and at first touch he knew an indescribable

elation, a certainty that she'd been made just for him, and he
for her. Her sigh passed through his slitted lips, and she tasted
so sweet that he craved to inhale her. He rubbed his lips back
and forth, and she swept her tongue across his teeth, then asked
uncertainly, "Am I doing this right?" He groaned in appreciation and bathed her chin with circling flicks of his tongue.

"You are nothing less than fabulous," he assured her, and
drew in a ragged breath. "However, kissing, like anything else,
always improves with practice. If you'd like to learn a few ad-
vanced techniques, I'm willing to offer my services."

Her hands shook as she sifted her fingers through his hair,
arched her neck, and raised her face to the sun. "How generous
of you." Her languorous sigh echoed the sensual tilt of her
smile. "Shall we proceed, Dr. Night—"

He answered her with a growl and a nuzzle at her throat.
He could feel her escalating desire in the rushing of her blood,
could hear her tiny whimpers between shallow pants of excitement that mirrored his own.

Heath vaguely began to wonder who was teaching whom.
She matched him stroke for stroke, nibbling bite for nibbling
bite. Ignoring caution, he pressed her down against the buggy
seat, and she lunged against him with a wild enthusiasm. The
jolt startled the grazing horses. The carriage lurched and Heath
grabbed for the reins.

Arms flailing, Annabelle tumbled to the narrow floor. She
clutched at a hard, flexed thigh. Her other hand reached higher
and closed around the likes of something she'd never before
felt. It was big and hard, and it grew even bigger with her
inquisitive search. What it was, she wasn't sure, but his tortured
plea of "Dear God, I can't bear this," was ample proof that she
had committed a terrible wrong by touching it.

Then his hand was suddenly covering hers and urgently pressing her fingers against him. "Oh!" she gasped. "I—oh, no!"

"Ohhh. Oh, *yes,*" came his choked reply. But his fingers now encircled her wrist, and gently, but firmly, he led her hand to his knee. He patted it once, then let go.

Annabelle was fervently praying they'd ride forever, or at least until she could face him again, but forever would probably come before that. She moaned quietly upon hearing his hoarse shouts of "Whoa! Whoa!" and fought tears of humiliation.

"Annabelle?" He gently stroked her bent head. "Are you all right?"

"No." She sniffled and vowed she would not disgrace herself further by crying. "Please take me home. If—if you never want to call upon me again, I do understand."

"No, my dear woman, I don't believe that you do." He hoisted her, resisting, to the seat beside him. He held her so tight and so sweetly that she buried her face against the crook of his neck. Once her sobs were spent, his murmurs of comfort stopped too.

"What you *must* understand, Annabelle," he said sternly, "is that after this ride, wild horses couldn't drag me away from you."

4

Humming a lilting tune, Annabelle kept time with her walking stick and fairly waltzed her way to the carved chest that had been her mother's pride and joy.

Kneeling, she lifted the top and felt for the length of satin ribbon. Heath had said he'd chosen it because its color, the color of bluebonnets, matched that of her eyes. He'd also said that he loved her eyes. And though today was just two Saturdays past and only the third time he'd asked to come call, she prayed that soon he might come to love more than her eyes. Heath she loved already.

She loved him for those thrilling sensations she relived again and again with each remembrance of their kiss. And though she knew she shouldn't, she couldn't help but imagine again feeling that manly part of him. She loved him for understanding her distress after touching him so, and she loved him for assuring her that he was just as distressed, but only because her touching him was so wonderful that he'd been hard-pressed to stop her before something else got started.

He'd laughed until she'd asked him what he meant. Then he made that "hmmm" sound he always seemed to be making.

She smiled secretively, remembering how he'd lifted her down from the carriage—oh, but his hands were so large and strong, fitting about her waist and drawing her close—then swept her into his arms before carrying her to a clover glade. Her back hadn't needed urging to rest against his chest, and when he fit his legs on either side of hers, she scooted to get closer. The feel of his hands in her hair sent shivers down her spine, while his voice sent shivers up it.

"Have you never had a talk with your father about the birds and bees?" he asked casually.

"Why, no, except to identify the different songs of one and the merits of honey from the other."

"Then surely you've heard women sharing tales of child-birth and how they came to the miracle of giving life."

"That's the sort of thing a mother shares with a daughter." Fingering the treasured locket, which was the last thing her mother had shared, Annabelle added, "And if women discuss such matters, they've never included me. Living on the farm with Pa, I haven't had much chance to hear private talk, since we mostly socialize at church."

"A farm . . . As a child, surely you saw animals mate?"

"Well, I do recall a stallion prancing about and sniffing a mare's tail on the wagon train. But when I asked Mama why they were behaving so funny, she said the horses were being indecent and sent me to tend Lorna."

"Perhaps you were too young to watch." He lifted her hair and brushed a tickling kiss to her neck. "But there's nothing indecent about mating, whether animal or man, because it's as natural as nature itself. God thought it all up, and if He wasn't embarrassed about the best way to procreate, then we have no reason to be embarrassed about discussing it." At that, she felt him slowly pull down the satin ribbon to her neck, which he caressed with a lingering stroke. Then hurriedly he began to plait her hair.

His touch was so hypnotic, she was lulled into an enthralled silence as he proceeded with a matter-of-fact explanation that ended with, "And that's how babies are made."

"It sounds very interesting. But a little disgusting."

"Oh?" He pulled her closer, closer, until she was sitting on his lap. He arched his hips, and that thing that made babies nuzzled her most private place. She instinctively sought a snugger fit. "Do you find me disgusting?" he said, smooth as the blue satin ribbon.

"I seem to stand corrected. What I'm feeling is far more interesting than that."

"And what I'm feeling is too dangerous to describe. Off you go and up goes the hair. The sun will be setting soon, and it's past time I took you home."

Annabelle realized that for the first time in seventeen years she hadn't taken notice of the sun's descent. Was it because she'd felt protected by him, despite the edge of darkness she felt in his shadow?

Their second ride hadn't been quite as eventful, but it was filled with personal confidences, secret kisses, easy laughter, and the absolute certainty that she did love Heath.

Her dreams didn't seem to realize that, however. They'd turned doubly horrible since she'd met him. The creatures still found her hiding place, but she no longer awakened with a cry of "Mama!" Instead, Heath had begun to appear, frightening away the hateful monsters, and then—

Annabelle shuddered, but snorted at the folly of her nightmare. Dreams were just that, and the man she was in love with would no more save her so he might bathe in her blood than she would writhe in joyous pleasure beneath him while he did it. Heath was a good, gentle person and she hated her dreams for trying to convince her that the man who brought her sunshine would bring her doom. His only sin was making her so happy that she sometimes hurt with the joy. Life had never been so grand—except for the wedge that had come between her and Pa.

"Gettin' ready to see your new beau?" he now asked quietly.

Hugging the satin ribbon against the locket, she managed to laugh lightly when what she really wanted was to throw herself into his arms and pour out her heart. She wanted to tell him that just because she loved Heath, that didn't mean she loved her father any less. And she wanted to hear his reassurance that the new dreams were normal, a funny way nature had of keeping a woman pure until she lay in a marriage bed, where all fear and bad dreams would leave.

Before she met Heath, she would have confided in Pa. But things had changed somehow, so she kept her own counsel and distanced the two of them further with an evasive smile.

Pa cleared his throat, and it sounded as awkward as the silence that had come between them. "Much as you've been stroking that ribbon, you'll need to wash it soon—if you aim to wear it with the new dress I ordered from Miss Joan."

Annabelle got to her feet and hugged him tight, as much in apology as elation. "You went to the dressmaker?"

"You mean you didn't notice I'd filched your best dress? Little girl, it's been missing since I went to town last Monday to hand it over to her. I found out word's passed faster than a telegraph wire that my daughter's got that Boston dandy up to his elbows in fancy chocolate to win her."

"Pa," she cried, "oh, Pa. You're sweeter than any candy I ever ate. A new dress! And it's not even my birthday. But . . . it will be Heath's a week from tomorrow. Is there a chance Miss Joan might be done by then? I would so like to wear it, and—well, if you don't mind, I'd like to have a little celebration for him after church. Heath's so far away from home, and I know that would mean a lot to him."

"Seems you've got your heart set on him." Pa swallowed so hard that she heard the dry click in his throat. "The doctor's a good man, and a finer woman than you there never was—except for your ma. When we fetch that frilly outfit next week, we'll visit Bud so you can buy what you need for a special dinner."

"A special dinner . . . Heath said he loves a good fish stew. I'll make him the best he's ever had—that is, if you're willing to trek to the lake."

"I'll head out with my pole the minute he whisks you away in that fancy buggy of his."

"And I'll make a cake! Chocolate, of course."

Pa rested his cheek against the top of her head and hugged her tight, then held her away. It was paternal pride she heard as he said gruffly, "I'm sure he'll enjoy the cake. But once he sees you in that new dress, he'll no doubt be thinkin' you're a sweeter treat than any he's ever had."

Heath stropped his razor while he whistled. His hopes were high that Dr. Purdue's package would be on the stagecoach that was running late.

So was he, thanks to a gun wound and a drunk who'd come compliments of the local saloon right about dawn. Laying down razor and strop beside the washbowl, Heath swirled his wet shaving brush into the mug of hard soap and lathered his face. The mirror told him that his stubble was heavy as ever, and unless he did a good job, Annabelle's tender skin would still be smarting when he met her for church tomorrow. Then again, if Jake caught sight of a whisker burn on his daughter,

the invitation to share their pew and a birthday dinner afterward could very well be withdrawn.

"Damn," he muttered when he nicked a cheek. He leaned
closer to the mirror to examine the cut and saw a thin slash of
bright red against the lather. The razor clattered as it fell into
the basin of wash water.

His mind insisted that a trick of lighting fabricated the leer-
ing image staring back at him, the gleam of hunger in his eyes.
And no, no he couldn't possibly be watching his tongue snake
out and struggle to capture the trickling drop of blood. The
pungent taste of soap mingled with the scent of roses and dank
air. He felt himself trembling, from revulsion he was sure, not
from the sick excitement that invaded his senses.

Struggling to draw a cleansing breath, he tore his gaze from
the mirror and frantically grabbed a towel. He pressed it hard
against his cheek, blotting away any traces of blood before he
looked again into the mirror. He didn't want to look into the
mirror. But if he didn't, that would give credence to the dark
presence he imagined was moving around and through him.
Ridiculous. Insane. There were no roses here, no unnatural
stillness after a last breath.

A dull thump sounded in the adjoining room. Relieved that
he had a valid excuse to put off confronting his reflection, he
strode to his living area. "Is anyone about?" he demanded. A
faint rustle came from the direction of his steamer trunk beside
the window. An uneasy sensation stitched down his spine, and
there was a tingling in his upper gums. The room darkened,
and he hastened to blame it on a thick cloud blocking the sun.

Heath went to the trunk, apprehension and the anger he
felt with himself for this foolish sense of dread increasing with
each step. Impatiently he worked the lock and thrust back the
heavy lid.

Peering inside, he saw nothing but the few sentimental treasures he'd stored: his first microscope, a wedding invitation, a pair of crocheted booties, an assortment of letters and handmade gifts, all from patients thanking him in their various ways. There wasn't much else in the trunk—just the journal that Grandpapa had given him on his ninth birthday. The memory was a fond one, and only for that reason had he brought along this ludicrous bit of family tradition.

A pecking at his window brought Heath's head up. A bird teetered on the sill and then took flight. That had to be what he'd heard. The bird had probably hit the glass, and the fluttering noise was no more than the sluggish flap of wings as it lay there, stunned. Heath shook his head at his addled imaginings. He was as bad as Grandpapa, bless his soul. Had the old man been there, with his propensity for superstition, he'd no doubt have insisted that the noises had come from the pages that chronicled curses and Nightingale lunacy.

Heath slammed the lid shut. A quick glance at his pocket watch assured him that the time he'd squandered could have put him well on the road to Annabelle's door.

He had to finish shaving. Damn if the soap on his face wasn't dry and burning his skin the way the sun had of late. He seemed to have developed a sensitivity to strong sunlight and had taken to avoiding it. Already his complexion held a slight pallor.

He grabbed the towel that he'd dropped beside the trunk and slung it over his shoulder. After walking back to the soapy bowl of water, Heath again lathered up, then carefully fished for the razor he'd dropped.

He shoved his face close to the mirror—and his mouth opened in astonishment.

Heath turned one cheek and then the other. Where was it?

The cut—he was certain he had one. He'd even stroked it while examining the trunk's contents. And if that wasn't proof enough, the red streak on his white towel was.

Was he losing his mind? First, seeing a ghoul stare back at him from the mirror—a ghoul that salivated at the sight of blood while an invisible, malevolent force made his entrails churn and raised gooseflesh on the back of his neck. And now, *this*.

Heath made short work of his remaining whiskers. As he did, he pondered the possibility that he was falling victim to the legendary Nightingale madness. It had convinced his ancestor Michael Nightingale that he was, of all things, a werewolf. Heath scowled. He, a man of science, was made of stronger stuff and he was determined to conquer whatever seemed to be afflicting him. That decided, he sloughed off the niggling fear that a cure was nowhere to be found.

5

Heath plucked a chocolate from the box and teased Annabelle's lips with it. She shook her head, and his gaze moved from her somber profile to the hand that stroked the carpet of clover on which they lay.

They lounged there, in their special place, lazy as two cats napping in the sun. The trees were thick, and the sun's light was dappled as it shone between the leaves. Nothing touched him here, except Annabelle. Everywhere he went, she was in his mind, his heart. He held the memories they shared close, so close that even his disturbing symptoms paled against their urgent kisses.

"You're so quiet." Heath tossed the chocolate back into the box and plucked a clover. Twirling it over her chin, he yearned to dip his tongue into the tiny groove of a dimple. "Is something wrong?" he asked, concerned.

"There is. But what it is, I'm not exactly sure."

"Perhaps something to do with your father?"

She scooted down until she rested on her side. She propped her chin with her palm and faced him. Her bare feet flirted with his shin. "How did you know?"

"I suppose it has to do with the way he hugs you as if it might be his last chance before we ride off. And he's taken to giving me a hard stare until we round the bend. He watches us even closer when we return. He's afraid of losing you, Anna-belle, but he loves you enough to let you go."

"You're wrong, Heath. Pa knows he could *never* lose me."

"Oh? Are you as close as ever? Think about it."

She didn't think long before reluctantly admitting, "Not since the first time you and I came here."

"You mean you haven't told him about our special place, the things we talk about, or the kisses we share?"

"Of course not. That's between you and me."

"As it should be." Giving into temptation, he leaned forward and lightly tongued her dimple.

"Stop it, Heath. I don't feel like sparking. This whole mat-ter's troubling me greatly."

Heath sighed heavily. He was direly in need of her physical comfort—in need of something real and good, rooted in the substance of touch and in earthy words of love and lust.

"Would you feel like 'sparking' if I told you about a prob-lem I had with my father? A problem that's just as troubling as yours?"

When she expectantly leaned forward and said, "Tell me what happened," his body responded in anticipation of the favors he'd reap before dusk set them apart.

"The cost will be a kiss. A long, wet kiss, once I'm finished with my story." At her quick nod he went ahead. "Very well, then. I grew up in a family of old money."

"Our cabin must look like a shack to you."

"Your cabin looks like a warm home. A much happier home than the one I grew up in." For a moment he remem-bered the soaring ceilings painted with murals; the maze of rooms with imported furniture; stately grounds, topiary gar-dens, and grimacing gargoyles. Lovely as their home was, he'd always envied his cousins, who lived at Cloud Castle. Ah, well, perhaps he'd take his final rest there, with his grandfather and other relations such as Michael and Katherine Downing Nightingale.

"What was your home like?" Annabelle gently asked.

"Cold as hell and filled with my mother's ghost. Grandpapa told me that she sang all the time. The music stopped when I was born. She died in childbirth."

"How terrible for you." Annabelle gripped his hand.

"I never knew her, so I never missed her the way my father did. He filled his empty hours with work and didn't have much time for his sons. I expect that's why my grandfather took a special interest in us. Grandpapa was good to my two older brothers, but he was always closest to me." Heath smiled, then draped his front teeth with his upper lip. That pain again. Except this time it was strangely arousing too.

"You were close to your grandfather, then?"

"Very," he replied, distracted. "Grandpapa was a great storyteller. His favorite was about a late relative who fantasized about his days as a werewolf."

"A werewolf! Tell me the story, Heath. Please?"

"Another time, when we have nothing better to do." The last person he wanted to think about was Michael Nightingale. The "werewolf's" story had begun to disturb Heath, a fact that he didn't want to admit. And so he stole a kiss and took heart that Annabelle's lips were making his mouth tingle.

"Anyway," he continued resolutely, "growing up, I told myself that had I been my mother's doctor, I could have done something to save her. I developed an interest in medicine early on and didn't hesitate to pursue what became my profession. I did so against my father's wishes."

"You mean he didn't want you to become a doctor?"

"What he wanted was for me to join my older brothers in

trying to salvage our shipping empire. When I insisted railroads were the way of the future, he tried to get me to marry a railroad baron's daughter. How sweet a revenge for my father to gain access to railroad money and sink it into our ships."

Annabelle worried her bottom lip. "Did you court her?"

"For all of a month, but I tired of her quickly. And though I didn't particularly like her, what my father wanted was wrong, and she deserved better." The wind danced through the trees, and a shaft of sunlight pooled over the locket resting against the swell of Annabelle's left breast. Heath reached for it, but caught himself. "I deserved better too." Pressing a feather-light kiss to her chin, he whispered, "I deserved you."

"If you hadn't come west, we never would have met. Did you come here to put miles between you and your father?"

"Partly, but I liked the idea of being someplace where my family's name didn't count. And I have to admit a fondness for Beadle Dime Novels. All that action and adventure in the wild West sent my imagination galloping with each page I turned."

Annabelle laughed. "There's not too much action and adventure in Eugene, except for the occasional bank robbery or drunk thrown out the local tavern. You must be disappointed."

"After meeting you? Hardly. The only disappointment I harbor is in myself."

"Because you did what was right for you, even against your father's wishes, doesn't make you worthy of blame."

"That's true. Listen to yourself, Annabelle. You're no more worthy of blame than I am, for having different needs from those of *your* father." Her brows knitted, and then she gave a nod of comprehension. "It's only natural for a child to separate from a parent, but the way I took my final leaving was no less than cruel. You see, I came west on the same railroad that crippled my family's business."

"But what's wrong with that? It's much faster."

"And that was my excuse. My father tried to make amends in his own way, by offering to see me off on the next Nightingale ship. But no, I had to get in the last word by taking the train to its end in Utah. From there I came to Eugene by way of stagecoach with a tip that the town was in need of a doctor. When I arrived, the smirk was still on my lips. But my petty revenge soon soured with the aftertaste of spite. The way I left doesn't set well with me."

"Which is exactly why you're being too hard on yourself."

"No more than you," he countered. "It's why you're upset about the distance that's come between you and your father."

"Hmmm," Annabelle mused, imitating the introspective sound she'd said he made a lot. "What a smart man you are, Dr. Nightingale. If trees could talk, this one above us would have plenty to repeat. You are inclined to impart quite interesting lessons, and it seems that I've just listened to a most meaningful speech." Her fingers found his chest. Laying her hand over his heart, she said sadly, "You're right, it's not the same as it used to be with me and Pa. And no amount of wishing can change what is."

"I'm afraid not, my love." The endearment had slipped out naturally, and he cherished the sound of those two words. "You're a woman sharing confidences with a man who's everything a father can never be. And your father is everything to you that I can never be. He is losing you, Annabelle. He's losing you to me."

"Is he?" There was hope in her voice. There was also disquiet. "Then you must have found something in me that you didn't find with that rich gal."

Heath stopped nibbling her chin. "If I didn't know better, I'd think you were jealous and no longer disposed to fulfill your promise of a kiss. As your official instructor I deem it my duty to make sure you don't renege."

"As I said, you're a very smart man. Too bad your mouth tends to be as smart as your brain."

Heath laughed, a deep belly laugh that only Annabelle could call from inside him. She called more. His groin was in extreme discomfort, and her impish grin only made it worse. He raised his gaze, and the sun glittered in his eyes. Wincing, he felt the stab of pleasurable pain that radiated from his incisors to his eyeteeth. In an effort to ignore them, he returned his attention to Annabelle.

His eyes quit burning, but the cinders of desire kindled higher. He ached to make love to her. He ached to plant his teeth against her neck. There, where her pulse rushed against his stroking thumb.

The locket that rested against her breast seemed to pulse in time with her rushing heartbeat. *Touch it.* The whisper was seductive and dark and swirled around and through him.

Heath forced his hand from her neck. He closed his eyes against the locket's eerie allure while he closed his ears to the repeated whisper of, *Touch it.* He didn't pray often, but he did pray now. *What is happening to me? Something is happening and I don't understand it. Please, stop this madness and tell me I'm not losing my mind.*

When he felt sufficiently himself, he allowed his narrowed gaze to return to the locket.

"Annabelle," he said in a deceptively even voice, "where did you get this locket?"

"It was my mother's. And before that it belonged to her mother, and the mother before her. The last thing I saw was this locket. Mama gave it to me before . . . before she sent me running into the woods and told me to keep Lorna quiet."

As long as he could keep her talking and his mind on what she was saying, maybe he could ignore the unthinkable scenario that bloomed in vivid crimson colors in his head. *Taking her. His teeth. The locket . . . touch it.*

"And after that what happened?" Heath focused hard on listening to Annabelle's voice. A real voice, not an imaginary whisper he wanted to purge from his ears.

"I—I can't remember much. Mama was screaming and Indians were whooping and I remember turning back, but as soon as I did, everything went dark and I never saw again."

He'd found it. The key that had locked her brain against all things visual. Could what was happening to him also be rooted in some memory of his own that was trying to resurface? Not probable, but then again, neither was blindness that was mentally induced. He was desperate for explanations. What were the causes, what was the cure? *Physician, heal thyself.* And what was he thinking, forgetting that he was a physician and any cures for Annabelle were dependent on his putting aside his own anxieties to probe the source of hers?

"Are you sure you don't remember what happened? Think, Annabelle. What happened when you turned back?"

"I don't know," she cried. "I don't know. Please, Heath, ask me something else, but not that."

"Shhh, shhh . . . ," he soothed. "All right, I'll ask you, where was your father?"

"With the scout. They'd taken off early that day to scope the trail and to bag some game to feed us till we were closer to Oregon."

"And when they got back, what did they find?"

"Me, wandering around with Lorna. She was fretting something terrible, and I was humming her the song Mama always sang me to sleep with. It was late that next afternoon

when they got back, and I was getting sick from the smell of
. . . dead people. I was stepping on dead people and inter-
rupting the buzzards' dinner." She gagged and Heath drew her
close, murmuring comfort until she rushed on.

"I have terrible nightmares, Heath. The Indians take me
down, and their painted faces are all I can see. Except for
Lorna, and Lorna's dead because I suffocated her, trying to
keep her quiet. They rip her from my arms and I—I see them
throw her on something that's reaching for my feet."

"What's reaching for your feet? Can you see it?"

"A hand. Mama's hand. I scream for her to help me and
then . . ."

"And then?"

"I wake up." Panting, she whispered, "At least I used to.
Lately something even worse happens. Don't ask me what that
is. I'm begging you, Heath, let this alone. My dreams are bad
enough without my reliving them." Her whimpered plea
speared his heart. "Hold me? Please, just hold me and make the
nightmares go away."

He gripped her to him, wishing he could make both their
nightmares go away. His own troubles bowed to the realization
that whatever Annabelle had seen must have been so beyond
horror and belief that she'd kept her sanity by succumbing to
total darkness. And here he was, asking her to relive the torment.

"Kiss me," he demanded. His mouth consumed her lips
until they trembled in passion rather than painful memory. He
soothed her with compassionate caresses until her desperate
clutches turned to a fevered embrace.

"We have to stop this," he said. And yet he continued.
"Help us stop," he groaned. "Annabelle, I can't do it alone."

"I can't do it at all, and even if I could, I wouldn't want to. Kiss me harder, deeper. Kiss me and never stop."

He was losing control, losing it so fast and completely that he was suddenly rendered blind to all but the images flashing through his mind's eye:

A trial amid fire. A glimpse of rent muscle and splintered bone spliced by the thrust of a silver knife. The sound of a weeping woman who shed the likeness of diamond tears over a fallen beast.

He felt caught between hallucination and the seductive reality that his knuckles were brushing Annabelle's breast and she was moaning his name over, over.

She needed him. He needed her. This was real, it was right, and he clutched at it like a tarp shielding them against a tempest. His mouth closed over her breast, and his tongue laved her through her dress until the fabric was soaked and her nipple was hard from the repeated thrusts he imparted.

Her cry of shock and ecstasy echoed in his mind, drowning out the sinuous whisper of *Touch it.* What he touched were the buttons of her bodice, and then he was peeling her blouse, along with her chemise, down to her waist.

Any hope he harbored for restraint fled as he gazed at her partial nakedness. He hiked up her skirt and petticoats and palmed her through pantalets. Annabelle was wet and whimpering. He was hard and hurting. *This was real.* And together they were stronger than any reflection in his mirror, any family curse, any nightmare.

Heath damned all three and unbuttoned his pants.

6

Annabelle had no idea when their kisses had turned to something out of control. *She* was out of control, begging Heath to do these unspeakable acts. His mouth was everywhere and his hands were spreading her legs open. Then something blunt was pressing and pressing against her. He was making her writhe with sensations that were magical and mad. He was making her scream. And the sounds he was making, beastly animal sounds, were so frightening, so thrilling, she could hardly bear them. The faint smell of roses mingled with the earthy scent of crushed clover. His breath was hot and entering her mouth in rushing streams.

"You want me," he murmured. "Even through your clothes I can feel what I'm doing to you."

"What *are* you doing to me?"

"Giving you pleasure, but not nearly enough."

"You mean there's more? That can't be. I couldn't stand it if you pleased me any more than you already are."

As if he were certain of some sacred knowledge, his low laughter filled her ears. "Let me," he whispered. "Let me give you something so wonderful, you'll wonder how you ever lived without it or without me, the giver."

Already she couldn't live without him. Not without his goodness or the humor he'd brought to her life. Not even without this formless shadow that was black as pitch, a growing presence that was now so strong, she could no longer deny it was somehow a part of him. Just as he felt no less for her because she was blind, neither could she love him less for the dark spot that shadowed his moving touch. With Heath she was safe, and no darkness, not even his own, could hurt her. Fear was her enemy, not him.

Fear gave way to desire and she touched his face. "Anything you want to give me I could never refuse. But it's only right for me to return the pleasure."

"Your pleasure, Annabelle, *is* my pleasure." His fingers were deft and skilled, flooding her senses with a sweet richness as he rid her of her undergarments. His mouth brushed the inside of her thighs, and she could feel soft bites where she'd never dreamed a man would think to put them. Something wet slid over her most private place. His tongue? *There?* How indecent. How . . . marvelous. She thought she might swoon from the luxurious, racking sensation. When he gently nibbled her, she arched her hips.

"Is the way I'm touching you exciting?" he demanded more than asked. "So exciting that you can't bear it if I don't touch you inside? Tell me. Because that excites *me.*"

Was this pleasure? Her heart drummed so fast, she was certain it would burst. Did heaven mean to strike her dead for committing a sin of the flesh? He covered her mouth with his, and she tasted herself on his lips, on his tongue. It swirled around hers, making the same motions she felt his fingers make before one entered her. What had felt so painfully hollow before was suddenly empty no more.

She cried out, "Heath, Heath," no longer caring if God did mean to strike her dead. She would die a happy sinner and even sought to sin further by squirming deeper into his hand.

At the first stroke, she marveled at the exquisite rightness of their being this close. At the second stroke, she ached to be much closer than this. Upon the third stroke, she was sure she would die from his denial before she would from any holy wrath.

Annabelle could bear his slow, measured slides no longer. She pumped her hips back and forth, faster, faster while he kept his own too far away. Reaching as far as she could, she managed to find his backside and urged him closer. With a start she realized that his shirt was on, but his pants were down. His behind was firm, and when she traced its shape, he went very still, then groaned so long and low, she knew an elation, an unfolding of womanly confidence.

If her pleasure was his, his was no less hers.

"Let *it* happen," he whispered sharply. "Be *there.*"

She felt his fingertips brush her breasts, and then his palm came to rest between them over the locket. His breath grazed her throat. Harsher, faster it came, hot as steam.

There was a stillness in the air, then a quiver as if the earth had tilted and turned upside down. He scraped his teeth against her neck. She felt a change in him that she couldn't define. It was something primal, something unleashed.

Something frightful and frightfully arousing.

"Heath?" she whispered haltingly. "Did you say, 'touch it'? Tell me what part of you to touch."

He couldn't answer her, could hardly hear her voice over the whispered command. *Hold it.* Something was suddenly, terribly wrong. The locket was burning his palm, and though he commanded himself not to, his fingers were closing around it. There was a poisonous energy that seemed to emanate from its core, and though he instinctively recoiled, he couldn't let go.

And he couldn't force words from his mouth, which planted itself against her neck. His jaws stretched so wide that they ached. And his teeth, heaven help him, they were raking over her pulse point. He was teasing and gently biting as if in a macabre dance of seduction meant to coerce a victim into submission.

Heath was desperate to hurl the locket away, to get his mouth off her and stop his plundering fingers. The first two were beyond his control, but he managed to force his hand from between their hips.

Too late he realized his error. With his hand gone, his lower body took command, as if his erection were obeying some profane order. His body was betraying them both, sending him into the throes of endless ecstasy. It was an insidious coercion, a wily device designed to trap him in the most humanly vulnerable moment. A time when reason was robbed and primal instinct reigned.

Heath struggled to break the connection that flowed from his erection to locket to teeth. They were like linked hands capturing Annabelle in the middle.

He could smell them again, the roses. He could smell her innocence. His teeth raked her neck back and forth while his hips thrust with ever-increasing speed.

He tried to call out a warning, to tell her to stop him. That something foul was in him and bent on using her trust against them both. But his vocal cords were locked. And, dear Lord, Annabelle was writhing beneath him, her body so ready that it easily accepted the plump end of his flesh. And as she moaned in delirious ecstasy, he fought the insistent need to bite her.

"Deeper," she pleaded. "I'm so empty. Please, Heath, let me feel you deeper inside."

In horror he felt her hand slide between them, intent, he

was sure, to lead him past the obstacle of her virginity. He flattened his abdomen against her belly, capturing her searching fingers. The flailing of her body, which was coming apart beneath his, drained his will until he teetered on the edge of succumbing to nature's course. It was a power in itself, leaving him to fight not one enemy but two.

The locket was growing hotter than hot. His teeth were quivering. He could feel them extending, vibrating with a wanton lust as they stroked over Annabelle's vulnerable throat. The sound of a carousel spinning out of control was filling his ears. Her sighs blended with her words that he felt more than heard.

"Why won't you let me touch you?" Annabelle pleaded. "If you won't talk to me, at least let your body speak for you and—*ohh.*"

His nuzzling teeth sparked sensations from her neck to her womb. And without warning, she was *there.* And there she wanted to be forever. A magnificent light seemed to surround her while their hearts raced as one. Ruby-colored tears rained down on them. They splattered against the back she clenched and streamed into a pool of red that was warm and comforting because it was theirs to share, to wallow in and partake together, a communion binding their bodies in love.

The vision passed and left her shaken. *She* was shaking. Drained, yet never more whole. Her flesh was his flesh. Her blood was his blood and their souls were sewn tight in a seamless circle of intimacy.

"Heath?" she murmured, "is my pleasure truly your pleasure? I do hope so, because you have pleased me ever so greatly, and . . . you're already sure to know it, but I love you."

She wished for reciprocal words of love, but all she heard was the cry of a bird overhead and Heath's labored grunts as he lightly teethed her neck and squeezed her nipple between thumb and locket. Was he not finished? Were they not done with the deed that he'd said made babies?

Her languor cleared abruptly. *Could she be with child?*

"Heath! Did you get me with child? Please, tell me."

Harder, harder he pressed into her, leaving her to wonder wildly if his silence had just verified the worst. She began to panic. Pa would kill him. No, he'd force Heath to marry her. But that would never happen because she'd live with her shame before taking a husband whose vows were prompted by the barrel of a gun.

She had to get away. She had to think. But when she tried to rise, he howled in outrage and nipped her neck hard enough to hurt.

What was she to do? She didn't know. This was all so new to her, and it was becoming extremely frightening. He was rutting between her legs, and she feared he would crush her beneath him or tear her apart.

In desperation she yelled at him. "Stop! Stop, Heath! You asked me to help you stop, and I am!" With her free hand she pounded at his shoulder and elicited a lusty growl. She aimed for his jaw, and the blow got his teeth off her neck. Taking advantage, she thrust with all her might and managed to roll them over. What was inside her slipped out.

Sitting up, she shoved him hard, but he grappled to get her back. "Heath!" she cried, sobbing. "Dear God, let me go." He didn't and she struck him again.

He snarled and bucked up, trying to put himself back in where she no longer wanted him to be. Instinctively she planted her knee between his legs. His wail of pain echoed in her ears while she tore herself loose from his slackened grip.

Fueled by adrenaline, she was on her feet and running, the

locket bouncing from one bare breast to the other. *Get away, you have to get away.* . . . The chant in her head ended with a gasp as she tripped on her sagging petticoat. Picking herself up, she again took flight—but to where? Home? How could she find her way home? And she had no shoes on, no pantalets or drawers. Heaven's mercy, *she'd left them behind with a madman.*

Heath was surrounded by a reddish black haze. His groin was in severe pain, and he welcomed the reassurance that he was human enough to feel it. He blinked, trying to get his eyes to focus.

"Annabelle," he whispered. His voice was barely a croak, but at least he could speak again. She didn't reply. He feverishly searched the clover glade trying to find her, to assure himself that he hadn't harmed her in those final moments when all he could see were raining drops of red. The scent of roses that were the color of blood had filled his nostrils and then . . . blackness, cloaking his mind, saturating his body. It was a void worse than death, and he now rid himself of its last traces by sucking in clean air.

A shriek reached his ears, and he turned to see a splash of color falling down the rise of a grassy knoll. *Annabelle.* He hitched up his pants and took off after her. With dismay he watched her get to her feet and raise her skirt. It flew behind her as she ran, as if pursued by the demons of hell.

"Annabelle, wait!"

She ran faster toward his buggy, and his heart sank with the certainty that she was running from him. He was the demon, he knew. She was alive but what crimes had he committed before she'd escaped?

Heath streaked ahead, slicing a trail through knee-high

grass. He watched the horses rear up while Annabelle stood rooted beneath their pawing hoofs. The endless distance that separated him from Annabelle was a blur of green and blue as he raced faster, faster. And then there he was, shoving her away and covering her body so his would take the deadly blow of the horses' hoofs.

Heath heard the pounding of dirt and snorts overhead as he rolled them out of harm's way. Her body was shivering beneath his, and despite Annabelle's heaving sobs, he took his fear and anger and relief out on her with a harsh chastisement.

"Dammit, why don't you watch where you're going?"

"I would if I could!"

Heath quelled the urge to inform her that her optical nerves were perfectly fine, and that if she could stop her mind from running as fast as her feet, she'd realize it herself. Instead, he gripped her to him, desperate for the assurance that she was all right.

Annabelle's sobs hurt him more deeply than the fists she beat against his chest.

"Let go of me," she demanded brokenly.

"Why? So you can kill yourself and take along with you the only reason I've got left to be living?"

"Why stop with just us? I asked you if you'd gotten me with child. Your silence was answer enough. Don't worry, I won't let Pa take a shotgun after you. Just be glad I don't have one myself right now." She turned her face to the side when he touched a tear.

A baby. Was it possible? When he'd revived, he'd felt stunned with pain. *A baby.* He was mute with a sudden awareness of the repurcussions if Annabelle had conceived.

The issue produced would surely be from a bad seed.

Never in his life had he considered such a staggering moral

dilemma. No, not even when a dying woman had beseeched him to give her ease and, with her last dregs of strength, thrust a pillow into his hands. He'd handed it to her husband and quieted her with an injection of morphine. But not enough to end the misery. His hands were meant for healing, not to act on behalf of the angel of death. After all, he was a doctor, not a spirit of terrible beauty that came with a final breath and left with the scent of roses.

Heath shuddered. Why didn't he have a ready solution, a sure cure to remedy this ill? His life was spinning out of control, and it was no longer madness he feared, but a terrifying premonition that he *wasn't* going mad.

He needed Annabelle more than ever. But she was stiff in his arms, remote, and he prayed that his words would reach her.

"I love you, Annabelle," he said with a rush of emotion.

"Do you?" she replied woodenly. "If that was love you were showing before, I want none of it. And I want none of you."

7

At first she thought it had begun to rain. But the drops that fell on her lips were as salty as the tears she had ceased to shed. And the rumble against her chest was too deep and close to pass for thunder. Against her better judgment, she touched his face to ensure her senses hadn't deceived her.

Heath led her fingertips to trace the stream that wound down his cheek.

"You're crying," she whispered.

"Twice in my life have I ever cried." He swallowed hard, and the hardness that was in her for his wrongdoing softened. "I cried when my grandfather's casket was lowered at Cloud Castle. And yes, I am crying now."

"Why? Because I didn't like what men naturally do when they want their way with a woman?" Her laugh was brittle. "But much as I hate to admit it, I can't put the whole blame on you."

"There is blame to be had, but it's not yours to share."

"No? I behaved no better than a strumpet, and us not even married. If I'd had any idea of the ways between men and women, I never would have led you on. Like I said, I won't let Pa make you pay for a mistake that's as much mine as yours."

"Do you actually believe that I'd get you with child, then desert the both of you?" he said, openly hurt. "Annabelle, how could you even think such a thing? I would never, of my own accord, dishonor you. Please, you must believe that."

"I did. And I want to." She weighed her answer, realizing how vulnerable he was to her, that she could cut him deeply with a single word. "It's just that—Heath, you scared me something terrible."

"I scared myself," he confessed quietly. "I'm as distressed, maybe even more than you are, by my actions."

"Then why did you do it?"

"Something came over me, and—and I can't explain what I don't fully understand myself. All I can ask is that you'll forgive me for what I'd give anything to erase."

Hesitantly, she hugged him. "I believe that to be true. I forgive you, Heath."

He held her to him and beseeched her, "Tell me that you know I could never mean you harm, that you're no longer afraid of me."

"I'm still a little shook up, but I'm not fearful. You're not at all the same person I ran from, and, well, I know that I hurt you just before I got away and—"

"You did us both a favor, because you're right, that wasn't really me." He kissed the tips of her fingers and pressed her palm to his cheek. "I need you, Annabelle. More than I've ever needed anyone or anything, I need you in my life. Say that you still want me in yours."

"I do want you in my life, Heath. But I need a promise that what happened won't happen again should we ever share a marriage bed."

"What happened was *wrong*. Intimacy between a man and woman is meant to be a beautiful thing. It grieves me to have made you think it's ugly and frightening and . . . I want badly to change that picture in your mind." His hands were gently persuasive as they sifted through her hair. "Have you enough faith in me to let me kiss you? If you could trust me that much, it would be good for us both."

"Like a spoon of sugar after a dose of castor oil?"

"Exactly," he whispered. His kiss was filled with such tenderness that she couldn't believe he had been capable of what he'd done. Except for the place on her neck that still stung where he'd bitten her, she wasn't hurt, not really. It was her heart that had taken the beating.

"Better?" he asked hopefully.

"Much." And she was. Enough that she was compelled to put things even more right. "I know you feel awfully bad about upsetting me, but maybe you'll feel better knowing that I liked what you were doing tremendously. Until I remembered myself, that is. I even enjoyed having your teeth on me, except for that last bite. It was a bit too rough."

Heath's gaze riveted to where she touched her neck. It looked as if he'd taken a small rake to it. Thank God he hadn't broken the skin, and the red streaks were light enough he was certain they wouldn't raise welts. But when he raised her hand to kiss it in apology, he saw a tiny puncture mark near her jugular. His hand shook badly as he tentatively touched it.

Something that felt like a hot current passed through his fingertip, and he watched in disbelief as a blue-white halo glowed against her skin where he touched her.

"What are you doing, Heath? My neck, it feels so warm and . . . ahhh." Her sigh was one of arousal.

He lifted his finger and his breath rushed out. There was nothing, not even a wound the size of a pinprick. He tapped his cheek where he'd nicked himself earlier. Quickly he brushed his fingertips over the streaks marring her neck. They faded and he jerked back.

The locket. He'd almost touched the locket, which appeared to pulse with an unearthly light. Heath eyed it shrewdly, with a wariness reserved for a formidable opponent.

"Annabelle," he said with feigned casualness, "your locket —I've never seen what's inside. Would you mind opening it for me?"

She fumbled with the clasp and it sprang open.

He was suddenly staring at a miniature likeness of Annabelle—except it wasn't she. The woman's hair was red and her eyes green. And the portrait was very old. He narrowed his gaze at a tiny diamond shaped in a teardrop and flawlessly grooved into a painted cheek. Two identical grooves were empty, giving the impression that the stones had fallen out.

Or had yet to be put in.

"Who is she?" he asked, certain that she was no less than some sort of witch whose influence he'd been under.

"It's been so long, I can't be sure. But I think Mama said her name was Rachael. Rachael Dobbs, that's it! She's an ancestor of some sort on my mother's side."

"Rachael Dobbs . . . Rachael Dobbs . . ." Why did the name sound familiar? He'd heard it before, he was certain. Or perhaps he'd seen it in print somewhere. He continued to stare suspiciously at the locket. Many women owned lockets, didn't they? And more than one had been passed down from mother to daughter.

But how many had the power to cast a spell?

Suddenly he knew: the journal that his grandfather had given him over twenty years ago! He'd never read it in its entirety, just bits and pieces when he'd been a boy who had deemed it nothing more than a fair piece of fiction by . . . Michael Nightingale. That's where he'd seen the name

Rachael Dobbs—Michael had linked it to a locket and the curse he'd battled.

What more, Heath wondered, was needed to prove the journal in his trunk was grounded in fact, not fiction? He'd ignored his grandfather's warnings, certain of his own logical superiority. He didn't feel so superior now, not when logic dictated that he had been very foolish to dismiss what was now becoming too true.

"You can close the locket, Annabelle. I've satisfied my curiosity on that, but not on something else." Leaning down, he pressed a soft kiss to her mouth. "Tell me truthfully, did I physically hurt you in any way?"

"Not really, though I am feeling that peculiar ache again." She frowned. "Considering our current position, I shouldn't be courting trouble like this."

"You're courting no trouble with me at the moment," he assured her. "In fact, I'd like to play a game of pretend. That is, if you trust me enough to play along."

He could see in her face that she wanted to trust him as much as he needed to right her perception of what men and women shared in lovemaking. No longer resistant, she was soft and vulnerable and nearly naked beneath him. He couldn't look at her and not want to touch her.

"Will you play the game with me?" he asked, and traced a fingertip around a rosy nipple. Her breath caught, and he seduced her senses further with the sway of his hips. Annabelle rubbed against him, a sign that she would trust him to make amends.

"I'll play," she agreed. "But . . . will you be putting your teeth on me again?"

"*No.*" They quivered as if possessed of a separate intelligence and displeased with his answer. He paused to consider the disturbing idea of his mouth wanting to open and feast upon her. "No," he repeated firmly, "I *won't* put my teeth on you. However, I will do something I hope you like even better." He wet his fingertip and flicked it lightly over each nipple.

"Ohhh . . . oh yes, I do like that. Do it again?"

"Gladly. But first, let's pretend that I never gave you a reason to run from me. I want you to 'forget yourself' again. Don't worry, this time I won't be forgetting myself."

She nodded, and Heath marveled at her willingness to let him do as he wished. He touched her with utmost care, each caress, each fleeting kiss an apology.

She forgave him with beauty and grace. Crouched at her feet, he stroked her soles and watched with amazement as the bruises she'd gotten from running in bare feet disappeared. Her wispy sighs stilled as he slowly pushed her skirt up her thighs.

"Easy," he whispered. "I'm not going to hurt you, I swear it."

"What are you going to do?" she asked anxiously.

"Pretend I'm a man who's madly in love with a beautiful woman—a woman who knows that I'll be very gentle while I touch her in the way a man should touch a woman when he wants to right a wrong he's done her. Will you let me?"

She hesitated, then said, "Will you stop if I ask you to?"

"I give you my word." The relaxation of her locked legs was the answer he craved. She believed in him again, he realized gratefully.

He bent her legs, placed a kiss on each knee, then parted them. His gaze traveled to the juncture between her thighs, and he was relieved when no traces of blood greeted him, only a sheen of moisture.

He slid a finger over her wetness, her gasp of pleasure aug-

menting his own desire. He held it firmly in check. He'd lost
the struggle not to take her before, had been robbed of his free
will, raped as surely as Annabelle had nearly been. But he was a
man, not a monster, and he desperately needed reassurance of
that.

As he circled her swelling cleft, he gloried in his own response, which was all too human. It was the solace he yearned
for, the proof of his humanity.

Heath held his breath. He was in pain, severe, sweet pain
and aching to be where he now had three fingers planted.
Through those fingers, he suddenly sensed her womb was
empty. He discerned no ill thing there, no echo of the darkness
he was.

"Annabelle," he whispered, "I want to put your mind at
ease. We didn't make a baby." *Or ungodly spawn.* The burden of
that horror lifted, he pressed a lingering kiss to her inner thigh.

"No baby. Oh." Her voice was small.

Her disappointment was surprising to him, but a balm to
his soul. That she could still want a child of his was testimony
to the depth of her love. His ran just as deep, and he put aside
his own needs to prove it.

"Tell me what's best for you now. If you'd feel safer with
me simply holding you, say so, and I'll stop what I'm doing.
Whatever it is you want, I'll give, as much or as little as you're
comfortable with. Intimacy, if it's right, should be a mutual
wish. *That,* my love, is the way between men and women."
When she didn't respond, Heath began to withdraw.

Annabelle caught his wrist. "Don't stop."

A smile wreathed his lips. And yet his happiness was overshadowed by the painful knowledge that their future was uncertain. Would he ever make love to her? Would they ever have
a home and children together? Until he bested this thing that

had turned his world into chaos, they could only pretend. It wasn't enough, no, not nearly, but should this be all they could have, he would make it a searing memory that would bind them forever.

"Pretend with me. Pretend we're on a ship, lying naked in our cabin." His fingers began their gentle stroking once more while her feminine sounds of arousal increased his rampant need. "What you feel is the most human part of me," he murmured, "the best way I know to show my heart. It's right and it's good that I should be inside you."

But he wasn't. For her sake, he couldn't be. He could, however, pretend otherwise. Heath hesitated only briefly before releasing the buttons of his trousers. How he ached for it to be her hand wrapped around him. Even more, that it was the sleek walls he fondled that were gripping the turgid flesh he pumped. His dual strokes came faster, matching the escalating tempo of their intimacy.

"The sheets smell of sunshine and soap," he continued in a roughened voice. "They smell of our lovemaking, musky and wet as the ocean around us. Can you feel it rocking the bed we share?"

"Yes," she said faintly. "I feel it. I feel you. You're very strong and you're holding me tight. It's dark out, but you make me feel safe and loved."

"You are. I love you, Annabelle Rawlings." He punctuated his vow with a thrust. "Hear me say it in our private chamber while the waves lap and our bodies slide together. Harder. Faster. Breast to chest. Hip to hip, your thighs locked around mine. The wind's whipping up, but the storm is inside. *I'm* inside you. Deep, so deep—"

"Deeper," she begged. "Yes, deeper. Please . . . *Heath*—"

He watched her climax, pretending it was his arousal, not his fingers, that she grasped tight. She moaned, long and sweet, then began chanting his name. Her voice mingled with his plaintive groan of release. As he spilled on the ground, his fleeting joy of oneness was eclipsed by a deep sorrow that they may never be closer than this. In truth, he wanted to weep.

After quickly restoring himself, he cradled her in his arms, and she wrapped hers around his neck. Her fingers tenderly stroked the damp hair at his nape.

"Thank you for taking me on your ship," she said, smiling.

"More than anything I want to take you there one day. I want to take you on a Nightingale ship and make love forever and for real."

"I'd like that ever so much, Heath." Laughing, she confessed, "But I do have to admit that I enjoy being 'there' tremendously—ship or no ship."

"So do I." Sweet heaven, how he wished he could laugh with her, hold her until he woke up from his nightmare. But even now the sun was descending, so he forced himself to carry her to the buggy, saying as he went, "It's getting late and I don't wish to court your father's wrath. I'll get your clothes."

Ridiculously, he didn't want to leave Annabelle alone with the locket. She'd worn it most of her life, and he obviously was a much greater danger. Still, he set out at a jog, vaguely aware that his surroundings were passing abnormally fast while he felt a sense of moving in slow motion.

When he returned with her shoes and undergarments, Annabelle said, "I thought you were going to fetch my things."

"I did."

"But how could you? Hardly a minute's passed since you headed for the glade."

Heath was beyond questioning what had to be another

manifestation of something supernatural at work. Numb, he groped for an explanation. "I . . . I, ah, brought them with me when I chased after you. They were dropped near the horses."

Staring hatefully at the locket, he helped Annabelle dress, then started the buggy on the path home. They were halfway there when he remembered the package that had arrived on the stagecoach earlier that day. He fished beneath the seat and placed his gift on Annabelle's lap.

"For you. Open it and see what you touch."

"Dots," she observed. "Why are all these dots on the paper?"

"Braille. I had a colleague send the book from Boston so you could read again. You told me the day I met you how much you missed reading, and whatever I can or can't do for your sight, at least I can give you this."

"You mean these dots are words?" she exclaimed.

"That's what they are." Heath wrapped his arm around her shoulder and drew her close. He'd planned for them to learn braille together; now he couldn't promise her that. He could only hope that Jake or her sister could read Dr. Purdue's letter of instruction. "Before you know it, Annabelle, you'll be reading that book."

"I don't know what to say." Tears laced her voice. "Just that I love you, and as soon as I get home, I'll bake you the best birthday cake you ever sank your teeth into."

Heath winced. He didn't think it wise to see her again until he knew just what he was dealing with. But her heart was so set on tomorrow that he couldn't bring himself to spoil her plans. Besides, Annabelle was the only solid thing left in his life, and he direly needed her presence in it.

"Just remember, my love, whatever the future holds, nothing can take away what we've shared. Never forget that." He pressed a kiss to her palm and let go of her hand only when they neared the cabin.

The sun was setting by the time Heath bade Jake good-bye and chastely kissed Annabelle's cheek. Both of them whispered they would count the minutes until they met in church the next morning.

Eyes set on the distance, Heath shouted the team of horses into a gallop. He had a journal to dig out of his trunk and answers to be gleaned before he slept.

8

Heath barred the door. He lit an oil lamp, out of habit rather than necessity. His eyes had become unusually perceptive in the dark. Grabbing up the lamp, he headed toward his apartment. His path led him past the mirror, which he'd taken down and set on the floor with the glass facing the wall.

After setting the lamp on a small desk that was cluttered with medical textbooks, he went to stand in front of the trunk. He took a deep breath, then throwing open the lid, stared at the journal, its pages rustling as if a thumb were riffling through them.

He glowered at the journal while a childhood memory flashed vividly through his mind. . . .

"Grandpapa, you know there's no such thing as werewolves. You're just trying to scare me, but it's not going to work." Jumping atop his bed, he formed a claw and swiped at the air. "Owwooo! Owwooo! Rarrrh!"

His laughter abruptly ended when Grandpapa slammed the journal shut and threw it on the feather mattress.

"What am I ever to do with you, young man?" he asked, stiffening in his chair. "Anything you can't touch or see yourself you refuse to believe. Foolish, that's what you are, foolish and disrespectful toward all that is beyond your ability to perceive. God exists, and it's a wonder you don't doubt Him since you can't plop yourself on His throne and demand proof of His divinity."

Heath climbed under the covers and lowered his gaze in seeming deference to his grandfather's wisdom. In truth, he didn't want the older man to see the doubt in his eyes.

"I'm sorry, Grandpapa. You were very kind to read me the story, and I was wrong to misbehave after you brought me such a nice gift for my birthday."

"A precipitate gift, it would seem. Three times three making nine, I thought this birthday the appropriate moment to pass on your heritage. Perhaps I should return the journal to Cloud Castle and take you to the toy store tomorrow."

"I'd rather keep this, thank you." The thing did possess a curious allure. Heath touched the thick volume, and something that felt like static pulsed between his fingertips and the leather binding. Certain there was a scientific explanation for the current, he lightly drummed his fingers against the book. "I thought you said this was old. It doesn't look it."

"Almost two centuries old, for your information. And as you can see, time hasn't touched it. Explain *that*."

Since he couldn't, Heath yawned. "I'll sleep on the possibilities and give you my conclusions on the morrow."

"I see through you, Heath Nightingale. If you can't win, you don't want to play." Grandpapa ruffled his hair and got up. "Ah, well, time is the greatest teacher, and you're bound to learn more from it than you ever will from me."

"Good night, Grandpapa. I love you."

"I love you too, boy." At the door he turned and pointed a gnarled finger at the journal. "Forewarned is forearmed. Just as Michael was, you are the third son of a third son. And though I know you don't believe in folklore any more than you do curses, there is an old belief I heard in Europe when our fleet docked there many years ago: when a werewolf dies, it transforms into a vampire. Sleep on that while you do the other." He shut the door.

Heath bared his teeth and rolled his eyes. His gaze settled on the journal. It was open. He didn't remember opening it, but quickly decided he had done so without being aware of it.

He turned his attention to the writing. "The locket was, and does remain, tied to the curse," he read. "The locket was the key to my release, but only if the diamond tear was returned to Rachael Dobbs. She has it now, bought by my beloved Kit's sacrifice, a sacrifice that no mortal woman would ever have made.

"Praise heaven she did, for had she not, I would still be trapped by that bestial agony and seeking my own destruction. The only other recourse would have surely ended the life of my true love. Even now I remember my lust for her soul, the hot craving to tear out her heart so it would eternally be mine as I stalked her in the form of a werewolf. No longer do I prowl the earth to prey on the unwary. But then, as now, I would be as the living dead without her. . . ."

Hmmm. The death part was a neat piece of fiction, but the love story that went with it Heath could do without. "Oh, Kit," he crooned, "I can't live without you." Embracing himself in a melodramatic hug, he simpered, "Even though I'm terribly hairy and want to chew up your bones, let me hear you say that you love me any old way and—"

The pages began to turn. Faster and faster they turned as if invisible fingers were flipping them in a rage. The room was icy cold, and the heavy curtains billowed with a blast of freezing air. The journal fell to the floor as Heath hurriedly got up to shut the window.

The weather was strange, even for Boston, but surely no stranger than his ancestor who had gone batty over a woman. She'd probably driven him to seek solace in his cups. . . .

The memory was one Heath often recalled, and always with a smile. He wasn't smiling now. He grabbed up the journal, ignoring the pulsating aliveness that called to something inside himself.

At the desk, he swept off his medical books. With only the lamp and an inkwell remaining, he laid down the journal and began to read.

Preceding Michael's entry, Heath discovered the agitated scratching of one Jonathan Nightingale, dated 1690. It was his record of a witch trial wherein he betrayed his betrothed, Rachael Deliverance Dobbs. The woman in Annabelle's locket, Heath learned, had burned at the stake, due to the cowardice of a man who had lived out his years in sorrow and regret.

Then Heath's gaze fell on the curse.

"The third son of every third son shall walk the earth as a creature of the night, trapped in shadows, no two creatures alike." Heath paused. If Michael had indeed been a werewolf, what might his successor be? If Grandpapa had been right about the folklore . . .

Scanning the lines, Heath read on. "Stripped of humanity, he will howl in concert with demons, never to die, always to wander in agony, until a woman entraps his heart and soul. . . . If that woman should find a way to set the creature free, it will be at great and terrible cost. . . ." Rachael's tears transformed into three precious stones, and then, "The curse will go on . . . until every tear I have shed is returned to me and I am whole again."

Heath glared at the words and in outrage grabbed the lamp's chimney and hurled it against the wall.

"I hope you can hear me, Jonathan Nightingale, you who make me ashamed to share your last name. And you, Rachael Dobbs, would you still have your revenge? Not only is it visited upon the Nightingales, but the women descended from you. Look for no pity here, because there's none to be had. Two strangers, that's what you are, dead and buried and deserving of each other. Take the spiteful curse and the profane accounting of it along with you. Ashes to ashes and the devil with you both. *Burn.* Burn together and leave the living be."

He put the journal to the lamp's flame, and as it licked the paper, a blast of sparks leapt from the binding and onto his face. The fire spread rapidly from face to groin, and though he knew he should be screaming in agony, he was not.

He raced for the pitcher and doused himself. A quick inspection showed that though his shirt and trousers were charred, his torso had miraculously escaped injury. But what of his face? Heath hurried to the mirror and put it back on its previous place on the wall.

"What are you?" he demanded as the image in the glass showed an untouched face. The eyes gazing back glittered with calculating intelligence, with hypnotic allure.

Heath pounded a fist against the mirror and, in horror, witnessed his teeth altering in shape. His canines lengthened and sharpened to needlepoint ends. They were as two straws, inhaling the cloyingly sweet, still air.

His fist dropped limply to his side as he leaned forward to study the creature that he had become. A creature that smelled of roses, that smiled serenely while he watched Heath Nightingale take his last living breath.

Annabelle pleated the folds of her fancy new dress—the color of a buttercup, Pa had said. It was just as soft as flower petals, too, but the joy she'd felt while slipping it on had diminished as she'd waited and waited for Heath on the front steps of the church.

When the service was over, her hopes were dashed. Worse, her disappointment was public knowledge. In her excitement, she'd bandied about that she was meeting her beau. His absence had been duly noted by the gossip mongers. Their whispers had followed her as she walked to a pew with Pa. Pa, whose arm was wrapped protectively around her shoulder, said in her ear, "Don't you pay those biddies any mind. They're just jealous 'cause you're fetchin' and they ain't. He's late, that's all. Till he gets here, I'll have the prettiest gal all to myself. Hold your head high and latch on to my hand."

Each swish of the church's doors had made her heart leap in expectation, only to die a little when the new arrival turned out not to be Heath.

"Was he in his office, Pa?" she now inquired anxiously.

"Nope. Checked his office and knocked on his private door too," Pa answered as he climbed into the rough cart and settled beside her on the weathered wood seat. He patted her hands when she continued to worry her new skirt. "The doctor didn't answer, but that's no reason for you to fret, girl. He's likely tending a patient that took sick and had to make a house call. We'd best be on our way so you can frost his cake while I stir the fish stew."

Jake shot a hostile glance at the drawn drapes in both office and apartment windows, then slapped the reins hard. He wanted to get gone before he stormed through town to hunt down the Boston dandy who had wounded his little girl's heart.

And wounded worse it would be if she knew that he'd also checked the livery stables. The doctor's horses were there, and so was the well-heeled buggy that carried her farther away from her Pa with each ride out.

Yep, Heath Nightingale had better have a good excuse for standing up his Annabelle. A damn good excuse.

Huddled in his closet that smelled of chocolate and funereal odors, Heath fought the urge to cry for help.

The pounding at his door ceased, and Jake Rawlings's grumbling voice faded with his heavy footsteps. Heath coveted the other man's freedom and took hope that there might be something human left in him. Not much, to be sure, but enough for him to have feelings of envy and anger and . . . fear.

Heath was well and truly scared.

He again catalogued the symptoms that had driven him, writhing and moaning, to crawl into the closet that was dark as a tomb. He identified them as the same as those he'd experienced that day at the telegraph office, but ten times more intense. Had the first signs begun only a month ago? He felt as though he'd aged a century. His hands were like claws, stiff with what he'd first mistaken for writer's cramp. He had spent most of the night penning his observations and heartache in the blank pages following Michael's entry.

Michael had actually survived and took for his wife the

woman that he had to thank for it. Kit had even worn the locket on their wedding day at Cloud Castle.

I, Heath Nightingale, take thee, Annabelle Rawlings, as my lawfully wedded wife. . . . And flying to the stars was just as likely as his making such a vow. If only . . .

Time passed too slowly, with his mind trapped in a paralyzed body. He was near to going mad when his eyelids snapped open, and the pores of his skin prickled as if a thousand pins had been stuck into him. Moving was painful, but not impossible. He crawled out of the closet on all fours.

The process of gaining an upright position was slow, but once he was erect, agility soon returned. Heath dressed in his best finery, then went to his desk, where he snatched up the journal and flung it into his steamer trunk. It thumped against the closed lid. Heath turned the lock with a vicious snarl that didn't sound human to his own ears.

In the cool shadow of dusk, he saddled up his fastest horse. The stallion was laboring for breath by the time Heath arrived at the cabin.

Annabelle sat on the porch, alone in the dark, the book of braille on the floor beside her and the locket in her fist. A deep sigh of longing escaped him as she stretched out her arms in eager welcome.

Forgive me, my love.

"Of course I forgive you, Heath." Her response to his silent plea took him by surprise. "I forgive you, but Pa might not. He's still fretting over your missing church and his having to eat jerky since I saved the fish stew for once you got here. I've been worried about you something fierce."

"Lord, but you've never looked so good to me." Throwing caution aside, he gathered her in his arms, desperate for the comfort of her embrace. They clung together even when the door banged open and Jake came out.

"Where've you been?" Jake demanded, glaring at Heath. "Git your hands off my girl unless you're a'planning to take her off mine. I don't take kindly to a man who trifles with my daughter's affections. You've got one minute to speak your piece before I run you out on a rail back to Boston."

"You'll do no such thing, Pa, not unless you run me out right along with him."

"That's enough out of you, young lady."

"I'm *not* a young lady." Annabelle whirled around to confront her father. "Look at me, Pa. I'm almost ten years older than Mama was when she ran away with you. Unless you want me to sneak off the same way, you'll let Heath be. Don't make me choose between the two of you. Much as I love you, my place is with Heath. Send him away, and you won't see me again until you ask him back."

Jake's big body slumped, and the hands he'd balled into fists fell limp in defeat. Heath felt a stab of pity for him and searched for a plausible lie.

"I owe you both an explanation and an apology. A man came banging on my door first thing this morning. He'd ridden several hours to fetch me so I might help his wife, who was having a difficult labor." *Jake had checked the livery stables.* Heath had no idea how he knew, but *he knew.* "I climbed into his wagon and returned only at sunset."

"Of course," Jake said with total acceptance. Heath was uncertain whether it was Annabelle's ultimatum or yet another ability he might now possess, the power of suggestion, that had swayed the older man. He confirmed it was the latter when Jake repeated verbatim what Heath willed him to say. "And I'm sure that you came here as soon as you could."

"That's right. Had I known the baby's delivery would take the whole day, I would have sent word. I love your daughter, Jake. Never doubt that fact in your mind."

"Apology accepted," Jake said. "Dinner's boiled thicker'n red-eye gravy. I'll serve up our bowls while you two keep company and . . ." He paused, seemingly confused. Then he shook his head and stared at his daughter. "Annabelle, what are you doing outside in the dark?"

"I was waiting for Heath. Don't you remember, Pa?"

Jake rubbed his furrowed brow. "Can't say that I recollect it. But I do wholeheartedly approve. Must be some real magic you've worked on my girl, Doc, and I thank you for that." Pointing sternly at Heath's hands, which were on Annabelle's shoulders, Jake grumbled, "But don't let me catch you two sparking till any vows are said."

Then he confessed, "I envy you two younguns. My life's more'n half over, but you've got your own still ahead of you, shining as bright as the Star of David."

9

"I'll help clear the table." Heath rose, needing to work off the strangely unsettling energy shooting through his veins. "The dinner was marvelous," he said, thankful that Annabelle couldn't see he'd barely gotten down only a few spoonfuls. *"You're* marvelous, my love."

"And you're out of your mind if you think I'm about to let you take cleaning duty on your birthday."

Quickly, Heath gathered up bowls and carried them to the washtub. Then, with preternatural speed, he went to work.

"Too late, Annabelle," he taunted good-naturedly a few moments later. "The chore's done, and I'll get the cake my-self." When Jake stared incredulously at the heap of dishes, Heath gave him a carefully guarded smile. Turning back to Annabelle, he said, "Your new dress is much too nice to soil in the kitchen. Did I mention how well you suit it? You're pretty as a picture." Scowling at the locket encasing the portrait of Rachael Dobbs, he returned to the table, cake in hand.

"You told me at least ten times, Heath. But please feel free to repeat yourself as much as you like in your old age." She laughed softly and stroked the locket. "My, but you move fast for thirty. However you cleaned up so fast is beyond me."

Too late, Heath realized his mistake. Avoiding Jake's narrowed gaze, he said uneasily, "Amazing what a chocolate cake can do to move a man along."

"Just don't eat it as fast, or you'll have me treating you for an upset to your system." Heath felt a fistlike twisting in his gut. If she only knew the illness already in his system . . . "Would you cut the cake?" Annabelle asked him. "I swear I can hear you drooling from here."

"I would be honored." He was certain her ears hadn't deceived her. His mouth was watering, but for something other than food. What it was, he was loath even to guess, and with all his might he tried to deny the perverse hunger.

Standing at the head of the table, he held the knife that he would gladly have driven into his unbeating heart. Sadly, he couldn't kill what was already dead. Filled with anger that Rachael Dobbs had decreed he was to be denied the grave, he viciously, blindly, sliced into the cake.

A stinging sensation in the palm of his free hand caused him to drop the knife. He opened his eyes and stared at his trembling hand extended before him. The color of crimson filled a gaping wound. He gazed at it, enthralled. Was this truly blood? No, nothing so human as that. It smelled more delicious than anything on earth, and the hue was so vivid, the texture so lush, it was like the richest velvet. The sound of its pooling tickled his ears.

Heath was captivated by the lure of sensual promises beyond description. With a dip of his head he sampled the sweetness. It didn't taste like blood from scrapes he'd inquisitively licked as a child, but rather like liquid ecstasy. It swirled around his tongue, seducing, entrancing, his senses.

Absorbed by the giddy experience, his eyes closed and he was only vaguely aware that his teeth had begun to drink up his essence. Suddenly he was drinking his first glass of champagne and feeling the intoxicating rush go to his head. He smelled the perfume of woman and sex as he danced his first dance between the sheets. He felt the joy of falling in love, and then Annabelle was offering herself freely to his touch in a clover-patch glade. Annabelle, his Annabelle, dear God how he loved her. Even more than this aphrodisiac that was so mesmerizing, so divine—

"Heath, Pa, why are you both so quiet? Is something wrong? Did the cake turn out badly?"

A hand suddenly shaking his shoulder intruded upon Heath's debaucher's delight. Instinctively, he began to snarl but stopped. He opened his eyes into predatory slits and saw Jake's ashen face.

"Just what the hell is the matter with you?" Jake whispered in a trembling voice.

"Something's wrong," Annabelle said anxiously. "I can feel it. Please, somebody say something, anything."

"Nothing's wrong." Heath was amazed that his voice could be so even while he grappled with revulsion for his actions. Ecstasy lingered in his veins. It was horrible, wonderful. His teeth vibrated with desire, wooing him with the promise that if he'd enjoyed his own taste, Annabelle would prove a much headier nectar.

He forced himself to cover the wound with his other hand and pinned Jake with a commanding gaze.

"That's right, girl," Jake said without inflection, then repeated word for word what Heath willed him to say. "The doctor had an accident, but nothing you need fret about."

"A superficial cut, nothing more." Turning his healed palm to Jake, he felt his teeth withdraw. He was too calm as he sliced the cake once more, his demeanor too smooth.

"Ready to make your wish?" Jake asked with absurd normalcy once he'd taken his seat.

"Yes, please do." Annabelle felt for her father's hand and once gained reached for Heath's.

"My wish is to say another prayer," Heath said as he clung to Annabelle and shut his eyes against the tempting sight of her jugular. "Lord, I ask You for resistance from all that is evil, and by Your blessing may we reap the joy of life and love."

His prayer was sincere, but his heartfelt plea he spoke in silence. *Dear Father in heaven, have mercy. Let me die and set me free from this curse. The evidence is too real, and I can't disregard what form of creature I've become.*

Heath knew with a terrible certainty the creature's nature: He was a vampire.

10

Annabelle was having the nightmare again, of ruby raindrops that poured down in torrents. Then she was suddenly awakened by an urgent whispering.

"Did you say something, Pa?" Annabelle asked groggily.

His reply was a snore from the bed across the room.

She heard the whisper again, only louder, more urgent.

Come to me, Annabelle. The porch, I'm on the porch. Waiting . . . for you. Come to me now. I need you.

Heath was summoning her. How in the world she'd heard him, she had no idea, but the message was clear. He needed her. But surely no more than she needed him. Five days had passed since his birthday, and after today's fight with Pa, she'd been told that there would be no more buggy rides.

Pushing aside the covers on the bed, she felt for her stick and made her way to the door. The metal bolt groaned as she slid it back, sounding unnaturally loud in the silent cabin. Annabelle held her breath until another snore assured her that Pa hadn't been disturbed.

Her steps were tentative. There was a blackness surrounding her that the full moon didn't dispel. The wind moved without a sound. There was no chirping of crickets or hooting of owls, just the rasp of her shuddering breaths. The thick, sticky sweet air she inhaled tasted of the ruby raindrops in her nightmare.

Had she really heard Heath's summons, or had she imagined it?

Her skin felt as though it were covered with leeches. Sweat made her scalp itch as if lice were in her hair. She shivered despite the long nightgown that clung to her like a smothering blanket. Annabelle turned to hurry back inside just as the boards nearby creaked.

"I'm here, Annabelle."

"Heath?" she whispered with a flood of relief. Why did his voice sound so cracked and brittle? And why did this tremulous blackness emanate from him, a frightful presence that somehow seemed something other than the man she loved more than life itself?

"What are you doing here so late?" she asked, reaching for him.

"I couldn't sleep." He caught her shoulders and gently pushed her away before she could hug him. The fingertips that stroked back the damp strands at her temples conveyed a barely supressed hunger, and she shivered again.

"It's warm out, but your hands feel so cold." She remembered the news that Mr. Mahony had brought from town when he'd paid an unexpected visit that afternoon. "Have you taken ill? The townsfolk are saying you won't answer their knocks during the day, and those who've come to you at night . . ." She couldn't bring herself to repeat the malicious, farfetched gossip.

"That's not all they're saying, is it?" His chuckle was without mirth. "It's all right, my love. I'm well aware of my demotion in public opinion. Amazing, isn't it, that in less than a week a man can go from worthy citizen to outcast. As you well know, people do have a way of fearing what they don't understand. And fear, sadly, is contagious."

"They're saying you have a contagious disease."

"Not exactly good for my practice."

"It's nothing to joke about. I got very angry when I over-heard Mr. Mahony running his mouth and filling Pa full of nonsense that only a fool would believe."

"And did your father believe it?"

"He swallowed enough of it to refuse driving me to town so I could make sure you were all right." She cringed, remembering the horrible fight they'd had and the frustration of knowing she couldn't see to walk the ten miles between the farm and Heath's arms. It was such a bitter thing to endure. No matter that the dark spot she'd sensed in Heath from the beginning had grown to a gaping abyss. He was her only love, and she embraced him fully, with total acceptance.

But she was so startled by what she felt that she drew back. "You feel so—so strange. You're hard . . . stiff as—"

A corpse. Her knees buckled with the memory of her stumbling over dead bodies, and Heath caught her. She forcefully shoved the memory aside and focused on Heath.

"Why is your body so rigid? You're a doctor. You have to tell me, what's ailing you?"

"Let's just say that I've recently developed a severe case of arthritis." Again that humorless laugh, followed by a tortured groan.

"You *are* ill, terribly ill, aren't you?" She clutched at his arms. Even through his coat they were hard as ice and just as cold. "Tell me it'll pass, that you'll be all right. I'm afraid for you, for us. If I lost you—I can't bear even to think it."

"Nor can I, my love. But you deserve better than a lie." He held her to him, and his hands, merciful God, they felt like claws. "I came tonight to tell you I've been stricken with a rather grave grave malady. And unless it miraculously improves, I'll have no choice but to leave. Soon. Very soon."

"Then I'll go with you and—"

"*No.*" His harsh refusal made her begin to weep in desperation. "I'm sorry," he said, his voice gentling. "But you must understand that I hold you too dear to expose you to any danger I might pose."

"And you think I care about that? Whatever illness has befallen you, let it take me too."

She heard a sucking sound just before Heath released her abruptly. But she gripped him to her, refusing to let him set her away.

"Hold me," she pleaded. "Hold me until I wake up. This has to be a bad dream. It can't be true."

If only he could tell her that. He had been telling himself as much in the endless days he'd huddled, paralyzed, in the closet that protected him until he emerged into the equally dark sanctuary of night. If only he could tell her of the agonizing hours during which his mind remained trapped in a body that he could scarcely bring himself to look at. Still, he faced the mirror nightly and duly recorded his slow decomposition.

Had Annabelle been able to see, she would surely run at the sight of him. A dead thing that had drained itself dry to appease its addiction to the taste, the smell, of blood.

He had none left. The final few drops that he'd consumed tonight were stagnant and foul, but enough to enable him to make his way on a horse that had damn near killed itself trying to race from the stall as Heath approached it.

The citizens of Eugene were banding against him. The few patients who had sought him out after dusk had wisely backed away to carry tales that were all too true. He couldn't blame them for shrinking from a creature who licked parched lips as he stared hungrily at a bleeding wound.

His own wounds had healed, but his heart bled painfully as Annabelle ran her hands over a framework of bones that encased his maimed spirit. His pitiful attempt at self-preservation had left him with a shell that was direly in need of new blood to restore the semblance of man.

"Walk with me," Heath said simply, and tucked her hand in the crook of his arm. "Walk with me and we'll play another game of pretend. We'll pretend that we've both awakened from the same bad dream and we're laughing at the folly of it because the sun is shining bright and here we are strolling down a garden path."

"I don't want to pretend, Heath," she answered firmly, and he drew upon his new powers to coerce her subtly. He led her down the porch to the corral, where his horse nickered in protest of his malignant presence.

The scent of wild roses mingled with death's bouquet as he laid her down in the soft grass he pretended was their marriage bed. Her hair shone like sunbeams in the moonlight. With gnarled fingers he sifted through the flaxen strands, while his tongue flicked against his demanding teeth.

"I love you, Annabelle. Nothing can ever change that."

"If you love me, then you'll promise never to leave."

"I will never leave you. No matter the miles between us or the time that passes, I'm always as close as this." Crouched over her, he refused to taint her body with what was left of his, but indulged them both with the luxury of pretense. "Pretend with me that this is our wedding night. Say you'll pretend it's true. I need that from you."

"Make it true," she demanded urgently. "That's what *I*

need." She reached up to search his face. Heath turned away before she could touch the gaunt hollows of his cheeks, or his teeth, which gnawed at his upper lip.

"You mustn't touch me." Fearful she wouldn't obey, he called upon his curious powers once more and commanded her to heed.

Her arms fell limp to her sides, spread in total submission upon the dewy grass. Fumbling and awkward, he released the buttons running down the bodice of her long white gown. He parted the cloth and wept in silence, wept without tears. Her breasts were full, healthy, beautiful. He dared not touch them. He dared not lower his mouth to suckle.

"Make love to me." She struggled to lift her arms but failed. "Let go of my arms and touch me while I touch you." Her hips arched in entreaty, and he drew up her gown to fill himself with the vision of her soft woman form.

Why was he torturing himself? Why was he subjecting them both to such danger? He bared his teeth to the night sky, raging at the forces that were so cruelly stealing their right to touch, to love.

"Pretending is too painful." Heath pressed her open legs together and rose to his feet.

"Then don't pretend. Kiss me. Kiss me and make all our hurts go away."

"I can't. I can't kiss you. I can't touch you." Forcing himself to keep a prudent distance, he released his invisible hold over her. She sat up, and her bare breasts swung freely, tempting his starved, empty mouth. "Button your nightgown and be quick about it. It's past time I returned you to your father. He needs you nearly as much as I do."

She sprang to her feet. "Damn you, Heath Nightingale. Damn you to hell for hurting me this way."

Her words cut him, and he knew his powers of healing could never mend the wound.

"I am well and truly damned and fast on my way to hell without your spurring me on." He grasped her shoulders, and her warmth took some chill from his flesh. His fingers uncurled, absorbing the goodness she gave. Did vampires have the ability to consume more than blood? As if in answer, a surge of energy coursed through him while Annabelle swayed, seemingly weakened by his touch.

He had to leave her, before he drained her of life *and* blood. But for now he would steal what precious time he could.

"Hell, my dearest Annabelle, is life without you. I beg you not to resent me for any slight that's beyond my control. I would never cheat you, and I would never betray you for my own gain. If you believe that's true, take off your gown, and I'll give you what you wish in whatever way I can."

Wordlessly, she dropped her gown and lay on the dew-kissed grass, offering her nakedness to his view. Heath plucked a nearby rose and dropped to his knees beside her. Down he stroked, the red petals tracing the peaks and dips forming each breast. Twirling the flower around first one nipple and then the other, he lingered in the pretense that his lips were the flower.

She gave him absolute access to her body but not to her mind. There he encountered a door to a memory that was as closed to him as it was to Annabelle. If only she would let him in, perhaps he might take with him the knowledge that he had been the instrument that returned her sight. Her memory refused his gentle probing, yet her bent legs parted.

"Wider," he whispered. He choked on the hateful thought that what was meant to be his—*his,* dammit—she would have every right to share with another man once his absence overshadowed the memories they'd forged. "You are so beautiful, outside and in. Loop your hand under your thigh and put your fingers where I'm meant to be. Yes, exactly. Feel how soft, how giving your body is, and pretend that it's me you're taking."

"It's you who's meant to be inside me," she protested.

"Never was a truth better spoken." Down her belly he skated the rose. He brushed it over the triangular patch of hair on her groin, then swept it back and forth over her ruby, wet peak. She cried out his name and arched her body, the sudden movement making him prick her thigh with a thorn.

She moaned, the sound a mingling of pain and pleasure.

Heath examined the small wound and had to struggle to ignore the luscious scent of blood. Wiping off the trickling flow with his fingers, he labored for breath as the glistening streak pulsed with the promise of ecstasy if only he would allow himself to taste.

Heath was beyond starvation. He was beyond hope and despair. He grappled for a tendril of reason, only to find none remaining.

He licked his fingers. Had he ever tasted anything so divine?

Annabelle's fingers sifted through his hair, and she urged him precariously close to the wound. A sip, a tiny sip of what would otherwise go to waste, and he might be restored and be whole again.

"Why are you so quiet?" she murmured.

"You're—" He swallowed. "You're bleeding and it's my fault."

"Then why don't you kiss me and make us both better?"

"A kiss," he panted. "Just a kiss. That's all." A kiss he couldn't deny, a single slow slide of his tongue. The taste of ecstasy trembled on the tip of it. His mouth hovered over the area where groin met inner thigh, then he lowered his head and claimed her with his lips.

His need made him linger too long. Before he could exercise intent over instinct, a single sharp tooth pierced the flesh she trustingly offered.

She arched up with a sharp cry and planted him deeper.

Heath tried to free himself, but he could feel the catch of her muscle and knew he would harm her before the enemy that was him would relinquish its hold. So he lay very still, moving only with each writhe of her hips.

11

Exulting in her tremulous sighs, he treasured each drop that flowed to him and that sang through his veins. Unlike his own substance when he imbibed it, hers seemed to expand within him, his body breeding with what she gave. It was new life he took in, not the remains of a man who had ceased to be.

He could feel himself absorbing her memories, the essence of her spirit. He wailed her first cry at birth. He took her first step and licked her first stick of peppermint candy. He was with her when Mama thrust Lorna and the locket into her hands and then they peeked from their hiding place and saw . . . no, no, it's too terrible to look.

And then, darkness. He shared her blindness, the protection it gave and the joy it stole. And Pa, Pa how good to me you are and how I do love you. But I'm so very lonely and please God might I have a beau of my own?

How sweet the taste of chocolate. Falling in love, falling, falling into the oblivion of sensual wonder, and has any woman ever known such happiness and lived to tell it? My heart's so full, it must surely burst.

But now it's breaking, and the pain of losing my only love so severe, surely I will die. Dying from the pain, dying from the ecstasy, dying . . .

Such peace she felt. Drifting . . . floating . . .

He was so warm, so flushed with their completion. And his body, it felt mightier than a legion of warriors.

But *her* body was lax, her limbs too still and too quiet.

Heath forced his mouth away.

"Annabelle." Her name was a plea to heaven, a curse consigning himself to hell. Sweet Jesus, what had he done? Had he killed her? His medical training fled in the wake of terror. Frantic, he tried to remember what he should do. A pulse. That was it—he should check for a pulse. Gripping her wrist, he wasn't aware of the strength he exerted until he heard a bone snap.

Heath dropped her wrist and stared in shock at his hands, disbelieving they were his. The taste of blood, Annabelle's blood, was still on his tongue, and he wiped his forearm over his mouth, desperate to erase his betrayal. But no matter how hard he scrubbed, he couldn't extinguish the joy of her taste or the exhilaration of the creature inside him.

Is this what he had become? This sick, twisted thing in a man's body that shuddered with insatiable hunger at the sight of a crimson streak staining a white sleeve?

In a rage he tore off his shirt and slumped over Annabelle's body. Feeling no movement beneath him, he wept the tears that Annabelle's life had bought.

"Forgive me," he pleaded. "Forgive me, Annabelle, because never will I forgive myself." He gripped the locket and snarled when the gold burned his palm, but he didn't let go.

He would lie with her until near daybreak. Then he would carry her to her bed, and if Jake shot him, so be it, but he doubted man's hand could kill the undead.

"Somehow I'll join you," he vowed. "I love you," he murmured over and over. "Love you always, Annabelle—"

"I love you, too, Heath." The faint murmur made him come up with a start.

"Annabelle? Annabelle, speak to me," he demanded. "Tell me I'm not imagining this, that you're—"

"Hurting. My wrist, it's . . . hurting something terrible and . . . are you crying?" Heath carefully raised her uninjured hand and pressed kisses to her palm, then led her fingertips over his restored face. "Why, you *are* crying. What's the matter? Did I say something, do something? I . . . I can't seem to remember much. . . ."

Nothing. You remember nothing except what I tell you.

"We went for a stroll and you blacked out," he suggested. "When you fell, you twisted your hand. I thought you were hurt worse than you were, and when you revived, I was so grateful that the tears just came—for the third time in my life. Three seems to be my fateful number."

Grateful was too inadequate a word for what he was feeling. His hands were shaking badly from the emotions flooding him, from relief, as he sought to harness his healing power. Cradling her wrist in his palm, he closed his fingers over the broken bone. He could feel himself draining into her, into the fracture, and he sealed that place he'd touched with a kiss.

"Move your wrist. Good. Now the other way." The obvious injury fully mended, Heath turned his attention to what he feared most: Had he caused any internal damage? And how much blood had he taken? She was moaning and her head slumped to the side. Shock was a possibility. There was still a chance he could lose her.

"I want you to rest while I check the rest of you. Never mind how I do it. I'm practicing a new technique."

Lying atop her, he again drew upon the marvel in his possession and scanned her body with his. He ascertained that she had lost ample blood for her to be woozy, fairly weakened, and mentally confused. That was no surprise, but the reason she'd collapsed in a dead faint was.

An overload of sensory demand. The intensity of their union had almost proved more than she could physically bear.

She snuggled close and nuzzled his neck. "Did I tell you there's a mean rumor in town about your health?"

"It seems I recall you mentioning such," he said tightly. The terror he'd endured was still too real. Heaven had been merciful and Annabelle's life spared, but he took it as a stringent warning, which he intended to heed well.

"I aim to set them straight, Heath, starting with Pa. You're perfectly fine, judging from what I can feel." Running her hands over his bare back, she murmured seductively, "But mayhap I should make sure with a more thorough inspection." She wound her legs around his, and he rubbed his thigh against the small incision. Willing it to close completely, he felt himself seep into her again.

He felt more. An urgency to fill her up with the man he'd once been. The temptation too great, he rolled off her and onto the rose he'd thrown aside. A thorn bit into his back, but the only pain he felt was in his hollowed-out soul. Hollowed out because he had no reason to stay. Yes, the madness had passed and the burning thirst appeased, but they would return. And return again. Never to leave until he found a way to destroy himself or break the curse.

Sitting up, he retrieved the rose. The stem straightened and the petals revived as he stroked the flower while staring into the night that was now his day. He felt the sweet hold of Annabelle's embrace as she pressed her breasts to his back and looped her arms around his neck. There, she kissed him.

"Do you have no sense of fear when you touch me?"

"I've always felt some," she admitted quietly. "Why, I don't know. But I love you too much ever to let you go."

"You amaze me. That you could see past a monster and still love me. God, how I need that from you." He pulled her into his arms and gripped her so tightly that she whimpered. Fearful of squeezing the life from her as a child's fierce affection could hug a puppy to death, he loosened his hold.

The sun would be rising in a few hours and memories would be all he would take with him. The loss was too great to endure. But how much worse for Annabelle, to think he'd deserted her for no reason. What could he tell her—that they were victims of a centuries-old vendetta?

"When I'm not hating her, I almost pity her," he whispered to himself.

"Who is 'her'?"

Silent moments lengthened to minutes of internal debate. Ultimately Heath decided she deserved the truth. The fact that she couldn't possibly give the story any more credence than he had as a boy was not an issue. His imminent departure was.

"We have a very serious problem, Annabelle, one that affects our future. I want you to open your locket so I can confront the source of our troubles."

Moonlight sparked off the diamond tear, and he shook his head as empathy and antipathy warred inside him.

"What could this old thing have to do with us?"

"Unfortunately, everything." Drawing a deep breath, and considering how he could say good-bye without breaking her heart, Heath prepared to unburden himself of what he could share with no one else. "I have a story to tell you about the woman in your locket. It's a very sad story that doesn't have an end in sight, even two hundred years later and thousands of miles away from where it all began. The bastard responsible for getting the whole business started was Jonathan Nightingale. And the woman whose likeness you bear was called Rachael Deliverance Dobbs. . . ."

12

As she rocked on the porch, Annabelle traced the tiny raised dots on the pages of the book in braille, but didn't feel the comfort Heath's gift usually imparted. She was trying very hard not to cry. If she did, Pa would want to know why, and she couldn't tell him the truth any more than she could lie.

Heath was no liar, either. For that reason she could almost believe his unbelievable story. Believing it was certainly easier than swallowing the bitter thought that he'd tired of her and the small town and was only seeking to protect her feelings. No more buggy rides to their secret glade. No more spritely discussions about their differences of opinion, no more private jokes, or confidences and dreams shared. No more whispered words of affection and vows of love, or the intimate touches and warm hugs that expressed more than words could ever say.

The painful knot in her throat tightened, and she choked on a heaving sob. Suddenly she rose. There were still a good two hours left of sun, and Pa was busy cutting trees near the barn. She'd sneak past him, that's what she'd do, and take off on her favorite horse. Betsy would know the way, and she herself had a good notion of which directions to take. As for what she'd do when she got there, she had no idea. But she'd think of something to make Heath realize a spiteful old curse had no more power over them than the locket she'd throw at his feet the second he opened his door.

Quietly rounding the corner of the cabin, she heard the too-near sound of ax to wood. "Annabelle!" Pa shouted. A replay of yesterday's heated argument caused her stomach to turn and her feet to slow. She couldn't outrun him, so she quickly decided a smile and an offer to clean stalls was her safest ploy.

"You're sure to be working up a sweat," she said, moving in his direction. "Why don't you take a break inside—I've made some lemonade—while I—"

"Annabelle—Anna—*move!*" Confused by his urgent yell, she had no idea which way he meant her to go. There was the sound of a tree splintering, and she felt herself get shoved hard. Then she heard the *whoosh* of a mighty weight hitting the ground.

Her scream faded with the sound of the sickening thud.

Heath heard a faint pounding and decided it must be coming from inside him. The creature was thirsty and demanding to be let out so it could satisfy its insatiable hunger. He'd come to recognize that feeling as the first sign of his nightly revival. Next was the sensation of as many needles pricking him as there were pores in his skin. The paralysis would leave, and what had been numb would come excruciatingly awake.

If only his mind could partake of that same deep paralysis. Then he wouldn't spend hour after hour forming desperate plans and solutions, only to discard them one by one and re-place them with tormenting thoughts of Annabelle. Not the least of which was wondering how much she would still love him if she could see what he'd been reduced to:

Barring his doors and locking himself inside a small cubicle, he drew into the fetal position and longed to cry like a baby. With even that release denied him in his deathlike slumber, he dredged up the only medicine available to him. True to the creature's nature, his humor was black.

He'd begun to amuse himself by debating the merits of making a revolutionary contribution to science. The dentists would be amazed! Oh, to see him pull out a tooth, then to watch it grow back before he could excise the other.

Better yet, he and Dr. Purdue could take turns at wielding a scalpel on a live cadaver. The medical scholars would have to look quickly, though, before the incisions closed.

Heath laughed. It must be night, he decided. His vocal cords were working again.

The pounding continued and he frowned. Now that he was rapidly gaining sensation, he determined what he heard came not from inside him, but from outside. Someone was at the door.

"A minute," he whispered, his throat feeling clogged with sand. Uncurling from the tight ball he'd been in he forced his jerking hands to unlatch the lock he'd installed on the cubicle. Crawling out into a lesser darkness, he focused on the sound of sobs accompanying the frantic pounding. Slowly he stretched onto the floor and extended his limbs until he resembled a flattened spider that twitched beneath a foot.

The process was agonizing, and he felt that whoever was on the other side of that door was in some sort of agony too. He felt . . .

"Annabelle." He battled the last vestiges of palsy to lurch forward, groaning as wave upon wave of her fright and distress assaulted him. With jerky movements he managed to pull back the metal bolt on the front door.

"Thank God you're still here. It's Pa. He's hurt something terrible, and—Heath, he might already be dead."

She was in his arms and he cursed himself for wanting her so much, he didn't care that tragedy had brought her to him. He'd never thought he'd touch her again, and another parting would be just as painful as the first, but for now he was rocking her back and forth, consoling her while she stammered out what had happened.

"And then—then I tried to drag him out and somehow lift him into the buggy, but—but—"

"Annabelle," he said sternly, and gave her a gentle shake, "you did the best that you could. Wait here while I go see to your father. I'll be quick as I can."

Lighting a lamp, Heath quieted her protests of being left behind. Time was of the essence, he said, and that was reason enough to convince her to await his return. Forsaking his horse halfway to the log cabin, Heath made a calculated trade of precious energy for even more precious time by running the remaining distance.

He wasn't even winded when he found Jake. Neither was he overly taxed after lifting the tree off the older man and carrying inside his unconscious form.

Fixing a broken body wasn't as easy, however. Especially when blood was flowing copiously and he was salivating to help himself to it. Heath wiped at the sweat beading his brow and shuddered when he realized it had tinged red the back of his hand. The loss was minor, but a loss just the same that increased his demanding thirst.

He sealed Jake's gaping cuts first, to guard against tempta-tion, then set several fractured bones, which nearly depleted his waning strength. It was the ruptured spleen that exhausted the last of his power. That done, Heath took a ragged breath and nodded with satisfaction when Jake's dry forehead indicated no fever and only a minor concussion. Jake would have a pounding headache when he came to, maybe a slight loss of memory, but otherwise he'd be fine.

It was more than Heath could say for himself. He'd analyzed this strange gift for healing and had come to two conclusions: his gift lay in his body's absorbing that which was faulty in another, then in his body's mending itself. And all this came with a price—blood. Blood was power, and what powers he used consumed the source of his energy supply.

It was now critically low. He was nearly sapped to the level he'd been before Annabelle had returned him to that place where he straddled humanity. It was her doing as much as his that her father would live.

"She's yours after all, Jake. Take good care of her for me." Staggering out the door, he wove his way to the barn.

The best he could do was sling himself astride the remaining farm horse, head for Eugene, and pray the nag would reach his home before dawn streaked across the horizon.

13

When would Heath be back? *Would* he be back? And Pa, how would she ever survive his loss, or the guilt that it was her blindness that had caused it?

Feverishly stroking the pages of a leather-bound book, she pretended it was braille. She'd discovered it in the closet where Heath had kept the chocolates. Though the cherished memory had drawn her there, it was the dank odor of a tomb, not chocolate, she smelled. That, and the faint scent of a rose she'd found crushed between two pages.

The front door creaked, then there was the sound of harsh panting, followed by the noise of something sliding to the floor.

"Heath!" She ran to find where he lay, overturning a tray in her haste. Metal clattered around her feet, but she paid it no mind, anxiety for the two men she loved sending her to her knees while she pressed kisses to Heath's drawn face. "You're hurt. I'll get help."

"No. Go to your father," he said in an old man's cracked voice. "He'll be wondering where you are when he wakes up. Hurry, go find the shopkeep. Bud will see you home."

Pa would live, and never had she been more grateful. But what had it cost the man responsible for her father's survival. Heath felt so cold, and she was taken aback by the sunken cheek he turned to her when she sought his mouth.

"I'm not about to leave you like this. Either tell me what's wrong with you and what I can do to help, or I will go to Bud and bring him here to tell me what you don't want me to see."

"No!" Groaning in pain, Heath pushed her hands away. "The scalpel. If you want to help, find my scalpel—I can see it on the floor a few feet behind you. Hand it to me and then leave."

Something, a voice of foreboding, stopped her from obeying. "Why do you want it?"

"Leave me, Annabelle. Leave me and I'll see to myself." Then he whispered faintly, "Pray to God there are still a few drops left."

"A few drops of what?" she demanded, heart palpitating. The darkness seemed to be emanating from him. Closer and closer it came as he tried to rise. Fear for his life, fear of the black fog surrounding them with a malodorous bouquet, made her press him back to the floor.

"Dammit," he snapped, and even that bit of anger seemed to tax him. Panting harshly, he bit out, "Dammit, I said *go*. Get out of here. *Now.*"

"I won't leave until you tell me what you aim to do with your blade." An inhuman snarl made Annabelle recoil, but a clawlike grip encircled her wrist and pulled her forward, forcing her near a shadow worse than night.

"Touch me, Annabelle. Feel my face, my body. See for yourself what I've become. If that doesn't send you running from me, nothing will."

"Dear God."

"The teeth. You forgot the teeth." His caustic laugh hurt her ears. "On second thought, don't touch them. They've developed a tendency to bite and not want to let go."

What could be more horrible, any more piteous than what

she'd already felt? Defying him, she worked a finger past Heath's tightened lips. She could feel a sudden vibration and had a sense of teeth rapidly growing, followed by a shifting movement as if those teeth were seeking her out.

And then, a snap.

Annabelle quickly withdrew her fingers, took stock, and found all still there. They shook uncontrollably as she stroked her hands over his rigid chest and touched the darkness that was in him. Because it was Heath's curse to bear, she would share it. No fear could overshadow her urgency to bind him to her, even past the grave that Heath was sliding into.

"Take me with you." She tried hard not to weep, but it was useless. "Whatever this is, wherever I can feel you going—"

"Hell," he moaned. "This is my hell, and if you don't leave before I drag you into it with me, you're madder than the madman who almost took your life last night."

"No." She shook her head in fierce denial. "You love me. You would never—"

"No? You're lucky to still be alive, my love. The same beast that almost raped you, and surely would have killed you, doesn't give up easily. You escaped the first time, and miraculously, the second. Don't give him a third chance." A few more shallow breaths and he wheezed, "Leave me and take with you what we had and . . . please don't cry. After all, we've had more happiness than most people ever find in a lifetime."

The darkness was slowly retreating, and its absence was terrifying, an omen that it would steal Heath from her and refuse to take her along with him.

"You're dying. *Please—don't die."*

"My dear, I'm already dead. What's left of me isn't much, but even that will be gone if you don't let me do what I must before the sun rises." His clawlike fingers gently patted her head, which she'd laid against his chest. "Dawn must be near. I can barely move or feel. Please, Annabelle, hand me the scalpel while there's still time. Give it to me and go. I'm begging you."

She felt for and found the instrument. "What are you going to do with it?" Holding it to her chest, she said, "I won't give it to you unless you tell me."

"Damn you, Annabelle, *damn you*. If you must know, the creature needs blood. Blood is what it demands, what it *takes,*to feed its existence, its powers. We're one, the creature and Heath Nightingale.

"They're constantly in battle, with neither side ever winning. I heal, it destroys. It's starving and now close to gaining the lead because . . . we're both lusting for more of what you gave us last night. Heath needs your love, it needs you to love him enough to give your life for him." He whimpered, then gnashed out, *"Get out! Get away!"*

"I'll cut myself," Annabelle said. "And give you what you crave."

"No! No!" he whispered harshly, whether to her or to himself, Annabelle wasn't sure. His next words, though, were directed at her. "I'm the one who takes the cut, not you. Annabelle, have mercy. I've got nothing left for you, not even a remnant of pride. If you won't put the knife in my hand, then do me a better favor. Slice open my chest and draw back the drapes."

She shuddered, knowing she would never be able to do as she was told. He intended to make the ultimate sacrifice any man could make. He would forfeit his life so she couldn't sacrifice herself on his behalf.

How right he was that she would willingly give up her life in exchange for his. And in so doing, might she not appease the curse's demand and release him from this torment?

Annabelle palmed the blade. If her sacrifice wasn't deemed worthy, then at least they would die together. Better that than to live without him.

"I will give you the scalpel, for a price. You must close your eyes while we play our game of pretend one last time. Will you agree?" She knew he had no choice, but still, she touched his closed eyes to make sure he didn't see her opening the buttons of her dress.

"Be quick," he whispered, then labored for what she was certain was near his last breath. "Say what you . . . wish to . . . pretend . . . my love."

"We're on your father's ship." Annabelle spoke quickly while she poised the scalpel's edge between her naked breasts. "It's our honeymoon, and we're on our way to Boston so your family can meet your new bride. Can you smell the salt air and the bittersweet chocolate you've just fed me in our marriage bed? It tastes good and rich, but not nearly so wonderful or right as the taste of your mouth." Her heart raced, but her hand was surprisingly steady as she made the decisive plunge.

The pain. The pain was so acute that she was choking on tears. Tears seeped from her eyes as she wrenched the knife free and leaned over Heath's mouth.

"Kiss me," she urgently whispered. "Kiss me while we pretend we'll never say good-bye."

14

A jolt shot through Heath, and his body jerked in every direction. The seizure was so intense, he was sure his limbs were being torn from their sockets.

He couldn't breathe; he was drowning on a thick, wet fluid that filled his mouth and spilled down his chin. *The taste. The smell.* They surrounded him, smothering him.

He came upright and spat out the sickening substance. His head spun, and sparks of white light momentarily blinded him to everything, but he could feel his veins rippling, expanding, heated by a sliding trickle that became a coursing stream. A demonic howl sliced through his lungs and ripped from his throat, splitting through the air that smelled of . . . blood.

The veil of showering light faded, and he blinked against a single sun ray that shafted through the slitted curtains. His gaze followed the beam that trailed to the scent's source. His cry of horror was her name.

"Annabelle." He crawled to where she was splayed like a rag doll, a ruby-red stream flowing from beneath her breasts and pooling around her motionless form. Frantically he put his ear near her mouth. No breath, not even a whisper of one. Fingertips to her throat, he searched for a pulse that wasn't there while his gaze locked on the gash over her unbeating heart.

His own should be racing, roaring in his ears, but there was only silence. Howling his agony, he covered the fatal wound with his hands, and felt a lurching in his chest. One thud, then two, and his heart was beating, bleeding, weeping. Alone.

There was no time to suture the skin. Hands joined, he pumped with a steady rhythm and beseeched God to take pity, to take him in her place. Because Annabelle, his beloved Annabelle, was dead.

The wrenching pain was gone, and a deep peace enfolded her. She felt the touch of Heath's mouth to the heart that poured out her love, her life, in exchange for his. Then she felt herself rising higher and higher while images flashed through her mind's eye:

The sorrow of losing Heath, the joy of their first meeting. Years spent in darkness amid everyday rituals, filled with laughter and tears. Young again, huddled behind a tree where she nearly suffocated Lorna as shrill whoops overrode her own muffled cries of "Mama!"

Mama running, running away from the woods so the Indian would chase her. Tomahawk taking her down. She's falling, have to help her, but she said *Don't come out, don't make a peep. Mama loves you, Annabelle. Take my locket and wear it always.* . . .

Holding the locket, creeping closer, so close she could see Mama's eyes that always looked at her with love. They were open, and so were the lips that had kissed her goodbye. Mama's mouth, stretched wide, froze around a gurgling scream. Her throat was split open and her hair, she saw Mama's beautiful hair, scalped from her head. And the milky-white skull, it was sheened with rivulets of red. Indian gone, Annabelle touching her now. *Mama? Mama?*

"Here, Annabelle."

She turned toward the voice that rang like a wind chime and saw Mama in a rainbow mist, her hair glistening with dewdrops. She ran toward Mama, who kissed her fondly, then stepped back. "We'll meet again once you've spent your years," Mama said. "But till then . . ."

She wanted to cry out when Mama gently pushed her away, but couldn't. Her mouth was filled with the taste of Heath's breath, and her lungs expanded to take in his air.

"Annabelle. *Annabelle.* Can you hear me?"

Her eyes opened and she stared straight at him. She touched his face, his beautiful face, drinking in the sight of him. He caught her hands and pressed them to his mouth. She could feel his lips moving as he murmured a fervent prayer of thanks between his vows of love.

Salty tears wet their cheeks while their lips met in a searing reunion. He gripped her tightly, fearful she'd slip away again if he let her go.

"I thought I had lost you."

"Not even death can separate us," she assured him. "Death is an illusion. I saw Mama, Heath. I saw her and she was whole again. So am I." Her smile was tremulous as she whispered, "You're a very handsome man. But even if you weren't, you'd be the most marvelous sight I ever beheld."

"You can see?" At her nod he gave thanks to God once more. "You can see, you can see," he said in wonder.

She wet a fingertip and wiped away a smear of red on his chin. It was then that she realized both their clothes were stained with blood. Shuddering, she tugged at his soiled shirt.

"What I see around us isn't any prettier than the sight of Mama's scalping."

A dark look crossed his face as they rid each other of their clothes. She was reluctant to let him out of her reach, even for the time it took him to fetch a large bowl of water and two towels.

As she bathed him, he ministered to her likewise. Pausing when he touched the unbroken skin of her cleavage, he said somberly, "Even evil, it seems, is capable of compassion. At least the vampire did his best to redeem himself before saying good-bye." With a reverent touch Heath stroked the wet cloth over the place where her heart beat. "I'm human enough to wish back his powers for myself. It wasn't I who sealed your wound with the laying of hands. And I've been humbled enough to realize that no amount of skill can perform a miracle. I was, am, and always will be the vessel, not the source of divine intervention."

He kissed her there, where evil and good had joined to heal. Heath lifted the beautiful wholeness of her body into his arms and carried her to his bed. The sun beat against the curtains, and dappled light streamed where they clung, naked, to each other.

Annabelle coaxed his head to her breast, and his mouth connected with the locket. It didn't burn. Yet it was warm and seemed to pulse against his lips. Heath drew away and ventured to touch it with a fingertip.

The locket sprang open.

"Look," he whispered in awe.

"A ruby! There was only a diamond there before."

They exchanged a poignant stare, each thinking of all the memories and sacrifices they had shared. Heath snapped the locket shut.

"Should this be passed on to any daughter we might have?"

"I'd rather lay it to rest. The family vault you mentioned sounds like a good place, don't you think?"

"I couldn't agree more. We'll see the locket and the journal to Cloud Castle after I wire my father to send his fastest ship—with two berths reserved. One for my father-in-law, and one for us. A honeymoon suite, fit for a bride who'll share a wedding bed with her husband."

"And they lived happily ever after," she whispered.

"Better than that, my love. No more pretend—we've won our future. The good times and the bad, for real and forever. God help the poor souls who inherit the burden of supplying the last tear. If they're half as hard to sway to reason as myself, they're going to need all the help they can get. We'll do what we can, but for the most part, it's out of our hands." Heath stroked her ring finger. "Not that I have any doubts, but I'd like to ask, anyway. Annabelle Rawlings, will you marry me?"

"Gladly, and then some."

He kissed her completely, and she shut her eyes to absorb the texture and taste of this man she was already bound to. They were twined together so completely that legal paper and spoken vows were mere nods to convention. Even so, Annabelle decided she'd wear Mama's wedding dress that was folded in white tissue and stored in her trunk. And Lorna, she could stand up as a witness and hold the bridal bouquet of . . .

Daisies.

"I've never seen Boston." Annabelle sighed wistfully, then added with a smile, "Well, actually, I haven't seen much of anything for a good many years."

Heath let go of a soulful laugh that only Annabelle had ever been able to call from him.

"We'll make up for lost time, my love. And since there's no time like the present, what do you propose we do with ourselves?"

Her nails skated down Heath's spine and her legs wrapped intimately around his thighs. Tracing her tongue over his teeth, she answered him with a suggestive, "Hmmmm . . ."

MAGIC
Charlotte Hughes

1

MASSACHUSETTS—PRESENT DAY

"Excuse me, I believe I have something that belongs to you."

Rusty Padget snapped her head up at the sound of the woman's voice. She'd been so involved in her book work that she hadn't heard this latest customer come in. "I'm sorry," she told the plump, blue-haired woman. "Have you been waiting long?" Rusty got the impression the woman had been standing there and watching for some time. Strange she hadn't sensed it. She seldom missed anything.

The woman reached into her lizard-skin handbag and pulled out a child's sock, slightly worn, slightly dirty. "I've gone to a lot of trouble to find you, Miss Padget." She offered Rusty the sock. Something solid had slipped to the toe. "Here, take it."

Rusty hesitated. She wondered if she was dealing with a crackpot. It wouldn't be the first time someone had wandered into her metaphysical-supply store making jokes about her lifestyle. "Look, madam—"

"My name is Bertrice Nightingale. My friends call me Beryl. I'm from Boston." She reached into the sock and pulled out a gold locket. "This belonged to one of your ancestors,

Rachael Dobbs. She was put to death in 1690 for practicing witchcraft."

Rusty was suddenly uncomfortable. Perhaps it had to do with the lady's black aura, she thought, which signified the woman was under a great deal of stress. But there was something else that bothered her. Rusty tried to remember where she had seen or heard the Nightingale name.

Intrigued, Rusty took the locket and almost jumped at the strange vibrations she received the minute her fingers closed around it. A sudden stark vision of a bleak winter sky, of men and women dressed in black, of shiny boot buckles, came to mind. She blinked and the images disappeared. Hands trembling, she opened the locket, then gasped. She could have been looking at a photo of herself.

"You see it too," Beryl said. "You and Rachael Dobbs could be twins."

Rusty studied the miniature portrait closely. It was oddly familiar, like something from a dream. Two stones, a diamond and a ruby, formed tiny teardrops on the woman's cheeks. Below, another teardrop seemed to be burned into the painting. "I've heard of this woman," Rusty said after a moment.

"Then you know about the curse?"

Rusty snapped the locket closed. Time to put a stop to the conversation. "I don't dabble in curses or black magic, Mrs. Nightingale. They tend to backfire."

"Which is precisely what happened in Rachael Dobbs's case. But don't take my word for it. Read for yourself." She reached into her handbag once more and pulled out a leather-bound book. "I recently discovered this journal along with the locket in our family archives. The entries were made by two of our ancestors. Men who were cursed."

"Mrs. Nightingale, please—" For reasons she couldn't

fathom, Rusty was reluctant to take the journal. She sensed an energy about it, some subliminal power at work, a sensation of such intense dread that the skin on the back of her neck prickled. "Look, I was about to close for the day," she said, trying to quell the sudden nausea that rose to the back of her throat. She swallowed hard. "Perhaps you could come back tomorrow."

All the warmth went out of the other woman's eyes. "There's no time, Miss Padget. My grandson is dying, and you're the only one who can save him. *You* have the power."

It was after three o'clock in the morning by the time Rusty finished reading the journal. With tears in her eyes, she placed the old diary on her bedside table and considered all she'd learned. As a practicing witch, she had never dabbled in black magic, not because she hadn't been tempted by boorish, ill-mannered people, but because she knew that curses often backfired. Rachael Dobbs had obviously not considered that possibility when she had put her curse on the Nightingale men. The women who'd fallen in love with those men, and who'd ultimately saved them, were direct descendants of Rachael. Unfortunately, neither Katherine Downing nor Annabelle Rawlings had been able to destroy the curse for all time. The Nightingale men, at least the third son of a third son, were destined to walk the earth as night creatures for as long as the curse went on.

Rusty reached for the sock holding the locket. Beryl Nightingale had not had to tell her the sock belonged to her grandson, who the woman suspected had fallen under the curse. Every time Rusty touched the sock, she caught a vision of a young brown-haired boy lying in a darkened bedroom. Rusty had to find out for herself if the child was indeed cursed.

Taking a deep breath, Rusty closed her eyes and went into a state of profound relaxation, clutching the sock in one fist as she visualized the boy in her mind. It didn't take long to reach the desired state. Years of practice had taught her to go into what scientists called the "alpha state" almost immediately. It was in this state that she performed all psychic and magical works, including mind travel and astral projection.

Within minutes Rusty felt herself float upward. It was a wonderful sensation, filling her with peace and tranquillity. Once she'd extracted her astral being from her physical body, she glanced back at the bed and saw herself lying there as though sleeping. A wispy cord attached her two selves. She turned to go. Strangely enough, she was not pulled in the direction of Boston and the Nightingale estate.

Rusty recognized Martha's Vineyard by the multicolored cliffs called Gay Head. But *why* there? she wondered. Then she knew. The Nightingale family were staying at their summer home, where prying friends and the media would not discover their dark secrets. Rusty pressed on, following the spectacular coastline, lured by a power that had nothing to do with logic. Vague pictures passed through her mind: the bereaved Nightingale family following a white casket out of a church; a dark-haired man trying to comfort his young sons over the loss of their mother; a newborn baby, fighting for his life. So fragile. So alone. The third son of a third son, and the present victim of a curse that had been set in motion three hundred years before.

The Nightingales' summer home was both cozy and awe inspiring, a Victorian mansion with turrets and fretwork and wide, sweeping porches. A six-foot stone wall surrounded the house on three sides, leaving the back open so as not to obstruct the view of the harbor. Rusty went inside.

Although the boy's bedroom looked like the bedroom of a

normal, healthy child with its bright decor and toy-lined shelves, there was an airless quality about it, a funereal gloom that made Rusty feel as though she were peeking into an open tomb. She shivered but made her way to the bed and gazed down at the youngest member of the Nightingale clan. He tossed and turned violently, and she knew he was in the throes of a terrible nightmare.

An inner voice told her the doctors thought he suffered from migraines because of the excruciating pain and vomiting, but Rusty knew his illness went deeper than that. She wasn't sure *how* she knew these things, only that she did. Because he was asleep, the child's aura was absent and offered no clues. But Rusty had learned long ago to trust her instincts for direction, just as other people trusted stoplights and road signs to get them safely from one place to the next.

The boy cried out, a sign that the nightmare had worsened. Rusty sensed something evil approaching the boy, an entity so fear inspiring, it left his young mind paralyzed, like a small animal trapped in the fierce glow of headlights. He thrashed in his sleep. His second cry was far worse than the first.

Suddenly the bedroom door slammed open and a man rushed in. He had thrown on his jeans hastily. They were only half-zipped, the snap falling open to reveal curly black hair, the same hair that started at his throat, crossed his chest, and plunged beneath his waistband. Rusty longed to see his face, but it was cloaked in shadows.

"Wake up, Tyler!" he said, shaking the boy gently.

The little boy's eyes popped open in horror. He started to scream, then stifled the sound as recognition hit. "Daddy!" He literally threw himself at the man. "Don't let the monster get me!"

At first Rusty was too dumbstruck to do anything more

than stare, taking in the man's wide back and shoulders with feminine appreciation. His voice was like liquid velvet as he comforted his son; it lulled and soothed Rusty as well, and she was drawn to him in ways she couldn't explain. It was indefinable, even to herself, a person who dealt with the unexplained on a daily basis. He was like a beam of light, inspiring deep emotions inside her that had been buried in darkness for a long time. At the same time, there was something oddly familiar about the man—the strong jaw, the set of his shoulders.

"It's okay, son," he said, embracing the boy. "It was just a bad dream. I won't let anything hurt you."

Rusty was struck with a vision, a fleeting but powerful image of this same man dressed in entirely different clothes in an entirely different time and place. She froze. Now where had *that* come from? She moved closer, until she stood directly behind him. The muscles rippled in his back as he lifted his son in his arms. His skin looked leathery with the moonlight streaming through the windows. Fascinated, Rusty reached out and stroked one shoulder blade.

The man snapped his head around, and his eyes darted across the room as though he sensed her presence. Rusty's jaw dropped when she saw his face for the first time. She recognized him! That same face had gazed back at her from billboards and public-service broadcasts announcing his candidacy for the U.S. Senate.

Peyton Nightingale. The People's Voice!

So they were *those* Nightingales, Rusty thought. No wonder they were so secretive. The Nightingale men had been entrenched in politics for years.

Rusty noted his black aura immediately. He was under as much stress as his mother. Was it because he was a widower who was constantly trying to compensate for the fact that his boys had no mother, a man constantly torn between career and single parenting? Rusty knew he had been the man following the white coffin in her vision, knew the body in that coffin had been his wife's. At the same time, she had the distinct feeling she had met this man. But where? They certainly didn't travel in the same social circles. She waited for him to acknowledge her presence, but he didn't. Instead, he turned to his son.

"You can sleep in my room tonight, Tyler," he said at last. He left the room carrying the boy in his arms, but not before Rusty noted one more distressing fact. Though she had clearly noted the aura surrounding the man, she had not seen anything of the boy's energy field. That absence could mean only one thing: death or worse. She shuddered to think of what the future held for little Tyler Nightingale. But that wasn't the half of it. If the curse was true, Rusty faced the chilling realization that someone from her own bloodline was in danger as well.

"You're the only one who can save his life and put an end to this dreadful curse," Beryl had told her. *"You* have the power."

Rusty had to try.

2

The Nightingale mansion looked inviting in the late-afternoon sun. A tall oak tree threw shade on the front porch, where high-backed rockers shared space with massive ferns and great clay pots of geraniums. An orange tabby cat stretched and regarded the sleek white limousine with lazy indifference as it pulled into the circular drive. Rusty smiled at the charming picture before her as the limo came to a halt. One would never suspect the family inside was cursed.

"Do we need to go over our story again?" Beryl asked.

Rusty turned to her. "I'm the daughter of an old friend," she said, repeating the tale they had fabricated on the three-and-a-half-hour drive, "here to help with the boys now that they're out of school for the summer."

"And you're perfectly qualified for the job since you teach school in Salem."

Rusty nodded. "First grade."

Beryl gave her one last look before the chauffeur opened the door. It was obvious she wasn't comfortable with the situation. Rusty looked anything but the teacher she was pretending to be. The black chemise with embroidered gold stars on the front and back was a little too short, and a little too snug across the hips, to appear respectable. Rusty's red hair tumbled about her shoulders like a flame out of control. Beryl sighed as she took it all in.

"Peyton is very protective of his privacy after the way the media reacted to Priscilla's death," she whispered. "This is the only way I know to get you close to the children and little Tyler. But if Peyton even suspects anything's amiss—"

"You never told me how Mrs. Nightingale died," Rusty said. Beryl had said very little about Peyton's wife's death other than that it had happened five years ago and had been very tragic.

"That's right, I didn't." The look on Beryl's face told Rusty she had no intention of sharing it with her now.

Rusty didn't press. She respected the woman for guarding her family's privacy so fiercely. She had already mentioned how they'd been scrutinized after her eldest son had been nominated to the Supreme Court. With her middle son working at the Pentagon and Peyton's eyes on the Senate, it was no wonder they were cautious. At the same time, Rusty was surprised Beryl had trusted her enough to divulge what information she had. The poor woman was obviously desperate. Why else would she bring a practicing witch into her house to try breaking a three-hundred-year-old curse?

Rusty tried to reassure Beryl as she followed her inside the house that her true identity would remain a secret. They found Peyton playing ball with the boys on the back lawn. "Don't worry, he won't suspect a thing," Rusty said.

That confidence sank to her toes the minute she was introduced to Peyton Nightingale.

"I know you," he said without preamble.

Rusty and Beryl exchanged nervous looks. "I beg your pardon?" Rusty said, blinking furiously. His hair was darker than she remembered, cut into a conservative style, now wind-blown rakishly about his face. His eyes were the color of gath-ering storm clouds—dark gray, fringed with thick black lashes that didn't so much as flutter while he perused her with a look that bordered on suspicion. Rusty suddenly wished she had worn something more respectable. That demure white linen suit her mother had sent her for her thirtieth birthday would have been just the thing for a first-grade teacher.

"Have we met?" he asked her.

"I don't think so." Rusty offered her hand in greeting as Beryl muddled through the introductions. That was her first mistake, she realized. The lightning bolt of recognition hit her the minute his fingers closed around hers. His eyes told her he'd felt it too. She snatched her hand away as though she'd been burned, and the action drew a deep frown from him. He opened his mouth to speak, but Beryl cut him off.

"You must meet the boys," the woman said as though sens-ing she had to move fast. The tension in the air was thick enough to chew. "Rusty, this is Josh and Peter." She sounded anxious. "Josh is nine—"

"Nine and a half."

"And Peter just turned eight." Beryl glanced around and found her youngest grandson hiding behind her. "And this charming young man is Tyler. He's five."

Rusty leaned forward and offered her hand, and the boy took it shyly. He was pale, thin, and hollow-eyed, and much too small for his age. "It's nice to meet you, Tyler," she said.

"Are you going to live here?" he asked.

"I'm just visiting," Rusty told him. "To help your grand-mother." While she chatted with the boys briefly, Peyton's gaze never left her face. Finally Beryl insisted on showing Rusty to her room so she could freshen up before dinner.

"What was *that* all about?" she whispered the minute she and Rusty were alone.

Rusty shook her head. "I'm not sure. But believe me, once I figure it out, you'll be the first to know."

The next morning Rusty almost slammed into Peyton as he came down the hall in a sweaty jogging suit that clung damply to all the right places. She'd stepped out her door, and there he was. He skidded to a halt the second he saw her.

"Sorry," he said, as she skirted out of his way. "I keep forgetting I'm on vacation and can relax. Did you sleep okay last night?"

A fine sheen of perspiration on his face and arms made him appear the picture of health and masculinity. His black hair was damp and curled at the ends. "Yes, I slept fine," she said, watching him mop his damp face with the hem of his shirt. She caught a glimpse of a hard, flat stomach. She wouldn't tell him how she'd slipped into Tyler's room several times during the night to make sure he was okay. Fortunately, the boy hadn't been troubled with bad dreams.

Peyton studied the slender woman in white shorts and navy pullover. She looked less flamboyant this morning, with that wild hair of hers pulled into a neat ponytail. He preferred it loose. Suddenly he had a vision of her in a long white nightgown with that hair tumbling down her back. He blinked, and the image was gone as quickly as it had appeared, leaving him to wonder what in the world had brought it on. "I didn't get a chance to thank you last night," he said.

"Thank me?"

"For offering to help with the boys. My mother swears they're no trouble, but I know she has a difficult time keeping up with them."

"I'm surprised you haven't hired someone to help," Rusty told him, knowing it had to be too much work for a woman Beryl's age.

Peyton shook his head. "Don't think I haven't tried," he said. "I've interviewed several excellent nannies, but Mother always finds something wrong with them. You must've impressed her for her to bring you here." He paused. "I'll have to say you don't look like any teacher I ever had when I was growing up."

"Oh?" She wondered if that was good or bad.

He smiled as he continued his perusal of her. Damn, but she looked familiar. "Do you get into Boston much?" he asked.

"No, I spend all my time in Salem."

"I thought maybe I had run into you at one of those boring fund-raising dinners." He paused then, feeling as though there were much more to say. Finally he glanced at his wristwatch. "Well, I'd better take my shower."

Rusty was so absorbed with watching him make his way down the hall that she didn't hear Tyler come up beside her.

"I'm all dressed," he announced.

She smiled at the adorable little boy, who looked so much like his father. He was dressed in play clothes and sneakers. "Ready for breakfast?" she asked.

"I'm not hungry."

Rusty offered her hand, and he took it reluctantly. She had watched him pick at his dinner the night before and knew he needed to get something in his stomach this morning. "Wanna know a secret?" she asked.

He nodded.

"I don't like to eat this early in the morning, either. But I'll try if you will."

He shrugged. "Okay."

Peyton joined them as they were finishing up the morning meal. Josh and Peter had eaten and were pitching a ball on the back lawn, Beryl was having a last cup of coffee. "Sorry I'm late," he said, as he made his way to the sideboard where a buffet had been laid out. He scooped scrambled eggs onto his plate from a small chafing dish. His gaze fell to his son's plate, where he was picking at his eggs. He smiled at the boy. "No bad dreams last night?"

Tyler shook his head.

Beryl met her son's gaze. "He slept through the night," she said proudly. "Says he feels fine this morning. No head-ache."

Rusty noted the relief on Peyton's face as he took a seat at the table. Although he and his mother were playing it very low-key, she could see the anxiety in their eyes. The cook appeared at his side, poured him a cup of coffee, then returned to the kitchen. Peyton sipped his coffee in silence for a moment as he regarded his son. "What do you say we pull the bicycles out of the garage and take a ride this morning?"

Beryl groaned. "In this heat? Count me out."

Peyton grinned at his mother. "That kind of attitude will make an old woman out of you."

"I'm *already* old. Take Rusty with you. She can use my bicycle."

Peyton looked at Rusty. "What do you think?" he asked. "We could go while it's still cool."

The idea sounded great to Rusty, who loved the outdoors. At the same time, she figured Tyler could use the fresh air and sunshine. "Sure, I'd love to." She pushed her chair from the table. "I'll call Josh and Peter in while you finish breakfast."

The weather couldn't have been closer to perfect. Once they'd pulled the bicycles out of the garage and dusted them off, Peyton led the group while Rusty brought up the rear, taking care not to go too fast for Tyler's sake. None of them seemed to mind the slow pace. There was so much to take in, the lovely homes and gardens and the harbor. They stopped at a small waterfront park so the boys could play.

"Your children are adorable," Rusty told Peyton as they watched the three boys climb on the equipment. "Especially little Tyler," she added.

"How much has my mother told you about him?" Peyton asked, watching his youngest struggle to keep up with the older boys.

Rusty glanced at him. "She told me about the headaches and nightmares. I assume he's been seen by a doctor."

"Several. So far they haven't been able to help him."

"It must be hard on you," she said.

"It's hard on everybody." He sighed. "I have to hit the campaign trail in a few weeks, so I won't be home as much. I'm afraid it will be too much for my mother." He turned to her. "How long do you plan to stay?"

"A week. Two at the most. I have to get back to Salem."

He looked surprised. "I thought you had the summer free."

She shifted uneasily on the bench. "Yes, well, I have other obligations."

"An impatient boyfriend, maybe?" he asked. When she didn't answer right away, he waved the question aside. "Sorry, it's none of my business. We're glad to have you for as long as you can be with us."

"How come you've never remarried, Peyton?" Rusty blurted out, then regretted it when he shot her a sharp look. She was famous for saying whatever popped into her mind. "I don't mean to pry," she said. "I was just wondering, what with the boys being so young and all."

"You think I should marry someone simply to give my children a mother?" he said.

"I would think after five years you would have met someone."

"I've met plenty of women."

"No one you really cared about?"

"None that I would want raising my children," he said. "I'm not sure I ever will."

"You're still in love with her, aren't you?"

He regarded her. "You ask a lot of questions."

"Curiosity has always been one of my biggest faults."

"Let's say that I haven't met anyone that even comes close to my wife."

"You mean your *late* wife, don't you?" she said gently, then knew she had gone too far. The ominous look in his eyes told her she had breached an unwritten law that forbade questions concerning Priscilla Nightingale.

"Why is my personal life of concern to you?"

Rusty fumbled for a reply. "I'm sorry if you thought I was being nosy. I was just trying to help. Sometimes it's better if you can talk about it."

"Cut the crap, Rusty," he said, "and tell me why you're *really* here."

She blinked. "I beg your pardon?"

"Why are you so curious about my family?"

"Why are *you* so paranoid?"

"Because I can't go to the bathroom these days without some reporter snapping my picture."

"You're in the public eye, what do you expect?"

"It started long before that. Even before Priscilla's death. People resent the wealthy. Look what the press has done to the Kennedy family. It doesn't matter how much we contribute to society or how hard we work. Everyone naturally suspects we use money to get what we want."

"Some people do."

"Not this family. We've worked hard to get where we are today. The reason I agreed to run for the Senate is because I thought I could make the world a better place. I wanted to make a difference. But the minute I announced my candidacy, I had reporters crawling all over me."

"Why do you put yourself through it?"

He paused for a moment. "Because when my children have grown and moved away, my career will be the only thing I have left. My other dreams were buried a long time ago."

3

Once they returned to the house, Rusty saw that Tyler ate part of a peanut-butter sandwich before she escorted him to his bedroom, where he could rest. The boy was not used to exercise, and the ride had left him completely worn-out. Still, she knew the activity had done him good. A child simply could not spend his days in a dark bedroom. She sat on the edge of the bed and read a story until he closed his eyes and drifted off. It was difficult to concentrate on the story, however, when all she could think of was Peyton. How sad that he was still in love with his wife after all these years. She sensed Peyton Nightingale needed love as much as his children, as much as the poor child beside her.

Once Rusty was certain the boy was sleeping soundly, she slipped out of the room and made her way downstairs. She found Beryl on a thick chaise longue in the sun room reading a magazine and sipping iced tea. She insisted Rusty join her.

"It's not often I have time to read a magazine from cover to cover," she confessed, plucking her reading glasses from the bridge of her nose and setting them down. "I must say it's a nice feeling."

Rusty smiled as she poured herself a glass of tea and sat on a chair close by. "Well, you deserve it," she said. "By the way, did I hear Peyton leave a few minutes ago?"

Beryl nodded. "He was invited sailing with friends, and I insisted he go. The man doesn't get out enough. I know it's because he doesn't want to burden me with the boys, but he should have something else in his life besides work." She paused and glanced around as though to make certain there was no one close by to overhear their conversation. Josh and Peter were playing a computer game in their room. "You've had the opportunity to observe Tyler," she said at last. "Can you help him?"

"I'll certainly try." Rusty took a sip of her tea and set it down. "He told me he was kicked out of kindergarten for fighting. Is that true?"

Beryl seemed reluctant to answer. "He didn't get along with some of the children. They made fun of him for being small. He was merely trying to defend himself."

"He's not allowed to play with the family pets?"

The woman seemed even more uncomfortable. "He was a bit rough with them, I'm afraid. The pets are off-limits until he learns how to be gentle. It's certainly not unusual to have to call a child down for mistreating an animal," she said defensively. "Especially a young child."

"I'm not trying to judge Tyler," Rusty said. "I'm trying to understand what's going on in his life right now." When the other woman turned away, Rusty became insistent. "Beryl, if you expect me to help, I'll have to ask questions. I can find out on my own, of course, but that'll take time. You and I both know we don't *have* a lot of time." The woman didn't look any more willing to part with information than she had in the beginning. Rusty went on, this time gently. "I know the press has taken advantage of your family. I'm sorry. But you're going to have to trust me."

Beryl seemed to struggle with the idea. Finally she turned to Rusty. "What do you want to know?"

"For starters, how did your daughter-in-law die?"

Beryl took a deep breath. It was obviously not something she wished to discuss. "She died giving birth to Tyler."

Rusty heard her own quick intake of breath. "How? Why?"

"She hemorrhaged. At least that's what her doctors said."

"Did you have reason to suspect the doctors weren't telling the truth?"

"Don't you think it's odd for a woman to die in childbirth in this day and age?" When Rusty didn't answer, she went on. "Peyton ordered a full investigation, of course, but there was no evidence of malpractice." Her lips thinned into a grim line. "I thought the poor boy would lose his mind."

"What do *you* think happened?" Rusty asked her.

"The truth? I think it has something to do with that curse. Priscilla was in perfect health before she went into the hospital."

Rusty pondered it. "I don't mean to change the subject, Beryl, but why do you suppose Peyton hasn't remarried?"

Beryl shook her head sadly. "He worshiped Priscilla," she said mournfully. "There's not a woman alive who could take her place." She blinked, and for a moment it looked as though she would cry. "Peyton and Priscilla grew up together, you see. They played together as children, walked to school together, then dated in high school. There was no separating them. They even insisted on attending the same college. Priscilla was like my own daughter." Beryl smiled. "We didn't call her Priscilla, of course. She was Prissy to the family." She paused. "Peyton doesn't like us to talk about it. I know that's not healthy, but that's the way it is. Sometimes I think he blames himself for her death."

"Why?"

"He wanted a daughter. Priscilla would have been happy with the two boys, but she got pregnant again in hopes of giving Peyton the little girl he'd always dreamed of. I wanted her to stop at two children. I'd heard of the curse. I didn't really believe it, but I figured why tamper with something we don't understand."

"Have you discussed this curse with Peyton?"

"I tried. But he was so offended by both the journal and locket that he wouldn't discuss it."

"Why was he offended?"

"I suppose because I brought it into the house. He doesn't want the boys to get their hands on it. Which is why I trust you'll keep it out of sight now that you have it." When Rusty assured her she would, Beryl went on. "That's not the only reason, of course. Peyton is a lawyer to the core, and he's not about to be swayed by the ravings of some ancestor. He needs proof that something exists. Evidence. You won't convince him there's a curse at work here."

The following night Rusty ushered the boys out to the terrace in their pajamas for bedtime stories. With dinner and baths behind them, the boys were no more ready for bed than she was. She decided it wouldn't hurt to let them stay up later than usual since they didn't have school. Beryl, on Rusty's insistence, had gone to her room with a book she'd been wanting to read, and Peyton was having dinner with the group of friends he'd gone sailing with the day before.

"Do you know any ghost stories?" Josh asked Rusty once they'd settled themselves in the comfortable wicker furniture.

"Ghost stories?" Rusty paused and glanced at Tyler, sitting beside her. She suspected he had enough scary things going on in his life at the moment without making it worse. Although he looked innocent on the outside, she sensed the negative energy surrounding him, felt it each time she got close. She had always been ultrasensitive to other people's energy, which was why she made it a point to surround herself with positive, energetic people. Nevertheless, she forced herself to get close to Tyler, not only because she knew he couldn't help what was happening to him but because she sensed he needed what positive influence she could offer.

"I *do* know one ghost story," Rusty said after a moment, "but it's about a *nice* ghost who watched over little children in an orphanage." Josh wrinkled his nose. It was obvious he wanted to hear something with blood and gore. To compensate, she seasoned her story with plenty of action-packed scenes. In the end, all the boys were delighted with her tale of a ghost called Aunt Martha who managed to save the mischievous orphans from calamity and find them loving parents as well. Afterward they gazed at the clear, star-filled sky while Rusty pointed out various constellations.

"Look at the moon," Peter said. "It looks like it's wearing a smiling face."

Rusty gazed at the moon and smiled. "Yes, she does, doesn't she? Maybe the moon is watching over us like Aunt Martha watched over the orphans."

"Why do you call the moon a *she?*" Josh asked.

Rusty hesitated. "Well, because the moon is like a woman

in some ways," she said. "Like now, she's waxing or growing in strength and intensity. Sort of like a young girl who is maturing and growing stronger."

"What about the full moon?" Peter asked.

"When the moon is full, she's like a pregnant woman."

"What's pregnant?" Tyler asked.

"It's when a man puts a baby in a woman's stomach, stupid," Josh told him. He rolled his eyes at Rusty. "He doesn't know anything about S–E–X yet."

Rusty decided to go on with her story in order to get their minds off sex and pregnancy. "And when the moon is waning or growing small, she's like an old woman who grows frail. You know, some people believe there's power in the moon."

Peter looked intrigued. "Magical power?"

"Uh-huh. Some people think if you go swimming in the moonlight, you can soak up that power like a sponge."

Three pairs of eyes stared back at her. Only then did Rusty realize she'd probably said more than she should have.

"Can *we* go swimming in the moonlight?" Tyler asked, gazing at the harbor where the moon's reflection fell like an iridescent orb.

"Not tonight," she said. Rusty decided it was time to get them to bed and was about to tell them as much when she heard a noise behind her. Peyton opened the back door and stepped out.

"Hi, guys," he said, grinning at his sons. "I've been looking all over for you. Aren't you supposed to be in bed?"

"Rusty's been telling us ghost stories," Peter said.

Peyton glanced in her direction, but before he could say anything, Tyler jumped up and ran to him for a hug. "Rusty says the moon has magical power, Daddy. Can we go swimming in the moonlight so we can be magic too? Maybe it'll make my headaches go away."

The smiled faded from Peyton's lips as he regarded Rusty. She was dressed in denim leggings and an oversized silk shirt with half moons and stars across the back. Her hair fell in coppery abundance across her shoulders, giving her a wild, untamed look. "Where's my mother?" he asked.

"In her room. I offered to get the boys ready for bed tonight. I hope that's okay."

He hugged Tyler briefly. "Why don't you guys brush your teeth and get ready for bed. I'll be up in a minute to say good night."

The boys put up somewhat of a fuss, but did as they were told, moving toward the door reluctantly. Rusty turned to follow, but was brought up short when Peyton closed his hand around her wrist. "Not so fast," he said. "I'd like to have a word with you."

This is it, she thought.

Rusty held her breath and waited until the boys had disappeared inside. "Is something wrong?" she asked. Peyton simply stood there and stared at her, his face giving nothing away. But *of course* something was wrong, she told herself. She had no business filling his children's heads with her own beliefs. She had learned long ago that people who practiced the old religion did not actively seek converts, nor did they begrudge those who found peace in Judaism or Christianity. Enlightenment being the ultimate goal, it mattered not the paths one chose to get there. There were times, however, that she longed to set people straight, those who put witches in the same league as devil worshipers. Still, that was no excuse. No matter how annoyed she became with ignorant people, she had absolutely no right to discuss her beliefs with young children.

She was going to have to answer for it now.

"You wanted to speak with me?" she asked when Peyton continued to stare in silence.

"The boys like you," he said.

This was not what she had expected. "I like them too."

"But they're very impressionable."

Here it comes, she thought. "And you don't want me filling their heads with nonsense, right?"

"I'm very protective of my children, Rusty. They've been through a lot. I want them to have the closest thing they can to a normal childhood." He paused and took a deep breath. He had made his point, and now it was time to tell her good night. So why was he standing there? And why was he feeling that there was more to say between them?

"Is there something else?" Rusty asked, feeling properly reprimanded despite the fact that he hadn't said much at all.

Peyton cleared his throat and stepped into his attorney persona. That was where he felt more comfortable these days. Comfortable and certainly less vulnerable. "Now, you and I both know the moon isn't magic, and that the only way you get what you want in this life is to work for it, right?"

"Whatever you say, Peyton."

Her voice was as soft as the night breeze falling on his cheek. His gaze drifted to her lips and lingered. They were the color of cinnamon sticks—slightly full, slightly wet. Something tightened in his gut as he imagined tasting them, imagined them on his body. He should have gone home with the petite brunette he'd met earlier. She had made it plain she was interested in seeing more of the future senator of Massachusetts. He had been so cautious these past few months, what with the primaries and trying to live up to the image his campaign man-

ager had painted for his constituents—an image that often over-
looked the fact he was a human being.

"That's not to say the moon doesn't create a *sense* of magic
sometimes," he said. "Like now, for instance, the way it shines
in your hair and turns the ends golden."

Rusty couldn't have been more surprised. "Are you flirting
with me, Peyton?"

He stepped closer. He was no longer Peyton Nightingale
the politician. He was a man with a man's needs. Needs that
had been ignored too long. "Maybe I am. Maybe the moon is
working its magic on me."

He really was a handsome son of a gun, she decided. Especially when he wasn't deep in thought over work or his late
wife or worried about his youngest son. "Anything's possible."

He reached for her. That luscious mouth of hers formed an
O of surprise, and he saw it as his invitation. He captured her
lips with his own and sank his tongue inside.

Rusty was so stunned, she couldn't process the information
in her dazed mind. Then, as the kiss deepened and his tongue
explored the depths of her mouth, she lost all coherent
thought. She simply stood there, fists grasping the front of his
jacket as though it were a lifeline and she a drowning woman.
He tasted wonderful, warm and masculine with a hint of mint.
That, combined with the musky scent of his after-shave, did a
number on her nervous system.

Peyton broke the kiss, gulped in new air, and captured her
lips once more. She felt small in his arms, and he realized that
abundant red hair, as well as her strong personality, made her
seem larger than she was. He slipped his hands beneath her silk
shirt and palmed her hips. They were clearly defined in the
snug leggings. He was instantly aroused.

Something flared to life inside Rusty the minute he cupped her buttocks and gave a gentle squeeze. His touch was both knowing and possessive, as though he had every right to be there. He pulled her against him, and the lump in his pants left no doubt in her mind what he wanted.

Rusty wrenched her mouth free and sucked in well-needed oxygen. "Peyton?" Her voice trembled.

Peyton was only vaguely aware she had said his name. The conservative politician and devoted father had lost control, thanks to the pert redhead in his arms. The only thing on his mind was getting her out of those damn leggings and into his bed. It was insane to want a woman so badly. Crazier still was this sense of urgency he felt, as if they should be making hot, furtive love by now. He opened his eyes and found her staring back at him. There was a vulnerability in her expression he hadn't noticed before. He captured her hand and pressed it against his zipper.

"You do crazy things to me, Rusty," he confessed. "I've been hard since you set foot into this house. Come to my room."

Rusty snapped her head up so fast, her vision blurred. His meaning was clear. Desire had turned his eyes smoky. Need had etched faint lines at the corners of his mouth. Mustering every bit of strength she had, she shoved him away. "Who do you think you are, mister?" she demanded, drawing a blank look from him. "Just who the *hell* do you think you are that you can use me like that?"

Shock rendered him speechless for a moment. "Use you?"

"I am *not* here to relieve your sexual frustrations so you can go on mourning your dead wife!"

He found his voice. "Lady, I don't know what you're talking about."

"Oh, yes, you do. I'm the one who had to listen yesterday to how perfect Priscilla was and how no woman could ever *hope* to fill her shoes. Is that supposed to warm my heart, Peyton? Is that supposed to sweep me off my feet and have me beating a path to your bed?"

He looked angry and more than a little put out. "I must've not done too badly," he said. "I seem to recall your kissing me back." When she opened her mouth to protest, he interrupted. "You're here for only a couple of weeks, Rusty. That hardly gives me much time to court you properly. Think of the time we'd waste." His smile was slow in coming. "Besides, we already know what we want. Don't try to deny it. You're hot as a pistol right now." He reached for her once more.

She stepped back, fists balled at her sides to keep from punching him in the face. Damn, but he could make her madder than anybody she knew. "For someone who hasn't had a meaningful relationship in five years, you certainly pretend to know a lot about women."

"I know enough."

"Oh? So that explains why Beryl is raising your children, why you're miserable and lonely, and why your boys don't have a mother figure to love and nurture them."

"So we're back to that, eh? And I suppose you think you could be their new mother?" He gave a snort of disgust. "You wouldn't believe how many women have suggested the same thing. Funny how money brings out a woman's maternal instincts. I can't help but wonder how eager they'd be if I weren't rich."

"I can't imagine they'd be very eager at all," Rusty replied matter-of-factly. He had to be the most arrogant man she'd ever met. "Other than your money, I don't see that you have a whole lot to offer." She turned to go, then paused at the door. "By the way, you misunderstood me. I wasn't applying for the job. As much as I enjoy your children, I wouldn't have you on a silver platter." She slammed the door behind her.

4

Rusty tossed and turned in her bed for more than an hour but couldn't get to sleep. All she could think about was Peyton and that kiss and the argument that had followed. She had lost her temper, and she knew perfectly well why. She was attracted to the man. She had wanted to go to his bedroom as much as he did. She had wanted to lie naked in his arms and make him forget Priscilla Nightingale had ever existed. For a moment she had forgotten the real reason she was there, and that reason had nothing to do with sharing kisses in the moonlight with Peyton! Besides, he was not likely to forget Priscilla. No doubt he saw her every time he looked into the faces of his children. She was as much alive today as she had been five years earlier. At least in Peyton's heart. And he wasn't going to let her go. Not for his children or his own happiness.

Rusty decided there would be no more kissing on the terrace. She could not compete with a dead woman!

Rusty was startled from her thoughts by a sharp cry from the next room. Scrambling from the bed, she flung open the adjoining door that led to Tyler's bedroom. Inside, she groped for the lamp on his night table and turned it on, then tried to still his flailing arms.

"Tyler, wake up!" she said, shaking him. He opened his eyes and stared back at her in horror before he recognized her.

"Rusty, they're coming!"

She took the trembling boy in her arms and held him tight. "It's okay, honey," she said. "It's only a dream." She pressed her lips against his damp forehead.

"They were coming after me," he said, choking on a sob.

"Who are *they,* Tyler? Could you see them?"

"They're bad. They were standing on the other side of something like . . . a sewer. They had a knife, and they were going to do terrible things to me."

"You're safe, honey. A dream can't hurt you." Rusty heard someone at the door. She turned as Peyton rushed in wearing jeans and nothing else. She was reminded of the first time she'd seen him. His face was etched with worry.

"Is he okay?"

She nodded. "A bad dream." She continued to hold the boy close. His pajamas were soaked with sweat. He shivered. "Could you get him fresh pajamas?" she asked Peyton.

He hurried to a dresser and fumbled through several drawers before he found what he was looking for. He turned, then froze at the sight of Rusty in a long white nightgown. Her hair cascaded down her back in fat, rowdy curls. She had never looked more beautiful, sitting on the bed holding his son against her breasts. Something stirred deep inside of him, a fleeting but powerful emotion that he thought long dead. As he continued to stare, he was swept up by a feeling of déjà vu that he had never experienced before. Where had it come from? Had the pressure of Tyler's illness and the upcoming campaign finally gotten to him?

"Peyton, what's wrong?" Rusty asked, noting the strange look on his face.

He blinked. "Nothing. I guess I'm still half-asleep." But he was clearly shaken by the incident. He continued to stare as

Rusty helped Tyler into dry pajamas—stare and wonder what was going on in his life.

Rusty didn't notice. She was more concerned with calming Tyler and getting him out of his wet clothes. She held him for a long time, rocking back and forth, soothing him. Until the trembling stopped. Until she heard his even breathing in her ear. Finally she laid him down on the bed and covered him.

By silent agreement they left the lamp on and made their way out of the room. Peyton waited until they were in the hall before he spoke. "He'll probably have a headache tomorrow."

Rusty saw the despair on the man's face, and it was easy to forget how angry she'd been with him earlier. He was human, after all. And lonely. He was a man reaching out the only way he knew. She sensed he needed to talk.

"Would you like a glass of milk?" she asked.

"A drink would be better."

Rusty followed him downstairs to a door off the main hall. "This was my father's study," he said as he motioned her through first.

Rusty recognized it as a man's room with the textured hunter-green wallpaper and camel-colored leather sofa and chair. In front of a draped window stood a massive library table, on it a dozen or more framed pictures. Rusty recognized Peyton and the boys. "I assume these are your brothers," she said, noting two men who bore a resemblance to him. Peyton nodded as he joined her. "The one on the left is John, the oldest. It was taken the day he was inducted into the Supreme Court. And that's Robert. He works at the Pentagon."

"Very impressive."

"Yes, well, my father expected his sons to do well, and none of us had the guts to let him down."

"He sounds like he was an ambitious man."

"Very. There was a lot of pressure for us to succeed. It wasn't enough to go to law school, we had to be accepted at Harvard and graduate at the top of our class."

"What did your mother have to say about all that?"

"She didn't like it. She thought it unhealthy to breed so much competition between brothers." He smiled. "My mother would have been satisfied if we'd grown up to be potato farmers as long as we were honest and happy."

"That sounds good to me," Rusty told him.

He regarded her. "You're obviously as much of a romantic as my mother," he said, looking slightly amused. "You think I'd make a good potato farmer?"

"I think you'd do well in anything you set your mind to," she replied, turning her attention back to the family photographs. She spied a picture of a pretty blonde with cornflower-blue eyes and knew it was the picture she'd been looking for all along. "Is that—"

"Priscilla," he said.

"She's beautiful."

The smile was gone. All the light had left his eyes. "Yes." Peyton turned abruptly and crossed the room to where a door concealed a wet bar and small refrigerator. He reached for a bottle. "What'll you have?"

"Whatever you're having is fine." Rusty moved to the sofa and sat down as she waited for him to pour brandy into two snifters. He handed her one, then took a hefty drink from his own glass. "I always have trouble falling asleep after Tyler has one of his nightmares," he said.

Rusty took a sip of the brandy. It warmed her belly. "How long has he been having them?"

"Six or eight months. On a regular basis for the past three."

Peyton took a seat beside her. "I've had him tested for everything from allergies to—" He paused as though unsure of
whether or not he should say more. "Did my mother tell you
we took him to a child psychologist?"

Rusty's smile was rueful. "Your mother keeps as many
secrets as you do."

"We have reason to be secretive."

"So what did the doctor say?" she asked, knowing if Peyton
dwelled on what the press had done to the family, he would get
paranoid again and clam up on her.

His eyes clouded. "He's afraid Tyler might be showing signs
of early schizophrenia."

Rusty could tell that it had cost him emotionally to tell her
that. "What do *you* think, Peyton?"

He drained his glass. "I don't know what the hell to think.
I *do* know there's a history of mental illness in our family."

"Oh?"

He nodded soberly. "My grandfather was unstable. Some
said it was early senility, but the man talked out of his head a
lot. I had an aunt who suffered a nervous breakdown and had
to be hospitalized. It was all hush-hush, of course. And then—"
He paused and set his empty glass on the table. "I remember
my brothers telling me once about ancestors who thought they
were night creatures or something."

Rusty felt a chill rush up her spine. "What do you mean
night creatures?" She tried to sound casually interested.

Peyton shook his head as though he found the mere
thought ludicrous. "Rumor has it one of the men thought he
was a vampire. I can't remember what was wrong with the
other guy, although both men claimed their malady was due to
some curse cast in the seventeenth century. I figured it was

nothing more than a rumor until my mother came across this old journal that supposedly details the events."

He stood, walked to the bar, splashed more brandy into his glass, then downed it in one gulp. "Of course, the term *schizophrenia* hadn't come into being at that time, so there's no way to know what these men actually suffered from other than serious delusions. Not that it really matters one way or the other. It happened hundreds of years ago. Unless there have been others since that time, I would suspect the bad genes played themselves out long ago." He set his glass down. "Maybe I should be worrying about my mother's genes," he said. "What with her talk of curses and night creatures." He smiled mirthlessly. "Or maybe the whole family is crazy, myself included."

Rusty, who had remained quiet while he'd shared his secrets, stood and walked the short distance that separated them. "I don't think you and your family are crazy," she said. "But I *do* think Tyler's illness and your campaign have put a great deal of stress on you all." Stress was putting it mildly, she thought.

Peyton stiffened visibly as though suddenly remembering all that was going on outside his home. "Please don't repeat any of what I've told you tonight," he said. "Neither my family nor my career could take the bad press."

"I'm here to help, Peyton, not make matters worse."

They gazed at each other in silence for a long moment. Rusty would have felt self-conscious in her nightgown and with Peyton bare-chested if he had been any other man. But with Peyton the small intimacy felt right. She had a sudden stark vision of him standing bare-chested beside a tall four-poster bed. He leaned forward, snuffed a candle on the night table before climbing in and reaching for the woman beside him. Rusty closed her eyes. She often received bits and pieces of both past and future events when she least expected it. Was she seeing a past vision of Peyton climbing into bed with his wife? The thought chilled her. She had no desire to watch Peyton make love to his precious Priscilla!

Peyton saw the look of horror cross her face, saw her pale visibly before him. "Rusty, what's wrong?" He reached out, grabbed her upper arms, and held her fast.

Rusty opened her eyes and found him close, the look on his face one of grave concern. "I'm sorry, Peyton. I suppose I'm just tired."

"You haven't slept much since you arrived, have you?"

She was touched by his show of concern. "I sometimes have trouble falling asleep because I'm afraid Tyler will call out and I won't hear."

"Oh, Rusty." He stroked her cheek with one finger. "I don't expect you to watch over my son twenty-four hours a day."

His look was so tender, Rusty feared her heart would leap right out of her chest. This was not the same man who'd offered her sex with no strings on the terrace earlier. This was a side of Peyton she had seen him exhibit only with his children. She turned her head slightly and kissed the finger that had touched her face so lovingly a second before.

Peyton thought the simple gesture one of the sweetest he'd witnessed in his thirty-five years. He felt the sensation low in his gut, and he wanted her all over again, as much or more than he'd wanted her earlier. Their gazes locked. Those green eyes did something to him, touched some part of him that he had not known existed until tonight: a darker side, a side that Priscilla, in her innocence, had not suspected he'd possessed. What was it about this woman that inspired tenderness one moment and made him want to carry her to his bed the next?

Without taking his eyes off her face, Peyton drew her closer, so close, his thighs brushed hers.

"Touch me, Rusty."

It was a gentle command, fraught with tension and a longing she had not heard before. Rusty raised a trembling hand to his chest and placed it over his heart, which beat out a steady message to her. His skin was warm, hazed with the same blue-black hair that covered his head. She stroked the taut muscle.

He closed his eyes.

She held her breath.

He reached for her.

She went willingly into his arms.

His mouth sought hers.

And then he was kissing her. Fully. Deeply. Desperately. It was the sort of kiss war-torn lovers shared once reunited. Fierce and hungry and consuming. The sort of kiss a man offered a woman just before he climaxed in her arms. It was poignant and sweet, and as Peyton thrust his tongue inside her mouth, he thought of thrusting his body into hers, of embedding himself deeply. Perhaps then he would find peace, not only with his physical self but with his emotional self. Perhaps then he would find answers to the questions that plagued him.

The kiss left them shaken and wanting more. Peyton lifted his head, and his eyes were filled with yearning. "Sometimes I feel as if I've known you forever. But how can that be? We met only a few days ago."

Rusty suspected he was closer to the truth than he realized. They *did* know each other from somewhere, another life probably, but she seriously doubted she would convince *him* of that.

"Life is full of surprises, Peyton. Surprises and little mysteries that are hard to explain."

"Why are you here, Rusty?" he asked.

"To help. Not to harm."

Peyton noted the earnest look on her face. He also noticed the ever-growing fatigue. As much as he wanted to take her to his bed and make love to her, he decided she needed her sleep more. All at once he swept her high in his arms.

Rusty gave a small squeal of surprise. "What are you doing?"

"Putting you to bed," he said. "You're not going to be of any help if you get sick."

"But what about Tyler?"

He was already out the door. "I'll sleep in his room tonight." He ignored her softly spoken protests to put her down as he climbed up the wide staircase, then deposited her at her door. He knew it would be dangerous to go inside where she slept, where her belongings lay and the bed covers carried her scent. "Try to rest," he said. He pressed his lips to her forehead, then moved quietly down the hall to Tyler's room.

When Peyton stepped into his son's bedroom shortly before lunch the next day, he found Rusty and Beryl with him, having kept a bedside vigil since Tyler had awakened at six that morning with one of his headaches. Peyton had checked on him periodically, between entertaining the other boys, assuring the servants Tyler would be okay, and taking calls from his campaign manager.

"He's not getting any better," Beryl told her son. "I've given him something for pain and nausea, but it hasn't helped much."

"Want me to call a doctor?" Peyton asked.

"A doctor!" Beryl said, her voice unusually shrill. "He's been to every kind of doctor there is. What good has it done?" She choked on a sob.

"Don't cry, Grandma."

Everyone turned in the direction of where the weak voice had come. Tyler's brown eyes were wide with alarm. Beryl gave a small cry and dropped to her knees beside the bed.

"Oh, Tyler darling, I didn't mean to upset you. Grandma doesn't like to see her sweet boy sick."

Rusty turned to Peyton. She'd been so busy caring for Tyler that she hadn't had a chance to say much to him. "I think what Tyler needs more than anything right now is quiet. Do you think you could take the boys out for a while?"

"Sure, if it'll help." He glanced at his son. "Isn't there something I can do?"

"Not at the moment." She glanced at Beryl. "You might invite your mother along," she said. "She needs to get out of this house."

Beryl snapped her head up at the mention of her name. Although Rusty had told her she needed to be alone with the boy in order to perform a ritual, it had not occurred to the woman that Rusty would send her away as well.

"That sounds like a good idea, Mother," he said, noting how tired Tyler looked. The boy wouldn't be able to rest with his grandmother fretting and pacing the floor. "I'll take you to lunch, then maybe we can drop by the museum for an hour. By the time we get back, Tyler will have had a good nap, and he'll be good as new."

Rusty felt her heart go out to Peyton as he tried to convince his mother everything would be all right. She was certain he felt the woman couldn't take the strain any longer. After having lived with her grandson's nightmares and headaches and other rather bizarre behavior, Beryl Nightingale looked like a woman on the edge.

Beryl opened her mouth to protest, but Peyton interrupted. "It's settled," he said. "I'll round up the boys and meet you downstairs in five minutes."

Beryl waited until he was gone before she spoke. "What are you planning to do?" she asked Rusty.

"Everything I *can* do. That's why you brought me here, remember?" She glanced at Tyler, whose eyes had finally closed after battling an excruciating headache all morning. "I want you to keep Peyton away for as long as you can," she whispered to the woman. "Tell the servants to stay away from this room. I don't wish to be disturbed."

Beryl gazed at the boy through emotion-packed eyes. "He's like my own son, you know."

Rusty nodded. She knew Beryl had cared for the child from the time he had come home from the hospital. The woman had changed diapers, prepared formula, and nursed her grandson's colds. She had refused to hire help because she didn't think an outsider could love him or her other grandchildren as much. And now she feared losing him.

"I know you're frightened," Rusty said, taking her hand. "You must trust me."

Their gazes locked. "I have no choice but to trust you, my dear. You're our last hope."

5

The nightmares and headaches continued over the next two days despite all Rusty did. Each night while the family slept, she spent hours at Tyler's side, performing what some referred to as the laying on of hands. Putting herself into a state of deep relaxation, she massaged and pushed negative energy away from the boy's body with her hands before channeling healing energy into him. She had been healing the sick and afflicted for years with that technique, but Tyler didn't seem to be responding. Come morning, he was much the same. On the second night, Rusty put herself into the alpha state before she placed her hands on the boy's head and began the healing process once again. She was so involved with her work, she didn't hear Peyton come into the room.

"What are you doing?"

Startled, Rusty whipped her head around and found him standing inside the doorway in a pair of sweats and a T-shirt. "Oh, Peyton, you scared me," she said.

He stepped closer. "What are you doing to my son, Rusty?"

"Trying to make him better, of course. What does it *look* like I'm doing?"

Peyton walked over to the bed and gazed at his sleeping

son, then back to her. His expression was clearly suspicious. "I haven't a clue."

"Do you believe in visualization?" she asked.

"I'm not sure I know what you're talking about."

"The power of positive thinking," she said, putting it in terms he would understand. She knew of one Christian minister who wrote at length about it.

"You mean the power of prayer, don't you?" he said.

"Call it what you like. Everybody prays to something. But we're all seeking the same result. Enlightenment. Strength. Healing."

He sat at the foot of the bed and regarded the woman at the other end. "What are *you* seeking, Rusty?" he asked.

She thought about it. "I suppose I'm looking for the same thing everybody else is. Love and happiness." She paused. "And a reason for being." He seemed to ponder her words. "I believe we all have a purpose," she went on. "So do you, or you wouldn't be running for senator. Your mother tells me you want to change the world. Make it a better place for your children and their children."

"My mother talks too much. But she's right. I *do* want to make a difference."

"She claims you're a wonderful lawyer. I suspect you're *already* making a difference."

Peyton turned his attention back to his sleeping son. "Right now I want to make a difference in my son's life," he said. "But what can I do? Should I let some shrink experiment with a bunch of mind-altering drugs and hope he finds the answer before he turns my boy into a zombie? Should I put him into an institution so they can study him like some laboratory rat?" He blinked several times, and it was obvious he was close to tears. "Or should I continue to hide him in a dark bedroom until this illness, whatever it is, eventually kills him?" He choked back a sob.

Rusty longed to put her arms around him, comfort him. "Please try to be patient a little longer, Peyton."

"I'm afraid," he said. "How much longer can I avoid making a decision? If Tyler is truly showing signs of early schizophrenia or other forms of psychosis, I have to do something." When Rusty didn't say anything right away, he continued. "You know he talks to himself when he doesn't think anyone's listening."

"All children do that at one time or another," she said, trying to ease his concern. "Didn't you ever have an imaginary playmate?"

"Not one who lived in a sewer and talked about disemboweling little children, no." He sighed, and it sounded as though it came from the very depths of his soul. "What sort of madness is this, Rusty?"

"I'm not sure," she told him. And she wasn't. The curse plainly stated those suffering from it would become night creatures, no two alike. Michael Nightingale had ripped beating hearts from his victims' chests, whereas Heath had sipped blood for sustenance. Rusty had a feeling that, once the curse took over Tyler's young body, it would manifest in a way that was even more horrific than the others.

"One of Tyler's friends from kindergarten claimed Tyler made the walls bleed in the boys' bathroom," Peyton said after a moment.

"Did anyone else see it?"

He shook his head. "There was a logical explanation for it, of course. His teacher told me they'd been finger painting that day. She was certain Tyler smeared red paint on the wall and simply told the boy it was blood. I punished Tyler for what I considered a practical joke. Then, the next morning—" He paused and wiped his hand down his face. "The next morning, when I went into his room—" He paused again and shook his head. His eyes misted.

Rusty saw that he was struggling to keep his emotions under control. "What happened?"

A look of horror crossed Peyton's face. "You're going to think this sounds crazy, Rusty, but I swear to God it's true. When I went into Tyler's bedroom the next morning, his sheets were saturated with blood. He was covered with it from head to toe."

Rusty shuddered at the thought of what it must have done to the man. "What'd you do?"

"I went all to pieces, naturally. I vaguely remember yelling for someone to call an ambulance." His eyes filled with tears. "God, it was awful! I thought someone had come into my boy's room during the night and butchered him."

Rusty moved to the foot of the bed and put her arms around him. He seemed to welcome what small comfort she could offer. But then, why wouldn't he? He had tried to be strong for so long. "What happened?"

He shook his head, and the tears fell down his cheeks. "It was the strangest thing. I couldn't find a wound anywhere on his body. I checked him head to toe, but there was nothing. I rushed into the bathroom and stuck him under the shower to wash off the blood, so I could find out where the hell it was coming from. There wasn't even a scratch. It was as though the blood were seeping from his pores." He closed his eyes as though reliving the whole thing again in his mind. "My mother ran into the bedroom, frantic, half out of her mind with fear, only to find there was . . . nothing."

"Nothing?"

"Not a speck of blood to be found anywhere. Not even on his sheets. It was as though I had imagined the whole thing."

"I'm sorry you had to go through that."

"Do you see why I'm beginning to think I'm crazy?" he said. "In another six months I'll be as crazy as my poor aunt was before they locked her up."

"You're not crazy, Peyton," she said. "Like I said before, life is full of little mysteries. Just because we can't explain things doesn't mean they don't exist. Physics professors are unraveling secrets of the universe every day."

"Don't try to make me feel better, Rusty. I know what I saw. I think it's all beginning to get to me. First Priscilla's death and the investigation and all those reporters. Trying to raise the kids without a mother. Next thing I know Tyler's sick and I'm running for senator. What a crock! How can I carry on a successful campaign when I have to keep my youngest son hidden from the public, when I'm constantly dodging reporters because I'm scared they'll discover what's going on here?

"And what if I have another hallucination out on the campaign trail? What if I get stressed out and start seeing things that aren't really there? They'll cart me off to the nearest asylum, and my children will be minus *both* parents."

"Nobody's going to take you anywhere, Peyton. You're as sane as the next person."

"You don't know that."

"Yes, I do." At the look he shot her, she went on, sorrowfully. "I've seen the blood, too, Peyton."

★ ★ ★

They spent the night in Tyler's room, holding hands, whispering to each other from time to time and watching the boy closely. They waited. For what, they didn't know.

Morning came and Tyler awoke without a headache. Rusty was moved to tears by the relief in Peyton's eyes, not to mention her own relief. They desperately needed a break, no matter how brief. The human psyche simply couldn't withstand uninterrupted hours of stress without the body eventually breaking down. Now Rusty sensed she could steal a moment for herself. She quickly excused herself, telling them she needed a hot shower.

"Rusty?"

She paused at the door and glanced at Peyton. He had never looked more handsome than he did at that moment in his rumpled clothes and unshaved jaw. "Yes?" Her voice trembled.

"Thank you. For everything."

She smiled. "You're welcome."

Rusty still felt torn between tears and laughter when she entered her bathroom a moment later and turned on the shower. She was certain the hodgepodge of emotions were born out of relief and exhaustion and had nothing to do with the fact that she was falling in love with Peyton Nightingale.

Rusty froze the minute the thought surfaced. *In love with Peyton!* A small groan escaped her. *But how could that be?*

She was a witch, for heaven's sake, and he was a future senator of Massachusetts!

Rusty caught a glimpse of her reflection in the bathroom mirror and stopped in her tracks when she spied the haggard-looking woman staring back at her. Her feelings for Peyton were pushed aside for the moment as she stepped closer to the mirror and studied her gaunt face and the dark circles beneath her eyes. *My God, what had happened to her?* Why hadn't Peyton said something? She was still trying to come to terms with the changes in her looks as she stepped into the hot spray of water.

With her shower behind her, Rusty felt somewhat better, although the look Beryl gave her told her she hadn't been successful in concealing the dark circles with makeup. "Try to get a nap today if you can, dear," the woman said as she poured Rusty a cup of coffee. "You look exhausted."

She *was* exhausted, but she knew she wasn't the only one. No doubt Peyton would be dead on his feet as well. "Isn't Peyton having breakfast?" Rusty asked as she fixed her plate from the buffet, then realized she wasn't the least bit hungry.

"He's on the phone with his campaign manager." Beryl shook her head. "You'd never know we were on vacation with all the calls he gets."

Josh put down his napkin. "I'm finished, Grandma," he said. "Can I go out and play?"

"As long as you stay in the backyard and don't go near the water," she said. Peter jumped up as well, and they dashed off toward the terrace. Beryl turned to Rusty. "There have been reporters out front all morning," she said. "I knew they'd find us sooner or later. Peyton asked me to make sure the boys didn't go near them." She slanted her eyes to Tyler, who was slathering jelly on a slice of toast, then back to Rusty. Her message was clear: Keep Tyler away from the prying media at all costs!

Peyton was still on the telephone when Rusty led Tyler out back to sit in the garden and watch the boats in the harbor. She hoped the fresh air would revive her and chase the cobwebs from her brain. Josh and Peter played with an assortment of cars on a picnic table in the yard, looking up now and then as a speedboat raced by, or a motorboat pulling skiers. Josh wandered over a few minutes later, picking at something in his hand. "Where's Grandma?" he asked.

"She's in her room resting," Rusty told him. "Did you hurt yourself?"

"Naw, just a splinter."

"Here, let me see. Splinters are my specialty."

The boy held out his hand, and Rusty used her fingernails to pull the sliver of wood from his palm. "See, good as new," she said. "And it didn't even interfere with your lifeline."

"What's a lifeline?"

"See this line across your palm?" she pointed out. "It tells how long you're going to live."

He glanced up at her, his look curious. "How long have I got?"

She chuckled. "Years and years."

"Are you a fortune-teller?"

"Sort of."

He looked intrigued. "What else can you tell by looking at my hand?"

Rusty studied his open palm. "I see you're very bright," she said. "Gifted, actually. You've been accepted into a special program at school, haven't you?"

He nodded, truly impressed. "They say I have a high IQ. Can you tell me what I'm going to get for my next birthday?"

"Hmmm. Well, I can't tell exactly what it is, but I *do* know it's going to be big."

He looked excited. "Is it a horse? I *love* horses, but Dad won't let me have one."

"I think you know the reason for that, young man," she told him matter-of-factly. "You gave your father quite a scare when that horse threw you last year. Lucky for you it was just a mild head injury and nothing serious."

The boy's eyes grew wide as saucers. "Wow, how did you know that?"

"Yes, how *did* you know that?" a male voice said, startling Rusty so badly, she jumped. Peyton stood there looking at her with a funny expression in his eyes.

"Oh, Peyton, I didn't hear you come up," she said.

"Did my mother tell you about Josh being thrown from that horse last year?" he asked.

"Your mother?" Rusty blinked. Once again she had not used caution. "Well, of course she told me. How else would I have known?"

Josh snatched his hand away. "You're not really a fortune-teller."

Rusty knew what it meant to be between a rock and a hard place, because she had certainly put herself there. It was her own fault. If she told the truth and confessed that she could indeed see fragments of the past and future, Peyton would send her packing immediately. Instead, she would have to lie and have Josh think she was a fake.

"Well, I *do* know what you're having for dinner tonight," she said feebly.

He gave a snort of disgust and joined his brothers in their play.

Peyton looked amused as he held out his own hand. "Tell me what *my* future holds," he prompted. "Am I going to win the election in November?"

Rusty reached for his hand. Just as before when she'd taken his hand, she felt the shock of recognition. She sucked in her breath. Nerves coiled in the pit of her stomach. The sudden tension in Peyton's shoulders told her he felt it also. She released his hand immediately. "Well, I'd have to say it depends on how much you want it," she told him.

"What kind of answer is that?" he asked. "And how can you tell? You didn't even look." Still, he couldn't help but wonder at the strange sensations that had hit him the minute she'd touched his hand. What was it with this woman?

"I didn't have to look," she said. "I felt it in my heart."

He studied her face, the strange look in her eyes. "Why do I get the feeling you know more about me than you're pretending?"

Rusty met the intense gaze. "Perhaps we met in a previous life."

Peyton grinned. Damn, but he liked her. As strange as she appeared at times, she had been indispensable the past few days. She had taken a load off his mother and shown nothing but affection for his children. But that wasn't the *only* reason he was glad she was there. He was beginning to look forward to seeing her at the breakfast table each morning, and he found himself trying to come up with excuses for them to be alone.

"I have to go to Boston for a couple of days," he said without preamble. "My campaign manager wants to talk strategy." He met her gaze. "I don't want to go, but he's *more than willing* to come here if I don't." He shot a look in Tyler's direction. "I don't think that's a good idea."

"I understand," Rusty said, although she was disappointed to hear he was going away. At the same time, she knew it was best. She had grown far too fond of the man in just a short time, and that could be dangerous considering their circumstances. Not only that, his absence would allow her to work with Tyler uninterrupted. "Don't worry about a thing," she told him.

"Are you sure?"

Rusty thought he sounded reluctant. Part of her wished it was because he couldn't stand the thought of leaving her even for a short period. But she knew better than that. His reluctance had nothing to do with her. He was simply worried about his son. "We'll be fine," she said.

Rusty set up an altar in her room that very afternoon, while Beryl, too afraid to get close, stood inside the closed door of the bedroom and watched.

"I never meant for it to go this far," the woman said. "I was hoping you might be able to chant a few verses from your spell book and be done with it."

"It's not as spooky as it looks," Rusty told her, hoping the woman didn't demand an explanation for everything. She was too weary for questions and needed all her concentration for the task at hand. "I simply have to charge some herbs that I plan to use for healing and protection. I couldn't do it before with Peyton in the house."

Beryl glanced at the altar once more and shook her head sadly. "If Peyton ever finds out about this, he is going to kill me."

"I have a gift for you," Rusty told Tyler that evening as she tucked him into bed. She knew he was afraid to close his eyes for fear the nightmare would return.

"For me?" He raised up, an expectant look on his face. Rusty handed him a chain with a funny symbol attached.

"It's a pentagram," she said. "For good luck. And to keep bad dreams away. Here, let me put it on you." She fastened the chain around the boy's neck. "There's only one rule," she said. "You have to keep it tucked beneath your shirt and out of sight. It won't work unless you keep it hidden." Rusty was stabbed by guilt as she convinced the little boy to keep secrets from his family, especially his own father. But she suspected Peyton would take great pleasure in ripping it off his neck and hurling it in her face. She had to do what she had to do.

It was easy to see why Fritz Armstrong was such a good campaign manager. He didn't miss a detail. "Peyton, I've been doing some serious thinking about your image for the campaign. Specifically, the way you dress."

Peyton looked surprised. "What's wrong with the way I dress?" he asked, taking in his own neatly pressed suit.

"We're trying to appeal to hardworking, middle-class people. You hardly look the part."

"Are you suggesting I start buying my suits at secondhand shops?"

"No, I'm suggesting you lose the suits altogether. Don't you have anything nice in denim?"

"Yes, but I don't usually wear it to the office." He shifted in his chair. "Besides, that's not really me," he said. "I've always taken pride in my appearance. Except in law school, where I was *expected* to dress like a slob."

"How do you hope to build a platform for blue-collar workers when you wear six-hundred-dollar suits?"

Peyton considered it. "By making changes in the system that will benefit them," he said. "Like strengthening safety guidelines and—"

"You don't have to sell me, Peyton, you've already got my vote. I want to see you get *their* votes." Fritz pulled off his glasses and twirled them by the stem. "I figure we can capitalize on the fact that you're a single father trying to juggle a career and raise your children all alone."

"I've never been alone," Peyton interrupted. "My family, especially my mother, have been there for me from the beginning."

"Speaking of your family, how's the boy?"

Peyton knew he was asking about Tyler. Although he'd kept most of the problems to himself, he'd had to tell Fritz the boy was seeing a psychiatrist. Better to tell him personally than let him read it in the newspaper. "He's better. My mother has someone helping with the boys for a few weeks."

"You mean you finally convinced her to hire a nanny?" Fritz asked. "I hope you checked her references carefully. We don't need any surprises before November."

"She's an old family friend," Peyton told him.

"So you know her well?"

Peyton looked surprised. "I haven't run an FBI check on her, if that's what you're asking." He shook his head. "You're getting paranoid in your old age, Fritz. I assure you Miss Padget is harmless. A little kooky at times, but perfectly harmless."

Fritz scribbled something on his pad, then pushed it aside as though it were a forgotten matter. "Just be careful who you bring into your house, Peyton. Now"—he paused and rubbed his hands together—"let's talk strategy."

6

Rusty literally had to drag herself out of bed the following morning. Much to her surprise, it was after ten o'clock. Unfortunately, the circles beneath her eyes had not disappeared with the extra sleep.

"You look awful," Beryl said the minute she saw her. "I wasn't aware Tyler had problems last night. Did you have to get up with him?"

Rusty shook her head. "No, he slept through the night." The housekeeper brought her a cup of coffee and offered to prepare something for her to eat. "Coffee is fine," she told the woman. "I don't have much of an appetite this morning." She turned to Beryl. "I must've picked up a bug."

Beryl insisted Rusty go back to bed. When Rusty started to protest, the older woman was adamant. "We can't risk Tyler catching it," she said. "This is the first time in weeks he's felt well enough to eat breakfast."

"You're right, of course," Rusty said, and turned for the stairs.

"Rusty?" Beryl called out softly to her. "Do you think it's over?"

"I'm not sure," she told her, feeling weaker by the moment. "All we can do is wait."

★   ★   ★

"She's burning up with fever. How long has she been like this?"

Beryl touched Rusty's forehead. "Since yesterday morning. I sent her back to bed, and she's been here ever since."

Peyton nudged Rusty gently, and she opened her eyes. It took a moment for her to focus. Her head throbbed. "Peyton?" Her mouth was so dry, she could barely say his name.

Beryl helped her sit up so she could take water. "Not too fast, dear," she said when Rusty tried to drain the glass in one long gulp.

Peyton waited until she had finished the water before he spoke. "How do you feel?"

"Better, I think," Rusty said, although that wasn't the case at all. She felt weak as a kitten. Her head spun. She saw that it was nighttime. "Did I sleep all day?" she asked.

"Honey, you've been asleep for *two* days," Beryl told her. "That must be some bug."

"Two days!" Rusty started to climb out of bed, but Peyton stopped her.

"Not so fast," he said, noting how pale and hollow-eyed she was. "If I had known you were this sick, I wouldn't have spent a second night in Boston." He felt truly guilty because when he'd called to check on things, Beryl had announced Tyler had never been better. He'd had no idea Rusty wasn't well.

For once Rusty didn't put up a fuss. "How's Tyler?"

"He's doing great," Peyton told her. "And eating like a horse from what I hear." He smiled, but it didn't erase the worry lines from his brow. "It's you we're concerned about right now. I think we'd better have a doctor look at you."

"No!" Rusty said, then wished she hadn't refused so strongly. She forced herself to smile. "What I mean is, I don't want to see *anyone* looking like I do. I haven't bathed in two days. Besides, it's late. Why don't we wait and see if I'm better tomorrow."

Peyton nodded after a moment as though convinced. "Okay, but if you're still sick in the morning, we're taking you in." He left her then so he could spend some time with the boys before they went to bed.

Beryl waited until he was gone before she spoke. "What's going on, Rusty?" she said.

"What do you mean?"

"You're not going to convince me this is a simple virus. You've been talking out of your head for two days about"— she paused—"awful things. Something's wrong. What is it?"

Rusty knew she would have to tell her the truth. "It's the curse, Beryl. The reason Tyler is better is that all the negative energy has left his body and entered mine."

The woman gasped in disbelief. "What are we going to do?"

"I'm not sure there's anything we *can* do," Rusty told her. "The curse plainly states that a sacrifice must be made, a sacrifice no mortal woman would ever make. And since we know curses always come back to those who cast them, it would make perfect sense that I should be the one to suffer. If not me, someone else in my bloodline," she added.

"Did you know this before you came here?"

"I suspected."

"Oh, my God!" Beryl sank into the nearest chair. "Isn't there some way to stop it?"

"I need time to think of something," Rusty told her. "In

the meantime, I can't afford to have Peyton dragging me to doctors."

Beryl sighed heavily. "Then you better put on one fine act come morning. Except for his worrying over Tyler, I haven't seen him like this since"—she paused and her eyes grew wide —"since Priscilla died." She shook her head as though it were too much to take in at once. "Oh, my Lord!" she exclaimed. "If I didn't know any better, I'd say Peyton had gone and fallen in love with you!"

"You look much better this morning," Peyton told Rusty over breakfast. "How do you feel?"

Rusty was warmed to her toes by the caring look in his eyes. "As if I just got over a forty-eight-hour virus," she said, giving him her best smile. She knew the only reason she looked better was because she had used concealer under her eyes and applied her makeup more heavily than usual. She still felt weak and had no appetite, but she wasn't about to let *him* know that. He smiled approvingly as she helped herself to a large serving of eggs and hash browns.

"I think the patient has recovered," Peyton announced to his mother with a broad smile. "She and Tyler are going to eat us out of house and home."

Rusty was glad to hear Tyler's appetite had returned. She had noticed him playing ball with his brothers earlier, and he looked wonderful.

"I'm glad to see you're better, dear," Beryl told her. She smiled at Rusty, but the private look she gave her told Rusty she wasn't falling for her act for one minute.

Beryl excused herself a moment later, telling them she wanted to discuss dinner with the cook. Peyton glanced up at his mother. "Don't plan on my being here," he told her. "I'm going out." He turned to Rusty. "Now that you're on the mend, perhaps you'd like to join me. An old friend is having a small dinner party, and I promised I'd drop by later. Once the boys are ready for bed," he added.

"Oh, that sounds like a wonderful idea," Beryl said. "Rusty hasn't had a chance to meet anyone on the island. Perhaps you could introduce her to some of the eligible bachelors you know," she added, and was rewarded with a frown from him.

Rusty knew Beryl was trying to discourage Peyton from entertaining any romantic ideas about her. Not that Rusty blamed the woman. Still, she couldn't have been more surprised with the invitation. "That depends," she told him, "on whether your mother has plans for the evening." She looked to Beryl for guidance.

"I'm free this evening," Beryl said reluctantly, then cast a look of warning in Rusty's direction. It was obvious she was counting on Rusty to keep her son at arm's length.

The small dinner party turned out to be a clambake and buffet for sixty held in Peyton's honor. As he led Rusty through a sprawling contemporary home and out back to the swimming pool, he was welcomed with rousing applause from old friends. Rusty took in the beautifully dressed men and women and the food-laden tables. Ropes of tiny white lights had been strung through wild cherry trees, giving the party a festive, fairy-tale appearance. An older man approached Peyton, shook hands with him, and insisted he be introduced to Rusty.

"Rusty, meet our host, Herman Dunfield," Peyton said. "He's an attorney on the island, and an old friend."

"I'm retired now," Herman said, shaking hands with

Rusty. "I can't tell you how many times I've tried to get Peyton to join our modest firm. But he's a bit too ambitious for the likes of us." He slapped Peyton on the back. "We were happy to hear of your success in the primaries. We need new blood in Washington. Our incumbent is getting lazy. I want you to know you can count on my support. Now, grab a glass of champagne and get out there and mingle with your future constituents." He winked. "And relax. I've already made sure there are no reporters in the crowd."

For the next hour Peyton reacquainted himself with old friends and made new ones. Rusty greeted each new person warmly, a smile plastered to her face in an attempt to hide the fact she felt so tired. Her tiredness did not prevent her from noting the envious stares she was getting from many of the women, however. Peyton Nightingale was obviously considered quite a catch in the area. When one of the women questioned her at length about what she did in Salem, Rusty fell back on the story she and Beryl had fabricated about her being a teacher. Yet she couldn't help but wonder what the group would do if she stood and announced she was one of the most active practicing witches in the country.

By the time they went through the buffet line, Rusty was beginning to feel better. It didn't take a genius to figure out why. Her body was slowly but surely dispelling the negative energy she'd absorbed from Tyler the past few days. That was the good news. The bad news was that without Rusty around to intercept it, Tyler would, sooner or later, play host to the negative energy again.

Once they had eaten, Peyton insisted on showing Rusty the grounds. She followed him to an elaborate rose garden that was set off from the rest of the area by six-foot hedges. Small lanterns placed in the trees lighted their way. "Watch your step,"

Peyton said, taking her hand so she wouldn't stumble. Behind them, the house and pool seemed far away.

"It's beautiful," Rusty said, gazing at the perfect star-filled sky. Laughter wafted from the pool area, carried on a balmy, flower-scented breeze. She turned to Peyton and found him watching her.

"So are you," he said. "I don't know how I would have made it without you these past couple of days. I wish you'd consider staying. At least for the summer."

"I would if I could." She thought about her life in Salem, a life that was so vastly different from his. She thought about the business she'd worked so hard to build and the classes she taught at the university on the science of witchcraft. Through her work she meant to change public opinion on the Craft and offer it as an alternative to those who had not yet found enlightenment. Hers was a calling she simply could not shrug off. It was her reason for being.

Peyton stepped closer. "Rusty, I thought about you the whole time I was in Boston. I can't tell you how long it's been since I lost sleep over a woman."

"You sound disappointed."

He pondered it, but his eyes never left her face. "I promised myself a long time ago I'd never put myself through another relationship and risk"—he paused—"losing someone I loved." He raised his hand to her face and palmed one cheek. "But the more I try to put you out of my mind, the more I think about you. The more I want you."

Peyton slid his arms around her waist and linked his fingers together at the small of her back. He tugged her gently so that she was pressed flush against his hard body. His gaze locked with hers. Finally he lowered his head. If Rusty had felt trembly before, it was nothing compared to the dizzy, weak-kneed sensation that hit her the minute his mouth came down on hers. Without hesitating, she slipped her arms around his neck and held on tight.

The kiss was different from anything she'd ever experienced, whetting her sensual appetite and stoking a fire low in her belly while evoking feelings of tenderness and deep affection. Peyton cupped her hips with strong hands and pulled her against him, telling her in a way that was as old as time that he was hard and eager for lovemaking. Rusty arched against him. He broke the kiss and swore softly in her ear.

All at once Peyton's hands were under her dress, pushing past slip and panties, searching for the heat between her thighs. He groaned when he found her wet. "Let's get out of here."

His meaning was clear. "And go where?" she asked.

"Someplace where we can be alone. We can go back to the house. The boys will be asleep by now. We can take a boat ride."

"In the dark?"

His gaze met hers in the moonlight. "There's a small cabin. We'll have all the privacy in the world."

"Peyton, I don't know—"

He silenced her with a kiss. Rusty knew she was lost the minute he slipped his tongue past her lips. When he raised his head, his look was tender. "Don't run away from me, Rusty," he said. "I need you now more than ever."

"Oh, Peyton, I'm so glad you're home," Beryl said the minute he and Rusty stepped through the front door. "I tried to reach you at Herman Dunfield's house, but he said you'd already gone."

All the light went out of Peyton's eyes. "What's wrong? Is it Tyler?"

"No, the boys are fine. It's Fritz. He's called twice. I told him I'd have you call the minute you got back."

Peyton glanced at his wristwatch. "At this hour?"

"He said it was urgent."

Peyton turned to Rusty. He was clearly irritated. "This won't take long," he told Rusty.

"I was just having a cup of tea," Beryl said once Peyton had disappeared inside the study. "Won't you join me?"

"I should check on Tyler first."

"I just did. He's fine."

Rusty followed Beryl into the kitchen and poured a cup of hot tea from a copper kettle on the stove. They sipped in silence for a moment.

"You look exhausted, dear," Beryl said. "Why don't you go to bed? I'll wait up for Peyton."

"He's invited me for a boat ride," Rusty said.

"At this time of night?" Beryl gazed at her curiously. "Is something going on between you and my son?"

Rusty was prevented from answering when Peyton pushed through the swinging door that led into the kitchen. He came to an abrupt halt when he spied Rusty sitting across the table from his mother. The look on his face was one of horror and disbelief.

Beryl shoved her chair from the table and stood. "What's wrong, Peyton?" she asked quickly. "You act as though you've seen a ghost."

Peyton's gaze remained fixed on Rusty. "Don't be silly, Mother," he said. "There are no ghosts in this house. Only witches."

7

The silence was deafening. Beryl was the first to break it. "Peyton, I can explain everything."

"Please do," he said, sarcasm slipping into his voice. "Please tell me why you brought this woman into our house, why you put my children and my political career at risk."

The angry look on his face was almost more than Rusty could stand. "Your mother didn't do it to hurt you. She was trying to help."

Beryl looked near tears. "I did it for Tyler."

"Doesn't Tyler have enough problems?" he snapped.

"That's why I asked Rusty to come. To destroy the curse."

"Oh, my God, are we back to *that*?"

Beryl's eyes glistened. "I know you don't believe in the curse, Peyton, but I do. That's why the doctors and the psychiatrists haven't been able to help him. Don't you see?"

"Tyler's not the one who needs a psychiatrist, Mother."

Beryl hitched her head high, obviously insulted by his insinuation. "I assure you I'm perfectly sane," she said. "And so is Miss Padget."

He looked from one woman to the other. "Do you have any idea what this could do to my candidacy?"

"That's why we've tried to keep it quiet," Beryl told him.

Peyton laughed mirthlessly. "Keep it quiet?" He glanced at

Rusty. "We spent the evening with sixty people, for Pete's sake!"

"I had no idea there were going to be so many people there," Rusty told him.

He wasn't listening. "I knew you were different," he said. "That explains a lot of things." His eyes narrowed into slits. "Tell me, have you cast some sort of spell on *me*? What did you have to do to get me to say those things tonight? How many toads did you have to kill to get me to kiss you?"

Beryl's mouth fell open. "You *kissed* her?"

Rusty blushed "I didn't *have* to do anything. You acted on your own free will."

"I don't want you here," Peyton said. "And I damn sure don't want you working your devil worship on my son."

"It's not devil worship, Peyton."

"Be sensible, Peyton," Beryl said. "I wouldn't bring a satanist into this house."

"I don't give a damn *what* she is. Stay away from my children." He glanced at his watch. "It's too late to do anything tonight. But I want you out first thing in the morning."

Beryl stepped closer to him. "Peyton, please listen to me—"

"First thing in the morning, Mother," he said. He turned and made his way up the stairs, dismissing them both.

It was several days before Rusty began to feel like her old self again. For two days she had dragged through the daily routine of running her shop, only to fall into bed exhausted once she closed for the day. She didn't know if it was leftover negative energy she'd absorbed from Tyler or if it was simply a matter of being brokenhearted over Peyton. On the third morning her energy returned. Still, she was an emotional wreck. She couldn't stop worrying about the Nightingale men no matter how hard she tried. Beryl had called the evening before to apologize for everything and to tell her Tyler was, once again, having nightmares and headaches.

"I know," Rusty told her, although she didn't bother to tell her *how* she knew. She had paid the boy a visit one night, only to find him in the clutches of a bad dream. He'd cried out, and Rusty thought her heart would break. Peyton had rushed in looking more handsome than he had a right to, and Rusty had decided she could not stand there and watch the people she loved suffer.

Then she realized the full extent of her feelings for Peyton. She loved him! Despite the fact he thought she was some kind of satanist, despite the fact he'd thrown her out of his house.

"I've never seen Peyton so depressed," Beryl had said during that same conversation. "Or torn between what to do. I tried to explain that you were a *white* witch and that your practices have been around since the beginning of time, but he wouldn't listen."

"I don't see what I can do to help," Rusty said, wiping tears from her eyes at the other end of the line. "Not when he won't even let me in the house." She was still crying when she hung up.

Now, on her third day home, Rusty no more knew how to help Tyler than when she'd first come back to Salem. All she knew was there was a little boy dying and not a damn thing she could do about it. She longed to share the information with some of her coven members, other white witches who shared her beliefs and were like family to her. But she couldn't. The pain was too fresh.

Rusty was in the process of closing her store for the day when she heard someone come through the front door. She glanced up and gasped out loud when she recognized the dark-haired man. "Peyton!"

He looked tired and haggard, as though he hadn't eaten or slept since she'd left. The stubble on his jaw told her he hadn't so much as picked up a razor in that time. Rusty stepped shyly from behind the counter and approached him. "What are you doing here?" she asked.

"We have to talk."

He didn't even sound like himself. "Are you okay?"

"No, I'm *not* okay. My son is dying."

"I'm sorry."

"I need your help," he said, glancing around her store, where silver-plated goblets and large black-handled knives shared space with ash pots and incense burners. He frowned. "I don't believe any of this hocus-pocus, but I'm desperate. If there's anything you can do, for God's sake, please do it." His voice cracked. He choked back a sob.

Rusty went to him, and the next thing she knew, she was in his arms. He kissed her, and she felt his tears on her cheek, mingling with her own. "Let's go upstairs where we can be alone," she said, reaching around him to lock the door and turn the sign around in the window. She took his hand, led him to the back of the store and up a flight of stairs to her apartment.

Peyton did not waste any time questioning her once she'd closed the door. "I have to know the truth," he said. "Did you cast a spell over me? Not that I actually *believe* in spells, but I have to know, regardless."

Rusty looked confused. "What kind of spell?"

"Did you make me fall in love with you?" When she simply stared back at him in disbelief, he went on. "Because I *am* in love with you, you know."

Rusty didn't know whether to laugh or cry over the news. Surely there could not be two people more poorly suited for each other. Nevertheless, her heart thumped wildly in her chest. "No, Peyton, I did not. I don't believe in tampering with matters of the heart. Call it feminine pride if you wish, but I like to think I don't *have* to resort to that sort of thing in order to find a man."

He looked enormously relieved. As he continued to gaze at her, Rusty sensed a change taking place, not only in him but in the very air around them. Suddenly, it was charged. It crackled like static electricity, unseen but real nevertheless. The look in Peyton's eyes changed from relief to desire. His pupils seemed to dilate and take on a feral look that was emphasized by slightly flared nostrils.

"I don't know who or what you are," he said. "I only know that I want you more than I've ever wanted a woman in my life."

He pulled her into his arms, flattening her breasts against his chest. Rusty was powerless to resist. It was like being under the influence of a hypnotist. As she gazed into his eyes, she felt the unmistakable pull of some invisible force at work. Was it fate drawing them together when they were so vastly different? she wondered. What other explanation was there for loving him so deeply when they had known each other for only a short while?

Unable to hold back any longer, Peyton captured her mouth and sank his tongue inside. He had missed her more than a man had a right to miss a woman. He had ached for her in the night, then cursed himself for sending her away in the first place. He had not counted on falling in love with her, not planned on needing her. But most of all, he had not planned on his children needing her.

Peyton did not know at what moment he lost control, only that he did. He sensed there was something else at work inside his head—had she lied to him when she'd denied tampering with his heart?—but he was not about to start asking questions at this point. His need was too great. Rusty arched against his body, and he was lost. He could not deny himself what he somehow knew was already his.

Peyton had no idea how they ended up on the floor. One moment they were standing and straining against each other, the next they were on the rug. Mouths twisted, tongues mated, hands groped frantically. It was lust in its purest form, but a lust combined with love, adoration, and deep devotion. Rusty had found that place in his heart that no one had been able to touch for five years. Peyton would go mad if he couldn't have her.

Their breathing was hard and ragged. The overwhelming urge to mate made them greedy and impatient. There was no need for foreplay, they were already hot. With his blood roaring in his ears, Peyton shoved Rusty's skirt to her hips and tugged her panties down. Through passion-glazed eyes, Rusty watched him lean back on his heels and unbuckle his belt. He slid his pants to his knees and swept her legs open, then guided his rigid sex to the moist opening. He thrust deeply, brutally, urgently, lifting her hips off the floor, grinding his body against hers so that she had no choice but to open herself fully to him.

The act was primitive and crude, carnal and hedonistic. Rusty raised her gaze to his. This was meant to be.

Her shyness disappeared like smoke in the wind. She met his next thrust. Their climax was explosive and left them shuddering in its aftermath.

They dozed, too emotionally spent to do anything more. Rusty's limbs felt heavy, weighted. A fog surrounded her brain, closed her in. She fought it, but it was useless. It covered her. She moved through it. Far away, light pierced the fog. The light grew, then shattered the fog completely.

She was in a meadow. Springtime. The scent of lilac. He was there, standing in the water, his wide back to her. He looked sleek and fit, more handsome than ever. His hair was long, tied back with a strip of leather. She gazed at his wide shoulders and followed it downward to the small of his back, his taut hips. On the bank lay his clothes, the dark breeches, the black coat. Puritan garments.

"Come into the water, Rachael," he called out, then turned slowly and extended his hand. She rose and walked toward him. Surely it was wrong to want a man so badly, when her poor sick husband had been in the ground only a few months. But she *did* want him. Jonathan Nightingale was young and fit, and her blood ran hot each time he kissed her. Her husband had been old and clumsy, a product of an arranged marriage. Smiling, she raised her gaze to his face, eager to tell him of her love. Her smile froze when she recognized him.

Peyton!

The fog closed in once more. When it cleared, she found herself in a meeting house of sorts. There he was, Jonathan her love, looking at her as though he wished he'd never met her. Did he believe what they were saying about her?

"Dost thou doubt me too, Jonathan?" she said.

He hung his head. "Methinks thou hast bewitched me, too, Rachael."

All at once the meeting-room doors were flung open, and they were there with their blazing pine torches, coming to get her. "Goody Brown's child is dead of the fits, and the witch must burn!" they shouted.

Someone screamed. The fog shattered around her, and Rusty bolted upright on the living room floor, eyes wide in horror. Beside her, Peyton tried to still her flailing arms.

"Rusty, stop it!" He saw the wild look in her eyes, the terror. She fought him, her nails aimed for his face. She drew blood. "Rusty, no!"

"You son of a bitch!" she cried. "I know who you are!"

Shock made him release her. "The dream? You had it too?"

"Damn right I did! Only it's not a dream, is it?" She slapped him soundly in the face.

He stared at her, too horrified to speak. His cheek stung, but he was too dumbfounded to acknowledge the pain. "If it's not a dream, then what is it?" he asked.

"It's our past, Peyton!" she all but shouted.

The blood drained from his face. "No!"

"You can deny it all you want, but it's true. That's why we kept feeling as though we'd met somewhere before. That's why—" She paused, understanding why their need to mate had been so strong. Their climax had opened the door to their former lives. "I suspected a past life, but I *never* suspected this!"

Peyton shot up from the floor, gathering his clothes together. He began to pace. "You can't expect me to believe something like that. It's . . . preposterous!"

She adjusted her own clothing, walked on her knees to a side table, and jerked open a drawer. She reached for the locket where it lay next to the journal and threw it at him. Peyton caught it with one hand, then jumped as though he'd been electrically shocked. "What are you doing with this?" he demanded, remembering it as the one his mother had shown him. He'd been repelled by it then, and he was now.

"Never mind what I'm doing with it. Open it."

He did so. "It's a picture of you."

"Wrong. It's a miniature painting of Rachael Dobbs, given to her by Jonathan Nightingale."

It all came rushing back to him. His head spun. Suddenly he remembered. The trial. The burning. The son and daughter he'd raised for her. The woman he'd eventually married but had never truly loved. His blood chilled at the memory. He dropped the locket and buried his face in his hands. "Oh, God, it *is* true! How can this be happening?"

"You betrayed me, Peyton," Rusty said, her voice as cold as a December wind. "You told me you loved me, but you turned your back on me and signed my death warrant." She stopped abruptly and her eyes filled with tears. "What happened to my children?"

He raised pain-stricken eyes to her. "They were well cared for."

"By your mistress, no doubt!"

"You can accuse me of being the worst kind of bastard, Rusty, but I saw to it your children were happy and had what they needed."

"I hate you!" she spat at him. "You destroyed my life and the lives of my children. And yet—" She tossed him a wrathful look. "And yet you expect me to save your son. How ironic."

"You can't blame Tyler for the mistakes of the past," he said. "You can hate me for the rest of my life, but keep him out of this."

"This is a hell of a time for you to start giving me orders, isn't it? After all, I hold your son's life in my hands." Rusty knew it was a cruel thing to say, but she couldn't help herself.

She wanted to hurt him, wound him, as he'd hurt her three hundred years before.

"Does this mean you're not going to help me?" he asked, then held his breath for her reply. When she didn't answer right away, he went on. "I made a mistake, Rusty. I was caught up in the hysteria of the times. If there was some way to go back and change it, I would." He held his hands out in surrender.

"You can't change the past," she said dully.

"Then name your price," he said. "I'll do anything, I'll *pay* you anything."

"I don't want your stupid money."

"This is my son's life we're talking about, dammit!"

Rusty sat there for several moments, trying to cool her anger. "I'll help you," she said at last. "Not because you deserve it, but because I'm the one who set this curse in motion in the first place. Somehow I have to stop it. Besides, *your* family isn't the only one in danger."

He looked relieved. "Can I help you pack for the trip back?"

"No, I'll do it." Rusty was already moving to the bedroom. "Call your mother," she said. "Have her pack Josh's and Peter's clothes and be ready to take them to Boston the minute we arrive. Dismiss the servants for a few days. I don't want anyone else around."

Now he looked confused. "Mind telling me why?"

"Because this is my last chance to put a stop to this damn curse once and for all. And because it's probably going to look like Armageddon before it's over." She disappeared into the other room.

8

The servants were gone, and Beryl looked as though she'd been crying when Rusty and Peyton walked through the door that same evening.

"Rusty, you're back!" Josh exclaimed, giving her a big hug. "We missed you."

"Are you going to Boston with us tonight?" Peter asked, refusing to let her go.

Rusty was deeply moved by their show of affection. She had missed them more than they could know. "I'm afraid not," she said. "Your dad and I are going to stay with Tyler while he's sick."

"He's always sick," Josh complained, yawning wide. Beryl had dressed them in pajamas, obviously hoping they'd fall asleep on the ride home.

The chauffeur loaded the boys into the limo and handed them a pillow. Rusty said good-bye and hurried inside to check on Tyler.

Beryl turned to Peyton. "You'll call if there's any news?"

He pressed a kiss to his mother's forehead. He often wondered how he would have made it the last five years without her. Had he taken advantage of her good nature, he thought, by expecting her to help him raise his children? "Of course I will," he said. "Try not to worry."

When Peyton entered his son's bedroom a few minutes later, he found Rusty sitting on the edge of the boy's bed, watching him sleep.

"How is he?"

Rusty shook her head sadly. The changes in the child were dramatic. He'd lost weight, pounds his frail body couldn't afford to lose. "He seems to have slipped into a coma," she said.

"Oh, God!" The blood drained from Peyton's face. His mother had told him she'd had trouble rousing the child that morning, but he'd had no idea it was this bad. "What the hell do we do *now?*"

"I need a minute to think," she said. What worried Rusty was the subtle odor in the room. She knew that when the body started shutting down, vital organs began to die. The smell of death permeated the air. Beryl had obviously noticed it as well because there was a box of potpourri and a can of air freshener on the bedside table.

Peyton gazed at his son through mournful eyes. "I'm scared, Rusty," he said, feeling guilty for the time he'd wasted, for making love to her while his son lay near death. "If he dies—"

"I'm going to try to prevent that," she said, peeking beneath the boy's closed eyelids. She didn't like what she saw. His pallor was chalky, his lips tinged blue. When she pinched his skin, the flesh stuck together.

"He's worse than he was this morning when I left." Peyton sat on the foot of the bed and buried his face in his hands. "Why couldn't this damn curse have fallen on me?" he said. "Why did it have to fall to my son?"

Rusty felt a giant fist squeeze her heart. While she hated him for betraying her in the past, she did not want to see his son die. "I'm sorry, Peyton," she said, knowing there was no way to make up for the mistake she'd made three hundred years before. All she could do was try to stop or destroy the evil forces taking place inside the boy, even if it meant taking on all the negative energy herself—even if it meant her own death.

A sacrifice no mortal woman would make . . .

"If only there was something I could do," Peyton said, tears streaming silently down his face. "If only I could go back and change it. Spare all those lives."

"That which is past must be left alone," she said.

His eyes were raw with pain. "You believe in psychic phenomena, don't you?" When she nodded, he went on. "And you believe in astral projection or out-of-body experiences, right? You believe the soul is capable of leaving the body for exploration and time travel?"

"Absolutely. I've done it a number of times. But it didn't happen overnight. It takes months, even years of practice."

"I could learn, Rusty. If time travel is truly possible, I could—"

"What would you do, Peyton?" she snapped. "Go back and try to put an end to the witch trails? They'd lock you up with the rest of them. I'm sorry if you're having a hard time dealing with your guilt, but—"

"If you won't help me, I'll do it on my own."

"Suit yourself," she said, knowing he would never be able to accomplish such a feat. "But first I need you to clear this room of furniture."

"Why?"

"Because I have to cast a circle. To perform rituals," she added when he continued to look confused and reluctant. "I can't help Tyler if you're going to question everything I do," she said.

Peyton sighed and raked his fingers through his hair. "I told you, I'm scared. I feel as if I should call an ambulance, get him to the hospital. And here you are telling me to get this place ready so you can practice magic. What am I supposed to think, dammit?"

"Do you trust me, Peyton?" She knew it was a heck of a thing to ask. After all, she had set the curse in motion in the first place.

He pondered it. "Yes. Even though I don't know what the hell you're doing, I know you have my son's best interests at heart." He paused. "But I'm not going to wait much longer, Rusty. If he doesn't improve rapidly, I'll have no choice but to take him to the hospital." He knew he wouldn't be able to live with the guilt if his son died in his own bed without the benefit of a doctor.

Rusty could see that Peyton was torn with indecision, and she felt sorry for him. No matter how angry and hurt she was about their past, she pitied him now. "I'm a firm believer in getting all the medical help you can, Peyton. But what have the doctors done so far for Tyler?"

"What do you want me to do?"

Once Peyton had cleared the room of all furniture except the bed on which his son lay, he begin to carry in the items Rusty had brought back with her from Salem. He couldn't resist peeking into one of the boxes. He froze when he spotted a large blackhandled knife.

"What the hell is *that* for?" he asked Rusty.

She regarded him. "You've no right to look through my personal belongings."

"I have every right to know why you're bringing a damn butcher knife into my son's bedroom," he said tersely.

"It's not a butcher knife. I use it in ritual magic, Peyton." Her eyes met and locked with his. "It's not for cutting."

He stood there for a long moment before he finally set the box down. "What do you want me to do with your books?" he asked, indicating a large cardboard box outside the door.

"Leave them. I have all I need for now." When he continued to stand there as though unsure what to do, she spoke softly. "You'll have to go now. I don't want any distractions."

He started for the door, and she followed. When she started to close it, he blocked it. "Rusty?"

"What is it?"

His voice pleaded. "Be careful." Finally he let the door close.

Peyton wondered if he was doing the right thing. What if Tyler died while she was in there performing her rituals? It would be all his fault for not taking him to the hospital where he could get medical attention. He would have to live with the guilt for the rest of his life. Peyton raised his fist to knock on the door, then stopped. He smelled something burning. Incense? He backed away. If he didn't at least give Rusty the chance to undo the curse, his son might die anyway.

He turned to go, almost tripping over the box of books he'd carried in from the trunk of his car. *The Old Religion. The Power of Modern Witchcraft. Drawing Down the Moon. The Path to Enlightenment.* He shook his head sadly. Fritz would be livid if he knew what was taking place this very instant, Peyton thought. Especially when he'd told him to get rid of her. Always on the alert for potential problems, Fritz had run a check on Rusty behind his back and discovered she was the high priestess for a coven of witches in Salem. "For God's sake, Peyton! Get that woman out of your house now!" his campaign manager had warned. "Before we all end up on the front page of some tabloid."

Fritz would probably resign as his campaign manager if he discovered she was back. Which was why Peyton hadn't bothered to return his calls. Not that he'd blame the man, of course. Rusty had told him on the drive down about the misconceptions people had about the old religion. As a lawyer, he'd been taught to rely on evidence or proof that something truly existed. In a court of law there was no room for speculation or abstract thinking. Everything was black and white; there were no gray areas. Now, in one afternoon, he was being forced to examine a lifetime of beliefs. He picked up several books and carried them downstairs.

It was going to be a long night.

It was late by the time Rusty had set up her altar and cast a circle around Tyler's bed. On a piece of parchment paper, she wrote the following words:

Goddess Moon,
Sky Above,
Fill this child with goodness and love.
Shine your light,
Shed your beam,
Fill this child with pleasant dreams.

Once Rusty had written the spell, she read it aloud, then burned it in the small ash pot on her altar. It was a simple spell, nothing like the more elaborate ones she sometimes wrote and chanted with her coven members. But it was direct and to the point. She knew, no matter what, she had to stop the bad dreams. Something in those dreams was feeding on Tyler's energy and dragging him further and further away.

Rusty gazed out the window at the waning moon and knew it was the best time to banish evil and neutralize enemies. She wrote another spell along those lines, chanted it several times, then burned it as well. Although she knew astrological patterns influenced magic works, she had not had time to study charts and calendars to determine which planets would be nearest the moon at what times. Some of her colleagues would never attempt to cast a spell without checking astrological signs first, but Rusty had learned a long time ago that successful magic centered not so much on what was happening in the galaxies, but what was going on in a witch's heart. If her spells were pure and focused, they should be successful.

It was well after midnight by the time Rusty completed her work. She catalyzed various herbs so she could concoct a protective potion. Once she had simmered the ingredients in a small enamel pot over a flame, she anointed Tyler. Before she put her instruments away for the night, she copied the three-hundred-year-old curse onto a piece of parchment paper, stuffed it into a bottle, and sealed a cork in place with white candle wax, which she melted over her flame. She would wait until the first light, then bury the bottle outside in a place where it would not be disturbed.

Once finished, Rusty opened her circle, climbed into bed beside Tyler, and closed her eyes. All they could do now was wait.

Morning came and brought with it a strange gray light. Peyton was dozing on the sofa in his den when he was awakened by a weird, unsettling noise. Startled, he raised up abruptly and knocked the stacks of books he'd been reading to the floor. "Rusty?" he called out.

Silence.

He jumped from the couch and made his way up the stairs to the second floor and Tyler's bedroom door. He tried the knob. It was locked. "Rusty?" He knocked. No response. He heard the noise again. It was a hideous, filthy sound. Squashing and sucking. He shuddered and pounded his fists on the door. "Rusty, open up!"

"Go away, Peyton," she cried from the other side.

He heard the hysteria in her voice and knew he had to get in. Something was wrong. He took several steps back, ran forward, and slammed against the door with all his might. The wood splintered and the door flew open.

For a moment, all he could do was stand there and stare. "Oh, my God," he said, his voice barely recognizable in his own ears. "What the hell is it?"

"I'm not sure," Rusty told him, her gaze fixed on the walls. "It started sometime after midnight, then went away after a few hours. It's worse this time."

Peyton gazed at the walls in horror and disbelief. The sheet rock had gone through some sort of transformation. A strange light coming from the walls cast an eerie glow about the room. The once-smooth surface seemed to pulse before his very eyes. It was damp and sweaty and corded with veins. Whatever it was, it was alive and meant to do them harm. He crept slowly into the room, unable to take his eyes off the breathing walls. "Tyler? How is he?"

"Not good," Rusty told him. She pressed her fingers against the child's throat. His pulse was almost nonexistent. He was cold. He was within death's reach.

It was then that Peyton noticed the smell in his son's room had worsened considerably. Suddenly his socks were wet. He glanced down at the floor and stepped back, his face contorted in disgust. Raw sewage seeped through the cracks in the wood floor. He felt sick. "My God, Rusty, what have you done?"

"It's not me, Peyton. It's Tyler." She choked back the bile that filled the back of her throat. "His dreams are somehow manifesting themselves."

9

For several long hours they sat in the eerie light and watched in
horror the workings of some awful poltergeist. Shadowy figures
danced along the walls, reaching out, moaning, while Rusty
and Peyton huddled around the boy. All the while, Rusty
chanted and anointed them with the protective oil she'd made
the night before. She burned incense and candles and did whatever else she could think of. For the first time, she wondered if
she would be able to handle it alone and wished some of her
coven members were there to help.

"Why the hell don't we grab him and go to another
room?" Peyton said.

"It won't do any good. It'll follow us. The good news is, it
seems to come in cycles. It should quiet down soon." She
didn't bother to add that it would probably come back even
more powerfully than before.

"So what do we do in the meantime?" Peyton asked.

"We wait."

By noon the room had returned to normal except for the
eerie light. Clearly shaken by all he'd witnessed, Peyton
glanced down at his son's face. "I know I'm probably imagining it," he said, "but his color looks better." When Rusty
didn't deny it, he became hopeful. "Is it possible that it's over?"
he asked, his voice a mere whisper.

Rusty shook her head. "It's not even close to being over. And I'm afraid it's going to get much worse before it is."

It was then that Peyton noticed how bad she looked. The dark circles under her eyes were worse than ever. "I'm going to run downstairs and get you some cheese and crackers and something to drink," he said. "Why don't you rest? You obviously didn't get much sleep last night."

For several days they battled whatever it was. Rusty had been correct about the cyclic nature of the strange entity. It lasted a couple of hours, then disappeared, and the room became normal once again. Except for the light. The eerie glow never went away. Each episode became worse. Afterward they rested and took nourishment. Peyton catnapped in the next bedroom so he could be alert to any sounds, but mostly he read. He spent hours poring over Rusty's books. Many of the questions he'd had over the years about life and death were answered in those books. He discovered witchcraft was not only a religion but a science, some of it backed by the laws of physics. Reincarnation made perfect sense to a man who had dealt with the legal system and seen firsthand that justice wasn't always served. It was only fair that a man be forced to make amends for any wrongs he'd committed in a previous life. A soul was reborn over and over until it learned the cosmic lessons of life and attained perfection. Time travel was also believable when applied to the laws of physics. Yet while believable, it could be achieved only in what was called the "alpha state." Peyton realized then that the alpha state was where Rusty went each time she performed magic. Studying the books carefully, he began to practice various techniques of relaxation, knowing that was the first step. He worked diligently. He was determined to succeed no matter what. This whole curse business was his fault, and it was up to him to do something about it.

On the fourth day, Peyton walked into the room after a brief nap and stopped dead in his tracks when he saw Rusty. "My God, what happened to you?" he said.

She turned away. "Get out, Peyton!" she cried, her voice sounding nothing like her own. "I don't want you to see me like this."

He stared at the ghostly pale woman before him. Her eyes were sunk back in her head, and the bones in her face were so pronounced, she looked as if she'd spent the last six months in a concentration camp. "Rusty, what's wrong?" He approached her, and she shrank away and faced the wall. She pressed her palms flat against it. It was as though a switch had been flipped. Something oozed from the sheet rock. Peyton took a step closer and realized the walls were bleeding. He shuddered in horror and revulsion. He buried his face in his hands, afraid to look at his son. "Is he dead?"

"No." Rusty still refused to look at him. "His pulse is stronger today. He's getting better, I think. He should wake before long." At least she hoped so. Despite all she'd done to protect his health, the boy was quickly becoming dehydrated. He could last without food, but his body desperately needed water.

"And you're getting worse." Peyton's voice sounded dead. "Why?" When she didn't answer, he yelled, "Look at me, dammit! I'm tired of all this secrecy. I want to know what's going on in here!"

Rusty turned slowly. "That should be obvious, Peyton. I'm absorbing all the negative energy that's being directed at Tyler."

When he merely stared back at her in disbelief, she went on. "What did you expect me to do, sit here and let him die?"

"Are you saying that in order for my son to live, *you* have to die?"

"It would make sense, wouldn't it? The curse plainly states that a sacrifice must be made."

"Then let *me* make it," he shouted.

"It doesn't work that way. When I cursed your bloodline, I cursed my own. To end the curse for all time, I will have to pay the ultimate price. My life," she added.

The news hit Peyton with the impact of a freight train. His body was immobilized with fear and pain. "No!" He went to her, arms stretched out.

"Please don't," she said. She couldn't bear for him to touch her or hold her. It was painful enough to look at him and know they wouldn't be together in this life either. As much as she loved him, had *always* loved him, it seemed they were destined to be apart.

Peyton had a lump in his throat the size of a goose egg. "I can't let you go," he said, tears stinging his eyes. "I lost you once. The thought of losing you again——" He was unable to finish his sentence.

Rusty moved back to the bed slowly and sat down next to the boy. "I'm not afraid of death, Peyton," she said after a moment, trying to sound brave. "What I *am* afraid of is not learning the lessons I was brought here to learn. If I don't pay my dues now, your son will die, and I will have to pay in the next life." She smiled wryly. "You've heard the saying that you give in life what you get back. It's true, Peyton. Don't ever forget it. Let it be one of the first lessons you teach your children." She sighed heavily. She was tired, exhausted beyond belief. "I want you to wear this," she said, reaching for the locket that she now wore around her neck. When he hesitated, she went on. "It has been charged with healing herbs. Its aura is both positive and powerful. It will protect you."

"I think you need protection more than I do," he said.

"No, I have all that I need." She insisted he fasten it around his neck. Finally she lay down next to Tyler. "If you don't mind, I really must rest now. No telling when this *thing*, whatever it is, will be back."

Peyton went to the room next door, where he tried to come to terms with all Rusty had told him. He had never known such despair. Rusty was dying. And she wasn't going to fight it, because if *she* didn't die, Tyler would instead.

Time was running out.

He lay on the bed and gazed at the ceiling for a long time wondering what to do. What *could* he do? Send Rusty away and let his son die? The locket felt heavy against his chest. He touched it, and his fingers tingled. He closed his eyes and thought of Rusty. *His* Rusty. As much as he'd loved Priscilla and grieved after her death, he knew there would be no getting over Rusty's. He and Priscilla had been husband and wife, but Rusty was his soul mate. If she died, something inside of him would die right along with her.

Peyton was not certain how long he lay there. The last few days had taken a toll on him. He was tired. So very tired. He closed his eyes. If he could only grab a few minutes of sleep, maybe then he could figure out some sort of solution. After all, he was a lawyer, and he was used to sorting through problems. Suddenly he felt weighted and more relaxed than he had in days. He gave in to the pleasant sensation, welcomed it. Then he saw it, a pinpoint of light in the midst of blackness. He gazed at it. It blinked on and off, but each time it returned, it grew larger, until it was the size of a half-dollar. It changed color, from yellow to orange to red, following a kaleidoscope of tones. Peyton felt the colors enter his body. He was bathed in the warm tones, soothed and cooled by the deeper ones. He experienced a sense of well-being. All was right with the world. Finally he was engulfed.

Rusty bolted upright in the bed, her heart racing, a scream poised on her lips. She choked it back when she realized it was another nightmare, this one more hideous than the last. No wonder Tyler had feared falling asleep.

Rusty gazed at the peacefully sleeping child beside her as she waited for her fear-induced trembling to stop. The dream had seemed so real. She could still smell the fetid odor, feel the dankness of that dark place she'd visited. She could still hear the hushed whispers of those *things* approaching her. She shuddered as she remembered the unspeakable crimes they'd committed against her, crimes that Tyler, in his innocence, wouldn't understand.

It was just a dream, she told herself.

And yet, so real, filling her with a sense of dread that refused to leave upon waking.

Finally Rusty nudged Tyler gently, and he opened his eyes. "Hi, kiddo," she said, trying to make her voice sound bright despite the heaviness inside. "How do you feel?"

Tyler blinked several times as though trying to focus. His color had returned, and the yellowish tint was gone from his eyeballs. When his gaze found hers, he frowned, and it was obvious he didn't recognize her at first. "Rusty?" His voice sounded like a croak. "My mouth is . . . dry."

She saw that his lips were parched. "Can you take some water?"

He nodded, and she rose from the bed slowly, taking a moment to get her balance. The room spun. She reached for a pitcher on the night table, filled a glass, and put it to his lips. Tyler sipped greedily, pausing now and then when water dribbled down his chin. Rusty cautioned him to slow down. "There," she said, thankful that he had finally taken liquid into his frail body. Now he needed nourishment. "Why don't you rest, and I'll ask your dad to heat up some soup for you," she suggested. He nodded again and closed his eyes.

Rusty discovered right away how weak she'd grown. As she crossed the room and opened the door, her knees trembled. She leaned against the door frame and called out to Peyton. No answer. She glanced around and found Tyler had gone back to sleep. She had to get some nourishment in him before the walls started their macabre dance. Using what little strength she had left, she opened the door to the next bedroom. Peyton was lying on the bed.

"Peyton, wake up," she said. "Tyler needs to eat." There was no movement. She stepped closer, noting the stacks of books next to the bed, *her* books. She froze when she spied the book on the bed next to him, *Astral Travel*. Fear clutched her heart. It was obvious he was in a state of deep relaxation. He had somehow managed to find the alpha state. But how? It had taken months for her to learn. She saw the locket clutched tightly in his fingers. But of course! She had known from the start there were magical qualities about the locket. Those qualities had obviously assisted Peyton in his quest to revisit the past.

The thought made her blood run cold. Although Peyton had told her repeatedly he wanted to try to go back, it had never occurred to her that he would be able to pull it off. Therefore, she hadn't bothered to tell him it would be a waste of time. Since he would be in his astral body, nobody would be able to see him, much less listen to what he had to say. What worried her was the chance that he might not find his way back to present day. He could spend eternity trying. In the meantime, his physical body would remain in a comalike state. Eventually he'd die.

Without wasting another second, Rusty lay down on the bed beside him and counted herself into alpha. She had never visited 1690, had never even had the desire, so this would be a new experience for her as well. She found the pinpoint of light. It flickered like a strobe, then burst into color. She immersed herself, giving in to the wondrous sensations the colors created. A coven member had once described the feelings as a cross between drowning and orgasm. Sweet death, she had called it. Rusty let it take her.

10

When Rusty opened her eyes she found herself in a meeting room facing a crowd of somberly dressed men and women. Two facts were immediately apparent: She smelled as though she'd spent the night in a garbage bin, and something was crawling on her. She raised her hands to scratch, then discovered she was bound. It was then she realized she had successfully found her way back to 1690. But before she had time to rejoice in the fact that she'd made it, something else occurred. Why was she itching? The astral body couldn't feel sensation.

"Rachael Dobbs, confess thy sins before this court and thy Creator," an authoritative-looking man said.

Rusty snapped her head up. The man was looking directly at her. He could see her. But how could that be?

Suddenly it hit her. She had entered her former self, that of Rachael Deliverance Dobbs! That possibility had not occurred to her.

The doors to the courtroom burst open, and a pack of men streamed in with blazing pine torches. "Goody Brown's child is dead of the fits," one shouted. "The witch must burn!"

The guards couldn't hold back the vigilantes. Rusty searched the crowd for Peyton but was unable to see past the pack of men who engulfed her. She was gripped by bruising hands and lifted off the ground. She could feel herself nearly being torn apart as they dragged her from the meeting room, but she did not cry out. She was too bent on finding Peyton.

Outside, the sky was leaden and cloudy, the ground frozen. Rusty shivered as the cold seeped inside the rags that covered her. But she was only vaguely aware of her discomfort and the fact that they seemed to be climbing a hill. Had Peyton not managed to find 1690 after all? Where were these men taking her? Then, as they mounted the top of the hill, Rusty spied Peyton on the outskirts of the crowd. He saw her at the same moment, and his look turned to horror.

"Rusty!" He waved wildly at her, at the same time trying to forge through the throng of people. It wasn't easy. Because of the cold, everyone was huddled together in a tight pack.

"Peyton!" She called out his name but was unable to wave because of the iron shackles binding her wrists. "Hurry, Peyton!" she cried. She had to wait for him. Together they could find their way back to the twentieth century. If she left him to his own devices, he might never get back. The crowd came to an abrupt halt, and Rusty glanced over her shoulder. She froze when she saw it: the stake where she had burned to death three hundred years before!

"Who is it Mistress Dobbs calls out to?" one of the men asked.

"I do not recognize the name," another said. "Perhaps it is Satan himself she beseeches."

Someone removed her shackles. She was tied to a post. "Peyton, please hurry!" she cried. "I can't leave without you."

"She's calling the devil!" a woman in the crowd shouted. "Bind her mouth before she summons her demons from hell."

A smelly rag was shoved inside her mouth. Rusty gagged and thought she would vomit. She turned frantic eyes to Peyton as he struggled to get closer. She would not leave without him.

"Release her!" he shouted, closer now.

"Who is that man?" one of her captors asked.

" 'Tis her betrothed."

"Why is he demanding her release? Is he not the one who brought the evidence against her?"

" 'Tis he, indeed. I fear Goody Dobbs hath cast another spell on him."

Breathing heavily from exertion, Peyton made it to the front of the crowd. He reached for Rusty.

"Capture him!" one of the men said. "She hath bewitched him with her powers."

Rusty watched in horror as several men lunged at Peyton. Pandemonium broke out. She tried to scream, but the rag in her mouth blocked all sound. The acrid smell of smoke suddenly rose around her. She wrenched her head around, saw one of the men put the torch to the hem of her dress. She turned pleading eyes to Peyton. Suddenly it was all too clear. Of course! Now she understood the full extent of the curse.

A sacrifice no mortal woman would ever be willing to make.

She was going to have to burn all over again!

Fear gripped her. This was why none of her magic had broken the curse. To stop it for all time, she would not only be forced to give up her life, she would also need to die a horrifying death. Just like before. Rusty sagged against the pole, fear rendering her too weak to stand. She recalled the feel of fire on her body. The blisters. The agony. To increase and insure that agony, they would use green wood. She remembered just how long it had taken her to die before.

"Let her go!" Peyton shouted, seeing the defeat in her eyes.

Why was she giving up? Why didn't she get the hell out of there? She had the power. Then realization hit him, and their gazes locked.

"Noooo!" he screamed, and his voice seemed to echo off the heavens.

Resigned to die, Rusty closed her eyes. She hated only that Peyton would be forced to watch it all over again. There were so many things she wanted to tell him.

How much she loved him.

That she forgave him for betraying her.

That she wished she'd never set this awful curse in motion to begin with.

That it was worth dying a second death to erase it forever.

That little Tyler was destined to grow up and make a success out of his life.

The flame climbed her skirt and touched her flesh, and Rusty bit down hard on the rag in her mouth. Oh, the pain! Fear raced through her blood like a raging river. Her eyes stung with tears. One fell to her cheek and hardened, the same emerald color of her eyes.

"Wait, Rusty!" Peyton cried. "I'm coming with you."

Rusty opened her eyes and watched Peyton struggle to break free from the men holding him. With superhuman strength he threw them off and ran the short distance to where she was tied. "I won't betray you this time," he said.

The crowd gasped in horror and disbelief as Peyton stepped into the fire. The pain was excruciating, and he bit his bottom lip to keep from crying out. He smelled burning meat and realized it was his own flesh. Let it be over soon, he prayed as he put his arms around Rusty. She writhed in agony. "I love you," he managed to tell her. "I would rather die . . . with you . . . than live without you."

Suddenly the flame roared out of control and became an inferno, chasing the crowd back. It leapt higher and higher, then sparked and turned blue. Peyton's eyes snapped open in surprise. The pain was gone. The fire turned cool and soothed their hot flesh like a healing balm. Rusty opened her eyes, and their gazes locked. They were suddenly filled with knowledge, the kind of knowledge that comes only when someone has touched upon some universal truth. They had made the sacrifice; the curse was broken. For all time.

Peyton snatched the locket from his neck and wrapped his arms around her. He linked one hand with hers and held it tight, the locket pressed between them. They closed their eyes once more and waited for the pinpoint of light to take them away.

11

"Peyton? Peyton, wake up." Rusty nudged the sleeping man gently.

Peyton jumped, knocking the book beside him to the floor as his eyes shot open and he found himself looking into Rusty's concerned face. His heart thundered in his chest. "Rusty?"

"It's okay," she said. "We made it back safely."

"Made it back? Then you mean it wasn't a dream?"

She chuckled. "Hardly."

With adrenaline gushing through his body like water through a fire hose, Peyton put his arms around her and held her close. "My God, I thought I'd lost you again. Where's Tyler?"

"Resting. I promised him you'd heat up a bowl of soup."

As though acting on cue, Tyler pushed the bedroom door open and stepped inside, still dressed in his pajamas. "I'm hungry," he told his father. "When are you going to make me something to eat?"

Relief softened the lines around Peyton's face. He released Rusty and sprang from the bed, sweeping his son up for a hug. "How do you feel?" he asked the child.

"Hungry," he said.

Rusty got up from the bed and hurried over to him. "Come on, honey, I'll make you something to eat."

"Not so fast," Peyton told her, blocking her way. He put his son down. "Go downstairs and get a slice of cheese out of the refrigerator. I'll be right down."

The boy raced from the room. Rusty turned to Peyton and found him watching her speculatively. "What is it?"

"Is it over?" he asked, afraid even to hope for as much. She met his gaze. "It's over."

"Are you sure?"

"There will be no more curses in our family, Peyton. The debt has been paid. Your family can finally go back to living a normal life, and I can go back to my life in Salem."

"No!" He pulled her into his arms. "I didn't mean to yell," he said, noting her startled gaze. "But you can't leave. I don't ever want to lose you again. Marry me, Rusty. Let's do it right this time."

She studied the hopeful look on his face. "Marry you? A senator with a witch for a wife?"

"I'm going to withdraw from the race, Rusty."

"Withdraw! But it's what you've always wanted."

"It's what my father wanted," he said. "But the more I learn about politics, the less I like it. There's still time to groom another candidate. I wanted to make the world a better place, but I think there are other ways to achieve that." He paused and pulled her closer. "Besides, I ran only because I thought it would give my life meaning. With you and the boys beside me, I have all I'll ever need."

"Peyton, are you sure about this?"

"I've never been more sure of anything in my life. I'll call Fritz today and tell him. We can even go back to Salem and live if you like. That way, you can carry on your practice, and I'll farm potatoes if I have to."

She chuckled. "I always said you'd make a great potato

farmer." Finally she grew serious. "I don't know, Peyton. I kind of like it here. It feels right. Remember when I told you I thought we were all searching for something? I think I've found it."

He studied her closely. "We don't have to decide today. I know I'd have a job here if we stayed, but we have plenty of time to talk about it. Right now I just want to enjoy my family."

Rusty suddenly felt shy. She couldn't help but wonder what Beryl would have to say about their marrying. Instinct told her Beryl would be happy as long as her son was happy. "Do you love me, Peyton?" she asked at last.

His look was sincere. "With all my heart. More than I did before." He paused. "Can you ever forgive me for betraying you?"

"You were forgiven the minute you stepped into the fire with me. That's what made it possible to break the curse once and for all." She handed him the locket.

Peyton opened it and gazed at the likeness inside, Rachael Dobbs. Rusty Padget. Three tear-shaped stones adorned her cheek: a diamond, a ruby, and an emerald. "It really *is* over, isn't it?"

"All of her tears have been returned to her, and she is whole again."

Peyton closed the locket, reached for Rusty's hand, and placed it in her palm. "This belongs to you," he said. "I want you to wear it always, as a reminder that I will never betray you again." He kissed her. Deeply. Tenderly. When he raised up, he was warmed by the love he saw in her eyes. "Will you marry me, Rusty?"

"Yes." Rusty thought her heart would burst with happiness. "But first, there's a little boy downstairs waiting to be fed." She started for the door. "Are you coming?"

"Darn right. I'm not letting you go." He grinned. "In this life or the next."